D0887677

GIRL WITH A GUN

GIRL WITH A GUN

An Annie Oakley Mystery

Kari Bovee

Copyright © 2018 Kari Bovee
All rights reserved, including the right to reproduce this book or portions
thereof in any form whatsoever.

Published by SparkPress, a BookSparks imprint,
A division of SparkPoint Studio, LLC
Tempe, Arizona, USA, 85281
www.gosparkpress.com

Published 2018
Printed in the United States of America
ISBN: 978-1-943006-60-1 (pbk)
ISBN: 978-1-943006-61-8 (e-bk)
Library of Congress Control Number: 2018933912

This is a work of fiction. Names, characters, places, and incidents either
are the product of the author's imagination or are used fictitiously. Any
resemblance to actual persons, living or dead, is entirely coincidental.

For Kevin,
who never lets me give up on my dreams.

For Jessica and Michael,
who inspire me every day.

April 12, 1885 – St. Louis, Missouri

Kimi sat at the campfire waiting for the water to boil. She winced as her baby, Winona, latched onto her breast with the greediness of a newborn bird. Kimi smiled as Winona looked up at her with bright indigo eyes. Her beautiful round face and her skin, the color of dark honey, gave the baby the look of a cherub. Tufts of Winona's straight black hair stood up on end. Kimi licked her fingers and pressed down the errant hair, soft as the fur of a jackrabbit, on her baby's head.

She placed a spoonful of tea in the porcelain cup and poured the boiling water over it, watching the minced leaves swirl as the water settled. Cuddling the baby to her chest, Kimi looked out over the camp. The peaks of the white tents shone bright against the backdrop of the violet mountains and endless fields of grass. The scene should have given her comfort—instead, a shroud of misery settled over her. She had displeased so many people of late, and she wasn't even sure how. Her mere presence seemed a blight to everyone, except Annie, her friend and boss. Annie had welcomed her from the start when the show's manager, Mr. LeFleur, told them they'd be living together.

Annie never made her feel ashamed or dirty for what she'd done or who she was—a Sioux squaw with an illegitimate half-breed baby.

Kimi frowned, disappointed she could not accompany Annie and the others to the saloon this evening, but Winona's teething had robbed her of sleep. A night of rest would be good for both of them.

The tea was unusually bitter, but the sting of Winona's two new teeth diverted Kimi. She hummed an ancient tune to distract herself from the baby's suckling and closed her eyes to shut out the sadness she felt in her heart.

A pain, deep from within her belly, started and spread into her chest. She coughed, thinking it might be due to phlegm in her lungs, or perhaps indigestion from the rich food she'd shared with Annie at lunch. She looked down at Winona, who had quieted, her eyes half closed, falling into a peaceful sleep with a full stomach. The pain increased, becoming so intense she pulled Winona from her breast and rose to go into the tent.

A cramp grabbed at her stomach. Kimi nearly doubled over, but caught herself so she wouldn't drop the baby. Quickly, she made her way across the tent and set Winona in her cradle. She arranged the blankets, tucking them close to the sleeping baby. Kimi drew back and her knees buckled. The pain oozed up her neck, closing her throat.

Something was terribly wrong.

She had to find Sitting Bull. His strong medicine could cure almost any ailment.

With a final look at Winona to make sure she was asleep, Kimi stumbled toward the tent opening, her agony growing by the second. She gripped the chair at Annie's desk to take a breath, but her lungs clamped down with crushing pain.

The tent started to spin as Kimi gasped for breath. She clutched at her throat, desperate to stop the spasms. Light dimmed as the pain surged through her body, paralyzing her limbs. She felt herself fall to the floor, clawing at the plush rug, her fingers sinking deep into the velvety softness. "Winona," she whispered, and then sank into the darkness of her pain. The light died.

CHAPTER 1

"Wild West Show's Frank Butler to Compete in a Shooting Contest Today at the Grand Terrace Hotel. Who Will Beat the Dashing Sharpshooter from Kentucky?"

Greenville Gazette – March 25, 1885

Annie Mosey struggled to negotiate Buck and the wagon through the bustling town square traffic of Greenville, Ohio. Carts and carriages crowded the tree-lined street. Annie swallowed down the dust, watching women parade up and down the hard, dirt-packed streets in their full-length satin and velvet dresses, twirling parasols above their heads. Men wore fine wool suits, beaver hats, and fancy shoes with buttons down the side. Annie looked down at her shapeless dress trimmed with old, tea-stained lace. It paled in comparison, but she didn't care. Her modest Quaker sensibilities dictated that clothes do not make the woman.

Annie guided Buck to the Grand Terrace Hotel's white columns then hopped off the buckboard seat to help down her mother, Susan. She motioned for her youngest siblings, John Henry and Hulda, to climb down from the back of the wagon bed.

"I wonder how many will be competing? I'm not sure I like this, dear."

Her mother's dark eyes strayed toward the pedestrians in the street. She pulled her shawl closer over her ample body, covering her large bosom.

"The show's manager, Mr. LeFleur, told me they would only allow twenty shooters. They don't want to wear out Mr. Butler. The Wild West Show has to go on the road next week."

"You mean that show that travels like a circus, with worn-out cowboys and Indians acting like a bunch of foolish boys? I don't see the attraction."

"Frank Butler isn't a worn-out cowboy, Mother. He's the world's most famous sharpshooter."

They made their way around the brick walls surrounding the colonial style building. An expanse of rolling green lawn led to a pristine lake, shadowed by weeping willows and soaring elm trees. Tables set up along the back wall of the hotel indicated where the contest would take place.

Well-dressed gentlemen and sophisticated ladies milled around the tables. Annie's gaze settled on Frank Butler. He appeared relaxed, laughing with some of the other gentlemen, all of them smoking cigars, a cloudy halo around their heads. He removed his hat, raked a hand through his thick, blonde hair, and winked at one of the passing women. Annie ignored his obvious charm and concentrated on her goal: winning the money her family so desperately needed.

Someone gripped her elbow.

"Hello, Annie. Are you ready for the big match?" Mr. LeFleur's Southern drawl, with the hint of a French accent, added to his sophistication. His hazel eyes flitted over Annie's face. A bit older than her mother, with grey at his temples and tiny white streaks through his mustache, his panache made him appear much younger. Today he wore a rich brown brocade coat and velvet vest with a gold watch fob tucked in the pocket. Annie stared up at him.

"I don't know . . . I'm afraid I'll let you down—"

"Let me down? What's this talk?"

"It's just so much." She waved her arms to indicate the hotel and its surrounding beauty, and then focused her eyes on Frank Butler, "and he's so . . . pretty. Like a peacock. I feel a bit out of my league shooting next to him." Annie chided herself for feeling inferior. Her father would be appalled.

LeFleur laughed. "I guess women do consider the Irish rake pretty. But you're the best shot in Darke County."

Annie nodded, mustering her courage. She'd been shooting game to make extra money since she was ten years old, and so far, she'd not missed a single bird, rabbit, nor squirrel. Pretty or not, famous or not, she *could* outshoot Frank Butler. She straightened her spine.

"Yes, I am."

"Believe me, he's not perfect. He's not even a perfect shot."

"What do you mean?"

"Oh, he's good. A year ago, no one could have beaten him. He still wins most of the time, but something's changed. If anyone's got a chance to win here today, it's you. This is your opportunity, Annie. Have faith."

Annie looked over at her mother, who frowned at Mr. LeFleur's enthusiasm. Annie's older sister was a proper Quaker and the pride of their mother. She led a simple life of humility and grace, and married into the servitude of God. But Annie had always been different, more like her father, and somehow she knew that a simple life would not be enough for her.

But there was more at stake here than her spiritual struggle. The

3

KARI BOVEE

simple truth prevailed. Despite her mother's protest at Annie showing off her shooting skills, she needed to win the $200 prize. The farm's mortgage could not be paid with the meager earnings she made hunting game. They needed to pay the farm's mortgage, and she needed to pay LeFleur the contest entry fee. If she didn't win, she would have to marry Friend Mick Easton, another member of the Friends community she'd grown up with, who'd recently asked for her hand. Her life would be far easier, but it would be a life of sewing and housekeeping, like the life of her sister. No more shooting, no more hunting, never to leave North Star.

When the sound of gunfire filled the air, Annie and Mr. LeFleur made their way to the weapons tables.

"See anything you like?" he asked.

Annie's eyes roamed over the fine rifles, shotguns, and pistols displayed on a gleaming blue silk tablecloth.

"Oh, yes," she sighed, "but I'm going to use my father's Henry. It'll bring me luck."

LeFleur reached for her rifle. "1860 .44 Caliber."

"Yes. My father was quite proud of it. I'm better with a shotgun, but today it seems to make sense to use a rifle."

"I agree." LeFleur lit a cigar and then pointed to the shooters. "Let's see what you're up against."

Annie trained her eyes toward the competitors and their weapons.

An assembly of people, many clad in western-styled, fringe-trimmed garments and fine leather jackets with glittering collars and cuffs, stood nearby. Next to them stood a group of Indians wearing buckskin and headdresses. Annie's eyes swept over them until a tall, barrel-chested man stopped her cold. She recognized his thick head of wavy brown hair and the beard that culminated to a fine point on his chin. She was

4

staring at the Honorable William F. Cody, Buffalo Bill, owner of the Wild West Show, standing just a hundred feet from her.

A woman with exotic features leaned into Buffalo Bill, her hand curled around his arm. Her olive complexion, almond-shaped eyes, and rosebud lips, along with her purple lace bodice and flowing black skirt, made her stand out among the group like an orchid in a cotton patch.

"Next up!"

The announcer's voice startled Annie.

"You'll go last." LeFleur leaned down, his breath warm on her ear. "It'll really pack a punch after all these gents."

Another man stepped forward and glared at Frank Butler, his face set in hard lines. Butler flashed him a confident smile and nodded for the stage to begin. A contest official threw a red glass ball into the air. The opponent aimed his rifle and shot, shattering the target into hundreds of sparkling ruby pieces. Annie gauged the toss to be about thirty feet high, definitely within easy range for her. Seconds later, the official threw a blue glass bulb into the air. Butler destroyed it with ease.

The glass balls flew up, one by one, and each man hit his targets. On the fifteenth toss, the opponent missed. The official threw one more in the air and Butler hit it. The crowd roared with applause. Another opponent stepped forward.

One by one, Frank Butler annihilated his challengers. As Annie's turn approached, she tried to calm the fluttering in her chest. She turned to look at Mr. LeFleur, and he gave her a wink, rolling the cigar between his teeth, a satisfied smile playing on his lips.

"Mr. Butler is shooting well today," a woman, standing just behind Annie, said in a raspy whisper.

"Today, yes—you should have seen him last week," her friend said. "Disastrous."

"I heard Cody and his manager are thinking of dropping him from the show, if he continues to shoot poorly."

"Such a pity if he loses. You know, he gives large amounts of money to the Darke County Infirmary, to help clothe and feed poor people."

The sound of gunfire diverted Annie's attention back to the competition.

"You're up next," said LeFleur.

Annie curled her hands fiercely around the rifle, her fingers aching from the pressure. She could feel the crowd stirring, searching for the last shooter, but her feet had grown roots and she couldn't move. LeFleur grasped Annie's elbow and pulled her forward.

"Mr. Butler, meet your last opponent, fifteen-year-old Miss Annie Mosey." LeFleur grinned.

Goose pimples rose on Annie's skin. She cast a glance in Frank Butler's direction only to be greeted with that wicked smile. Annie tried to return his smile but couldn't make her lips work. She didn't want to be thrown off her aim.

"How do, Miss Mosey," he said, removing his hat with a polished flourish.

"Ready!" The announcer crowed to the audience. "Best of two rounds wins. Miss Mosey, the first shot is yours."

The official threw a glimmering, translucent yellow ball into the air. Annie drew her aim and shot, shattering the bulb into sunny fragments. Butler took aim at the next ball and shot, a pop echoing through the breeze as the shards fluttered to the ground. One by one, Annie and Butler took turns hitting the glass balls, their aim steady and sure. After fifteen hits each, the announcer stepped forward.

"Well, at this rate, it's going to take all afternoon," he said. "Let's make it a bit more challenging—two at a time!" The crowd roared.

Annie let out her breath. The shooting calmed her, made her feel more herself, as long as she didn't look at Butler. His ease in the limelight was only overshadowed by his swaggering confidence. Annie fought to maintain concentration, to not feel completely intimidated by his undeniable skill. She'd never met anyone like him. Friend Easton came close, but even he never radiated such self-assured coolness.

Two glass balls soared into the air and Annie hit them in succession with ease, gaining back her momentum. Butler hit the next two. Annie's arm began to tire. Used to the weight of the Henry, it had never taken her this long to make a day's wage in the field.

They progressed to three balls. Her eyes followed the targets. Bang, bang, bang, she hit them all.

At Butler's turn, he took aim and missed the first ball, but hit the other two. The crowd stirred behind her, their excited voices floating on the air. If she missed one of the balls, they would have to shoot again. If she hit all three, she would win $200—money her family desperately needed. But if she won, Butler could lose his job—and be ridiculed for letting a woman win. She'd win the opportunity to help her family keep the farm, but *he* could lose everything. She'd be responsible for bringing down a hero, the greatest sharpshooter in the world. Annie turned to him, her gaze meeting his.

"Think of what you could do with $200, sweetheart. Shoot straight." He winked at her.

The official launched the targets. Annie hesitated, thrown off by his patronizing words still ringing in her ears. She missed the first one, but hit the next two. A collective gasp rattled through the crowd.

Annie clenched her jaw. How could she have missed? She *never* missed.

"Next shot wins." The announcer's voice echoed throughout the grounds. "Mr. Butler's turn."

Annie glanced at Butler, praying he would miss, and then silently admonished herself for wishing another ill will. Butler pressed a thumb and finger against his eyes, looking as exhausted as Annie felt.

"My money's on the little gal," a man shouted. "Double or nothing, anyone?"

People around them laughed, and some men raised their hands to join the bet. Butler steeled his eyes forward and lifted his rifle.

The crowd murmured—the tension in the air was so palpable, Annie could feel it slicing into her bones. The ball went up and she watched it drift toward the heavens, each moment going higher and higher. She held her breath. When would he shoot? She could feel him calculate the timing of when to pull the trigger, when to destroy the shining piece of red glass in a perfectly cloudless sky—a tiny object with the power to hold or mold a future.

Frank fired and the glass ball shattered into sparkling red fragments, raining blood from the sky.

The crowd roared with delight. Frank Butler, the most famous sharpshooter in the world had won again.

Frank turned to her to shake her hand and when his palm pressed against hers, she felt as if the ground shifted beneath her feet.

"You're quite an excellent shot, Miss Mosey. You had me worried for a minute there."

Now so close to him, Annie noted that the glint of arrogance in his eyes had faded to a complacent resignation. His smile, radiant from a distance, displayed a jaded and practiced stiffness.

"Thank you, Mr. Butler. It's a pleasure to meet you."

With his right hand still holding hers, he used his other hand to lightly encircle her arm. "The pleasure was all mine." His eyes roamed over her face and then met her gaze, lingering for a moment, as if she beguiled him. Annie's face grew hot.

Seconds later, the masses, like a dark cloud, pushed forward and swept him away.

"You did just fine, Annie. Just fine." Her mother came up behind her.

"I lost, Mother. I lost the money."

"It doesn't matter." She pressed her palms to Annie's face. "You had your chance. God will provide. We'll get by somehow."

"Of course. Let's find the children. I want to go home."

Annie took her mother's arm and headed towards the main thoroughfare. She felt all the eyes of the spectators on her as they passed by. Several people shouted, "Great job, excellent shot, you sure had him worried." Annie nodded or offered a tight smile, tugging her mother through the throng.

"Miss Mosey, wait." LeFleur pushed his way through the crowd. They all three stepped aside—away from the wave of people.

"I'm so sorry, Mr. LeFleur," Annie said. "I owe you the entry fee. I'll pay back every penny, I promise."

"You are a wonder, Miss Mosey. The crowd loves you." LeFleur grabbed both of her hands and laughed.

"But I lost."

"It doesn't matter, Annie. They loved your spunk, your talent. They've never seen a girl like you. Listen, I want to take you and your mother to dinner at the hotel. There's someone I want you to meet."

Annie and her mother exchanged glances. Her mother frowned again, in obvious disapproval.

"Well, I suppose we will then, thank you." Annie hoped Frank Butler wouldn't be there. She didn't want to face him again. "We'll have to bring along my brother and sister."

"Meet me in the hotel restaurant at six o'clock. Bring everyone." LeFleur tipped his beaver top hat and pushed into the crowd again.

"Eating at the hotel," Susan said. "I'm not sure we should. I'm not sure it's proper, and we certainly haven't enough money for the week."

"But it would be rude to refuse, Mother. The grouse are coming back. I'll have a good week next week. Don't worry."

Annie's mother gave her a dubious look. "Eating at the hotel—as if I were the Queen."

The main door to the Grand Terrace Hotel revolved in a circle, sucking people in and spewing them out, all in one fluid motion. Annie and her mother watched for several minutes before stepping into one section of the orbiting door and scooting their way into the interior, plush with velvet chairs and potted palms. A grand marble staircase soared in an upward arc to the next floor. Large tapestries decorated the walls. One depicted sleek horses, red-coated riders, and a pack of long-eared dogs, galloping in pursuit of a fox. Others illustrated pastoral scenes and grand houses.

"Excuse me?" A man wearing a dark red suit and a tiny cap approached them. "Are you Annie Mosey?"

"Yes."

"Follow me, please." He tipped his hat and led them through the elegant lobby into the restaurant filled with silk brocade upholstered booths and gleaming marble tables. They paused in front of a set of cream-colored velvet curtains, and the man pulled them back to reveal a small group of people chatting and sipping champagne.

Mr. LeFleur, Buffalo Bill, the exotic woman, and a stocky Indian wearing a full-feathered headdress, engrossed in their conversation, didn't seem to notice Annie and her family.

No Frank Butler. Annie didn't know if she felt relieved or disappointed.

"Mrs. Mosey, children. Please come in and join us." LeFleur stood up.

"It's Mrs. Brumbaugh" Susan said.

Annie's shoulders tensed at hearing her late step-father's name. He'd turn in his grave if he knew her mother had taken up with Joshua Anderson—a man she had nursed back to health after a farming accident. Joshua wooed her and promised to marry her. All he'd done so far is live off of Susan's kindness and drink all day. Since her step-father died, Annie and her family's quality of life had shifted from moderately comfortable to achingly poor, and now the burden of providing for the family fell on her. She spent her days hunting food and game to sell to the grocer, to keep her family fed.

"Of course, my apologies." LeFleur ushered them in and offered them champagne.

"No, thank you." Annie held up her hand in refusal, as did her mother.

"How charmingly prim." The exotic woman's lips turned up into a smile, but her dark eyes narrowed. Annie bristled at the woman's tone.

"And you are?" Annie asked.

"Allow me to make the introductions. This is Miss Twila Midnight, Colonel Cody—also known as Buffalo Bill, but we call him Colonel—and Chief Sitting Bull." LeFleur swept his hand toward the group. "The Chief particularly admired your marksmanship today, Annie."

"The real Buffalo Bill and Chief Sitting Bull!" John Henry shouted, nearly jumping out of his seat. "I've read about you two in the newspapers. They're famous. Annie, they're famous!"

"John Henry, where are your manners? It's not polite to gush." Annie placed a hand on John Henry's arm.

"But it's Buffalo Bill and Chief Sitting Bull, Annie!"

Everyone laughed, except Twila Midnight. She lowered her sparkling gold eyelids and flashed them open again, the fire of her stare aimed at Annie.

"Chief Sitting Bull and Mr. LeFleur are quite taken with you, Annie." Buffalo Bill leaned forward to pour more champagne into his glass.

"I've been trying to convince the Chief here to join our Wild West Show for a while now, in the hopes we can kindle a certain . . . solidarity between our peoples. He's been bullheaded about it until today, says you inspired him. Now he thinks it might be a good idea if you both joined the show."

Annie's eyes darted from Buffalo Bill, to the Chief, to LeFleur. She opened her mouth to speak, but words wouldn't form.

"Watanya Cecilia." Chief Sitting Bull leaned forward and pointed a finger toward her.

"He's just christened you 'Little Miss Sure Shot.'" Buffalo Bill raised his champagne glass to her. Sitting Bull said something to the Colonel in his native language.

"The Chief would like to consider you his adopted daughter."

"Oh, my goodness!" Susan gasped.

"But—why?" Annie whispered to the Colonel.

"Says you remind him of a girl he held special once, long ago. A spirited girl, like you. It may also be that the Chief never had a daughter, only sons.

"My manager, Mr. LeFleur here," the Colonel slapped LeFleur on the back, his voice taking on a more serious tone, "thinks that you and Mr. Butler have a certain . . . chemistry. He thinks you two competing against one another will draw huge crowds."

Annie ran a finger under her lace collar, its stiffness suddenly strangling her. She hoped they didn't notice the perspiration pooling on her upper lip.

"Annie," LeFleur said, "you made Frank Butler shoot his very best today, and we need him to shoot his best. Plus, the Chief has decided that he'll only join if you join, and we want both of you."

Annie looked at her mother, who sat open-mouthed and red-faced.

"We'd like to offer you a contract to go on tour with Buffalo Bill's Wild West Show. Your salary will be $100 a month, and there aren't any women, let alone girls, earning $100 a month in the business. You're the best and will be treated like the best."

Annie drew back, clamped a hand on her chest.

"You want me in your show, squaring off with Frank Butler, traveling—"

"Yes, that's exactly right," said the Colonel.

Annie's mind tumbled with the possibilities. She could support her family entirely and experience something other than North Star. She glanced at her mother's dubious face.

"Your offer is very, very generous, sir, but I can't leave my family. They need me. I—"

"We'll make out just fine, dear." Susan grabbed Annie's arm, smiling to the group, her lips twitching with uncertainty. Annie's mouth dropped. Thank goodness her mother understood the direness of their situation and knew this opportunity could save them.

"Annie's my little worrier. Takes such good care of us, right, children?"

John Henry and Hulda nodded, their eyes wide.

Chief Sitting Bull, a giant grin spreading across his face, turned to Buffalo Bill and offered him a weathered hand. The Colonel shook it, then both men turned to Annie.

"What do you say, Miss Mosey?" The Colonel waited, stroked his tawny, pointed beard.

"May I bring my horse?" she asked.

The Colonel and Chief Sitting Bull exchanged glances.

"A mounted female shooter. By golly, that's a heck of a good idea," the Colonel said, his eyes twinkling. He cocked his head to the side. "Mosey. Not much of a show name. Got anything else?"

"My grandmother's name was Ogle. But that's not very catchy—what about Oakley?"

"Annie Oakley." The Colonel slapped his thigh. "I like it. Welcome to the show, Annie Oakley."

CHAPTER 2

"Darke County Ohio Darling 'Annie Oakley' Joins Buffalo
Bill's Wild West Show. Crowd-Pleasing Competition and
Entertainment Ahead for All."

St. Louis Times – April 1, 1885

Annie's body trembled with excitement as the train, pulling Buffalo
Bill's twenty colorfully painted boxcars, arrived in St. Louis. Mr.
LeFleur explained to her that they would camp near the train tracks at
the city's newest marvel, Forest Park, an expanse of fourteen hundred
acres of meadows, trees, lakes, and streams along the River de Peres.

It surprised Annie at how quickly the crew assembled the makeshift
camp she would consider home for the next four weeks. Large, white
canvas tents lined up in three straight rows—as neat as her late father's
fields—made the center of the camp. Adjacent to the white tents stood
a large, circular tent, red-striped, like one she'd seen in a picture of the
circus. Smoke billowed from the top indicating that the mess crew was
already busy preparing the performers' first meal.

Across from the big top, a couple dozen tipis dotted the grounds.
Indian men and women gathered in groups, talking and laughing
as they sat outside, tending their fires. Behind the tipis stood a large

wooden structure with fenced paddocks to house the show's many horses, cattle, and buffalo. Buck's new home.

Annie bit a fingernail. Buck had never resided indoors, in any sort of barn. He'd always lived in fields, with only the shelter of several large elms. She hoped he'd adjust to the confinement.

LeFleur escorted Annie to her new lodgings. She stepped inside the tent and sucked in a breath as her feet sank into the plush carpet, her eyes scanning the room. An elaborate wood-framed bed with a thick mattress stood in one corner, while a more modest bed graced the east corner of the tent, and next to that bed, a small cradle. A mirrored vanity with matching velvet stool and a wooden wardrobe painted in a bright floral pattern completed the furnishings.

She'd never imagined living in this kind of opulence. It flew in the face of everything her family believed in. She could hear her mother's voice in her head: "The heart of Christian simplicity lies in the singleness of purpose, which is first to seek the Kingdom of God. The call to each is to abandon those things that clutter his life, like wealth and worldly goods, and to press toward the goal unhampered."

Annie dismissed the voice, and the uneasy doubt it pressed upon her juxtaposed feelings.

"You will be sharing your accommodations with an Indian girl named Kimimela," Mr. LeFleur grabbed the lapels of his silk jacket. "We call her Kimi. She is here to assist you with whatever you need, and she will be designing and sewing your costumes. Kimi has a little girl, named Winona."

As if on cue, a tall, statuesque girl walked into the tent, holding an infant in her arms. The girl looked fourteen at most. Not much younger than Annie. The fringe on her suede dress brushed against her long, brown legs as she walked across the room and lowered the bundled child into the cradle. When Annie turned to ask Mr. LeFleur a question, he had vanished.

Kimi went to her bed and picked up a package wrapped in brown paper. She handed it to Annie, her dark chocolate eyes opened wide.

"For you."

"What is this? But I can't—" Stunned, Annie took the package.

"Please. I am so grateful."

"Grateful? I haven't done anything."

"Please, open."

Annie tore open the paper and underneath lay a beautiful sky-blue suede blouse with intricate embroidery and shiny beads sewed onto the yoke.

"Your first costume," Kimi beamed.

"You made this? It's beautiful. Thank you. But I—" Annie smiled, touched at Kimi's thoughtfulness, but how could she tell her she couldn't possibly wear such an extravagant thing?

Annie and Kimi stared at each other in silence, both grown suddenly shy. Kimi's face crumpled and she began to cry. She ran over to her baby.

Annie followed, horrified that Kimi had taken her silence as a sign of disregard, when a freckle-faced boy of about twelve years old appeared at the open tent flap.

"Miss Oakley, Mr. Butler would like to see you."

Annie's hands went immediately to her hair, which she knew must look like she had been caught in a dust storm, then silently chided herself for her vanity.

"I'm Bobby Bradley." The boy offered his hand. "I'm one of the youngest sharpshooters and all-around cowboys—and I do whatever Frank Butler needs me to do." Bobby's eyes traveled to the back of the tent where Kimi kneeled at the cradle, cooing to her baby, apparently no longer crying.

"Well, I'll be going." Bobby leaned to his right to get a better look at Kimi, who ignored him. Disappointment written on his face, he tipped his hat to Annie and hurried out of the tent.

Annie, still wiping the dust from her face and clothes, saw Frank Butler's silhouette appear just outside the canvas wall.

"Miss Oakley, care for some target practice?"

"Good day, Mr. Butler." Annie stepped out from the tent.

"Call me Frank. Shall we go?"

"My rifle is still in the wagon, I'll just go and—"

"You can't rely on your Henry for everything. You'll need to be a well-rounded shooter, especially if you're going to be mounted." He pushed a pistol toward her, almost crushing it into her chest.

Annie bristled. *She did just fine with her rifle, thank you very much.*

She took the proffered pistol, glancing down to admire the finely etched floral design on the barrel. The gleaming mother-of-pearl handle felt cool and smooth in her hand.

With a cocky tilt of his head, Butler bade her to follow him. They passed by the corrals and Annie noticed an older man attempting to lead Buck into a barn stall. He tugged and pulled on the rope halter but couldn't coax Buck inside. Annie knew Buck saw the stall as a small black hole where he might go in and never come out, probably still traumatized by the two-day train trip. They hadn't been able to get Buck into the train car until the Colonel insisted Twila give him some calming herbs. The herbs seemed to take the edge off his terror, but Buck kicked and thrashed all the way to St. Louis.

Annie stopped and watched as the man dangled a bucket of food in front of Buck. The horse finally followed him inside the stall. Oats worked—sometimes.

Frank led her to an open area where a series of targets were lined up against a fence. He turned to face her and handed her the other pistol.

"Let me see you hit all those targets."

"Mr. Butler, you know I can shoot."

"With a rifle. I want to see how you shoot a pistol."

He put his thumbs into the waistband of his pants and cocked a hip. Annie tried to ignore the way those grey-blue eyes slowly surveyed her face. She raised both of the pistols and pulled one trigger after the other, until she'd hit every target.

"That's what I thought." Frank took back both pistols, emptied the chambers, and then locked his eyes on hers. "You never miss. LeFleur thinks you're a wonder, and the Colonel thinks you'll make him money, but I swear on everything that matters to me that if you let me win again, I'll make sure you're fired." He shoved his pistols back into their holsters. "Welcome to the show, Miss Oakley," he said, striding off.

Annie's insides crumbled, and she swallowed down her disappointment. She never should have considered Frank Butler's feelings during the contest. She never should have missed.

She sighed, feeling as welcome as rain at a picnic.

On the way back to her tent, Annie heard banging and shouting coming from the barn area and then saw Buck running free, his lead rope trailing behind as the old man chased after him, cursing at the top of his lungs.

Buck must have spotted Annie, because he slowed to a trot and headed toward her. He circled her once, came up behind her, and pushed his nose into her back, his nostrils flaring and his rib cage heaving. She grabbed the line and stroked his neck.

"You're okay, fella."

"Damn horse struck at me then pulled away from the hitching post." The winded and sweaty man approached them. Stick thin and balding, with a grey beard straggling well past his chin, he plopped his beaten, dirty, sweat-stained hat back on his head.

"I'm sorry," Annie said. "I think it's the barn. He's not used to being confined."

"Well, he's gonna *have* to get used to it. We can't have the son-of-gun just wanderin' around." The man spit out a hunk of chaw.

"I'm sorry." She held out her hand. "My name's Annie."

"Post. Rusty Post."

"Oh, my. That's really your name?"

"Since the day I was born. I keep care of the animals around here. We got a herd of forty horses, twenty head of cattle, and twelve buffalo, and none of them ever once tried to strike at me—not even them wild Indian ponies."

"Again, I'm sorry," said Annie. The man bore a slight resemblance to Vernon McCrimmon, the man from home who had made her and Buck's lives a living hell for a year. A man she'd hoped she'd never see again. No wonder Buck resisted. "I'll work with Buck, Mr. Post. I'll try later to get him into the barn."

"I can make him a pen outside of the barn, but you're gonna have to come up with something to keep him settled while he's contained. Talk to Twila about giving you some of them herbs again, like she did for the train ride from Ohio. We need to calm that boy down."

"I will, thank you."

Post strutted his bow-legged way back to the other animals.

Annie let Buck munch on grass. She rested against him, surveying the surrounding purple hills, dark as velvet, and the miles of long green grass.

"You're going to have to find a way to deal with our new life." She ran her fingers through his ebony mane, taking advantage of his lowered head to pick through the tangles. At the sound of gunfire, Buck raised his head, pricked his ears and whinnied. Annie followed Buck's gaze to the cowboys practicing in an unfenced sandy field behind the barn.

Annie walked Buck back to the barn and tied him to a hitching post outside. She spotted her saddle, bridle, and saddle blanket resting on top of a wooden chest.

After she got Buck tacked up, she rode him over to the area where the cowboys were practicing. They had devised a course that included glass ball targets perched upon wooden tripods. One of the shooters made his way through the zigzag course, his body leaning this way, then that, the horse's legs in perfect harmony under him. Still weaving, he pulled a pistol from his belt and deftly fired at the targets, shattering the colored glass. He pulled his horse to a stop and let out a wild whoop, while another man repositioned and reloaded the targets. A group of mounted cowboys watched, their arms resting on their saddle horns. One of them approached Annie.

"You the new shooter we've heard about?"

"Yes. My name's Annie."

"Doc Hanson." He extended a hand. "Wanna give the course a whirl?"

"I'd like to see how Buck handles it first. He's having a little trouble adjusting to his new situation. Could you explain the course to me?"

Doc Hanson waved for her to follow him, and they made their way to the other riders. He explained what corners she should take and how deep she should take them, what targets to go for first, and the various patterns they used to maneuver through the field.

Annie squeezed Buck into a lope, circling the field a few times, letting him work his legs and burn through his nervous energy. He pulled at the reins, wanting to go faster, but Annie sank deep into the saddle, moving with his rhythm, and he soon let up. After Buck settled into a slow, rhythmic cadence, Annie ran the course. As she approached the targets, she held out her arm, as if shooting a pistol, and aimed for each one.

The second time around the course, she laid the reins over Buck's neck and held her arms up as if carrying a rifle, and practiced aiming at the targets. She used her legs and her seat to veer Buck in and out of the turns, marveling at the synchronicity she felt as his body flexed and surged through the obstacles. After a few turns through the course, Annie brought Buck to a stop. The cowboys whooped and hollered, obviously impressed with her skill. Annie felt heat surge through her body and up into her face.

She spied Frank Butler leaning against a fence post near the barn, watching her, a cigar glowing red between his lips. Nervousness settled in the pit of her stomach. She hoped he'd approved of her performance, but the look on his face told her different.

"That's a thing of beauty, Annie." Doc broke the silence. "You and your mount are gonna fit right in. Now, take my pistol and give the course another turn, this time shooting the targets." He handed her a Colt .45.

"Kid, reset the course!"

Bobby, the boy who'd entered her tent earlier, jumped to his feet. Once the course was reset, Annie squeezed Buck into a gallop and maneuvered through the obstacles. Buck, sure-footed and stable beneath her, made it easy for her to hit every one of the targets, bursting each colored glass ball. To her surprise, Buck never flinched when broken glass soared through the air. She brought him to a stop to another round of wild applause, and turned to get a glimpse of Frank, but he was gone.

Annie opened the flap to her tent to find Kimi straightening Annie's clothes and toiletries, the girl's previous distress gone. At least that's the way it appeared. The girl greeted Annie with a warm smile.

"Hello, Miss Oakley. I'm sorry about before."

"No apology necessary."

"It's not you. I just want you to know that."

A cry came from the baby, and Kimi went over to comfort her. She picked up the bundle and brought it over to Annie.

"This is Winona. The name means 'firstborn child' in my language, Sioux."

Bright blue eyes stared back at Annie from the baby's full, round face, her skin the color of gently tanned rawhide. The baby gave her a gummy smile.

"She's beautiful. May I ask, if you are staying with me, where does your husband stay?"

"No husband. Only me. I'm fortunate to have a place here." Kimi looked down into the face of her baby.

"Me, too." Annie smiled, wondering if Kimi's husband died, or if she never had one at all. She didn't think it polite to pry.

"The Colonel was once a scout and Indian fighter. It was his job to come into our villages and capture us for assimilation into the white man's world. Some of his men killed our people." She cast her eyes to the floor. "My parents."

Kimi motioned for Annie to sit at the vanity and then placed the baby in her arms. The warmth radiating from the little bundle melted into her and a surge of affection for the precious baby bloomed in Annie's chest. Winona cooed and blinked up at her with blue eyes and wrinkled her nose in an attempted smile.

"I was just a small child then." Kimi picked up a piece of fabric off the table. "The Colonel made amends for what his men did to our village and, instead of turning us over to the government, he took my two brothers and me with him back to his home in Kansas. They had lost their only child, so the Colonel brought us to his wife."

"How did you come to be here? With the show?"

"The Colonel came and got us a few years ago. Said he wanted us to work in the show with him. My brothers play the Indian warriors who try to ransack the white town or hold up the stagecoach. The cowboys always win, of course."

Even though agreeable and quick to smile, a lingering unhappiness hung about Kimi, like a cloud of gloom.

"What did you do—before I arrived?"

"The Colonel made me work for Twila." Kimi rolled her eyes. "She's awful. She hates me. In fact, if you had not come to the show, I don't know where I would be right now. Perhaps turned out."

"But why?"

"My people are less accepting of me now that I have Winona, because of her blue eyes." Kimi threw down some of the fabric she'd been holding, her face full of resentment. "She scares them. The Colonel is barely tolerant of me and . . . well, Twila." Kimi paused, her lips lifting to a smile. "I'm so glad you joined the show."

"I'm glad I joined the show, too. And I'm glad to be living with you and Winona." Annie handed the baby back to her. "I have felt out of place my whole life. I don't have anything in common with the rest of the girls I know. They want to live their lives inside, sew, cook, and prepare themselves for marriage. I want to be outside, breathing in the fresh air, on my own, answering to no one. The boys I grew up with were either jealous of me because of my shooting skills or they didn't take me seriously. I know what it's like to feel lonely—but now we have each other, and Winona."

"Hello." Bobby flipped open the tent flap and stepped in with a package and handed it to Annie. He sought out Kimi again, but she turned her back to him. With a tip of his hat, he ducked out as quickly as he'd come.

Annie thought the parcel might be from home, so she tore through the paper. Inside rested two pearl-handled, engraved Colt .45 pistols, nestled in a tooled-leather holster belt. She pulled one out and turned it over in her hands, admiring its beauty. A card inside the box said, "Best of luck, partner. Frank."

Annie gasped in disbelief.

"Kimi, I'll be back in a minute."

"Yes, please." The young woman resumed her task of perusing fabrics and sorting Annie's belongings.

Annie found LeFleur and Twila in LeFleur's tent, arguing about something. The Colonel, wearing a white suede bead-embellished jacket, sat at the desk smoking a cigar. He sipped at a silver flask like a king on a throne, amusement written on his face.

"I am sorry to interrupt." Annie walked further into the lodging, awestruck by its immense size and expensive furnishings. Her tent, though beautiful, did not compare. An oversized, rustic trunk with a bulky and heavily scratched padlock seemed out place next to the desk.

"It's no problem, dear," LeFleur said. "What can we do for you? Are you settling in all right?"

"Yes, thank you, but I can't accept this gift."

"I'm sorry. I don't know what you mean." LeFleur shook his head.

"Mr. Butler sent me these gorgeous pistols."

Twila twirled around, her dark eyes blazing. Surprised at her reaction, Annie blinked and then looked at LeFleur, unwilling to engage with the woman.

"It seems you have a fan, Miss Oakley," LeFleur said.

"But it's too much. I can't accept them."

"Do you have a set of pistols, Miss Oakley?" The Colonel let his chair down with a loud thud and stood up.

He seemed a giant to her, standing there, twirling the cigar in his mouth with one hand, the other hand resting on his gun belt.

"No sir, but—"

"You'll need those guns before you get paid. You've got routines to learn, practices and rehearsals to attend, lots of targets to shoot. Am I clear?"

"I see," Annie said, not pleased.

"These are fine pistols." LeFleur peered into the box. He pulled one out, holding it up for the others to see, then placed it back into the box.

"Yes, they are beautiful, but I'd rather buy my own guns."

"Right now, you can't afford them, and Butler's a generous man. He doesn't expect anything in return."

Annie took the box and turned her attention to Twila, trying to ignore the insistent glare of the woman's coal-black eyes. Mr. Post had told her to get some herbs for Buck from this unfriendly woman who always seemed offended by Annie's mere presence. Would she give him something harmful?

Annie took in a deep breath, weighing her options. If she wanted to continue with the show—the best opportunity she'd had thus far to help her family—she would have to trust Mr. Post's word that Twila could help Buck again.

"I am sorry to bother you, Miss Midnight, but I need to talk to you about my horse. He won't go into the barn, and Mr. Post thought you could use your herbs to make a calming tonic for him."

Twila's lips turned up in a smile, but the smile never reached her eyes.

"I will speak with Mr. Post," she said, dismissing Annie with a wave of her hand.

CHAPTER 3

"Tickets to First Six Performances of Wild West Show at Forest
Park Going Fast. Get your tickets before they sell out.
Show to run from April 5 to April 30."

St. Louis Times – April 5, 1885

On the morning of her first performance, Annie knew the but-
terflies swirling in her stomach traveled through her body right
into Buck's, making him agitated and nervous. She tried to speak to
him in soothing tones, but the words came out clipped and sharp, and
Buck would have none of her attempted sweet talk. She tried to steady
her shaking hands by combing her fingers through Buck's mane, but
only succeeded in ruining Mr. Post's fine grooming job. He'd polished
and waxed Buck's coat to gleaming gold and his black mane and tail
glowed midnight-blue in the sunshine.

Kimi's gift, the form-fitting, blue suede blouse and silk-lined riding
skirt—the most luxurious things Annie had ever put on her body—
threatened to roast her alive. Her protest to Mr. LeFleur about the
extravagance of the costume fell on deaf ears.

"Wearing the costume is part of doing your job," he'd said.

The silver diamond-shaped Conchos that trailed down her sleeves and down the legs of the riding skirt, though stunning, felt like burning pools of silver against her arms and legs.

Adding to her stress, they'd pasted flyers all over St. Louis announcing that Buffalo Bill's Wild West Show would introduce "its newest pride and joy—the beautiful, petite, and most excellent female sharpshooter in the world: Miss Annie Oakley." When Bobby showed Annie the posters and told her the tickets had sold out "faster than a late summer wildfire," the blood drained from her head.

Annie walked Buck in tight circles, trying to get him focused. She calmed herself by breathing slowly in and out, counting her breaths to keep a rhythm.

Frank Butler came into the paddock area riding a stunning brown-and-white paint with a striped mane and tail.

"You're going to be fine." He pulled his horse to a stop beside her. His mare immediately lowered her head and closed her eyes. "You'll get used to the nerves."

"Easy for you to say, your horse looks like she's taking a nap."

"Once Buck starts to run, he'll burn off that nervous energy and be as calm as Fancy here," Frank grinned.

"Fancy? Isn't that kind of a sissy name for the famous Frank Butler's mount?"

"You're such an itty-bitty thing," he said. "Amazing you can wrangle that skittish horse. You might try wrangling me, sometime." Frank tipped his Stetson, his eyes scanning her body. Annie blushed at his forwardness.

"Simmer down, Mr. Butler." Annie knew she wasn't pretty in a girlish sense, but she had a pleasant face, long, lustrous hair, feminine curves, and tiny waist, even without her corset.

"How'd you like those pistols?" Frank nodded toward her holster. His gloved hands rested on his saddle horn, and the mirrored silver accents on his suede jacket—made to match hers—blinded her with their brilliance.

Annie brought Buck to a stop, dropping the reins onto his neck. The horse finally exhaled a great breath and stood still, his ears pricked forward, his head high and straight, the muscles on the sides of his neck bulging.

"They're beautiful, but I really didn't—"

Frank held up a hand.

"LeFleur told me you were uncomfortable about the gift, but don't think twice about it, Annie. We're in this together. If you look good, then I look good."

Annie feigned a smile at the disappointing reality of his self-serving gift.

The crowd inside the stadium gave a mighty roar.

"It's showtime, darlin'." Frank snapped down the brim of his hat. "You're on."

The gates opened, revealing a massive arena with tiered grandstands soaring to the sky. Box seats lined the floor of the ring, decorated with colorful swags and pots of flowers. Top hats, parasols, pennants, and banners created a tapestry of color among the masses. Annie reminded herself to breathe as the roaring crowd chanted, "Annie, Annie, Annie," so loud it sounded like thunder.

Annie swallowed her nerves, forced the biggest smile she could muster, and gave Buck a squeeze with her legs. In his enthusiasm, the horse leapt off of all four feet simultaneously and charged into the arena.

Annie galloped Buck around the arena, his speed threatening to take off her hat. She eyed the targets—the familiar colored glass balls set upon tripods, arranged in an intricate course of turns and circles. She breathed in determination and breathed out her anxiety, visualizing her bullets hitting each and every one of them. The image of glass flying like confetti at a parade settled her mind.

Sensing her fortitude and sense of purpose, Buck's rhythm steadied. She turned him left onto the course and drew her pistol. It felt heavy and sure in her grip, like it had been molded to fit her hand. She leaned her body to the left, lining up for the first target, and pulled the trigger. The yellow ball exploded, and the crowd roared. She leaned to the right, her body and Buck's body as one, as they raced through the serpentine course, hitting all the marks.

For the last set of double targets, set up on two parallel straight lines, Annie turned Buck to position him in the center of the targets and, leaning her weight forward, urged him into a run. She laid the reins on his neck, pulled out her other pistol, and with both weapons shot the elevated glass balls, one at a time on each side of her.

The crowd rose to their feet, their shouts and cheers a cacophony of music in her ears. Annie felt adrenaline, along with happiness and exhilaration, racing through her body. She never knew she could feel so proud or so fulfilled. Her actions made people happy, and that made the apprehension of living a glamorous life dwindle. In her own way, she could serve God and mankind at the same time.

To close her shooting stage, emboldened by the crowd's obvious enjoyment of Buck's and her performance, Annie sat deep in her seat, shifted her weight back to allow Buck's hind end to crouch as he slid to a dramatic stop. He raised his upper body into a rear, his front legs pawing the air, and Annie leaned forward, riding the upward momentum. She gave the audience an enthusiastic wave, a giant smile radiating on her face.

"Ladies and gentlemen," the announcer said, "the brilliant Annie Oakley and Buck the Wonder Horse!" The crowd thundered their approval. "Next up, the most amazing, most charming, most handsome, fiercest shootist on the globe—Frank Butler!" Again the crowd roared.

Annie loped Buck to the far end of the ring to allow Frank his turn. Fancy sped into the arena so fast, Annie blinked in astonishment. Frank galloped two laps around the arena, waving his gun in the air, coaxing the crowd to cheer louder and louder, raising them to their feet before turning Fancy and aiming for the targets. One, two, and three broke into shards, but he missed the fourth and the fifth. The spectators moaned in disappointment. Three more targets. He hit them all, then made two more laps around the arena. The crowd cheered with abandon.

He made his way to Annie, and she noticed the same tightness around Frank's eyes she'd seen before. His face had gone pale, and his smile lacked its usual confidence. Together they rode to the center of the arena, waving to the crowd.

Several of the crew ran out to meet them. Annie and Frank dismounted, and one of the crewmen took the horses by the reins, leading them out of the arena. Several other crewmembers quickly brought out a small table, several rifles, and a deck of cards.

Annie held up the ace of diamonds for everyone to see and rushed to her mark, holding the card at arm's length. Frank snapped up one of the rifles, aimed, and fired a hole clear through the diamond. The crowd whooped and hollered.

Next, Annie held another playing card, its face perpendicular to the ground. Frank peered through the sight, paused, then raised his head, as if refocusing—something he'd never done in practice. He again lowered his eye to the sight, aimed, fired, and split the card half. The crowd bellowed with cheers and laughter.

Frank ran toward Annie and before she could stop him, he swept her up and swung her around in a circle, squeezing her so tight, she could barely breathe. The firmness of his arms and the aromatic mixture of his sweat and musky cologne jarred her in a way she didn't expect. She wanted to pull away from him, tell him to get off her, but she didn't, surprised at the giddy feeling in her head as his arms held her tight. It must be the excitement of performing in front of the audience for the first time, she thought. Annie put her druthers aside and let the wave of the crowd's adoration crash over her, soaking her to her core.

No longer Annie Mosey from Greenville, Ohio, she was now Annie Oakley, "Little Miss Sure Shot," star of Buffalo Bill's Wild West Show.

Annie performed flawlessly for the next several shows, her aim sure and straight. Buck seemed to love the adoration and affection the people lavished upon him after every performance.

"Heck," Bobby said after one of Annie's acts, "we could become powerful rich just selling tickets for people to give Buck a pat on the nose."

Bobby, LeFleur, the Colonel, and especially Kimi seemed excited about Annie's contribution to the show, but Frank grew increasingly aloof. Annie knew it bothered him that she'd become the crowd favorite, but as a team they sold a lot of tickets and made the show a boatload of money.

After one of her performances, Mr. LeFleur called her to a meeting in his tent. The show was a resounding success; she couldn't imagine what the manager wanted. When she went inside, the Colonel, Twila, Frank, and a robust girl of about thirteen all turned their attention toward her.

"Annie," LeFleur pulled her toward the group, "this is Miss Lillian Smith, a local sharpshooter."

"I go by Lillie," the girl said, barely glancing at Annie.

Annie glanced at Frank, reclining in a chair, his legs crossed at the ankles. He raised his chin and winked at her, and she returned the greeting with a wave of her hand. Twila approached Lillie and caressed a lock of the girl's long, curly, brown hair—her only pleasing feature. The Colonel said nothing, but the pinched look on his face indicated his displeasure.

"Lillie is Twila's adopted sister." LeFleur inclined his head toward Annie. "We'd like to add her to the act. How would you feel about that?"

Annie pressed her lips together, shrugged a shoulder.

"Will my wages change?"

Her family needed all the money she earned to keep their nearly foreclosed family farm—and they all knew that.

"All will stay the same."

"Then I guess that would be fine."

Annie had no reason to complain, but something in Lillie's demeanor irritated her. Perhaps Lillie wouldn't prove as prickly as she appeared.

"Lillie will be bunking with you and Kimi." LeFleur smiled.

A sour feeling curdled in Annie's stomach, but she smiled back at the manager anyway.

When Annie got back to her tent, she heard yelling and arguing from inside. She walked in to find Kimi and Bobby at odds over something. At Annie's sudden appearance, Kimi turned her back to both of them, burying her face in her hands. Bobby, his cheeks mottled pink and his face grim, tipped his hat to Annie and stormed out of the tent.

Annie glanced down at the mound of fabric, beads, feathers, and other costume accessories on the table. Kimi spun back around and feigned a cheery expression, her smile crooked and false, the life in her eyes dimmed like the flame of a dying candle. Crescents formed below her lower lids and her cheeks flushed with color.

"What's the matter, Kimi?"

"It's nothing. I must be tired. You know, the baby and all."

"Is there anything I can do to help? It looks like you have a lot to do here. I'm a pretty good seamstress myself, although my sister, Hulda is better." The words tumbled out of Annie's mouth in a rush. It didn't seem right—this girl, this woman, this mother, working for her.

"I have another person to sew for now. It's just a bit overwhelming."

"Yes, the new girl, Lillie. Really, I can help you with the costumes. I have nothing to do when I'm not practicing. It would make me feel so much better."

"I could use the help. Sometimes Winona wants nothing but for me to play with her." Kimi sniffed and rubbed the back of her hand across her nose.

Annie's heart warmed. It would be good to use her hands again.

"I wanted you to take a look at this color." Kimi rose from her chair. She turned to pick up the bolt of fabric lying on the end of the table.

Black, blue, and yellow bruises stained the skin on Kimi's upper back.

"Your shoulders!" Annie gasped.

Kimi gently picked up the bolt of fabric and sat back down, her eyes trained on the table, avoiding Annie's.

"What happened to you, Kimi? Who did this?"

Kimi pulled in a breath and raised her large, sorrowful brown eyes to Annie's.

"It doesn't matter. Please, I don't want to discuss it."

"Was it Bobby?" The words came out of Annie's mouth before she could stop them. He seemed the obvious culprit, given his ill temper a few minutes ago.

"No! Not Bobby, never Bobby. Please, I don't wish to discuss this."

An alarm, like the sound of cast iron kettles being struck with hammers, rang in Annie's head, remembering all too well the kind of pain Kimi might be experiencing.

At the trial two years ago, Annie had felt petrified and enraged at the same time when the sheriff questioned her, urging her to tell her story.

"Let's start from the beginning, Miss Mosey. Did you work for Mr. Vernon McCrimmon?"

"Yes, sir, I did."

"In what capacity?"

"I was hired out by the Darke County Infirmary to take care of his ailing wife and child."

"How long did you work there?"

"One very long year, sir."

Snickering throughout the courthouse quieted when the sheriff lifted his gavel.

"Did they treat you well?"

"No, sir." Annie clasped her trembling hands together in her lap.

"She's a liar!" McCrimmon shouted, jumping up from his chair, his bony body swaying with drunkenness, reeking of moonshine.

"Silence!" Sheriff Brody clanged his gavel down so hard the sound block bounced. *"Mr. McCrimmon, you are to sit still and remain quiet until I ask for your testimony. Now, please tell me, Miss Mosey, in what way were you mistreated?"*

Annie coiled her hands into fists and held them steady on each side of her knees.

"They beat me. Especially him. They would lock me in a closet for days. No food, no water. Once, they threw me out into the snow in the middle of the night, wearing only my nightdress."

Annie shuddered at the memory of that night, and her fear that she might die like her father did from the aftereffects of being frozen in a storm.

"Kimi, I understand. I've been in your position before. Please let me help you."

Kimi pressed a hand to her mouth, as if debating whether to speak.

"I suffered beatings from a man I worked for, Vernon McCrimmon. He abused Buck, too. I know what you are going through, and you don't have to put up with it, Kimi. We are all equal in God's eyes."

Kimi turned her head away from Annie, hiding her face.

Interrupting them, Lillie showed up at the tent with several of the crewmen.

"Boys, put my bed over here, by the entrance. Never know when company might drop in." She gave her helpers a mischievous, deep-dimpled grin.

When they returned carrying a small wardrobe, the noise woke Winona and she began to wail. Kimi rushed over to pick up the crying child.

Lillie thrust her chin toward Kimi, but fixed her eyes on Annie.

"What's she doing here?"

"She lives here. She makes our costumes, helps take care of us."

The baby's crying intensified. Kimi bundled baby Winona close to her chest and wove her way between them to slip out of the tent. Lillie grabbed her by the arm, and Kimi looked into Lillie's hardened face with surprise.

"Don't test me, squaw."

Kimi shook her off and scooted past them through the tent flap.

"They aren't sleeping in here with us, are they?" Lillie, placing her lace-clad fists on her hips, fired a look at Annie. "We'll have to sleep with one eye open. Damn Indians."

"They are. And you'll not speak to or about Kimi, or any of her people, in such a demeaning way in my presence. They are just as important to the show as we are. Do you understand?"

"So I not only have to share the stage and my tent with the do-gooder Annie Oakley, I have to share it with a squaw and her half-breed?"

"You do." Annie stepped forward and glared hard in Lillie's eyes. "And, like I told you, watch your mouth. It would benefit you to be friendly."

Lillie snorted.

"You threatening me? I don't think that's a good idea, Miss Oakley. And as far as being friendly goes, I'm friendly, all right—just ask the boys."

~

Later that night, Annie, LeFleur, Frank, and many others met at a saloon in St. Louis to celebrate the success of the show.

Annie wanted to ride Buck into town, but LeFleur insisted he escort Annie in his horse-drawn carriage.

They entered the establishment to find Frank Butler entertaining the crowd with his effusive charm. His relaxed posture—an elbow resting on the brass railing of the bar, and his long legs crossed at the ankles—showed his clear understanding of his power to enchant. He leaned closer to a group of men and two women to emphasize a point, and they all laughed, their eyes and attention completely focused on the famous sharpshooter. He ran a hand through his thick mane of blond hair, like a lion showing off to the pride. Annie smirked, seeing through his vain pretense, but then frowned when Lillie squeezed her way into the group to whisper something in Frank's ear.

Several polished and poised ladies at a nearby table shook their heads in disapproval as Lillie blew smoke rings into the air, let out a shrieking laugh, and wrapped her arm around Frank's shoulders. When she felt Frank's gaze on *her*, Annie turned towards LeFleur and pretended to be engaged in conversation with him, but she could feel Frank's eyes lingering. She didn't want him to see her observing him in his glory, or to see him flirting openly with Lillie. *He'd do anything to rankle me.*

Performing with him in the arena had proven surprisingly easy, but outside of the act, he made it known to her and everyone else that he remained a celebrity—and deservedly so—but very much out of her league, professionally and personally.

A gentleman tapped a glass with a spoon and asked for everyone's attention.

"To the shootists and players of Buffalo Bill's Wild West Show." He raised a glass.

Chief Sitting Bull and a group of Indians at a nearby table raised their tankards of beer in the man's direction. Annie caught the Chief's eye and he smiled and lifted his cup again to her, and she returned the tribute with a lift of her own glass filled with sarsaparilla.

"To the expertly talented star of the show, Frank Butler," the man continued.

The crowd raised their glasses and cheered. Frank removed his hat with a flourish, bowed at the waist, and flashed his trademark smile as he popped back up. Annie couldn't help the small grin that crept across her face at the spectacle of Frank in his element, surrounded by his fans. How she longed to possess his sunny confidence.

"A toast to the newest member of the group, rifle sharpshooter Miss Lillian Smith."

Lillie removed the cigar from her mouth and raised her whiskey glass to the group. A smaller round of applause circulated throughout the room.

"And last, but not least, a toast to the expert and accomplished mounted shooter, Miss Annie Oakley!"

Loud whoops and hollers, whistles and shouts filled the room.

Annie wanted to clamp her hands over her ears. She smiled and waved to the crowd. It felt good to be so appreciated.

She sensed Frank's eyes on her, and his hard gaze made a chill snake up her back. He snatched his hat off the bar and strode out of the restaurant, Lillie trailing behind him.

LeFleur and Annie left after midnight, returning to camp in his carriage. Her limbs and mind heavy with fatigue, Annie stared out the window as the carriage slipped through the trees in the inky dark of night. She felt calmer, the adrenaline from all the attention abating, but couldn't stop thinking about Frank's cold glare, and Lillie fawning over him, acting like a fool.

By the time they got back to Forest Park, few people stirred in the camp. Some of the Indian players sat at campfires outside their tipis, smoking pipes and playing cards, but most had retired to their beds.

LeFleur escorted Annie to her tent, his hand firm on her elbow.

"You've become the sweetheart of the Wild West Show." He turned to face her. "I knew you'd be a success. You were worth every penny of that ten dollars I paid to enter you in the Greenville shooting contest and more, my dear, far more."

Annie met his gaze.

"Thank you, Mr. LeFleur, I'm afraid all that fuss rather tired me out, so I will say goodnight."

Suddenly, he drew closer and leaned his head toward hers, as if he meant to kiss her. Annie stepped back, her hands gently pushing him away.

"What's this, Mr. LeFleur?" She thought him handsome but felt no attraction to this much older man—and had done nothing to encourage him.

"Ah, nothing. Well . . ." He planted a kiss on her forehead. "You go rest. We'll see you in the morning."

Her brain swimming with the effects of her new celebrity and LeFleur's boldness, Annie stepped inside the darkness of her tent and made a beeline for the soft featherbed she'd come to love. When her foot caught and she went sprawling, she reached out to break her fall and felt the unmistakable firmness of a human jaw beneath her hand.

Heart jangling, her skirt tangled around her legs, Annie scrambled to get upright. She fumbled in the darkness trying to get to her desk. Once there, she grabbed a candlestick and scrabbled her hands along the desktop for a box of matches. She found them, her fingers trembling so violently she failed to light the flame three times. Finally, it caught.

As soon as light illuminated the tent, Annie spun around to see what she had stumbled over and gasped—Kimi lay motionless on the ground.

"Kimi! Oh, my God, Kimi!" Annie placed a finger on the girl's neck, seeking a pulse, and couldn't find one. She laid a hand on Kimi's forehead. The skin had gone cold.

Kimi was dead.

CHAPTER 4

"Spring Heat Wave Gives Way to Possible Thunderstorms"

St. Louis Times – April 12, 1885

"Where's the baby?" Annie said aloud.

Winona's cry from the crib answered her. Stepping over Kimi's lifeless body, Annie made her way over to the baby.

This couldn't be happening.

Annie's head spun. She felt detached from her body, suspended in time as if in a dream. She had to get to the baby, yet her feet felt like lead, her limbs heavy, the air in the tent thick as water as she fought her way through to get to Winona.

Finally, she reached the crib and scooped the bundled Winona up into her arms. The child wailed even louder, breaking Annie out of her stupor. Annie bounced her up and down, trying to quiet her. Walking back over to Kimi, her mind still foggy, her heart pounding, she looked down at Kimi's face. The dewy, honey-colored skin had gone grey with a hint of blue. A swath of straight black hair covered the chin, and the eyes stared open, their light snuffed out.

Annie choked back a sob and hurried to the opening of the tent, holding Winona close to her chest, the baby's frantic crying piercing her ears.

"Somebody, help!"

Annie's scream brought an immediate response. LeFleur rushed over, and Annie slipped back inside her tent. LeFleur stepped through and saw Kimi on the floor.

"What's this? What happened?"

"I don't know. I came in to go to bed and fell over her. I don't know how long she's been here. Help her!" The moment the last two words came out of her mouth, she realized the absurdity of them.

LeFleur knelt down and ran his hand down Kimi's face, closing her eyes. He then lifted her gently to the bed.

"I just can't imagine what happened." A sting started behind Annie's eyelids, her voice shaking. "Kimi, Kimi, Kimi."

LeFleur stood back from the body, one hand tucked into his pocket, the other cupping his chin, his face grey.

Winona's urgent yowl snapped Annie's mind back into focus, and she hugged the baby close, swaying from one foot to the other, alternating the motion with bouncing up and down. In moments, Winona's cries turned to whimpers. Annie took the corner of the blanket and dabbed at the baby's face.

"Shhh," she murmured. "It's alright, Winona."

Annie looked up to see the Colonel and Twila enter the tent, several others on their heels. They all crowded around Kimi, gasping, talking, their voices raised in alarm.

"What happened?" The Colonel shouted over the din.

"Hush, everyone, stand back." LeFleur urged people to move aside.

The gathering crowd took a few steps back, still craning their necks to catch a glimpse of Kimi.

"Tell me what's wrong with her. What is this, LeFleur?" The Colonel rushed forward.

"There's no heartbeat, no pulse, no breath, she's cold, and her fingertips are blue."

"Are you saying . . .?"

Twila, who had shoved her way closer, drew in a sharp breath.

The Colonel stared hard at LeFleur, his face draining of color, his lip twitching, waiting for an answer.

"Yes," LeFleur said. "I'm afraid she's gone."

Murmurs circulated around the tent.

"Are you sure? Positive?" The Colonel grasped LeFleur's arm.

LeFleur nodded.

The Colonel dropped to his knees and gently lifted Kimi's lifeless body to his chest. "Why, why, why?" He buried his head in her neck and rocked her back and forth, as if she were a child merely sleeping.

A few of the cowboys pressed forward, causing the others to do the same. Bobby came up from behind, put his hands on their shoulders, dragging them backwards, trying to push his way to the front.

"Kimi! What happened? Oh, God. Is she—?"

"Everyone, clear the tent." LeFleur shooed all of them back. "Let's give the Colonel some room."

Most heeded LeFleur's command and shuffled out of the tent into the cold night air, but Bobby and Twila stayed.

"Out, Bobby," LeFleur said.

Annie's heart crumpled as she watched Bobby walk backwards toward the tent opening, his eyes fixed on Kimi, his freckled cheeks pink from running in the crisp night air, his chin trembling.

Annie stepped next to LeFleur, bouncing the whimpering Winona gently in her arms, trying to soothe the baby, whose cries had quieted to little snuffles and short intakes of breath.

"Give me the baby." Twila stepped forward.

"No, I have her." Annie pulled Winona closer, cradling her tiny head, pressing her small body against her heart.

Twila narrowed her eyes, but Annie held firm, glaring as hard as she could in return. Twila huffed, spun around, and returned to the Colonel's side.

"Come, Annie," LeFleur said. "You and the baby can rest in my tent for now."

"Wait, don't leave yet." The Colonel gently released Kimi and raised himself to his feet, suddenly looking much older than he had minutes ago. "What happened? Who did this?" He directed his question at Annie.

"I don't know. Kimi was on the ground when I came into the tent. I called to her, checked her pulse, but—nothing. Then I called for help."

"I was here within seconds." LeFleur said. "From the temperature of her body, it appears Kimi expired hours ago."

The Colonel raked his hands through his hair.

"She's so young, so healthy. How could this happen? How?"

Twila placed her hand on the Colonel's arm, looked into his eyes.

"We may not know how or why for some time, my darling. Some people have weak hearts. I've seen many pass within seconds from a weak heart. Even young people are not spared."

The Colonel buried his face in his hands.

"Leave us alone." Twila trained her eyes on Annie.

Clutching the baby tighter to her chest, a wave of sadness rolled through Annie. This little child would have no mother. The father, whoever he was, if alive, made no claim on the child. What would happen to this precious little baby?

Once inside LeFleur's tent, he pulled out a chair for Annie, signaled for her to sit, and pulled a chair up for himself.

"I can't believe she's gone. How could this happen?" Annie stroked Winona's cheek, soft and downy as a baby bird's chest.

"Did Kimi seem all right before you left for the outing?"

"Yes . . . well, no. She'd been crying, upset about something, but she wouldn't tell me what was wrong."

"Had you seen her upset before, recently perhaps?"

"Just today. She and Bobby had a spat. I could hear them arguing as I approached the tent, but when I came in, they stopped and he left. I asked her if she wanted to talk about it, but she shook her head and went back to sewing my new costume. That's all I remember. I didn't hear what they were arguing about."

"She never was a talkative sort. Always shy, quiet." LeFleur ran a finger over his mustache.

"Had she ever been sick or complained of any physical ailments?" Annie asked.

"No, quite the contrary, she always appeared to be well. I don't recall any illnesses or weaknesses."

Annie gasped, suddenly remembering.

"She had bruises all over her back."

"Bruises?"

"Yes. I asked her about them, but again, she gave me no information. Lillie walked in the tent, interrupting us. We never finished the conversation." The last words died on Annie's tongue.

"Were the bruises fresh?" LeFleur avoided her gaze.

"I only saw them yesterday, and most were still purple, some yellowed."

The baby squirmed in Annie's arms and began to fuss.

"I think the baby needs to eat," Annie said. "How will we feed her?"

"I'll see if I can find some milk." LeFleur stood up. "I also need to go find Kimi's brothers, before they hear what's happened from someone else. They will take this news very hard . . . as we all have." He left the tent.

The baby fussed harder, so Annie rocked her back and forth, trying to comfort her. She thought walking would help so stood and attempted to scoot the chair away with her legs. She lost her balance and almost fell into the oversized trunk she'd noticed the first time she saw Mr. LeFleur's tent. She righted herself and sidled past the trunk, banging her knee on the bulky padlock.

"Ouch!" Annie stepped around the trunk and moved to the center of the tent, where she would have more space.

She paced and rocked the baby, her feet sinking into the luxurious plushness of Mr. LeFleur's Persian rug. She admired the stately four-poster bed, the large oak desk, the velvet chairs, and expensive trunks. Had he always been rich? Of course, she hadn't seen the Colonel's tent yet. LeFleur's might be modest in comparison—but far more lavish than the one she shared with Kimi. Once shared.

The baby quieted again, but Annie knew she'd have to eat soon.

Bobby suddenly rushed into the tent, eyes wide, unblinking, frantic. Sweat glistened on his forehead.

"What happened? What happened to Kimi?" He stood inches away from Annie, clenching and unclenching his fists. "She was fine when I left her."

Annie raised her eyebrows. *Kimi had not been fine when he left her.*

"I know you heard us arguing, and I know she was upset with me, but she was fine. What could have happened to her?"

"I'm sorry, Bobby, I know this is a terrible shock."

Bobby walked toward the bed and settled onto it, balancing himself with his arms as if he might collapse. Annie noticed a crystal decanter filled with liquor and two crystal glasses on LeFleur's desk. Consuming liquor went against her beliefs, but Bobby looked as if he needed fortifying. Still holding the baby in one arm, she filled one of the glasses with the amber liquid and took it over to Bobby.

"Here, this might help. You look as if you are going to buckle."

Bobby wagged his head back and forth.

"No. I'm fine." He took the glass and swallowed the liquor down in one gulp.

"I don't know what to say . . . or what to think," Annie said.

Bobby sat the empty glass on the bed and covered his face with his hands. "I shouldn't have—"

"What's that?"

"—gotten angry. I was so angry with her."

Annie had known Bobby for only a short while, but she couldn't imagine anyone with his freckled, boyish face and sweet demeanor hurting anyone, emotionally or physically. Certainly not the young girl he so obviously adored.

"Why were you angry?"

"It's not important now; it really wasn't that important then. I overreacted. I shouldn't have been so angry with her." He raised his head to look straight into Annie's eyes.

"I loved her . . . she was my girl." The last words came out in an emotional croak.

Holding Winona close, Annie sat down next to Bobby and used her free hand to rub his back, making small circles like her mother used to do to comfort her.

"I'm awfully sorry, Bobby."

Bobby shook off her hand and sprang to his feet.

"I don't deserve your pity, miss." He lowered his eyes. "I thank you for your kindness, but I don't deserve it."

He ran out of the tent, almost bumping into LeFleur as he returned.

"Where's he running off to?" LeFleur asked.

"He's upset, which is understandable. I think we're all upset that such a young girl would die suddenly, for no apparent reason."

"Did he say anything about their argument?"

"Only that it wasn't about anything important. He regretted being angry with her and claimed he loved her. I believe him."

"Yes, I suspected as much." He held up a glass jar. "I found goat's milk in the ice box, but I couldn't find Twila . . . she would know what to do."

"Winona is too young to drink milk from a jar, she's only had her mother's . . . We'll have to find something she can suckle." Annie bit her lip, thinking. "There's some chamois on Kimi's sewing table, in our tent. Would you mind getting it? I'd go, but . . . I just can't go back in there, not yet."

The baby issued a piercing cry.

"My dear, I fear it will be much quicker if you go yourself." LeFleur winced at the sound.

Annie sighed and thrust the wailing Winona into LeFleur's arms.

"I refuse to let this child see her mother's dead body again." She ignored his panicked look and ran, as quickly as she could, to her tent.

She found Twila still in the tent, looking for something. Kimi's body was gone.

"What are you doing here?" Twila said.

"This is my tent. I'm looking for chamois to feed the baby. What are *you* doing here? Why are you rummaging through our things?"

"Where is the baby?" Twila straightened her shoulders, glared at Annie.

"She's in Mr. LeFleur's tent. She's very hungry."

Twila dismissed Annie with a wave of her hand and continued her search.

"Miss Midnight, please leave my tent." Annie needed to get back to the baby, but she wanted Twila out of her tent. What could she be looking for?

"Very well." Twila stood. "But the girl stole something from me, a necklace with a butterfly pendant. I want it back."

"A necklace? I've never seen Kimi wearing a necklace."

"Of course you didn't, she stole it. Why would she wear it?" Twila stormed from the tent.

Annie scratched her head, amazed that at this time, during this tragedy, Twila could only think of a necklace.

More concerned about the hungry baby than Twila, Annie grabbed a swath of chamois and fled back to Mr. LeFleur's tent.

She found the baby screaming, her little face red with anger, and LeFleur frozen, his face blanched, holding little Winona at arm's length.

Annie removed the wailing bundle from his arms.

"For heaven's sake, Mr. LeFleur, she's a baby, not a monster." Annie cradled the baby, sat down on the bed, dipped the cloth into the milk, and held the moistened corner up to the baby's mouth. It took a few seconds, but when Winona realized the liquid dripping into her mouth was nourishment, her wails diminished to tiny grunts and coos. Annie let out her breath, her whole body sinking in relief, finally able to give some comfort to Winona's needs.

Annie looked up to see Mr. LeFleur staring at the baby, his face etched with fear, or nervousness, or something.

"Mr. LeFleur, are you all right?"

He blinked out of his frozen stare at the baby.

"Yes, yes. I just didn't realize—"

"Realize what?"

Instead of answering, he clapped his hands together as if rallying the troops, and the expression on his face shifted from concern—or maybe fear—to its usual charming demeanor, like a practiced artisan playing a role.

"Oh, well. Nothing. I mean, of course I'm distressed about our poor Kimi, and Winona, but it looks like you've solved the problem for the time being. I'll leave you to finish feeding her. Take your time."

"Thank you. Oh, before you leave, I was wondering if you knew— who was, or is the baby's father?"

LeFleur stopped in his tracks, his back to her, holding the tent flap open. Slowly he turned his head, but only far enough that she could hear his raised whisper.

"The Colonel."

The sleeping baby in her arms, Annie stood to take Winona back to the cradle in her tent, when the Colonel and Twila appeared.

The Colonel, stooped over with grief and grey in the face, came over and stared down at the sleeping baby. Annie wondered how he felt now that the mother of his child was dead. A child herself. Annie's stomach flipped, and she couldn't meet the Colonel's eyes. He reached out and with a weathered finger stroked Winona's cheek.

"The sheriff and coroner will come retrieve Ki—the body, after we've done right by her with a Sioux funeral," the Colonel said. "Said they would let us know what happened to her." His voice sounded tight, gravelly, like he struggled to speak every word.

"Good. That's good. Where is she now?"

"Her bothers are preparing her body. We're going to move her in here. LeFleur said he'd bunk with the cowboys tonight. You can go back to your tent, get some rest. Twila will care for the baby for the time being."

Twila stepped forward, a look of smug satisfaction on her face. Did she know that the Colonel fathered Winona? If so, Annie now understood Twila's resentment of Kimi. Could she have resented her enough to pummel her with angry fists? Resented her enough to kill her? Annie, too, wanted to hear the report from the coroner. As soon as possible.

Twila held out her arms for Winona.

Every instinct told Annie not to hand the baby over to this sullen woman.

"But—" she started to protest.

"I don't have the time, energy, or the inclination to argue with anyone at this moment, Miss Oakley. I know you were fond of Kimi, and I know you have a special attachment to this child, but please do as I say," said the Colonel.

Twila's lips pursed in smug gratification, and Annie swallowed down the retort on her tongue. With stiff and reluctant arms, she held Winona out from her body and placed the baby into Twila's grasp.

Sick to her stomach at Twila's victory, Annie rushed out of the tent and ran through the torch-lit camp to her tent, the crisp night air cold on her face. She noticed the fire from the morning still smoldering, and the tea tin that usually resided on her trunk sitting on a rock next to the fire pit. One of the porcelain teacups she and Winona shared lay on its side, partially empty.

Annie picked up the cup and stared into the remaining liquid, its color darkened by the mashed tea leaves, and then dumped the contents into the fire. It spit and sizzled, then died, a trail of fragrant smoke winding up to the sky. With tea tin and cup in hand, Annie stepped into her tent, retreating from the ugly realities outside.

Annie set the tin and cup back on her trunk and slumped onto her bed. She pressed her hands to her face, her mind still reeling with the shocking reality of Kimi's death. Would Kimi be able to rest in peace with the fate of her child in Twila's grip?

Unable to relax, Annie got up from the bed and paced the floor of her tent. Her gaze fell to Kimi's calico scarf lying in the corner. She picked it up and held it to her chest, thinking she'd have to remember to give it to Twila for Winona. The thought of Kimi's scarf, too, in Twila's possession disturbed Annie further, so she tossed it into her wardrobe. Giving the scarf to Twila could wait.

Back on the bed, Annie stared at the candle on her desk, still lit, but soon to go out. Secure in the knowledge that the flame would snuff itself out at any moment, and not caring that it would burn out before Lillie's return, Annie tilted back to lie on the bed again when she noticed a glint of something on the ground next to her trunk.

Curiosity propelled her to get on her hands and knees and crawl over to the shimmering object.

A gold coin lay on the carpet next to some ground tea leaves.

Annie reasoned that the leaves fell to the floor when Kimi prepared her evening tea, but what about the coin? Kimi didn't have access to anything that valuable. Neither did Annie, for that matter. Lillie hadn't been in the tent ten minutes before she'd headed to the saloon, so who did this coin belong to, and why was it on her tent floor?

The next morning the Colonel called a quick meeting, stating he didn't want anyone in the camp discussing Kimi's death. Annie assumed he didn't want the newspaper reporters, and the public they entertained, to know that he'd fathered Winona.

Later that day, the Colonel conducted a small service for Kimi in LeFleur's tent. The crew had pushed all the furniture, except the bed and the massive, weathered trunk, against the canvas wall. Kimi's brothers Michante and Nakota placed Kimi's body on an ornately carved wooden table in the center of the room.

Kimi's brothers, wearing deerskin tunics decorated with multicolored beads, seashells, and animal teeth, bore the same high cheekbones and strong jaw as Kimi. Eagle feathers adorned their long, ebony braids, and their formal attire glittered in the tent's candlelight.

The Colonel, LeFleur, Twila, Bobby, and Annie stood in silence as the brothers painted Kimi's face with a watery red paste made from oil and clay.

Annie snuck a look at Bobby, his face crumpling with emotion. He plunked his hat on his head and left. Annie thought about going after him, but staying for the service seemed more important.

Michante, the tall brother, his face streaked with tears, took a buck knife and cut a lock of hair from the left side of Kimi's head, wrapped it in a piece of calico and placed it in a small muslin bag. Nakota placed bundles of food, her hairbrush, and jewelry around Kimi's body to be buried with her for the afterlife. Annie noticed the butterfly necklace placed strategically around Kimi's neck.

Michante continued to weep, occasionally pushing the tears from his face with the back of his hand, but Nakota stood proud, his face a mask of stoicism—or anger.

The Colonel spoke kind words of his affection for Kimi, and how he loved her like a daughter. Annie's stomach churned. She did not understand the relationship between Kimi and the Colonel, but couldn't help her disappointment at the Colonel's blatant disregard of his true feelings.

Annie glanced at Twila standing just behind the Colonel, her attention focused solely on the whimpering baby. She wondered if Twila's apparent disinterest in the service indicated a need to seem nonchalant. Was it an attempt to disguise guilt?

The Colonel turned to LeFleur and gestured for him to say a few words. He cleared his throat, placed his fist against his mouth, and then lowered his fist to his chest.

"Kimimela was a good girl. She never shirked her duties and lived with quiet dignity. We shall miss her." He stared straight ahead, without even a glimpse in Kimi's direction, then shook his head. "Such a tragedy."

After a few quiet moments, the Colonel removed his hat, approached Kimi's body, kissed her on the cheek, then strode out of the tent. Twila and the baby followed. Twila did not pause to pay her respects to Kimi, and baby Winona gurgled, happily unaware of what had transpired in the last few hours.

LeFleur, too, wordlessly departed, leaving Annie with Michante and Nakota, their eyes remaining transfixed on their sister's body. Annie felt compelled to stay with them.

After an hour or more of silence, LeFleur escorted two deputies and the coroner into the tent and asked Michante, Nakota, and Annie to pay their final respects so the men could remove the body. The brothers bowed their heads for several minutes, clearly reluctant to depart from their sister, who looked so beautiful, even in death.

Annie walked to the bier, raised her hands and pressed them together.

"May God bless you, Kimi, on your journey. May he bless your brothers and sweet Winona."

She motioned for Michante and Nakota to follow her out of the tent. Michante strode toward the Indian quarters holding his hands against his face, but Nakota turned to Annie.

"I appreciate the friendship you showed my little sister. She spoke highly of you."

"I admired your sister." Annie smiled at him. "She was so kind. I wish I could have done more for her. She seemed so . . . unhappy, troubled."

"She was never the same, after he . . ." Nakota's chin quivered and he crossed his arms tightly over his chest.

"I know that the Colonel is Winona's father. Is that what you're trying to say?"

Nakota gave a curt nod.

"Did he . . . did the Colonel force—"

"No." Nakota answered, perhaps to spare her the embarrassment of saying it aloud. "Kimi is—was young, her feelings for the Colonel, confused. She cared for him, and at one time she did give her heart to him, but because he raised us as his children, she recognized the inappropriateness of their relationship. Kimi turned away from him. When the Colonel learned Kimi was with child, he could not bear it. He denied Winona. I know in my heart he felt ashamed of what they—he did."

Annie could see why.

"You don't think the Colonel would ever harm Kimi, do you? He would not have raised a hand to her, would he?

"I do not believe he would harm her. He promised never again to bring violence against another. He vowed that his battles were behind him, and he treats us with more dignity than most. His family has cared for us."

Kimi had said the Colonel's wife raised them for a time. Annie wondered what the Colonel's wife, who was miles away, would think of his dalliance with Kimi. Did she know about the baby? Did she know about Twila?

"What about Twila Midnight?"

"The woman is not kind." Nakota's face darkened. "She was never kind to my sister, and when Winona arrived, she was angry, very angry."

"Jealous probably. That necklace, the one with the butterfly pendant, around Kimi's neck, Twila told me that it belonged to her."

Nakota's brow wrinkled in confusion.

"No, it was a gift from the Colonel. Kimimela means 'butterfly' in Sioux. He gave it to Kimi long ago, when we were children. When Winona was born, Kimi did not feel it was proper to wear the necklace anymore. She gave it to me for safekeeping."

Annie considered this new information. Twila's behavior was

growing more and more characteristic of the jealous lover by the minute. Annie redirected the conversation.

"Is there a reason, any reason, why you think Kimi would have fallen to the ground unconscious like that? Had she been weak or sick? Have others in your family . . . had troubles with their heart?"

Nakota shook his head, his mouth set in a grim line. Annie wanted to ask him if he knew of anyone else who would wish to harm Kimi, but it seemed too harsh for the moment, and she didn't want to stir up a hornet's nest if her suspicions were wrong.

"Sitting Bull says you have a fierce heart with a kind and gentle spirit," Nakota said. "I am glad my sister enjoyed her last days with you."

"That's a very kind thing to say." Heat rose to Annie's cheeks.

"I must go now. I will be leaving soon."

"You're leaving? But why?"

"I was here to protect my sister and I failed. I can no longer honor the Colonel knowing the shame he feels in his heart. Bad feelings will now grow between us. I can bring him no peace, nor he me."

"Don't you want to know what happened to your sister?"

"She is gone. Nothing will change this."

"What about Michante—and Winona?"

"Winona is the Colonel's responsibility. My brother is simpleminded and will be happy here. He will stay for Winona." Nakota looked into Annie's eyes for the first time. "Will you look after him—and her—when I have gone?"

"Yes, of course, you can rely on me." Annie laid a hand on his arm. "But are you sure you won't stay?"

"I cannot." Nakota held up his hand, palm facing her—his face morphing back to its stoic mask—and then turned and walked away.

59

CHAPTER 5

"Wild West Show Performances Temporarily Cancelled.
Ticket Sales Will Resume at the End of the Week."

St. Louis Times – April 13, 1885

Annie woke early the next morning and tiptoed out of her tent, curious to know if the county sheriff and the coroner agreed that Kimi's sudden death was suspicious. They had not. LeFleur told her that they did not find the bruises on Kimi's body damaging enough, or recent enough, to be related to her death. The coroner announced his conclusion that Kimi died of natural causes.

Back in her tent, flipping through her Bible, Annie ruminated on the news. She slipped her hand in her dress pocket and pulled out the gold coin she'd found last night. She turned it in her fingers, studying it. Heavy scratch marks marred the image and lettering, making them impossible to decipher. She let the coin fall into her palm and closed her fingers around it.

Where had it come from?

Annie considered asking Lillie if it belonged to her, but would Lillie tell the truth? She might use the opportunity to claim the coin as hers.

Annie decided to hang onto the coin for a while longer. It might mean absolutely nothing, but still would probably be worth keeping.

Annie thought the announcement of Kimi's "death by natural causes" perplexing. When she had to face Vernon McCrimmon in court, the trial didn't last an hour, but more questions had been asked in that time span than had been asked about Kimi's death in the last two days. In fact, no questions had been asked about Kimi—no deputies or sheriffs queried her about anything. LeFleur asked a few questions right after they discovered the body, but then stopped talking about it, seemingly no longer concerned about Kimi's death. No one else talked of it either, except maybe Nakota, but he too accepted the coroner's word and planned to leave the show, his brother, and his niece behind. Annie figured Nakota knew that white men didn't show much respect for the lives or deaths of Indians, particularly a female Indian with a half-breed child, and felt powerless.

Bobby popped his head through the tent flap.

"Lillie in here?"

"No, I haven't seen her this morning." Annie didn't tell him Lillie never showed up at all last night. She didn't think it her right or responsibility to keep tabs on the girl.

"Well, if you see her, tell her that the Colonel wants her at practice today. He won't put up with her missing any more."

"Will do."

Annie's irritation still lingered at Lillie's refusal to attend Kimi's service. Many people held grudges against the Indians because of the Indian Wars, and maybe Lillie did, too, but her resentment seemed more hateful than a grudge.

Bobby cleared his throat.

"Was there something else?" Annie asked.

Bobby hesitated, started to leave.

"I'll let Lillie know if I see her," Annie said, not sure if she would.

Bobby nodded but didn't move. His eyes sought hers, and Annie could see the pain in them, their bright blueness now dark and dull. His once-buoyant face looked like it had been dragged down into the depths of sorrow.

"Are you all right, Bobby?

"I can't believe we go right back to our routines, as if nothing has changed." Tears welled in his eyes.

"If you want to talk about Kimi, I'm a good listener."

Bobby placed his hat back on his head.

"The Colonel says the show must go on and told us to be prepared for a full house tomorrow, at both the morning and afternoon performances." He shifted his weight from one leg to the other and twisted his mouth as if he had something more to say.

"Bobby, please tell me what's wrong."

"She didn't die of natural causes," he said, his voice so low Annie couldn't be sure she heard him correctly.

"What's that?"

"You heard me."

Before she could reply, he ducked under the tent flap and left.

Annie shook her head, confused by Bobby's behavior. Why did he feel the need to say that to her? Annie sighed, not sure what to believe. She knew one thing, though, she needed to see her horse—a being who, by nature, could not deny, avoid, or hide his feelings, and whose nearness always made her feel better.

Approaching the stables, Annie saw Buck in the distance, picking at a stack of hay on the ground, not munching with his usual abandon. Even from this far away, she could tell he still didn't have much of an appetite. He hadn't eaten much at all since they'd arrived in St. Louis.

Buck raised his head and whinnied at her, galloping to the fence line. He hung his head over the railing and nudged her with his nose.

"Hey there, fella." Annie stroked the soft skin of his ebony nose. He closed his eyes, luxuriating in her attention.

Like a darkening thunderstorm, a sudden cloud of sadness bloomed in Annie's heart. Bobby's words played over and over in her mind. Did he know what happened to Kimi? She'd have to see if she could get him alone again, to talk. If Kimi didn't die of natural causes, then what? It didn't appear she'd hurt herself—she had Winona with her, and Annie couldn't imagine Kimi abandoning her child. Kimi hadn't complained of feeling ill or hurt, despite her bruises, which had been ruled out. The only other conclusion was murder.

Thinking the word *murder* sent a cold river of chills down Annie's spine. She couldn't imagine taking another's life, although she'd been accused of attempting it—something she hoped she'd never hear about again. She could still see the villainous look on McCrimmon's face when Sheriff Brody questioned her:

"Miss Mosey, were you provoked to shoot Vernon McCrimmon?"

McCrimmon jumped up so fast, his chair screeched across the dusty hardwood floor. "You aren't going to let her go on with these lies are you? You don't believe her?"

"Sit down, Mr. McCrimmon, and don't interrupt my questioning again." Sheriff Brody leaned forward, glared hard at him.

McCrimmon plopped back down in his chair with a snort.

"Miss Mosey, were you provoked?"

The image of Buck's legs crumbling under his body as Vernon whipped him over and over sprung to Annie's mind.

"Yes. He was beating the horse."

"His horse?"

"Yes, Buck was his horse, but he kept him half-starved and near death. Buck couldn't pull the load, so Mr. McCrimmon thrashed him with a whip, again and again. I shouted for him to stop, and then he came at me with his fists balled up, full of rage. I knew if I didn't do something, he would kill me."

Annie aimed for his ankle, never intending to kill him. She was brought up to believe that violence was sinful. If she had wanted to kill him, she would have aimed for his heart—and she wouldn't have missed. She never missed.

Thinking about the past, Annie stroked Buck's golden neck, sad at the injustices of the world, sad about Kimi. They'd been like sisters. Soul sisters, both out of place among the players of the show, and both with a past filled with sorrow and unhappiness. In Kimi's company, Annie had felt a little less alone in the world, and she felt compelled to find out what had happened, who had *murdered* Kimi.

Buck sensed her uneasiness and again nudged her with his head. She scratched the soft spot between his ears.

A few cowboys and Indians gathered with their horses, getting ready for their rehearsal of the cabin scene where the Indians surround the cabin, the cowboys emerge, and a great gun battle ensues. The scene always entailed lots of whooping, yelling, and shooting, and the crowds loved it.

Something behind Annie diverted Buck's attention. She followed his gaze and saw Lillie walking toward them, the fringe on her jacket and chaps swinging. The plump figure stalked toward Annie with a man's gait, all of Lillie's femininity lost in the unisex cowboy outfit.

"So this is the 'Wonder Horse.'" Lillie reached up to give Buck a few stout slaps on the neck.

The girl didn't have a soft moment about her. Loud, aggressive, and attention grabbing, which became worse when she drank too much whiskey—which she did often—Lillie always had to make her presence known.

Not in the mood to deal with her, Annie sighed.

"Hey, I'm sorry about Kiki . . . Mimi . . . your friend."

"Her full name was Kimimela. It means 'butterfly' in Sioux."

"Huh. Well, isn't that lovely? Hey, we need to talk about the act. I have an idea that people will be wild for—"

"You need to run it by the Colonel or Mr. LeFleur," Annie said. "They come up with most of the ideas."

"Frank and I have already discussed it. We just need you to go along with us." Lillie took a cigarette out of her pocket, ran a match down the fence post, and lit it. "Think you can shoot this out of my mouth at thirty paces?"

"I think I could shoot it out of your mouth at fifty paces," Annie glared at her. "Not that it's a good idea. It's the most ridiculous thing I've ever heard."

Lillie's eyebrows shot up. "Fifty paces? Okay, you're on. But I get a shot, too."

"How do you know *you* won't miss?"

Lillie squinted at Annie, took the cigarette out of her mouth and snubbed it on the fence post.

"Well, we'll just have to find out, won't we?" She blew smoke in Annie's face and then walked away.

Annie's hand squeezed hard around Buck's lead rope, so hard her nails sank into the fatty part of her palm. What *did* Lillie Smith bring to the Wild West Show, except trouble? Only Twila wanted her there, but since when did Twila make those kinds of decisions?

"Hey, Lillie!" Annie called after her.

Lillie stopped, but didn't turn around.

"Better show up for practice. The Colonel doesn't cotton to slackers."

Annie saddled Buck so they could take some warm up laps around the arena. Despite Buck's dwindling appetite, when Annie urged him forward, he performed with his usual amount of enthusiasm. The heat and humidity of the rare early Missouri spring seemed to sap the energy out of everyone. Already, Annie's cotton shirt clung to her arms and neck, and the lining of her wool riding skirt stuck to her sweating legs, making them itchy and uncomfortable.

Fiddling with the guns in his gun belt, Frank and his horse Fancy trotted into the arena, almost running Annie and Buck down.

"Whoa! Gosh, I'm sorry about that, Annie. Didn't see you."

Annie tilted her chin up in a greeting.

"Hey listen, I'm awfully sorry about Kimi. She was a sweet kid." Frank ran a hand over his blond mustache, smoothing it.

"Thanks, but something is bothering me about her death."

Frank frowned. "Really? Like what?"

"Did you know her well?"

"Not really. I saw her around some, but I'm not sure we ever exchanged two words. Why?"

Annie tapped her fingers on the saddle horn, wondering if confiding in Frank might be reckless. She couldn't help herself—she had to know what happened.

"She had bruises on her back."

"No kidding? Bad bruises?"

"Yes. I can't stop thinking about it. Who would do that to her?"

Frank tilted his head back, as if thinking.

"I saw Twila get after her once, pretty rough about it, too. In case you haven't noticed, Twila isn't the nicest person in the Wild West Show."

"I have noticed. I thought she only hated me."

"Nope. She hates everyone. You're in good company." He flashed her his signature smile, his eyes lingering on her face, causing a tingling feeling to crawl up and down Annie's arms. Must be the heat, she reasoned.

"Lillie told me about your new act idea. The cigarette?"

"That gal is plumb crazy."

"She said you wanted to add it."

"I said nothing of the kind. We got a little drunk last night and—"

Annie turned her head away, not really wanting to know more about their escapades last night.

"Well, let's just say I might have agreed just to get her to shut up about it. Believe me, I would never aim a gun anywhere near that beautiful face of yours."

Annie felt a flush creep up her neck and Buck started to dance, feeling her discomfort. She fiddled with Buck's reins, trying to feign indifference at Frank's infuriatingly charming stare.

"Say, Miss Oakley." Frank rested an arm on top of his saddle horn. "Let's get our practice session in, and then why don't you join me for a late dinner?"

Annie sucked in a breath, not sure how to respond. Early on, the man made it clear he didn't like her sharing his limelight, and now he asked her to dinner? Would it be appropriate? She knew he was a good ten years older than she. But did that matter? She couldn't deny that she found him attractive—everyone did—but why did he also make her feel like she wanted to jump out of her skin? She patted Buck's neck, trying to calm him, acting like that was her major concern.

"Where?"

"My tent."

"I don't think that would be appropriate, Mr. Butler."

"Very well, how about a restaurant downtown?"

"I can barely hear myself think in a restaurant."

He smiled. "The mess tent it is, table for two." He pulled one of his guns out of the holster, fired it into the sky, and took off, Fancy's feet flicking clouds of dust into the air.

Annie's amusement at Frank's behavior dwindled as soon as Lillie showed up for practice—drunk. Lord only knew where her bullets would fly.

The crew had set up a line of several metal targets for one stage of shooting, and an assortment of glass jars set upon different objects of varying heights for another stage. They also brought out a table for the card trick stage.

Lillie stood nearby, flirting with the cowboys and crew. When Frank walked up to the group, Lillie's light-hearted laughter accelerated to something brash and obnoxious. Annie took in a deep breath to steel herself for whatever lay ahead.

"Say, handsome," Lillie said, swinging her hips as she walked toward Frank. "Watch this."

She chose a rifle from one of the tables, and then picked up a hand mirror. Standing thirty paces away from the metal targets, she turned her back, set her rifle on her shoulder, used the mirror to aim at the target, and fired off shots. Her first two shots hit, then she missed one, hit two others, and missed the last.

Frank rested his thumb and forefinger on his chin, as if deep in thought.

"Interesting. I'd like to give that a try."

Annie bristled at the eagerness in his voice. What was it about Lillie that lured men like moths to a flame?

Frank followed Lillie's lead and hit all the targets. They both turned to look at Annie. "Have at it, Miss Oakley," Frank said, that dazzling grin on his face.

Annie swiped the mirror out of Frank's hand. She didn't want to play their game, but she didn't like the idea of being bested by either one of them.

She set up with her back to the targets and hit each one. *Child's play.*

"Very nice, Miss Oakley, but let's up the ante," Lillie said, sneering at Annie. "Let's do the cigarette trick."

"No can do, Lillie," said Frank, "you're drunk. It's too dangerous."

Lillie stuck out her bottom lip in a pout and draped herself on his arm and shoulder.

"Well, since you're so worried about 'Little Miss Sure Shot' over there, why don't you let *her* shoot the cigarette out of *your* mouth?"

"I can guarantee she wouldn't miss." Frank winked at Annie.

Annie smiled. If she didn't know better, she'd say Frank Butler had grown to appreciate her talent.

"Course she wouldn't. She's *Annie Oakley*." The words came deep from Lillie's throat. She flung her arm in the air with a sloppy wave and then pointed to the group of Indian players as they rode in on their ponies to start target practice, bows and arrow in hand. "We could always use one of them Indian scum as a target."

"Watch your mouth, Lillie," Annie said. "We all work together, as a team. No one wants to hear your nasty comments."

Lillie smirked. "They're cheap labor is all."

"We're done here for the day." Frank unwrapped Lillie from his shoulders. "You need to go sleep it off, Lillie. And if you show up drunk at one of the performances, you're out."

"You're threatening me?" She staggered away, walking backwards.

"I am. It's too dangerous to mix whiskey with our act. Don't think I won't go to LeFleur, or the Colonel."

Lillie gave Frank a seductive grin and turned toward the cowboys. "Come on fellas, drinks are on me."

"Exactly why was she hired?" Annie asked.

"She's Twila's family." Frank spit into the dirt. "Not by blood, but she's like a daughter to her."

"But why would the Colonel want someone like that in the show?" Annie snapped her rifle back into its ready state.

Frank ran his fingers through his blond mane, staring off into the distance after Lillie and the cowboys.

"I don't reckon he does, but Twila usually gets her way."

CHAPTER 6

"Buffalo Bill Spotted in Local Saloon with Former Business
Partner Dick Carver. Conversation Ends When Carver
Draws Pistol, Is Escorted from Establishment."

Missouri Chronicle – April 13, 1885

Following practice, Annie settled Buck in the barn and took her time wandering back to her tent. A faint breeze rustled the sun-kissed grasses, and Annie enjoyed the warm spring air—despite her trepidation that she had a dinner date with the legendary Frank Butler. What would the Quaker Friends in North Star have to say about that?

Twila and the Colonel emerged from their tent and headed in the direction of the mess tent as Annie approached the camp. *Where was the baby?*

Twila's aggressive fervor to get her hands on Winona worried Annie. Twila might want to harm that sweet baby, jealous of the fact that she had been brought into the world by Kimi and the Colonel.

To avoid them, Annie stopped and leaned over to pick a long blade of grass, running her fingers along its smoothness. Once they were out of sight, Annie scanned the area near the tents. A few people hung around their campfires, cleaning tack, tending to their costumes, or engaged in quiet conversation. She scurried toward the Colonel's tent and managed to slip inside unseen. Once her eyes adjusted to the darkness, she made her way to the baby's pram. *Empty.*

Annie spun around, wondering where the baby could be, or if she could find anything that might prove that Twila wasn't taking good care of the baby—or that she had beaten, and possibly even murdered, Kimi.

Various herbs and plants, tied with twine, hung from the ceiling, and a mortar and pestle sat on a small table. Just as Annie was about to reach out and touch the pestle, light engulfed the tent and disappeared again as the flap closed. Annie sucked in her breath and whirled around.

"Who's there?" The voice was stern. Male.

"It's me, Annie."

As the figure moved closer in the dimness, Annie recognized LeFleur and let out a breath of relief. But still, how would she explain her nosing around in the Colonel's tent?

"What are you doing in here, Annie?"

Annie bit her bottom lip, thinking fast.

"I saw them leave without the baby, and I just wanted to have a look at her. I've been worried about her. It was foolish—"

"Stop talking," LeFleur held up a hand. "Do not ever come in the Colonel's tent without asking permission."

"I didn't mean any harm. I'm just concerned about the child and—"

"You have no business in the Colonel's tent."

"And you do?" Annie cocked her head. She realized instantly her presumption in asking the question of her boss and superior. She couldn't see him very well, but his tension filled the room.

"I would hate to have to write you up for insubordination, Annie." His voice lowered, emphasizing the seriousness of the threat.

"It's just that I'm not sure Twila is the appropriate caretaker for Winona."

They stepped outside into the glow of sunset. The sky had deepened to crimson red, and a welcoming breeze brushed across their faces. LeFleur's expression softened slightly, masking his impatient smile.

"Annie, you are new here. You don't know Twila or the Colonel. You didn't even know Kimi well. How can you possibly know if Twila is an appropriate guardian for the baby or not? And truthfully, it's not your business. You are an employee of the show. You'd best keep your mind on your performance."

Annie crossed her arms over her chest. She had so much more to say, but decided it could wait.

"I don't mean to be so harsh, Annie, but you need to focus on your job, being the best sharpshooter in the show, not on the rest of the company. I get paid to worry about *everything* and *everyone* else. If you lose your focus you may not be able to keep sending your family money."

Another threat. This one could have serious consequences. She raised her eyes to his and nodded.

Yes, she had trespassed, but only because things didn't feel right. Just like it didn't with Vernon McCrimmon, but, in that case, she'd waited too long to do anything about it and Buck suffered. She didn't want anyone else suffering because she didn't act on her instincts. Wasn't it her duty to help others, to "hold them in the light", as her mother always said? People could be devious. Someone likely murdered Kimi, and even if her curiosity and determination to find the truth jeopardized her livelihood, Annie knew she wouldn't stop probing—not until she identified the culprit.

To prepare for her dinner with Frank, Annie asked a crewmember to bring a copper bathtub and buckets of hot water to her tent. While she waited for the hot water to arrive, she collected wild flowers and a few sprigs of lavender in the glow of approaching darkness.

Back home, a cold splash in the creek took care of the necessity to be clean. Now, she was about to luxuriate in hot water, bathing like a manor-born lady. She wrinkled her nose at the thought of her mother having to make her way to the icy water spring a few times a week. How Annie would love to be able to provide her mother with a proper home, one with good heat, good solid bones, and a copper bathtub. But for now, keeping a roof—no matter how dilapidated—over her family's heads seemed hard enough.

Once the tub had been filled, Annie sank in up to her neck in the deliciously fragrant, warm water when she heard a man's voice outside the tent.

"Miss Oakley. You have mail. I'm going to leave it under a rock right here, just outside your door."

Unable to resist the sensation of her muscles melting in relaxation, Annie lingered awhile longer in the tub. When she got out, she reached for a dressing gown from the trunk LeFleur had brought to her tent shortly after she arrived. The gown's sleeves hung several inches past her hands. Probably one of Twila's castoffs. Annie winced at the thought but knew she should be grateful, as she had arrived with only her mother's wedding dress, her buckskins, a blouse, a nightdress, her Bible—and little else.

Annie lit another candle. The letter from her mother revealed that Joshua had quit drinking and secured work at the blacksmith's forge. He claimed to have turned his life around and wanted to make good on his promise to marry Susan. Her mother reported feeling relieved, and her words denoted a more positive attitude in general. The money Annie sent provided good food and new boots for both children.

Annie folded the letter and placed it back in the envelope. Her mother made no mention of making a payment to the bank but had probably been so excited about Joshua's employment that she'd forgotten to mention it. Annie said a silent prayer that Joshua would be true to his word this time, but in her heart she knew that if they married, she'd be hearing again about more family troubles. She only hoped her mother wouldn't let Joshua squander the money he made, or that she sent home.

Annie chose the most modest dress in the trunk, a burgundy velvet dress with a high-necked collar and black lace cuffs. She brushed and braided her hair, then piling it all on her head, secured it with a tortoiseshell comb. Looking in the mirror, she noted her skin looked a bit sallow. Ignoring her mother's voice in her head, she pinched her cheeks to make them pinker.

In the mess tent, Frank sat by himself. A candle in a glass jar on the table glowed, lighting his face, and a bouquet of spring flowers cheered the Spartan atmosphere. Annie wanted to laugh at the formality he'd attempted but was afraid she might hurt his feelings—or his pride. He'd gone to great lengths for this dinner date, and she needed to be appreciative. She though it rather sweet.

Frank stood up, removed his silk hat, smoothed his mass of wavy blond hair, and held his hands out to her. Annie placed her hands in his. Their comforting warmth seeped up her arms, and the tingling feeling returned. Their eyes met, and Annie wondered if Frank felt the same kinship she felt developing between them. He released her hands and pulled a chair out for her.

"You look beautiful." He settled his chair close to hers.

"Thank you."

"I have to apologize to you." Frank picked one of the daisies out of the vase and handed it to her. "I've been a little testy with you since you've joined the show. I'm not used to someone outshining me in a performance, but the truth is, I'm not shooting as well as I used to."

Annie tilted her head, impressed that his ego allowed him to admit defeat.

"I thank you for your apology, but you are overrating my abilities and underrating yours. I thought you shot fine today. You never missed, even when you were shooting backwards."

"Today was fine. It comes and goes. I'm not sure what's happening to me, but I'm not as steady as I once was."

"Why are you telling me this?" She twirled the stem of the daisy between her fingers.

"It disappoints the crowds when I'm off my game, and the Colonel is getting impatient with me. They love you, for obvious reasons, but old Bill may decide to edge me out."

"There wouldn't be much of a Wild West Show without you," she said, alarmed at his words. "Have you spoken to Mr. LeFleur about this?"

"I haven't spoken to anyone—but you—about it." Frank's eyes softened.

"But why me?"

"I want you to back me when Lillie comes up with her hair-brained ideas, like a burning cigarette in someone's mouth as a target. She knows my aim isn't what it used to be. I can't risk shooting you, or anyone else . . . but especially you." His smiled faded.

Annie sympathized with Frank's predicament. It took a lot for a man like him, a legend, to admit his recent inaccuracy with the targets.

"Well, then, if it makes you uncomfortable, we just won't do it." Annie wanted to ease his mind.

"But Lillie's got some sort of pull with Twila, and she may convince the Colonel to go with it."

An older gentleman appeared at the table, his hands clasped behind his back.

"This is not a restaurant, but I'm doing Mr. Butler a favor." He offered a warm smile to Annie. "What would the lady like to drink?"

"Champagne," Frank said. "We'll have a bottle of champagne. I'm sure you can rustle some up, somewhere, back there." He pointed to the kitchen.

"I'll have tea, thank you."

"You don't drink?" Frank raised his eyebrows.

"No, I don't. Is that a problem?"

"Not by me."

Annie glanced toward the kitchen and noticed Twila hovering over one of the stoves. *Where was the baby?*

To her relief Annie heard Winona gurgling—babbling in the contented way babies do. The pram must be somewhere near, perhaps behind the large row of cabinets in the center of the kitchen.

Seconds later, LeFleur appeared at their table.

"Hello, folks." He picked up a chair from another table and set it down next to Annie. His eyes roamed over Annie's dress and her upswept hair.

"Are you two conducting some sort of private meeting?"

"We're just trying to have a pleasant dinner," Frank said, not hiding his displeasure at LeFleur's appearance.

"Don't mind if I have a drink, do you?" LeFleur took off his hat, set it on the table, and winked at Annie. She hoped it was a sign of forgiveness for sneaking into the Colonel's tent. "How's the act coming along?"

"Aside from some of Lillie's crazy ideas, fine," Frank said.

"Horse doing okay?" LeFleur focused on Annie, ignoring Frank.

Annie shrugged. "It's taking Buck a while to adjust."

Buck still had no appetite and still hated going into the barn. Annie worried that his condition would cause an inability to perform and ultimately lead to her losing her spot in the show.

The older man entered with the tea and champagne.

"You're going to have to bring another glass," LeFleur said.

The "waiter" rolled his eyes and left again.

Frank drummed his fingers on the table, his patience growing thin, but LeFleur failed to notice—or noticed and didn't care.

"I'm sure Buck will be just fine," LeFleur said, assurance in his voice. "Now what's this about shooting a cigarette out of each other's mouths?"

Annie let out a snort, then covered her mouth, afraid her opinions would get her in trouble again.

"I was not in favor of Lillie joining the show." LeFleur's eyes locked on Annie's. "The Colonel and I went round and round about it, but, ultimately, it's his show."

"She's not even that good of a shot," Frank said.

"She's not bad," LeFleur countered. "Annie's been such a hit, the Colonel argued that it was a good idea to bring in another female sharpshooter to set up a competition between them."

Annie tried to keep her face placid, but couldn't help sighing. Just what she needed—more rivalry.

She glanced around the room, noticing Michante and Nakota in a far corner with a group of their friends. She'd thought Nakota had gone, but clearly something had changed.

"Is there any news on Kimi's death?" Annie asked LeFleur.

"No." LeFleur's posture stiffened. "Why would there be? The coroner ruled it a natural death, so there's no reason to investigate further. It's a tragedy, but we must move on."

Annie bristled at LeFleur's dismissive tone, his apparent lack of regard for the death of her friend. She couldn't say what, but something made her think the coroner was mistaken—she'd just have to find a way to prove it.

A banging ruckus in the kitchen drew their attention to Twila, rummaging through trunks and storage bins. She looked up and saw them all staring at her. Her eyes traveled to the candle and the flowers, and her face drew downward, her bright red lips flattening to a hard line. She then disappeared into a section of the tent behind the kitchen and came back out with the pram, stalking out the back entrance.

"Well," LeFleur stood, breaking the tense silence. "I'll let you two get back to your dinner." He hitched up his pants and tipped his hat before leaving the tent.

"Finally," Frank said. "I thought he'd never leave."

Annie studied Frank's face as he sipped from the dainty champagne glass. Tiny, white, feathered lines etched the outer corners of his eyes and the rough stubble of his blond whiskers contrasted with the tanned smoothness of his cheeks. He stared down at the tablecloth, obviously preoccupied, probably with what he'd just disclosed to her about his failing performance.

Annie sensed his vulnerability, and she finally understood—Frank Butler knew he was flawed, like all people, with self-doubts, foibles, and misgivings. No different from her, no different from anyone else. He raised his champagne glass to his lips.

"I don't know anything about you except that you're a world-class shooter—and a philanthropist," Annie said.

Frank froze mid-sip, lowered his glass, and raised his eyes to hers, caution written in his face. His surprised expression amused her.

"I heard you donate money to the poorhouses, which is very kind."

"I've always had everything I've needed." Frank shrugged. "Never been hungry. Never not had a roof over my head, or a warm place to sleep. If anyone should be offering a helping hand, it's people like me."

"Still, it's admirable."

"Nothing to crow about." Frank swallowed a large gulp of champagne.

Sensing his discomfort, Annie changed the subject. "Do you ever get to see your family?"

He poured himself more champagne and twirled the stem of the glass between his fingers once again.

"I haven't seen them for years. Left when I was sixteen. We didn't get on too well. Not since my brother died." He tapped his fingers on the tablecloth.

"I'm sorry . . . do you mind if I ask what happened to him?" Annie lifted her teacup to her lips.

Frank leaned back in his chair, placed his thumbs in the waist of his pants, then flopped his chair back down.

"I killed him."

Annie nearly choked on her tea.

"That didn't come out right," Frank said, waving his hand in the air. He drained his champagne glass.

"It's a long story. I'll have to tell you about it some time . . . some other time."

Since their arrival in Missouri, the rare spring heat wave had scorched its way through the Midwest, St. Louis in the heart of its wrath. The audience numbers plummeted, and Annie hoped the lack of participation was due to the heat—not their performance.

At the early show the morning after their dinner, Annie and Frank worked their way through the mounted course as usual. Annie executed the task with perfect panache, her aim dead on, but Buck's enthusiasm waned. Fancy outran Buck at every turn, which meant Frank and Fancy won the competition.

"I'm worried about Buck," Annie called out to Frank as they galloped their farewell lap. "He's not himself."

"Tell Rusty," he said, his face bearing his trademark smile for the crowd. "He'll know what to do. He's the best horse hand we've got. It's probably just the heat."

Annie leaned back in the saddle, giving Buck the cue to rear and paw at the air. Buck strained underneath but gave his best effort. She lovingly patted his shoulder and dismounted.

Rusty ran over to retrieve the horses.

"Buck's not feeling well," Annie said.

"He didn't eat this morning." Mr. Post took her reins. "I'll give him a good rub down and some fresh water."

Annie let Buck go and placed a hand on her chest, worried about the slow decline of Buck's health, trying to figure out what could be wrong.

"He'll be fine." Rusty winked at her and stroked Buck's neck.

Frank took Annie by the hand and led her over to the area designated for the shoot off between her and Lillie. Rifles, pistols, and shotguns lined the table. The first stage included hurdling a low fence, then, with their rifles, shooting four live birds released at the other end of the arena.

"First up is Miss Lillian Smith." The announcer's voice boomed through the arena.

Lillie grabbed her rifle and headed for the fence. Her skirt caught and she stumbled, almost falling, until the fabric ripped, releasing her. She somehow managed to hit all four birds and lifted her rifle in a triumphant salute to the pleased audience.

Annie grabbed her rifle, waited for the whistle, then hopped the fence without issue. She aimed, pulled the trigger—and heard a hollow click. Nothing happened. She lowered the weapon, turned it over, opened the release, and gasped.

The chamber was empty.

She immediately looked up at Lillie, and hot blood rushed to her face as Lillie's lips curved into a smirk.

"And she misses!" the announcer bellowed.

A round of boos rumbled from the crowd.

"Ladies and gentleman, this is a Wild West Show first! Come on Annie, shake it off and grab those pistols!"

Determined not to face any more humiliation, Annie took up her pistols and hit all her marks. She scored the highest of the two in the shotgun round as well—still, Lillie won.

Annie wanted to sink into the ground as she, Frank, and Lillie joined hands and bowed for the crowd. The humiliation of failure in front of thousands made her throat close up and her lungs freeze. She could scarcely breathe, and she knew Lillie basked in the light of her embarrassment.

A group of barebacked ponies with yelping Indians astride came bounding into the stadium, taking the audience's attention away from the three shooters as they left the arena.

Safely behind the gates, Annie turned to Lillie, her heart racing with anger.

"Did you tamper with my rifle?"

"I don't know what you are talking about." Lillie smiled. "Aren't you responsible for loading your own weapon?"

"I did load it!"

Frank came between the two, placed his hands on Annie's shoulders.

"I can see you're upset, Annie. It doesn't hurt for you to lose once in a while. It keeps things interesting."

"Interesting? I looked like a fool out there. Lillie emptied my rifle on purpose."

"You think Lillie would stoop to that?" Frank released her shoulders.

Annie took in a sharp breath, her blood boiling.

"Either she did, or someone else who isn't shooting as well as he used to did, but I loaded that weapon."

"You're saying I did it?" Frank's smile vanished.

Annie refused to look away from him, her glare hard and unbending.

"I'll let you two have your discussion in private." Lillie twirled her suede skirt as she walked away, looking back at them with a satisfied grin on her face.

Annie's rage bubbled out of control. If Frank could do something as unethical as tamper with her weapon to make her look bad, then what would prevent him from killing someone who might know a deeply hidden secret? Maybe Kimi knew something about Frank that would interfere with his fame. Could Frank have killed her? He'd admitted that he killed his own brother.

"I can't believe you'd do something that low. Did you treat me to dinner to throw me off? Did you intend for me to blame Lillie?" Annie knew she'd just said something stupid, something she didn't mean.

Frank opened his mouth like he was going to comment but instead shook his head, slapped his hat against his thigh, and stalked off.

Coward. Annie kicked at the dirt with her boot, angry at her outburst.

Now that he'd left, her head cleared. She'd been caught up in vanity and competitiveness, and it balled up in her stomach like a knot. Lillie's smug expression practically broadcast her own guilt. Annie shouldn't have accused Frank, shouldn't have thought him desperate enough to do something so petty, or something as evil as killing Kimi. Yet, he'd admitted to killing his brother and then went mute on the subject. What would he have to gain by Kimi's death?

If she'd just made an enemy of Frank, she would never be able to find out about his past, about his potential to kill. It would be best to remain on his good side, if she could make it up to him. He'd seemed so sincere in his attempt to connect with her last night.

Confused by her thoughts and emotions, Annie almost didn't hear the announcer close out the Indian act. She realized she'd be run over by thundering horses if she didn't get out of the way.

She spun around to walk away from the arena and bumped right into a scowling Vernon McCrimmon.

CHAPTER 7

"Ticket Sales to Wild West Show Performances down
Twenty Percent. Buffalo Bill Announces Discounted
Tickets on Sale Tomorrow."

St. Louis Times – April 14, 1885

Annie's knees went wobbly as she stared into the face of her former abuser.

"What are you doing here?" she asked.

"Thought I'd see me a *ro-de-o* circus." Spittle seeped out from the corner of McCrimmon's mouth. "Buck is slowing down, girl, and you weren't up to your usual snuff today."

"You've been following me?"

"Might be. Can't find no work. Got nothin' better to do but hobo around."

"But . . . your wife? Your child?" Annie could barely catch her breath.

"Dead. Both dead. Got sick and I couldn't afford to get a doctor. You done took everything I ever had."

Annie swallowed hard and her armpits dampened, sending an icy chill through her body.

"What do you want from me?"

"I come to get what's mine. At the very least, Buck will make a decent meal."

"You can't have him. I bought him." Annie tried to steady her hands by placing them on her hips, wishing she had her gun belt, but she'd left it and her guns in the arena.

"I never got payment. You got a bill of sale?"

"I laid it on the table. You wouldn't take it." Her hands trembled and she tried to keep her voice steady.

The judge had ruled Annie's shooting of McCrimmon as self-defense, and if she agreed not to press charges for suffering abuse, McCrimmon would be forced to sell Buck to her for one dollar.

It took a full year to nurse Buck back to health. During that year their bond solidified. Buck became part of her, and she promised him, and herself, that no harm would ever come to him again.

She couldn't lose Buck. She wouldn't.

"No transaction took place, so I reckon he's still mine." McCrimmon spat in the dirt. "But that's beside the point. I'm here to ruin you like you ruined me. I told you I would make you pay for what you did, ruining my leg and my name, taking my wife and child, not to mention stealing that old two-reined widow maker."

The gates to the arena opened and Indians and ponies flooded out. McCrimmon grabbed Annie's arm and pulled her to the side. LeFleur, behind the Indians in a wagon, pulled the horses to a stop.

"Is there a problem here?" he asked, staring hard at McCrimmon.

McCrimmon stepped away from Annie.

"No problem. Miss *Annie Oakley* knows why I'm here." McCrimmon tipped his hat and grinned, revealing brown, rotting teeth. "Have a nice evening." He backed away from them, his unblinking eyes and hideous grimace turning Annie's stomach.

"You're trembling. What was that about? Who is that man?" LeFleur jumped off the wagon and walked over to her.

"You don't want to know." Annie let out her breath. She felt tears prick behind her eyelids and swallowed to keep the flood from coming. "He's—" she couldn't keep her voice from wavering, the emotion seeping through like a crack in a dam. Annie couldn't speak or the dam would break.

LeFleur pulled her to him and wrapped his arms around her. She let him, letting his embrace lift some of her burden. After a few seconds, he gently released her and raised her chin with his fingers. He lowered his head and pressed his lips against hers.

Annie stood stock still, not knowing what to do. She didn't want to offend him, but the shock of his inappropriate behavior paralyzed her. Finally, she placed her hands on his chest and pushed him away.

"I'm so sorry. I didn't mean to . . . take advantage." He let go of her arms. "I was just overcome by seeing you so upset."

"I didn't know you had those kind of feelings for me." Annie felt the blood drain from her face.

"I didn't either. Well, I suppose I did. I just never thought I would be so impetuous." LeFleur let out a self-conscious chuckle. "Truly, Annie, I apologize for being so forward."

Annie tried to sort out her emotions. She liked Mr. LeFleur, maybe more than she'd realized, but not in *that* way. In that moment, she realized she wanted Frank to reach out to her, hold her up when her legs didn't have the strength—and she'd just rudely accused him, the man she . . . loved, of sabotaging her rifle.

"That man—he upset you." LeFleur broke her train of thought.

"He did. But I don't want to burden you, Mr. LeFleur." Annie let out a shaky rush of air.

"Why don't you call me Derence?" He smiled and pushed a stray lock of her hair over her ear.

"I don't know if I can. I don't feel—" Annie wrinkled her nose. She didn't know how to soften the blow of not returning his feelings.

"Again, I'm sorry I kissed you." LeFleur raised his hands in the air, as if in surrender. "It was wholly inappropriate. You are clearly upset. Please, tell me what's wrong. Who was that man?"

"It's a long story," Annie said, suddenly feeling the need to rush to the corral. "I want to check on Buck. That's why he's here. Vernon McCrimmon. He wants to take Buck from me."

"Let's go over to the barn together to see Buck, and you can tell me all about it."

As they walked toward the barn, Annie saw Buck lying flat out in his pen and Rusty Post, elbows resting on the fence, watching him. Annie ran over to them.

"What's the matter? Is he all right?" she asked, breathless.

"He's been down like this since I brought him over after your act." Rusty chewed on a long stem of grass. "Doesn't seem distressed, not sweating, just plain wore out."

In the past, Buck would lie down once in a while but never for long periods of time. Annie climbed through the wooden rails and knelt down at his head. He gave her a pathetic nicker and closed his eyes.

"Something is wrong. He doesn't act like this." She looked up at LeFleur and then turned to Rusty.

"Has he been eating?"

"Nope, like I said, he didn't eat this morning, but he did have a big healthy poop. His system seems to be working just fine, he just don't have any pep."

Annie stroked Buck's jowl, remembering his eyes reflecting a similar vacancy after Mr. Post administered Twila's herbs.

"Have you given him Twila's sedative?" she asked.

"Nope." Rusty pulled the stem of grass from his mouth shaking his head. "Twila only gave us a couple of doses, and we used that up those first few days. You might want to see if she has anything else up her sleeve to pep him up."

But could Twila be trusted again? Annie and Twila's relationship hadn't improved—in the least.

"What about the Chief? I've heard he has medicine," she said.

"Yep, but only for human folk, only for some things. Twila's your best bet."

"Oh, my God." A horrible thought entered Annie's mind. She lifted her hand to her mouth in horror.

"Annie?" LeFleur climbed through the fence to kneel at her side.

"McCrimmon . . . that man." Her eyes filled with tears, but she refused to cry. "He said he was here to ruin me. He threatened to take Buck. Maybe he wants to—"

"What in Tallahassee are you talking about, girl?" Post asked.

"Have you seen any strangers walking around the barn?" LeFleur asked.

"Mr. LeFleur, you know I never leave the horses unattended." Rusty straightened his spine, offense written on his leathery face. "I've been here all day. I ain't seen any strangers."

"Well, you're going to have to keep an extra eye out now. I think this fellow is just trying to scare Annie, but we can't be too careful."

"I'll have the boys put in some more hours," Post said. "Don't you worry, Miss Annie. We'll take good care of your friend." He secured his hat back on his head and gave her a reassuring nod.

"I'm supposed to ride Buck in the act tomorrow." Annie looked up at LeFleur.

"Do you think he'll rally by then, Post?" LeFleur asked. "We're expecting a sold-out crowd."

"Don't know. Even if he does rally, he probably needs to rest his bones for a few days, least till we find out what ails him." Post pulled a dirty hanky from his pocket and wiped his face.

Annie lifted Buck's head and let it rest in her lap. Buck blinked his eyes contentedly and let out a big sigh laced with a groan.

"We're going to have to come up with something for you to do to spice up your act." LeFleur said. "Feel up to trying Lillie's cigarette trick? You'll be the shooter, of course, not the target."

Annie opened her mouth to argue against it, but too worried about Buck—and her possible future at the Wild West Show—to care, she held her tongue.

"We'll see if Butler's up to standing in as target—as long as you're willing to hold the cards for him later in the act."

"Of course," Annie said. LeFleur and the Colonel might be losing faith in Frank's skill, but she hadn't. She couldn't blame him for this temporary confidence issue. They'd brought her on as a rival to him, and the crowds fell in love with her. She'd inadvertently taken his place in their hearts. She bit her lip, too hard, and the coppery tang of blood filled her mouth. She shouldn't have snapped at Frank like she did.

Buck lifted his head from her lap and raised himself to an upright position, curling his sturdy legs beneath him with another stout sigh. He shook his head, making his forelock swing to chase away a pesky fly. Annie and LeFleur stood up, still watching his every breath. The horse closed his eyes again. He seemed comfortable, content. For the moment.

"Let's let him rest. Rusty will keep an eye on him." LeFleur tugged on Annie's arm.

Afraid to leave the barn, afraid that Vernon McCrimmon might show up again and steal her horse right out from under Rusty Post's nose, Annie scanned the area around the barn and over toward the main arena. Would the Colonel let her move her tent next to the barn? If anything happened to Buck . . .

LeFleur slipped a hand around her waist and guided her to the fence. They all three crawled through, but Annie turned around to look over at Buck again. He hadn't moved, but he seemed relaxed.

"Make sure he has enough water," she said.

"I'll make sure that's full. Don't you fret." Rusty pointed to the left end of the corral to a large wooden water trough.

"And McCrimmon?" Annie turned to LeFleur.

"I'll have some of the boys keep an eye out for him. What's the best way to spot him?"

Annie felt a momentary flash of satisfaction.

"He has a limp."

CHAPTER 8

"Wild West Darling, Annie Oakley, Loses in Rifle Round.
Rumors Abound about What Went Wrong."

St. Louis Times – April 15, 1885

Annie and LeFleur approached the Colonel's tent as Frank emerged.
He made eye contact with Annie and politely tipped his hat, but
Annie could see the anger and hurt she'd caused in those blue eyes. She
wondered if Frank had come to see Twila, and her disappointment at
the thought surprised her. Although preoccupied with helping Buck,
she had to do something to make peace with Frank.

"Frank, wait."

He turned around, his hands in his pockets. His eyes scanned her,
then LeFleur, then back to her.

"Mr. LeFleur," Annie said, touching his elbow. "Do you mind?"

LeFleur's eyes widened in insulted surprise, but Annie offered a
pretty smile and his expression softened. He turned and walked in the
direction of the mess tent.

Frank faced Annie head on, a calculated anticipation in his eyes.

"I'm sorry I accused you of emptying my rifle. I know you would never
do something like that. I was upset, and you didn't take me seriously."

"I would never do anything to make you look bad, or hurt you, Annie." He ambled closer, took his hat off with one hand and smoothed his hair with the other.

"I know it's been difficult for you since I joined the show, Frank, and I'm sorry. I didn't know what it was going to be like, performing and everything. It's been rather overwhelming."

"You've been good for the show, Annie, and good for me. Don't ever apologize for your talent. Embrace it."

"I should have known it was Lillie. She's been out to sabotage me from the beginning."

"You don't know it was Lillie."

"But who else?" Annie shook her head, blinking up at him.

"You don't *know* it was her."

"There you go defending her again. Why, Frank? Is there something between you two?"

"I invited *you* to dinner, not Lillie. But you're jumping to conclusions and accusing Lillie out of the blue. Is it possible you forgot to load that rifle?"

Annie gritted her teeth, but didn't want to argue anymore. She didn't have time. She had to make Buck her priority now.

"I suppose you're right. I shouldn't accuse someone when I don't know for sure."

"She's a pistol, Lillie, but she really means no harm."

I couldn't disagree more, Annie thought.

～

Frank tipped his hat to her and left Annie, still feeling flustered and bewildered, standing in front of the Colonel's tent. Annie knew Lillie wanted to make life difficult for her whether Frank believed her or not, but if Vernon McCrimmon had followed them from Ohio, he posed the most obvious threat.

She drew a breath and stepped closer to the Colonel's tent.

"Miss Midnight?"

"Come in," Twila sang out.

Annie ducked her head into the interior of the tent and gasped when she saw Twila Midnight with a giant snake wrapped around her middle, its head and flicking tongue next to the sultry woman's ear. Nakota was right. In a crimson bustier with black stripes and a black lace skirt, the woman's mysterious aura and the snake wrapped around her middle made her look like a witch.

"You're shocked," Twila said.

Annie's eyes traveled to the other side of the room where the English-style pram rested in the corner. Winona must be sleeping. She lifted to her tiptoes to see into the pram, but she was too far away and too short.

"Not shocked. Just surprised you'd have a snake near an infant."

"He eats mice, not babies." Twila looked at Annie as if she'd just fallen from the moon.

"Oh, I see."

"I'll bet you didn't know that I'm a snake charmer." Twila looked into Annie's eyes, her feline lips curling upward. "It used to be one of the more popular acts in the show. I've given that up, but I couldn't give up Hank. He's like a child to me."

She unwrapped the snake from her body and, holding his giant coils in her hands, lowered him into a large wicker basket, closed the lid, then strolled over to the pram to peek inside. She then turned her attention to Annie, the same feline smile curling her lips.

"What can I do for you?"

Annie hesitated. It still bothered her to ask Twila for herbs to give to her horse. He'd improved before, but . . . Annie had no other option.

"It's Buck, my horse—"

"Still bouncing off the walls?" Twila's eyes flashed, and she placed a hand on her tiny corseted waist.

"No. The opposite. He doesn't seem to have any energy."

Twila tapped a long, pointy fingernail against her cheek.

"Have you changed what he's eating?"

Annie shook her head.

Twila walked over to where herbs hung from the rafters, obviously her little corner of the tent. The rest of it was all Buffalo Bill, with rugged, masculine accouterments—a thick, sturdy, four-poster bed, a weathered armoire, and at least a dozen pair of thigh-high leather boots with decorative beaded straps and feathers dangling from them lined up against the tent wall.

Annie felt a twinge of apprehension as Twila used a large, bone-handled bowie knife to snip twigs and branches from the hanging plants. A flicker of light bounced off the thick blade, and Annie darted her eyes back to the pram. How safe could Winona be in the care of this odd woman? A niggling sense of unease climbed up Annie's spine. Why was the baby so quiet?

"May I see the baby?"

Twila gave a curt nod and continued selecting and cutting herbs.

Annie tiptoed over to the pram and leaned over the black accordion hood to see Winona, her sweet brown face in peaceful slumber; such a beautiful baby with her poker-straight, jet-black hair and a bowed little mouth, ripe as a plum. She looked perfect, and perfectly content. Annie released a breath.

"Here you go." Twila suddenly appeared at Annie's side, startling her. The woman stood so close Annie could see light of the lantern reflecting in her coal-black eyes.

"Crumble this up and put a small amount in his food each day. He should feel better in less than a week." She held out a bundle of herbs.

"Thank you." Annie took the proffered twigs and leaves.

Twila broke her gaze, leaned over the pram, and stroked the baby's cheek.

"How is the Colonel? He seemed to take Kimi's death quite hard." Annie swallowed hard, hoping she wouldn't get a tongue lashing, or worse, but she wanted to see how Twila would react.

Twila's face turned to stone as she slowly she raised her dark eyes to Annie's, but she said nothing.

"You didn't care for her much, did you?"

"Are you implying something sinister?" Twila's lips twitched.

"No, just an observation. Some of us took it harder than others, and I was worried about the Colonel's state of mind." Her eyes drifted over to the multitudes of dried plants and flowers hanging from the tent's ceiling. What if some of those plants were dangerous? Poisonous? Deadly? Who would know besides Twila? Could she have poisoned Kimi?

"The Colonel was naturally upset. The girl was like a . . . daughter to him."

"Yes. Of course." Annie managed a tight smile.

Twila moved closer to her, enveloping Annie in a cloud of perfume that smelled like black licorice.

"You *are* a pretty one." Twila reached out to stroke Annie's mane of braided hair. "No wonder he's smitten."

Annie pulled back and Twila's smile deepened, revealing a dimple on her left cheek. "He's married, you know."

Frank married? Annie tilted her head in confusion.

"The pitiful Mrs. LeFleur is ailing and bed-ridden somewhere in the South." Twila grinned. Annie felt a surprising sense of relief.

"I am sorry to learn of Mrs. LeFleur's illness, but there is nothing beyond friendship between her husband and me."

"You don't return his love?"

"I was not aware of love." Annie's cheeks grew hot under the woman's penetrating gaze.

"I have great respect for Mr. LeFleur; I do not have romantic feelings for him."

"Poor LeFleur," Twila said, a smug look on her face. "Take some advice, my dear, watch yourself. It can be dangerous to break hearts in the Wild West Show."

Annie delivered the herbs to Mr. Post, who reassured her that Twila Midnight would not give Buck anything that would harm him.

"That conniving woman could get the Colonel to dismiss any one of us simply by crooking her finger the right way, so why would she involve Buck?"

"I suppose you are right."

Annie longed for nothing but to stop thinking about everything, go back to her tent, and sink into her comfortable bed. It had been such a long, confusing day. But the image of Twila's feline grin, the bowie knife, the snake, and sweet Winona under that woman's roof haunted her.

Annie hurried toward her tent, trying to push aside her anxieties and hopeful of rest. When she opened the flap and slid in, she found a cowboy on top of Lillie, his pants down to his knees. Hearing Annie, they broke apart and erupted with raucous laughter. The cowboy jerked his trousers up over his hips.

"Oh, my. We might have offended the sensibilities of the ever-popular, but oh-so-proper Annie Oakley!"

The cowboy tossed Lillie back onto the bed and pressed his face into her neck, causing another screech to come out of Lillie's brazen mouth.

Annie's every instinct made her want to leave, but this was her tent. She'd lived here first, with Kimi and Winona. Lillie had no right to "entertain" when the two of them had to share the same space. A sour taste filled Annie's mouth.

"I need to get some sleep," she said, her voice flat.

"Oh. Did you hear that, Slim? Baby needs her sleep. Guess you better run along." Lillie sat up, pushing the cowboy off her.

The cowboy stood, hitched his pants higher up on his waist, and fastened his belt. He leered at Annie with the dull, watery eyes of a drunken simpleton.

"I'm gonna go smoke a pipe with the Injuns, anyhow. They invited me to one of their pow-wows."

Annie turned away from his leathered face.

"You're cavorting with the enemy?" Lillie rose from the bed, her lacy robe falling open to reveal huge, pale breasts.

"Well, I'm not sure what 'cavorting' means, but we occasionally like to have a snort of whiskey and a puff." The cowboy tucked in his shirttails.

"Don't come near me again, you damn red-man lover!" Lillie shoved him, nearly knocking him off his feet. She then grabbed one of his boots and threw it at him. He flinched, spun around. She grabbed the other boot and flung it, making contact with his back. Gathering his discarded footwear off the floor, he left with an angry snarl on his face.

Annie, transfixed by the outburst, didn't say a word.

"What are you looking at?" Lillie plopped herself onto the bed and tilted back the flask she brought out from under the covers. "Damned idiot," she said, staring after the tent flap.

Lillie never hid her antagonism towards the Indians, but the depth of her hatred surprised Annie. Did it come from something in her past? For the first time, Annie noticed despondency in Lillie's eyes—but it was no excuse for her behavior, now or during their act.

"I didn't appreciate what you did today." Annie went to the wardrobe on her side of the tent.

"I'm not sure what you mean." Lillie took another sip from the silver flask and leaned back onto her rumpled pillows, busily rolling a cigarette.

"The bullets. My rifle."

"Oh, that." Lillie let out a deep-throated chortle. "It was just a little joke. It was funny to see the look on your face." Her head swayed and bobbed, the alcohol getting the better of her. It took three tries to light her cigarette.

"What is your problem with me?" Annie couldn't keep the sound of exasperation out of her voice.

100

"It must be hard to be so perfect." Lillie took a long drag on her cigarette. She blew the smoke out in a pointed line.

"I'm not perfect. Far from it."

"Then why don't you try some of this?" She held up the flask, threw back her head and laughed.

"I don't want your liquor, but I don't know why we can't be friends."

"Friends?" Lillie spat out the word. "Oh, that's rich." She took another swig from the flask, then a drag from her cigarette. "You're a red-man lover, too. Or rather, a squaw lover. I'm glad that bitch is dead. I don't know what I'd have to do if I had to live with her and that spawn of hers one more day."

Annie's breath caught in her throat. Did Lillie just admit to something? She balled her fists, staring hard at Lillie, trying to decide if Lillie would have the audacity to kill someone.

Lillie's face bunched up and tears streamed down her pudgy cheeks. She looked away from Annie and then raised a shaking hand to her mouth.

"They killed them all. My whole family. Damn Shawnee." Sobs wracked her plump shoulders.

Annie took in a deep breath, pulled her nightdress off the wardrobe hanger, and walked over to Lillie's bed, suddenly aware there might be more to Lillie than puffed-up bravado and unbridled brazenness. She'd not seen this side of her.

"I'm sorry for your loss, Lillie."

"Yeah, I bet you're sorry. You've never had to suffer a day in your life." Lillie lowered her hands, her face instantly regaining its usual cynical expression.

"Pardon me?" The sting of Lillie's words hit Annie hard, as if Lillie had physically slapped her. How dare this . . . this *person* assume anything about her life? "You have no idea what you're talking about; my family has suffered every day since my father died."

"You are the darling of the Buffalo Bill Wild West Show. People in the audience shout your name. You can outshoot Frank Butler with shotgun, rifle, everything. You're so busy being humble you don't even know what you have. I'll never be able to shoot like you."

Annie paused, realizing the truth of Lillie's words, suddenly understanding Lillie's insecurities—that she'd never measure up.

"You have your own . . . abilities."

"Oh, sure. I'm a lot of fun." Lillie gathered the hem of her robe to dry her face.

"I truly am sorry about your family. Losing my father—" Annie fiddled with the dressing gown in her lap, trying to figure out a way to press her about Kimi.

"Did you see him slaughtered in front of you? Butchered? Scalped?" Lillie raised her bloodshot, tear-stained eyes to look into Annie's.

"No. He died as the result of a snowstorm."

"Hardly the same thing." Lillie took another swig of the whiskey.

"No, it isn't, but it hurt the same."

Lillie burrowed deeper into the pillows and raised her eyes to the ceiling, as if searching for words.

"I can't look at them, the Indians, the *savages,* and not feel such hatred that it claws into my bones."

"Then why did you agree to work with them?"

"It was this or the whorehouse."

Annie knew desperation, the ache of hunger and the fear of losing her loved ones to poverty, but she had never had to consider selling her body. She hoped she—and Hulda—never would.

"The Indians in the show aren't Shawnee, you know. Most of them are Sioux."

"Don't matter. They're killers. All of them. Turn your back on them and they'll snuff you out." Lillie reached down and stubbed her cigarette out on the earthen floor beneath her bed. She leaned back onto the pillows and closed her eyes.

"I think you're wrong. We killed their families, too. War is never fair. Kimi wouldn't have hurt anyone. You would have grown to like her if she hadn't—"

"Wouldn't happen. Hate them all."

"Did you kill Kimi?"

Lillie opened her eyes, sat up.

"Kill her? You think someone killed her, you think *I* killed her?"

"Maybe."

"Huh." Lillie scratched her head and lay down again. "That's funny, Annie."

"I don't think there is anything funny about it."

"Don't you have something else to do?" Lillie flung an arm over her eyes and yawned.

Annie sighed, knowing she wouldn't get any more from Lillie tonight.

"Good night, Lillie."

Lillie answered with a resounding snore.

CHAPTER 9

"State Government Negotiates Indian Land Affairs
with Surrounding Area Chiefs"

St. Louis Times – April 17, 1885

Annie woke the next morning, quickly dressed, and rushed to the stable to check on Buck, anxious to see if Twila's herbs had helped—and half afraid they might have made him worse. Halfway to his pen, Annie saw Buck, head down, eating. A good sign. She quickened her pace, and when she got there, she leaned her elbows on the railing to watch him eat. Buck lifted his head, pricked his ears in her direction, gave her a long gaze, and resumed chewing.

Relieved to see Buck feeling better but not wanting to disturb him, Annie walked back toward the camp. On her way she saw Sitting Bull standing by the stagecoach.

"Watanya Cecilia," he said as Annie approached.

"Hello, Chief. Going somewhere?"

"I am going to visit a man called Thomas Reed. A government man."

"So you are going into town?"

"Yes, I am attending a meeting to discuss illegal settlers on Indian lands."

Annie wondered if a visit to the coroner's office might settle her mind on the matter of Kimi and how she died. She had a few hours before the next performance.

"I see. May I have a ride? I'd like to walk a bit in the city."

Chief Sitting Bull held his arm aloft, inviting Annie to climb into the coach.

Once they were settled, Annie let her eyes rest on the Chief's smiling face. He seemed amiable. Maybe she could ask him about Kimi's death, if she slowly eased into a discussion.

"This Mr. Reed, what does he do?"

"He is a Congressman."

"He sounds important."

"Yes, very important man, with important friends. I met his friend, the writer Mark Twain. He, too, has interest in Indian affairs."

Annie's mouth popped open.

"The man who wrote *The Adventures of Tom Sawyer*? Friend Easton gave me that book for my birthday, and I loved it. How exciting to meet him in person!"

The Chief's smile deepened. Annie decided to press forward.

"Chief Sitting Bull, I'm awfully sorry about Kimi. I miss her so much. I was wondering—how are her brothers and, well, your people faring after her death? Do they find it suspicious?"

The Chief's eyes drifted from the window to her face.

"Why do you ask, my daughter?"

"I don't believe such a healthy young woman just . . . died. Perhaps you and your people also found that odd?"

"We are deeply saddened by her death, but we cannot question what the spirits want for us, Watanya Cecilia."

"I see. I mean no disrespect to you, but I don't believe in spirits. I believe in the Holy Spirit, but somehow it sounds as if we mean the same thing. I find the reasons for her death questionable, and I'm determined to find out what happened to her. Even if no one else questions the circumstances, I want answers that will satisfy my doubt."

"Perhaps the spirits, or your Holy Spirit, call you to seek answers. You have my blessing." Sitting Bull leaned over and placed his large, warm hands over hers.

"Thank you." Annie's eyes followed his gaze out the window. It hadn't occured to her to ask for his formal blessing, but the fact that he bestowed it led her to believe that perhaps, deep down, he also questioned the young girl's death—and perhaps he took solace in knowing that at least one white person valued an Indian girl enough to inquire about her untimely end.

Arriving at the city's Four Courts Building, Annie thanked the Chief for the ride. They both agreed to meet again at this place in an hour, and Annie set out to find the coroner's office. The driver directed her to the building on Clark Street.

As soon as Annie entered the building and spotted a door with the title *City of St. Louis Coroner's Office*, her heart flipped. Did she really have the courage to pull this off?

A short, scrawny man with bulging brown eyes and enormous grey eyebrows opened the door. Annie recognized him from his visit to the Forest Park campsite.

"Hello, sir. I'm Annie Oakley. I'd like to ask you a few questions."

"The famous Miss Annie Oakley has come to see me? What can I do for you?" He beamed.

"Could we possibly speak in private?"

"Yes, of course, my dear, come in."

Annie's boot heels clicked on the wooden floor as she made her way to the chair in front of the coroner's paper-strewn desktop. How he could make sense of such a mess, Annie couldn't fathom. Charts of human musculature and skeletons lined the walls and a faint hint of cigar smoke hung in the air. A large potted palm in one corner proved the only non-medical decoration in the office.

"I'm Dr. Chaney." He settled onto a rickety wooden chair, the wheels of the chair legs squeaking and the floorboards groaning as he scooted closer to the desk.

"Dr. Chaney, as you may know, Kimi, the young Indian girl you examined after her death, was my assistant, a confidant and a friend."

Dr. Chaney's eyebrows pulled together, pointed downward, creating a *v*.

"I don't mean to sound impertinent, but are you quite certain that she died of natural causes? Because I am not." Annie licked her lips, garnering courage. "In fact, I believe it's possible that someone set out to intentionally hurt her, perhaps even to murder her."

The coroner's eyebrows sprang up in surprise. He leaned forward, pressing both hands against the desk.

"Miss Oakley, I conducted an investigation, and I informed the show's manager of my findings. I really cannot discuss the case with you—even though you knew the girl well. I suppose you think your celebrity status entitles you to—"

"Oh, Mr. Chaney, I don't presume—"

"That is exactly what you are doing Miss Oakley, bringing your presumptions to my attention, which you really have no right or cause to do." He stood. "Is there anything else I can do for you?"

"Mr. Chaney, I don't mean to offend, but the bruises on Kimi's back—"

"Good day, Miss Oakley. Best of luck with the show." Dr. Chaney nodded toward the door.

Annie jumped when the door slammed behind her. *Oh dear. That did not turn out as planned.* She had another hour and a half to continue her research before the Chief would return for her. Where else might she find answers?

Annie walked down Eleventh Street, admiring the store windows, when a hansom cab with two beautiful black horses pulled up next to her. The driver, a fat, jolly-looking man wearing a silk top hat, leaned down toward her.

"You're Annie Oakley, aren't you, miss?"

"Yes, I am." Annie blushed, still unaccustomed to strangers recognizing her.

"May I offer you a ride?"

"I thank you, but it's a fine day for a walk. Could you possibly direct me to the nearest library?" Annie hadn't brought any bills, only the gold coin she'd plunked in her reticule for safekeeping, and she didn't want to use that.

"The nearest library is over past Lafayette Park. It's quite a way, but really, I would be honored to offer you a lift, and I refuse to take your money."

Annie smiled. "That's kind of you, and I am grateful to accept."

The driver climbed down from his perch, his ample body rocking the coach. Annie took his hand, and he helped her into the cab. After several blocks, the driver pulled the black horses to a halt.

"St. Louis Public Library," he called out.

Annie stepped out of the cab, rummaging through her reticule and found two nickels and the gold coin. She grabbed the two nickels and held them up to the driver, but he waved them away.

"I can't wait to tell folks I had Little Miss Sure Shot in my cab!"

"Again, I thank you." Annie didn't necessarily want anyone to know that she'd been in St. Louis investigating Kimi's death, but she supposed the driver wouldn't figure out why she'd gone to the library. She could merely be borrowing a book.

Once inside, Annie took in the stateliness of the interior of the building. Wood bookshelves covered the walls, and stone bricks soared to the dizzying heights of the ceiling. Large tables with plush armchairs dotted the massive space, and stained-glass windows threw rainbows of light upon the floor. She'd never seen anything like it. Annie stood staring at the architecture for a minute or two, then hurried on her way.

At the main desk, a large, very tall woman—the tallest Annie had ever seen—peered at her from behind round-rimmed spectacles.

"May I help you?"

"Yes. I would like to conduct a little research. I'm trying to find out ways a young and vigorous person might unexpectedly die."

The librarian raised her eyebrows.

"Not for ill intent." Annie looked behind her, suddenly self-conscious. "A friend of mine, who appeared quite healthy, recently died, the cause not obvious. No wounds or visible ligature marks on her neck, no signs of suffocation. The sheriff and the coroner both concluded that she died of natural causes, but I'm not convinced." Annie leaned in closer. "I'm sure you will be discrete. I wouldn't want her family to know I'm poking around in this."

"Of course." The librarian nodded, her brows pressed downward, indicating the seriousness of her promise.

"I believe there might be more to the story, so I'd like to ease my mind by researching causes of unexpected death in someone so young, and I don't know where to begin."

"You think someone deliberately killed this young woman."

"Let's just say that I am curious."

"You know," the librarian's brown eyes lit up, "there was a story, long ago, about an entire family found dead in their home, right here in St. Louis. No trace of an intruder, no outward cause of death. It was quite the mystery."

"Did they ever find out what caused the family to die?"

"I don't recall. I'm sure we have the newspaper. Our archives are quite extensive." Annie noted pride in the librarian's voice. "I can also find books on poisoning or other nonobvious causes of death."

"That would be most helpful."

Once they secured the books, the librarian led Annie to a secluded desk in a corner, lit up with a rainbow of green, yellow, blue, and red from the stained-glass window above. She handed Annie a pencil and small notebook.

Annie unfolded the newspaper dated April 12, 1866, around the time of the end of the Civil War. A headline on the front page caught her eye.

"Missing Confederate Gold Thought to Have Been Found."

A stash of gold, stolen from a Confederate treasury in Atlanta, Georgia, reportedly had been found. Annie peered closer at the illustration depicting burlap sacks rumpled with folds and bumps. The story reported the find a hoax, the burlap sacks filled with lumps of coal.

Annie reached into her bag and pulled out her coin purse. She studied the gold coin, trying to make out the marks on the front and back, but the scratches on the surface were etched too deep. The article didn't mention coins; the gold could be in many other forms—ingots, bars, bricks.

A quick look at the large clock reminded Annie that she'd best stick to her investigation. She plunked the coin back into her coin purse and focused on the newspaper.

She turned page after page, searching for the story of the unfortunate family. Finally, she found it on page thirteen. As the librarian stated, the Matson family, a husband, wife, and three children, had been found dead in their beds one morning—no apparent illness, no injuries, and no foul play detected. The coroner reported the family died of natural causes. *All five of them?* Annie scratched her temple and jotted their names in the notebook.

She flipped through the books the librarian had given her about toxic plants and substances but couldn't find anything that might explain what happened to Kimi. It seemed that most poisons caused foaming of the mouth, vomiting, or other physical signs of ingestion. Kimi had displayed none of those effects—she'd still looked beautiful and calm, as if she'd died in her sleep. Annie still wanted to know about the bruises on her back and who had beaten Kimi, even though the coroner claimed it had nothing to do with her death.

Frustrated, Annie slammed the book shut, a little too loudly, judging by the sour expression on the face of a gentleman seated at a nearby table. He scowled again at her before turning his attention back to his paper.

Annie glanced at the clock. She'd have just enough time to go back to the Four Corners Building to meet the Chief.

Back at camp, Annie put on her costume and immediately rushed to the stables to see Buck. He stood in the middle of the pen, munching on a large stack of hay.

"Is he doing any better?" Frank came up behind her and leaned his elbows on the railing next to hers. He smelled of leather and cinnamon, and she couldn't help noticing the attractive way his hair curled around his ears and over his collar.

"He's up and eating, which is a good sign." She forced her gaze back to Buck. Looking at Frank often unsettled her, setting her off balance, and she needed her mind clear and focused.

"LeFleur and the Colonel want us to perform without the horses today. Buck is almost as popular as you are, and they feel the audience will be disappointed if Fancy is there but Buck isn't."

"I see. I'm sorry, Frank."

"Don't be sorry. You and Buck make a great team. People sense your connection with him. It's partly why the act is such a success. You're both natural stars." Frank lowered his elbows from the railing and turned his body to face her, resting his thumbs in the waist of his leather pants.

Annie quickly glanced at Frank's face, afraid that meeting those blue eyes head-on would make her mind go blank.

"So it's the cigarette trick."

"Yep."

"Okay."

"You and Lillian will do the shooting in that one."

"But the crowd will be expecting—"

Frank held up his hand, stopping her.

"I've talked it over with LeFleur. Splitting cards is my specialty." Damaged pride simmered under the surface of his face, pulling the light out of his eyes. He lowered his gaze to the ground and kicked at the grass.

One of the cowboys emerged from the barn, holding his watch in his hand.

"Almost showtime."

Frank flashed Annie his rehearsed smile.

"You heard the man. Let's go."

In the paddock area, outside of the arena where they waited to go on, they saw Bobby working with Isham—the Colonel's favorite horse, a white Arabian with a long gray mane and tail—filing one of Isham's hooves. Fully absorbed in his task, Bobby crouched low, his back bent over the horse's hoof resting between his knees.

"The Colonel performing today?" Frank asked.

Bobby looked up at him. "Naw. Just wants to watch on horseback."

Come to think of it, Annie rarely saw the Colonel off his horse, unless he was in the mess tent or meeting with the crew and staff indoors.

"Something wrong with his feet?" Annie moved closer to inspect the hoof.

Bobby dropped the file to put both hands on the hoof, cradling it, checking the heel, then the toe, making sure the edges were clean and to the shape he desired.

"Just long in the toe. The Colonel said he'd been stumbling a bit."

Something on the file glinted in the sunlight. Annie picked it up and examined it. She couldn't be sure but thought the substance in the file, mixed with horse hoof, looked like gold. The image of the coin popped into her mind, the inscriptions on both sides filed down to a scratched and marred blur. She ran her finger along the protruding ridges.

"Miss Oakley?" Bobby held out his hand.

"Oh, sorry. Here you go." Annie deposited the file in Bobby's out-stretched hand. He bent his head and continued filing.

"That's a sharp file. Is it new?" Annie asked.

Bobby didn't look up. "Dunno. Seems like it's new. Got it in the barn. Mr. Post has a few hanging around."

Annie knew that most cowboys carried their own files and farrier tools with them. She remembered what her father used to say. "Horse don't have good feet, you don't have a good horse." From the sound of it, this file didn't belong to Bobby. That didn't mean he wouldn't use it, like he was using it now.

What would Bobby be doing with a gold coin? The Colonel always paid them in bills. And how had did the coin get on *her* floor, next to *her* trunk? If the coin belonged to Bobby, it made sense that it ended up in her tent. He often went there to visit Kimi. Had he gone there one last time—to send Kimi on her way to the afterlife?

For the performance, LeFleur dictated that they should enter the arena in the Deadwood stagecoach, surrounded by a dozen marauding Indians on horseback shooting blunt-pointed arrows. Lillie and Annie played damsels in distress, while Frank burst out of the coach and single-handedly shot all of their attackers. Once all the Indians had sufficiently and dramatically fallen off their horses and rolled to the ground, Frank redirected the audience's focus on himself as he jumped to the driver's seat of the coach and drove the team of six to the other side of the arena. Lillie and Annie emerged from the coach, firing their guns into the air.

The crowd loved it.

They all transitioned quickly to perform Frank's famous card trick. Annie and Lillie lined up, each extending her left or right arm, holding a playing card flat between her thumb and forefinger. To Annie's relief, Frank seemed to be gaining back his shooting momentum and hit his targets dead on. His smile made all the women in the audience swoon— his western cowboy charm never failed to fascinate the crowds.

Annie lifted her gaze from Frank back to the audience and saw three women pointing at her, speaking behind their hands. Uneasiness settled into her bones.

Frank lit his cigarette and patiently waited. Lillie fired and the cigarette exploded from Frank's mouth. He held his arms up, mugging to the crowd, making them laugh. He lit another one, turned toward the other side of the arena, and Annie fired, smashing the cigarette into nothingness.

The three of them came together, held hands, and bowed for the pleased crowd. Annie again noticed strange, disapproving expressions on some of the faces. The stagecoach came barreling across the field to pick them up. She and Lillie hopped in through the opened door and hung out of either side, waving to the crowd.

They circled and came back for Frank, who hopped onto the stagecoach roof, arms outstretched, pumping his hands in the air to gin up more applause. The team of six galloped out of the arena. When they cleared the gates, Annie glanced over at Lillie, who had a bemused smile on her face.

"What?" Annie asked.

"Theft and attempted murder? You? I never would have guessed."

"What are you talking about?"

"You obviously haven't read the newspaper this morning."

"No, I haven't."

The coach, now outside the arena, slowed to a stop. Lillie flipped up the door handle and then turned to fix Annie with a raised eyebrow and that same, smug smile.

"Well then, maybe you better."

CHAPTER 10

"Annie Oakley an American Inspiration. Four Girls Enter
Shooting Contest Today in Cleveland."

Cleveland Post – April 17, 1885

As Annie walked toward her tent, some children rushed up and
handed her autograph books to sign, their faces shining with joy
at meeting their idol. Their mothers stood back, frowning, something
Annie had not experienced. Women usually felt a connection with
her, rooted the loudest for her. After the children scampered off, leaving Annie alone, the strangers staring and talking in whispers behind
gloved hands slowly moved away. Swallowing hard, she made a beeline
for her tent.

She pulled the tent flap aside and entered to find LeFleur standing next to her vanity, and the Colonel sitting on her vanity stool. The
scenario would have been comical, but the expressions on their faces
sucked any hint of humor out of the situation. LeFleur handed her a
newspaper.

"Wild West Show Shooting Star Annie Oakley's Wild Past" it read.
Annie felt the color drain from her face and her limbs grow weak. She
read further:

According to an anonymous informant, Buffalo Bill's newest shooting sensation has some secrets in her closet. After a romantic tryst, Miss Annie Oakley allegedly shot a man and stole his horse. Looks like the petite darling of the famously popular show ain't so sweet.

Annie lowered the paper and raised her eyes to the Colonel's and LeFleur's expectant faces.

"I don't know what to say. It's not true. Well, it's not all true."

"Not *all* true? We didn't expect any of it to be true. Explain yourself, Miss Oakley." The Colonel's pale blue eyes assessed hers.

Annie didn't like the disapproving tone of the Colonel's voice. Her mouth went dry as dust and her mind reeled, making her feel faint. She walked toward her bed, forcing her legs to carry her there. She sat down on the edge of the mattress and placed her hands on her knees to steady herself.

"Well?" the Colonel said.

"I certainly have not had any romantic trysts." Annie met the Colonel's eyes.

"We knew that couldn't possibly be true," LeFleur said, palpable relief in his voice.

She could tell he wanted to rescue her, but she knew she'd have to do it herself.

"I did take the horse. Buck. His owner, Mr. McCrimmon, the man following me, abused him, whipped him, and starved him till he was near death. The court awarded Buck to me for the price of $1, which I laid on the table, but Mr. McCrimmon refused to accept payment. If I'd left Buck with him, he would have killed him. I couldn't let that happen."

"Is he the man you shot?" the Colonel asked.

"Yes. I did shoot him, but I only nicked him in the ankle. He was beating Buck and came at me when I tried to stop him, he . . . he . . ." Annie's throat closed and she looked into Mr. LeFleur's eyes.

"Then it was a clear-cut case of self-defense."

"Yes sir, Sheriff Brody said it was self-defense and that was the end of the matter."

LeFleur and the Colonel exchanged glances.

Annie leaned forward, trying to keep the desperation out of her voice.

"He said I ruined his life, and he came to seek revenge. I've been afraid that he could be the one making Buck sick. He might even be trying to kill him."

"And maybe he cornered one of the reporters and gave them the false story about Annie." LeFleur looked over at the Colonel.

"Maybe." The Colonel ran a hand down his perfectly trimmed beard and let out a growl. "But this has Carver's stink all over it. Maybe Carver bumped into this McCrimmon fellow at an opportune time, likely in some drinking establishment. The man has been out to get me ever since we parted company."

Annie knit her brows in confusion.

"The Colonel is speaking of Dick Carver," LeFleur said. "The show was once called 'Buffalo Bill and Dick Carver's Rocky Mountain and Prairie Exhibition,' until Carver got himself into a financial mess and Bill here bought him out. Carver blames the Colonel for his misfortunes and has been out for revenge ever since we took over the show."

The Colonel chuckled. "Could be him, out there skunking around, trying to find manure to fling at me. Unfortunately, our popularity—now your popularity—" he nodded at Annie, "has made us vulnerable to him, and to others. It could be that Carver struck up a conversation with this McCrimmon fellow and they hatched a plan together . . . or it's all Carver's handiwork. Either way, it's not your fault, Annie, and I'm not about to let the press ruin your good reputation."

"I'm so sorry," she said.

"That's show business, sweetheart." The Colonel stood, grabbed the lapels of his tawny buckskin jacket and snapped the collar forward to straighten it. "Comes with the territory. I just needed to hear your side of the story. Now, don't you fret. Quite honestly, I'm more worried about that horse of yours than anything else. Does he seem to be improving?"

Annie nodded, not entirely convinced.

"Might have to get you a new mount." The Colonel strode past her toward the opening of the tent.

"Oh, no sir, that won't be necessary. Buck will be fine, I promise."

The Colonel didn't answer, just paused to tilt his head toward the tent's entrance, indicating for LeFleur to follow him outside. They stood just outside the tent, exchanging a few words. Annie tried but couldn't hear their conversation.

When LeFleur returned, Annie went to him, wringing her hands.

"What should I do?"

"Nothing. We're going to ignore this and keep moving forward." LeFleur took her hand and held it between both of his.

"I can't be without Buck, Mr. LeFleur. I don't know what I would do if . . ."

"Don't worry yourself too much, Annie. Let's just see if we can help Buck feel better. Get to the bottom of his ailment."

"I'm grateful. Thank you. But what about McCrimmon? He's caused so much trouble—because of me."

"Well, now, we don't know for sure that this was his doing, but even if it is, this isn't a situation we can't handle. Carver's tried before to damage our reputation, but the crowds still love us, and they keep coming, which is all we care about."

"Why is Mr. Carver out for the Colonel?" Annie looked into his eyes. LeFleur released her hands and took a small step backward.

"He's always getting riled up about the Colonel. He's dug and dug to find something to slander the Colonel but hasn't been able to uncover anything detrimental. He's likely the reason reporters were buzzing around after our last show, and it's possible McCrimmon approached one of them and purposefully distorted the facts of your story. They're both scoundrels, not worthy of our time."

"I wouldn't expect Mr. McCrimmon to be that smart, but someone could have drawn the story out of him, if they knew he knew me. He came to St. Louis to ruin me."

"I'll find a way to deal with McCrimmon. You just continue to perform at your best, and people will see you for who you are. Believe me."

"Thank you, Mr. LeFleur." Annie stepped closer and placed her hand on his arm. Just as she pulled her hand back, LeFleur captured it again in his hands.

"I will take care of you, Annie, if you let me."

Pinpricks ran up her neck. She didn't *want* anyone taking care of her—and LeFleur's pleading eyes made her want to run. He'd misinterpreted her moment of vulnerability in the worst way.

"Mr. LeFleur, you are a married man with a wife at home."

"How do you know about my wife?" His dark eyes registered shock.

"Twila mentioned it to me yesterday."

"Of course she did. She can't stand to see anyone happy."

"Happy?"

"Yes, Annie. You make me happy. Being around you makes me happy. My wife is my wife in name only, she's has been very ill for years."

"But if she's sick, how does she get on without you?"

"She comes from a very wealthy family who insist on providing a companion and nurses who are always with her. We've all accepted that I have a show to run, and even if I were at home with her, I wouldn't be very useful."

"But surely you love her."

He shook his head. "Our families have known each other for decades. I'd always known we were expected to marry, and although I was quite fond of her, it wasn't a matter of love."

"I'm sorry. I didn't mean to pry." Annie turned away from him.

"Annie—" LeFleur rushed to her, firmly grasped her by the shoulders, and pulled her back to his chest. He breathed into her hair. Annie wriggled out of his grasp, her heart pounding.

"Mr. LeFleur, you must know by now that I don't return your affection. I've come between man and wife once before—"

"McCrimmon? You and that man were lovers?"

"No, no, no," Annie spun around, shaking her head. "I never encouraged him, but I remained in their house after he made advances, and one day he—he—"

"He forced himself on you?" Anger tinged the edge of his words.

"He tried. I did whatever I could to stay out of his way, but I should have left sooner."

"If that man laid his hands on you, it wasn't *your* fault. I'll make sure he doesn't bother you anymore."

Suddenly, they weren't alone—to Annie's relief, Bobby had entered the tent. He seemed uncomfortable at finding them together.

"Come in, boy. What is it?" LeFleur said.

Bobby stepped forward, his body tense, a piece of paper crumpled between his hands. "Excuse me, Miss Oakley. I have a letter for you." Bobby handed it to her and hurried out of the tent.

Annie recognized her mother's handwriting.

"It's from home. Do you mind if I read this in private?" She held the letter next to her heart.

"Yes, of course." LeFleur brushed his hand against her shoulder, as he left.

Dearest Annie,

I am sorry to report distressing news. Joshua has been drinking again and lost his position at the Forge. John Henry and Hulda are miserable with him around, and some days my headaches are so bad, I don't leave my bed. The money you send is a like a gift from God, but this last time, Joshua went to the Mercantile, and convinced Mr. Shaw to give him the money, to bring to me. We barely saw a penny. Mr. Shaw promised to safeguard your future letters and parcels, but we are now short on the mortgage, so whatever you can spare will be sent directly to the bank. The folk in North Star who read the newspapers say you have become a sensation. I'm proud of you, Annie, and don't you worry about us. Joshua won't lift a hand to any of us;

he's basically a milksop. Don't go letting some cowboy steal your heart, as I miss you dearly.

Your loving Mother

Annie paced in the small area next to her bed and raised a hand to her throat in exasperation, her pulse thudding faster and faster. *Everything will be fine*, she tried to tell herself, but why did she feel so helpless? Her family's suffering, her tainted reputation, and her uncertainty about Kimi's death felt like an anvil settling on her chest. Her hands went cold.

Annie tossed open the tent flap and ran to the barn. She found Buck standing in his pen, his head drooping and one of his back legs cocked. He sensed her, raised his head and whinnied. Not wanting to startle him, Annie slowed her pace. She climbed through the fence railings, and reaching him, she wrapped her arms around his neck and pressed it to her face. The scent of dust and hay and horse reminded her of deep-blue mountains, fields of flowers, and dense pine forests, instantly calming her.

She breathed deeper, inhaling Buck's scent, feeling the warmth of the sun radiating from his golden coat. A rumbling nicker from deep inside his lungs provided a welcome vibration, soothing her body. His tail swished at a fly and flicked against her arm, and she ran her hands along his neck, in deliberate, meaningful strokes.

She sensed someone behind her and turned to see Frank, his arms resting on the fence railing.

"Rough day?"

Emotions blocked her throat. Annie nodded and continued to run her hands down Buck's neck.

"I've never seen anyone love a horse like you love that one."

Annie smiled at him, gratified that he'd seen her deep affection for Buck.

"He's a lucky chap." Frank placed a spear of grass between his lips, chewed on the end. "Want to talk about it?"

"Do you know about the article?"

"Anyone who knows you knows it's not true." Frank climbed through the fence and came to stand next to her and Buck. He stroked the horse's black nose.

Annie slowly raised her eyes to meet his. The compassion and tenderness in them rendered her speechless.

"I know what it's like to be judged for something you didn't do, Annie—or rather, didn't mean to do." Frank's gaze drifted back to Buck's head. He stroked the horse's forelock and Buck closed his eyes, basking in the attention. Annie put her arm up over Buck's withers and leaned her weight into him, allowing the rise and fall of his ribcage to gently rock her to and fro.

"You remember I told you that I killed my brother," Frank said.

"Yes."

"Not intentionally. I loved my brother—more than anyone. We were playing down at the lake, near my family's horse farm."

Annie smiled at him, surprised to hear about the horse farm.

"Yes, I grew up raising horses." He must have read her thoughts. "That's why I understand your connection with Buck."

"You *do* understand. I love that." She leaned harder into Buck's side.

"We'd hung a swing on a tree branch, over the lake. You know, a board with a couple of holes drilled into it. We shoved the ropes through each of the holes, tied a knot. I climbed the tree and secured the ropes at the top. We wanted to soar out over the water and then jump from the swing. It was like flying for a few seconds, just before a huge splash into the drink." He laughed at the memory, showing every one of his perfectly straight, white teeth. As quickly as the smile had come, it vanished.

"I hadn't tied the ropes tight enough. When it was my turn, as I flew over the water, the ropes came loose and the swing came down into the water with me. I got tangled and panicked, and then went under. Kenny dove in to help me, but I thrashed about so hard, I struck him in the side of the head. Knocked him out cold. I frantically pulled at the ropes, but when I finally broke free, it was too late. He'd taken on too much water. I struggled to get him to the shore, but he outweighed me by about thirty pounds."

Frank, hands on hips, turned away from her, his head dipping down in shame or sadness, she couldn't tell. The leather of his jacket bunched at the collar, showing off his square shoulders. Not able to resist, Annie reached out, placed her hand at his collar and let it rest there, feeling the softness of the leather and the strength of his hardened muscles underneath. Her eyes stung at the beautiful gift—more beautiful than the shiny pistols—he shared with her. He'd opened himself up to her.

"Thank you," she whispered. His personal confession made her feel less alone in the world, less isolated. LeFleur had tried to do the same, but it meant so much more coming from Frank. He turned around to face her again, his mustache twitching with emotion.

"Frank, if you could overcome such a horrible tragedy, then who am I to cry because of a little bad press?" She smiled at him. "I'm going to fight it. Fight the story. I'm going to find out who wrote it and set the record straight."

Frank tilted his head, squinting his eyes.

"You might be careful about that. Sometimes it doesn't pay to get in the slop with the pigs. They like rolling around in all that mud."

Annie let out a boisterous laugh.

Frank reached over, grasped her around the waist, pulled her to him and kissed her. A kaleidoscope of light spun behind her eyes and electricity zinged through her body, leaving her limp, like a rag doll in his arms, surrendering to him at last.

Frank pulled away from her.

"Are you all right?" he asked, laughing. "I didn't mean to be so forward—"

"You just took my breath away, is all." She wrapped her arms around his neck and kissed him again.

In that moment, nothing else mattered but her melding into him and his fusing with her. She had never before felt so complete.

Buck nudged Annie and Frank with his nose, breaking them apart.

"Someone's jealous." Frank patted the horse's neck.

Annie laughed and ran her fingers through Buck's tousled mane.

"He's used to having all my attention." Her voice faded, a catch forming in her throat. "The Colonel is thinking about replacing Buck. I don't know what I'd do without him, and what would happen to him."

"Has he gotten any better?"

"His energy is high some days and really low on others. I'm hoping to ride him in the act tomorrow. Mr. Post said he's been eating a little better, and drinking enormous amounts of water—"

Annie noticed a flash of bright colors and saw Twila—wearing a long, multi-colored skirt, looking more like a gypsy that a witch — rushing out of the barn, marching steadfastly away from them. Had she seen Annie and Frank kissing?

"What's *she* doing in the barn?"

Frank shrugged. "Who knows? She sticks her nose into everything concerning the show."

To defuse her emotions, Annie played with Buck's black mane, sectioning shanks of hair to plait them.

"How long have you *known* Twila?" She hoped her voice sounded lighthearted, not suspicious—or jealous.

"For a while now. We knew each other before the Wild West Show."

"Can I ask you a question about her?"

Frank nodded, smiled.

"Is she really a snake charmer?"

"So, you've met Hank." He threw his head back with a laugh.

"He's a beastly thing."

"Indeed he is. Why are you asking about me and Twila?"

"I just wondered if you'd once been . . . you know." Annie concentrated harder on braiding Buck's mane.

"Ah, I see. You've been hearing gossip about us. That was before she and the Colonel became an item."

"Well, did you love her?" Annie couldn't imagine him loving such a manipulative woman, but then again, she'd seen him flirting with Lillie more than once—though not since he'd invited Annie to dinner, which seemed so long ago now.

Frank shrugged again. "It never turned that serious. She wasn't for me."

"Was it the snake, her odd clothing, or her witchy ways?"

Frank laughed. "You don't think much of her, do you?"

"I don't know what to make of her. I know she doesn't like me, and she was downright cruel to Kimi. Mr. LeFleur told me that the Colonel fathered Winona, but do you think Twila was capable of hating Kimi enough to beat her . . . or to purposefully harm her?" Annie looked into Frank's eyes to gauge his response.

"Whoa," Frank took a step back. "How did we get there? What are you talking about?"

"I told you about the bruises on Kimi's back. Even you said Twila was always mean to her."

"Twila has a temper, that's for sure, but I've never seen her raise a hand to anyone. I understand your concerns, but are you implying that Twila might have—"

"Maybe. I don't want to sound unkind, but why does a healthy young girl just drop dead? One day she's fine, and the next she's found dead on the floor."

"I surely hope you are wrong." Frank let out a lungful of breath.

Relieved to share her fears, and relieved that Frank hadn't made her feel foolish for them, she reached up and cupped his whiskered cheek in her hand. He did the same, running his thumb from her temple to her chin, pulling her face closer to his.

"I'm here for you, Annie," he said. "I've lost my heart to you. We'll find a way to set things right. All of it."

CHAPTER 11

"Wild West Show's Ticket Sales Plummet. Annie Oakley
Accused of Attempted Murder."

St. Louis Times – April 18, 1885

The next day, the attendance numbers proved dismal—only five thousand tickets had been sold for the morning show and four thousand for the afternoon show. The numbers had been three times that on other days—before the article about Annie surfaced. To make matters worse, Buck, too weak to perform, lay listless in his outdoor pen, breaking Annie's heart.

The Colonel instructed Rusty Post to get Isham ready for the next performance. He also told his publicity man to contact all the local newspapers and let them know that Buffalo Bill would saddle up and perform in the show, once again.

Annie stood in the wings of the arena by herself, watching as the people flooded into the great stadium, making a thundering noise like a herd of buffalo. The air all around Annie vibrated with excitement. Excitement strung on a thin thread of gloom.

She spotted Frank, on his noble Fancy, in conversation with the Colonel on his stallion, likely going over the details of the act; a reenactment of a buffalo stampede with the Sioux fighting against the famous Buffalo Bill and his troop for control of the herd. The act had been a standby in the past, and the Colonel could probably do it backwards and blindfolded.

A commotion erupted behind her, and she turned to see LeFleur and Bobby arguing. From the looks of it, LeFleur tried to calm the boy, but to no avail.

Annie remembered Bobby being upset with himself for his anger at Kimi—stating he didn't deserve Annie's pity. Could it have been an admission of guilt? At the time she didn't believe that he could be capable of violence, although the look on his face now made her think twice. Annie imagined his balled up fists striking Kimi's back, or him accidentally smothering her with a pillow in a fit of rage. It didn't seem possible. And what about the matter of the coin and the gold flecks in the file? Annie couldn't wait to get him alone to question him further.

Their voices grew louder. LeFleur pointed a finger in the boy's face and seemed to be admonishing him or warning him against something. Bobby returned the gesture with an expression so full of loathing, his eyes like glowing coals, that Annie gasped. When Bobby turned heel and stalked off, LeFleur cast a furtive glance around him, as if afraid someone had witnessed the scene. Annie spun around so he wouldn't know she had seen them arguing.

The Colonel and Frank approached the gates where Annie stood, preparing to go in. The Colonel tipped his hat to her, and Frank gave her an astounding smile—a smile reserved for her alone, not the smile he used for the thousands waiting for him to perform. The tingling sensation returned, making her feel giddy.

In moments, several mounted cowboys guided the herd of buffalo toward the gates. Whoops, whistles, and the cowboys' long, swirling ropes kept the herd in check. Dust formed in thick, billowing clouds, breaking the magical spell and making Annie cough. She thought about moving to another vantage point but didn't want to lose sight of Frank, his performance always a pleasure to watch.

When the announcer's voice boomed through the stadium introducing the show, two of the crew opened the gates wide, and the cowboys ushered the thundering stampede of buffalo into the arena. The crowd got to their feet, whooping and hollering. Within seconds, the Sioux warriors mounted bareback on their ponies, their faces brightly painted and their chests shirtless, rumbled through the gates with the ferocity of an angry waterfall. They carried long spears decorated with straps of leather adorned with feathers and seashells.

Nakota and Michante came in toward the back, looking proud and fierce. Frank and the other cowboys entered the arena, causing a new set of thunderous applause to fill the stadium.

The Colonel, bedecked in powder-blue buckskin, readied himself for his entrance. Large silver Conchos donned his sleeves and leggings, and his saddle, with finely polished silver accents along the skirt, at the stirrups, and along the cantle, gleamed in the sunshine. Isham pranced in excitement, but the Colonel held him in check until they entered the arena at top speed, Isham galloping full bore ahead. The crowd's cheers resounded in response as the battle re-creation began.

Once the gates closed, Annie could no longer see the action, but she could see and hear the cheering audience. She could tell what happened behind the closed gates as she watched the crowd, their faces changing with each unfolding. So immersed was she in the spectacle, she jumped when LeFleur suddenly appeared next to her, his face glowing red and sweat trickling down his sideburns.

"We don't have a full house today," Annie said.

"Nope. Sure don't."

"Do you think it's because of the story?"

LeFleur took off his hat and swiped at his sweaty forehead with his right hand, which was stained with something black, like . . . gunpowder. She'd never seen LeFleur carry a gun, much less shoot one.

"It could be anything. We've been here for a couple of weeks. Interest usually wanes after a while. Maybe it's time to move on."

"When do I go on?" Annie asked.

"After the intermission. We'll have you, Lillie, and Frank work the mirror, the hurdle and birds, and the cigarette trick. I've got to hand it to Lillie—the people sure do love that trick."

Annie hated to admit it, but had to agree.

"Everything all right with Bobby?" she asked.

LeFleur fidgeted with his hat and then placed it back onto his head. "He's in a snit about something. Nothing to worry about." He crossed his arms over his chest and rocked side to side, resting his weight first on one foot and then the other. "You just get prepared for your act." He turned abruptly, leaving a wave of anxiety in his wake.

Annie lingered, worried about LeFleur's odd behavior, but also hoping to speak with Frank for a moment. As she moved away from the gates to intercept Frank, she saw Twila standing near the paddock area, behind one of the cattle chutes—talking to Vernon McCrimmon.

A rush of weakness seized Annie's knees. What were *they* doing together?

Annie fought an urge to rush over and confront them head-on. Instead, she tried to read their lips to see if she could figure out their words. She couldn't make much out except Twila's flinging arms, directive in their movement, suggesting that she wanted McCrimmon to do something. But what?

Startling her, the herd of buffalo, cowboys, and Indians stampeded past Annie, dragging a storm of dust clouds that blocked her view. By the time the dust cleared and Annie could see again, Twila and McCrimmon had vanished, as if Annie had blinked them away.

Annie headed straight to the Colonel's tent and found Twila inside, feeding the baby. She had Winona propped up in the pram and spoon-fed her something from a container that read "Nestlé's Milk Food."

"What are you doing here?" Twila's perfectly arched brows pressed down toward her aquiline nose. "Don't you go on soon?"

"Soon, yes, but we need to have a conversation about that man you were just talking to at the arena."

"What man?"

"I saw you talking to Vernon McCrimmon. Chews tobacco. Smells like a whiskey still."

Twila lifted the spoon to the baby's mouth, her face expressionless. Winona flailed her fists in the air with delight.

"People ask me questions. Where do I buy tickets? Can I meet Buffalo Bill? Is it really true about Annie Oakley nearly murdering her lover?"

"How dare you!" Annie moved closer to Twila, ready to throttle her. "I bet you're the one who fed the reporter that rubbish, knowing it wasn't true. Maybe you and Vernon McCrimmon teamed up on that. Maybe it's been you trying to do me in from the start."

"Stay away from Frank Butler." Twila's words came out low and menacing. Annie squared her shoulders.

"You've got no say about what I do or don't do with Frank Butler. He told me it's over between you two and has been for a very long time."

Twila calmly laid down the baby's spoon, but when she turned back to Annie, her face bore an expression that darkened the room.

"Look, you little two-bit runt from nowhere. You may be the show's biggest star right now, but we created you, and we own you. If you're as smart as you want everyone to think you are, you'll stick to being a sharpshooter and making that big money to take care of the family that depends on you."

Annie bit back her rage at Twila's insolence.

"If you're helping McCrimmon take my horse, or harm him in any way, I'll make sure the Colonel knows about your interference."

"Don't cross me, 'Little Miss Sureshot,' or you'll regret it."

Startled by the volcano of tension the two had built in the room, Winona began to fuss, but Twila seemed unmoved. Her venomous stare didn't waver, making Annie almost certain that this mean-spirited, jealous woman would be capable of poisoning Buck—and murdering her rival, Kimi.

"Showtime," Twila said, waving a hand to shoo her away.

"Leave Buck alone, let him recover."

"I don't know what's wrong with that beast, but I've given him my best herbs."

Winona's wails grew louder. Annie wanted to rush to her but knew doing so would create more animosity. Instead, she left the tent, an odd mixture of certainty and uneasiness settling into her bones.

CHAPTER 12

"Buck the Wonder Horse Ails from Mysterious Sickness.
Annie Oakley Performs without Her Beloved Sidekick."

Missouri Chronicle – April 18, 1885

Annie, Lillie, Frank, and this time Bobby all entered the arena hanging off the Deadwood stagecoach. Frank drove the team of six, and Annie and Lillie stood in the coach, their upper bodies leaning out through the windows. Bobby stood on the rear boot in the back. They all fired their pistols in the air as the stagecoach circled the arena at top speed.

When Frank brought the horses to a halt, Annie, Lillie, and Bobby hopped off the coach and waved to the audience. Frank pumped his fists in the air, egging on the spectators, while crewmembers hauled out the table, targets, and weapons. Annie took the first stage with the mirror trick. She finished quickly, turning her attention to the audience with her eager show smile and endearing wave, but she earned little applause. She and Frank exchanged glances, both stunned.

Spontaneously, one of the crewmen came out of the wings with a honey-colored, long-eared hound and a stool. The crewman set the stool down about thirty paces from Annie and motioned for her to pick up her rifle. He then cued the dog to jump on top of the three-legged stool and sit. Annie dragged her rifle off the table, not sure what he wanted her to do.

The crewman pulled an apple from his pocket and placed it on the dog's head.

Annie smiled. *Pure genius.*

Annie took aim and splintered the apple into a pulpy mess. The spectators roared with approval as the dog leapt off the stool and ran to Annie. Standing on his hind legs, he lifted up, resting his paws on Annie's shoulders, and gave her a sloppy, face-licking kiss. Relief swept through her when she heard laughing, cheers, and shouts from the crowd. She'd have to remember to thank the crewman for such a brilliant idea.

Next up, Lillie, sober for once, hopped over the hedge prop without effort and downed all six pigeons in a flash. Frank picked up two pistols from the table and meandered toward the hedge, flashing his dazzling smile for the crowd. When the buzzer sounded, he leapt over the hedge, graceful as a jaguar—

And missed. All six pigeons.

Stunned silence filled the arena. Annie's heart sank. He'd never missed *all* the targets before.

"Quick," Bobby said to Annie and Lillie, "stand me on my head and let me take a crack at those glass jars."

He ran to the table, tossed a rifle to Annie, and moved into a headstand. Annie handed back the rifle, and, now turned upside down, Bobby blasted ten glass jars in rapid succession. The audience thundered their appreciation.

Annie and Lillie moved seamlessly into the card trick. First, Annie shot the card out of Lillie's hand, and then Lillie held the card for Frank. Annie watched his face as he raised the pistol and steadied his aim, taking longer than usual, his sudden lack of confidence making him hesitate.

He split the card in two. Everyone, especially Annie, sighed with relief.

Lillie lit a cigarette, ran a few yards away and mugged for Annie to shoot it out of her mouth. Annie shot clean through the glowing ash. Lillie faked that she'd been shot and fell to the ground. The spectators gasped, then laughed when she leapt up, ran over to Annie, and pretended to strangle her. Laughing, Lillie then wrapped her arms around Annie in a bear hug. Annie felt a surge of affection—but only for a second, as she was skeptical of Lillie's sincerity.

Finally, their act complete, they all took their places on the stagecoach. Frank, driving the team once again, offered his radiant smile to the crowd, but Annie could see the humiliation in his eyes.

When the gates opened to release them from the arena, the Colonel and LeFleur stood waiting for Frank. Annie wanted to say something reassuring to him before he faced them, but what could she say? She glanced at Lillie, whose smile displayed a sympathy Annie had not seen on the girl's face before. They all knew Frank's career might be in jeopardy, and they all hated to see a fellow sharpshooter, one larger than life—a legend in his field—go down.

Bobby jumped off the back of the coach and rushed over to shake Frank's hand. Frank received it in silence and then jumped down from the seat. LeFleur, his arms crossed over his chest, and the Colonel, sucking on a fat cigar, watched Frank stroll past them, gave each other a knowing look and followed him away from the crowd.

~

Still stunned by Frank's degradation, Annie, Lillie, and Bobby made their way to the public area to greet the spectators as they filtered out of the stadium. Men, women, and children rushed over to them, asking for autographs.

A flaxen-haired, pink-faced girl handed Annie a straggly bouquet of wildflowers.

"She admires you so much," the girl's mother said, placing her hands on her daughter's shoulders.

Heat rose to Annie's cheeks. She'd never get used to this adulation.

"What's your name?" she asked the little girl.

"Rose."

"Well, Rose, you look like you could be a cowgirl in the show." Annie bent down to peer into the girl's eyes. She didn't have to go far; the girl stood almost as tall as she. "Do you want to learn how to shoot?"

"I help my daddy shoot squirrels and rabbits in the forest." Rose's smile revealed several missing baby teeth.

"Well," Annie said, widening her eyes. "I did the very same thing when I was about your age. Perhaps you could be a sharpshooter for Buffalo Bill when you get a little older."

The girl giggled, holding her hand over her missing teeth, reminding Annie of her own siblings, John Henry and Hulda, at home. Annie hadn't had time to figure out what she would do about the situation at the farm, or about Kimi, or Frank, or Bobby. And now, with Twila threatening her . . .

The girl's mother leaned closer to speak to Annie, her voice hushed.

"I just want you to know, we don't believe that story printed in the papers. You keep your chin up."

"Thank you," Annie said, pleased at the woman's sincerity.

Someone bumped her from behind. She turned to see an elderly man.

"Miss Oakley, I sure do love to watch you shoot." Toothless as the little girl, he offered his hand, and Annie shook it.

A boy held out a school primer and asked her to sign the inside cover, also handing her a feathered pen. The din of noise and the crush of the crowd—and worrying about Frank and her family—pressed in on Annie, and she gritted her teeth against the panic starting to take hold. *Just breathe.*

"Hey, Miss Oakley." A skinny, scrappy-faced, older teenage boy shouldered his way through the crowd and raised his chin in her direction. "How about a tumble?" He snickered to the men standing near him.

"Show some respect, boy," the older man said.

The teenager snickered again, quickly raising and lowering his eyebrows at Annie. She swallowed hard, wanting to deny the rumors, wanting to explain her innocence, but she held her tongue, not giving the boy the dignity of a response. When he leered again, the older man shoved the boy, jostling a few others standing nearby.

"Hey!" someone shouted. "Knock it off."

The crowd stirred, people started shouting and shoving one another. Fists started to fly. An arm slipped around Annie's waist and pulled her away from the chaos—Bobby. He held his arm out in front of him and pushed and shoved their way through the crowd, finally breaking free when a woman's shrill scream pierced the air.

Everyone stopped and turned to see where the horrendous sound originated.

The scream came from the stands.

This time, Annie grabbed Bobby's hand and pulled him toward the shrieking woman, pushing and shoving through the throng of people. They soon spotted her, holding her hands over her face, wailing. The man next to her sat slumped over on the wooden bench, blood streaking down his face and into his open eyes.

Annie rushed to the trembling woman and with gentle arms, pulled her away from the body, pressing her tightly to her side

"Oh, good Lord," Bobby said.

"What? What is it, Bobby?" Annie strained over the woman's shoulder to see.

"It's the Colonel's old partner, Dick Carver. He's dead. He's been shot in the back of the head, near the neck. Someone either shot from up top in the bleachers or just behind him."

Annie patted the woman, trying to calm her violent sobs. She cried so hard that Annie worried she'd throw them both off balance and they'd both tumble down the steps. She coaxed the woman to sit down, and they sank onto the bench together.

"Bobby, you go get Mr. LeFleur, I'll stay here with her and the"—she cast a glance at the upright corpse—"Mr. Carver."

Bobby steadied the body and stood up, facing the crowd of people who'd come to gawk. "Folks, please stand back. Please, don't anybody touch him. Everybody, just go on about your business."

People stood around, murmuring to each other about what could have happened. Several women sniveled into handkerchiefs, their spouses consoling them.

"Are you all right here, Miss Oakley?" Bobby cast a glance at Annie.

"I'm fine, Bobby. Please go get Mr. LeFleur. Hurry." She peeked down at the woman she held in her arms. The woman's hat had fallen off, spilling her cottony hair onto her shoulders.

"Were any of you here with Mr. Carver?" Annie asked those standing around them. "Did anyone see what happened?" The gawkers shook their heads no and began to saunter away.

"He was sitting right next to me the whole time." The woman lifted her head. "I didn't hear anything. Didn't notice anything, until we got up to go down the stairs after the show. Then he just sort of fell over against me."

She started trembling again, so Annie pulled her in tighter.

"You're going to be fine. Help is on its way." *Hurry up, Mr. LeFleur.*

Moments later, LeFleur appeared, winded from his climb up the stairs, his face ashen. The Colonel followed, right on LeFleur's heels.

"Carver! What the hell was *he* doing here?"

Twila and Bobby bounded up the steps, and Twila immediately rushed to the woman in Annie's arms. She knelt down next to her, holding some green and brown herbs close to the woman's nose.

"Here, take a whiff of this. It will restore you."

Annie released her hold on the woman so she could breathe in deeply. The woman blinked her eyes several times, then straightened.

"Yes, yes. I do feel better." She looked at Twila with gratitude and Twila trained her eyes on Annie.

"I will take her now."

Annie couldn't imagine that Twila would harm the woman, so released her grip and helped the woman stand. Twila then took the woman's arm, and they inched their way down the steps.

"Is someone going to get the sheriff or something?" Bobby asked.

"We'll have to." The Colonel swiped a hand across his forehead. "I'll have one of the boys ride into town to get him. Meanwhile, I don't want people gawking at him." He paused, shook his head. "This is most unfortunate—and very bad publicity, so let's go ahead and move Mr. Carver into my tent."

LeFleur, who would normally jump into action, seemed paralyzed by the sight. Sweat glistened on his pasty forehead. His lips, nearly white, trembled.

The Colonel leaned over to pull Dick Carver up from the bench and turned to LeFleur. "Derence. A hand here?"

LeFleur snapped out of his paralysis, and together they lifted the body to standing. The Colonel leaned into Carver's stomach, hefting him over his shoulder. Annie winced as blood splattered onto the Colonel's immaculate buckskin tunic and the footboard of the wooden stands.

Struggling with his load, the Colonel made his way down the stairs, LeFleur trailing behind, his face frozen in fear.

"Mr. LeFleur, you don't look well," Annie said as he passed her.

"I . . . uh . . . haven't seen a death like this since the war."

Annie knew full well that the men who fought in the Civil War had seen terrible things. Her father would scream in his sleep, often get up from bed and wait for morning, afraid to dream again.

"You okay, Miss Oakley?" Bobby asked.

Annie tried to smile. "Yes, Bobby. Thank you. Are you?"

Bobby's jaw flexed. The Adam's apple in his neck bobbed as he swallowed.

"It just brings back the pain." He rubbed his forehead. "Nobody in the show died before. Now we've had two since we got to St. Louis." He looked down at his hands and picked at a callus on one of his palms.

Annie tried to ignore the sinking sensation in her stomach, tried to ignore the feeling that *she* might be the catalyst that started the downward spiral of the show—starting with Buck's illness, then Twila's jealousy, then McCrimmon's mischief, and now possibly two murders. Though not entirely sure that someone murdered Kimi, she knew for absolute certain that somebody wanted Mr. Carver in the ground.

Her stomach in knots, Annie felt a desperate need to see Buck. If he were well enough, she'd saddle him up and take a twilight ride to clear her head. Buck, nature, and solitude always calmed her down.

But first she'd try to find Frank to find out what happened with him. She brushed past the remaining onlookers and made her way to his tent.

"Frank, it's Annie. Are you in there?" She pressed her sweaty palms together and rubbed them on her skirt, now ruined with blood splatters and smears from the woman's hands. She heard rustling inside and then he appeared, sticking his head outside the opening.

His crestfallen expression broke her heart. He looked utterly defeated.

"Won't you come in?" he said, his voice flat. He turned and headed back inside.

Should she go in? Would it be proper? *To hell with propriety.*

She stepped into the darkness of his tent—all the window flaps had been closed and a pall hung in the air.

Frank's appearance startled her. Usually impeccably attired, one of his shirttails hung over his leather belt, the other still tucked in his pants. His thick hair, normally groomed and tidy, stood up and out at awkward angles as if he'd raked his hands through it in anguish.

A small lantern glowed dimly upon a table, illuminating an open, half-empty whiskey bottle and a glass full of the amber liquid. Frank made his way over to the table and sat down, flung a leg up onto the tabletop, picked up the glass, and cradled it in his lap.

"What's all the commotion out there?" His raised the glass to his lips.

"There's been a murder," Annie said, too traumatized to say more.

"Murder?" He pulled his head back, his brows furrowed in confusion.

Annie shifted her weight from one foot to the other, uncomfortable standing, but couldn't see anywhere to sit except the bed, and that seemed inappropriate. Suddenly exhausted, she raised a hand to her forehead, dizziness making her knees weak.

"Forgive me." Frank jumped up. "I've forgotten my manners. Please, sit here."

Relieved, she made her way over to the chair while Frank quickly neatened up the table, corked the whiskey bottle, and set it in an open trunk.

"What's this you said about murder?"

"Someone shot Dick Carver in the head while he was in the stands, in the stadium. It must have been when all the shooting was going on, because no one seemed to notice until almost everyone had left."

Frank plopped down on the bed, the palm of his hand pressed against the right side of his forehead. Annie noticed that his usually bright eyes looked bloodshot and bleary. How much had he had to drink?

"Dick Carver. Well, I'll be damned."

"Do you know that he used to be business partners with the Colonel?"

"Yes, a long time ago."

"The Colonel said he thought Carver might be behind the story about me. Said he's been out to get the Colonel for years. I still think the story was Vernon McCrimmon's handiwork."

"McCrimmon wouldn't have the clout to get someone to print that story. He's just an old sot. He'd have to have help." Frank rested one of his elbows on his thigh.

Annie thought about telling him about Twila talking with McCrimmon earlier that day, but thinking about it made her head hurt—and she couldn't bear to hear Frank take up for Twila once again. She only wanted to soothe Frank's wounds.

"I'm so sorry about today, the performance."

"I'm finished." Frank shook his head and rested both elbows on his knees, training his eyes to the ground. "They only dressed me down this time, but one more day like today and they'll cut me out of the show for sure. I've been skating along, even before I competed against you in that contest in Greenville."

"No." Annie sprang from the chair and rushed to the bed. She sat next to him and placed a gentle hand on his broad shoulders.

"What is it, Frank? Why did you miss?"

"I don't want to talk about it." He straightened up and locked his eyes on hers. "I don't want to talk at all."

Frank reached for her, wrapped his arms around her, pulled her close, and pressed his warm, soft lips against hers. Her heart pounded, and she could feel the rhythmic rush of blood pulsating in her ears. She pushed him away, bolted to a standing position, and pressed her hands against her corset, gasping.

Frank stood and gently placed a hand on each of her arms. "I'm sorry, Annie, I frightened you."

"I'm not frightened. You didn't frighten me."

Frank wrapped his arms around her waist and held her so close she felt her body melding into his. She sank against him, not caring about anything else in the world except his body, his breath, his hands.

He kissed her again.

Annie knew she was lost—forever.

CHAPTER 13

"Local Man Vernon McCrimmon Missing. Last Seen Two
Weeks Ago at North Star Mercantile, Owner Mr. Shaw Says
McCrimmon Threatened Him with His Life."

Greenville Gazette – April 18, 1884

Annie woke and opened her eyes to see Frank sleeping peacefully
beside her. Her stomach plummeted. She'd just shared intimate
relations with a man out of wedlock. It flew in the face of everything
she'd ever believed in. What had happened to her? She'd let her fame
and celebrity overtake her good judgment, making her someone she
didn't know. A fornicator. How could she have betrayed her beliefs?

She crawled out of the bed, pulling the sheet with her to cover her
body.

"Hey," Frank said, drowsiness in his voice. "Where are you going?"

"I shouldn't be here, I shouldn't have done this." Annie couldn't keep
the tremor out of her voice.

Lord knew if word got out about this, her reputation would be
doomed forever. She thought about the article that had recently been
printed about her, and her stomach flipped again, her throat went dry.

She'd compromised everything. She had given in to her weakness for

Frank. What would her mother think of her? Her poor mother, alone, was pining over a man who'd done nothing but cause her heartache. She'd be so ashamed. Susan didn't raise her daughters to give themselves to the first man who'd made them breathless.

She knew in her heart she loved Frank, but this was wrong.

Annie pulled the sheet tighter around her body, embarrassed at her own wantonness. Where were her clothes? Her boots? Panic rose in her chest. She had to get out of here. She hoped and prayed no one would notice her leave, but before she could, she had to be dressed. Perfectly, like before. Where was that blouse?

"Not yet. Don't leave." Frank's arms slipped around her waist. He tried to pull her back onto the bed.

Annie wriggled out of his embrace, her heart thudding in her ears and heat crawling up her neck. How could she have done something so careless?

"Please, Frank. Let me go."

"C'mon. Just for a while longer."

"No!"

Frank's smile fell. "What's the matter?"

"Nothing. Where is my skirt?" She walked around the bed, her sweating hands gripping harder at the sheet.

"Annie, why are you upset?"

She stopped searching and looked him full in the face.

"This was wrong. We never should have done this. I have people depending on me, I should never . . ."

Frank sat up, leaning his weight on the palm of his hand.

"Annie, just because you have people depending on you doesn't mean you shouldn't be happy."

She spied her blouse on the floor at the foot of the bed and swiped it up.

"I am no better than that article that was printed about me. It's shameful what I've done. I hardly know you. I can't believe I walked away from Friend Easton. He was ready to spend his life with me—the right way, not taking me to his bed the first chance he got."

"Easton? Who's Easton?" he asked.

"Never mind."

She fumbled her way into her shift without letting the sheet drop. She grabbed her corset off the floor. Dear God, what a mess. Her shame overwhelmed her like water breaking free from a dam.

"Annie." Frank got out of the bed. "I think you are overreacting. I love you. This isn't wrong."

Annie found her petticoats and grasped them to her stomach. *He loved her.* She couldn't look up at him but instead stepped into her bloomers, still grasping the sheet. Frank chuckled and she glanced up at him, appalled.

"What is so funny?" Couldn't he see she had ruined her life? *He'd* ruined her life. What if she carried his child?

"Honey, you're overreacting."

Fury rose in her chest up to her throat, making her choke.

"Don't you 'honey' me! You don't understand. This is not me. I have to get out of here. Where is my skirt? Put your pants on, for heaven's sake."

Frank raised his hands in surrender and grabbed the pants that he had carefully hung on the bedpost and pulled them on. How had he been so meticulous in their passion? She couldn't find anything. She'd never get herself pulled together. Frenzied, she looked under the bed, near the chair, next to the table. Where was that skirt?

Unable to keep it together any longer, she slumped to the floor, sob-bing. How had she made such a mess of things?

Frank knelt down beside her. His warm, strong hands pulled her up, and he held her close to his chest. The steady rhythm of his heart comforted her as she cried into his shirt.

"It's going to be okay," he said. "I'll make this right. No one has to know, Annie. We can keep this secret until we can get married. I can wait for you."

She pulled back. "You want to marry me?"

"Yes, I do. Will you?"

She released herself from his grip. "I—I—"

"Don't answer now. We both have enough to manage at the moment. We can worry about it later."

She sniffed loudly, remembering that her faith preached that true happiness and joy in marriage depends first on devoted love, a love that is not about just a passing attraction, but that includes real respect for the whole person. Didn't she and Frank have that?

Frank pulled a handkerchief from his pocket and handed it to her. While she blew her nose and wiped her face, he gathered up the rest of her clothing, her stockings, her corset, and her boots. He gently led her to the bed and sat her down, placing all her things next to her.

She had just stuck her big toe into her stocking when light from the tent flap flooded the room.

"Frank, the Colonel wants to see—"

It was LeFleur.

"See you . . ." His voice faded as his eyes widened to see Annie sitting on the bed.

A lump the size of a tin can filled Annie's throat.

"What in God's name—?" LeFleur lunged toward Frank, ready to grab him by the throat. Frank ducked below LeFleur's arms and skirted past him.

"Derence, get a hold of yourself. What's wrong with you, man?"

LeFleur wound up to deliver a blow to Frank's face. Annie jumped from the bed and grabbed him.

"Stop!"

"How could you?" LeFleur's eyes cut through her.

Annie took him by both arms and squared him in front of her.

"I know what this looks like, Mr. LeFleur. I am so sorry."

"Looks like? You mean to tell me it's something else?"

Annie shook her head, the blood draining from her face. She liked and admired Mr. LeFleur. He'd been her champion from the beginning and disappointing him in any way left her hollow. She couldn't bear the disgust written in his face.

He shook free from her grasp and turned to Frank.

"The Colonel wants to see you. About the abysmal performance you gave earlier today." He turned back to Annie. "And the police would like a word with you. They are in the mess tent." The words came out slow, calm. Without looking at either one of them, he strode out of the tent.

Annie raised her hands to her face, the tears threatening to flow again, but she was too mortified to cry. She wanted to crawl under the bed and never come out.

Frank reached out for her and pulled her to him again.

"How could anything be worse than this?" she whispered into his chest.

Light from the tent flap illuminated the dark interior once again, but this time it wasn't LeFleur. Twila stood in the light, holding the tent flap aside. Her eyes narrowed at the two of them, and her mouth screwed up in a smirk. She whirled around, her skirts slapping against the chair at the entrance, and she stomped out, the bells on her boots jangling.

"This isn't going to be good," Frank said.

After they had dressed, Annie and Frank sat in silence, Annie at Frank's desk and Frank on the mussed bed.

"You know we're going to have to face the Colonel and LeFleur soon. Or, at least I am." Frank had both hands resting on his knees.

"I don't think they'll let you go."

"The Colonel is a perfectionist, and I have fallen far short of perfection for some time. He's run out of patience with me."

Annie stood and walked toward the bed.

"I'd put in a good word for you, but I don't think my opinion is going to count for much. There's been nothing but trouble since I joined the show."

Frank stood up too and reached for her, smoothing her tangled hair.

"You have been nothing but a godsend to this show . . . to everyone, but especially to me. Being who we are, Annie Oakley and Frank Butler, everything we say and do is examined and judged. I don't think you were quite prepared for what being famous entails."

"I wasn't. And I don't know how I'd face all this without you. I don't want you to go anywhere."

"If they fire me, you could come with me."

Annie met his eyes. "Come with you, where?"

"Back to Kentucky. I need to make amends with my family. I've been running from them for far too long."

Annie ran her hand up his arm. "I have a family to support. My mother's—Joshua—quandered almost all the money I've sent home. My mother is ill, and my brother and sister are too young to carry such a burden. I should go home and take care of matters there. What good is sending money to them if they never receive it?"

"But you signed a contract, right?"

"Yes, for one year."

"You shouldn't break the contract."

"What about you? If you signed a contract, they can't fire you, right?"

"It expired a month ago. They haven't pushed for a new one, possibly because they wanted to see if I could shake off this slump. I'm only here because the Colonel likes me."

Annie stiffened. "You mean you're only here because Twila likes you."

"Yeah, her too," he said with a chuckle.

Annie balled up a fist and playfully punched him in the ribs.

"Ouch!" Frank wrapped his arms around her and held her in a quiet embrace. Annie felt comfortable in his arms, like they were a perfect fit for her body, a warm, securing blanket of safety and protection from the world.

"If they don't fire you, will you stay on?" she asked, her voice hopeful.

"I'll stay . . . for you."

Annie smiled, nuzzled into his chest.

"We'll just have to change some things in the act. I'll have to astound the audience with my amazing horsemanship. Maybe I'll take up roping buffalo. It works for the Colonel."

Annie pulled back and looked him square in the eyes.

"You are the best marksman in the world, Frank Butler. You'll get it back. I know it." She laid her head on Frank's chest, her ear next to his heart.

"Yeah, maybe you're right."

Annie left Frank's tent and tried to muster her courage to face everyone in the mess tent. The smoke from a campfire lingered in the air and she turned to see Chief Sitting Bull, cross-legged on the ground in front of his tipi, stoking the flames. A flutter of hope arose—if anyone could advise her on this impending disaster, it would be the Chief.

"Watanya Cecilia!" The Chief raised his hand in welcome and then gestured for her to join him.

Annie sat down with him, pulling her skirt up over her knees and crossing her legs. She held her hands to the fire, welcoming its warmth.

"What brings my daughter to visit me?"

Annie searched his weathered face, grateful for his consistent kindness towards her.

"I'm troubled, Chief Sitting Bull."

"Is it the matter of Kimi's death? Did you find your answers?"

"I haven't yet found anything conclusive. I have other problems right now."

"Tell me what troubles you, child."

Annie took a deep breath and told him about Joshua stealing the money she'd been sending home, her mother's illness, Vernon McCrimmon's threats, Buck's continuing ailment, Twila's threatening resentment, and her feelings for Frank.

Once she stopped talking, the Chief picked up a pipe and took a draw from it, enveloping them in fragrant smoke, as if it would form the cloud of protection she needed.

"Think hard, Watanya Cecilia." He blew out another puff of smoke. "Do you love Frank Butler?"

Annie nodded.

"And he loves you?"

"Yes." A blush crept up her cheeks.

"A love such as this is sacred."

"Mr. LeFleur and Twila just discovered us together. I'm worried about our reputations, particularly mine, and neither of them is happy about our being together."

"Then you must stand firm. Your love is not wrong."

"Frank thinks the Colonel might fire him after his performance today. Now my relationship with Frank may make things worse. Twila hates me, and she may convince the Colonel to fire me as well."

Chief Sitting Bull drew in and released another stream of sweet-smelling smoke. Annie fumbled with the hem of her skirt.

"The Colonel's mistress has darkness inside. You must be wary of her."

"Yes, I agree. That's why I need your help. I don't wish to burden you, but I wondered if you could say something to the Colonel to convince him to keep Frank on as part of the show."

Chief Sitting Bull tamped the residue out of his pipe.

"I will speak with the Colonel, Watanya Cecilia. He is a wise man. He has weathered many storms. This is but a small one. He has had to rise up against many foes, including his past business associates."

"You know about the murder of Mr. Carver?"

Chief Sitting Bull nodded.

Annie wanted to ask him more questions, to solicit his advice on her quest for answers about Kimi's death, but she'd just remembered that the sheriff and his detective were waiting for her.

"May I come to you again?" she asked.

"Yes, my daughter, you are most welcome at any time."

CHAPTER 14

"Dick Carver, Former Partner of Buffalo Bill Cody,
Shot Dead in Stands of Wild West Performance.
Wild West Show under Investigation."

St. Louis Times, Evening Edition – April 18, 1885

Annie entered the mess tent to see two men seated at separate tables, interviewing crew members one at a time, recording notes on small pads of paper. Her eyes drifted immediately to Twila, who rolled Winona's pram back and forth in what looked like a half-hearted attempt to comfort the fussing baby. LeFleur stood in the corner in conversation with the Colonel. The woman who had been sitting next to Carver at the ill-fated incident sat quietly on a stool, her handkerchief pressed to her face suppressing tears.

Before Annie could take it all in, a young woman wearing burgundy moiré taffeta trousers that ballooned out at the thigh approached her, notepad and pencil in hand.

"Miss Oakley, I'm Emma Wilson, a reporter for the *St. Louis Times*." The woman beamed, her dimples receding into her creamy white cheeks.

Miss Wilson's demeanor and expensive-looking attire exuded an air of well-to-do confidence. Her wool coat's collar and cuffs, adorned with colorful, intricate embroidered designs, reminded Annie of Kimi's fine needlework.

"Are you the reporter who wrote those horrible lies about me that were printed in your paper?" Annie looked directly into Miss Wilson's sage-colored eyes.

The smile on Miss Wilson's lips softened.

"No, Miss Oakley, but I wouldn't worry about that story. Fame breeds sensationalism. Sarah Bernhardt, Lillie Langtry, and even the great Susan B. Anthony always have salacious stories published about them which we know aren't true. Reporters have a tendency to embellish, make their stories a little more exciting. It sells more papers."

"But Miss Wilson, are *you* the type of reporter who embellishes stories to sell more newspapers?"

"I most certainly am not," Miss Wilson's said, her eyes widening, "I assure you. I'd just like to ask you a few questions—about the shooting."

"Very well. I don't wish to be quoted, though."

"I can make you an anonymous witness. Now, about this business with Mr. Carver. Did you know him?"

Annie shook her head. "No. I only learned about him when the Colonel thought Carver might have been behind the story about me, that he might have sought to discredit or harm the Colonel and the show."

Miss Wilson glanced around, making sure no one might overhear her.

"Well, I'm here to tell you, he didn't."

"Then who did?"

"I don't know. Honest. Cross my heart. Hope to die." She ran her finger above her left breast, creating an invisible cross. "Do you know any details about this bad blood between Carver and the Colonel?"

"Only that they had been business partners once, and that it didn't end well."

"And what about Bobby Bradley? What can you tell me about him? I understand he was one of the first people to discover Mr. Carver."

"What about Bobby?"

"I overheard Colonel Cody tell the police that he's disappeared."

"Bobby disappeared? If that's true, I have no knowledge of it." Annie thought the statement odd. Why would Bobby disappear? Unless he feared the police. Unless he had something to hide. Annie's mind flashed back to Bobby's argument with Kimi, his hateful expression when quarreling with Mr. LeFleur.

"Well, from the looks of it," Miss Wilson nodded towards the detectives, "this will be a huge case, widely reported in the newspapers—locally and across the country. Colonel Cody apparently called in his friends at the Theil Detective agency to assist in the investigation. This is usually Pinkerton territory, but Theil and Colonel Cody were soldiers together in the Civil War."

"That's wise of the Colonel, given his relationship with Mr. Carver, but I'm certain the Colonel is innocent."

Miss Wilson scribbled something on her pad, and then gently took Annie's arm, leading her to a more private location.

"Listen, Miss Oakley. May I call you Annie?"

"Of course you may."

"I admire you, Annie. With your sweet face, you look like a prim little girl in those sparkly cowgirl outfits, but you are fierce—you are making a difference in the world of women, inspiring women to be stronger, to let the world know that women can be mighty without losing their femininity. Have you thought about joining the suffragette movement?"

"Well, no, I haven't."

"I understand that the Colonel pays you the same wage he pays Frank Butler."

Annie raised her eyebrows. She didn't know that, but didn't really care.

"I make a decent wage, and I am grateful."

Miss Wilson grinned. "Positively charming. You are simply adorable, Annie. I'm here to cover the story of Carver's murder, and I will, of course, but I have another agenda—one that you can help me fulfill." She raised her eyebrows. "Are you game?"

"I don't know, Miss Wilson. I have plenty of things to worry about at the moment, and I doubt that I could be of much help to you."

"What if I told you I could get the story about you retracted? Perhaps even get the editor to issue a formal apology in the newspaper?"

"I would appreciate a retraction, but it depends on what would you want me to do."

Miss Wilson's eyes widened beneath her large brimmed hat.

"Join the crusade for women's rights, share your knowledge of guns and shooting with other women, teach them to defend themselves. Whether you know it or not, Annie, you have become a powerful national sensation. Use that power to inspire and uplift the so-called 'fairer' sex."

Annie smiled at the possibilities. She *could* empower women, cultivate their independence, ensure that girls and women would not have to be dependent on others for their livelihood—even their very lives, like her poor mother.

"You say you can get that story retracted, and a formal apology published?"

"I promise you that I can, and we'll make sure it's printed in newspapers all over the country."

Annie felt a rush of excitement. She would have an opportunity to help other women—people like her sister, her mother, and Winona.

"Then I will join your crusade, Miss Wilson." She held out her hand.

"Emma, please call me Emma, now that we're going to be sisters in the fight for women's rights." Emma took her hand, squeezed it.

"Emma it is then. But I need some time to tend to pressing matters first." Annie saw the Colonel wave his arm to get her attention.

"Of course. You won't regret it, Annie. I'll leave you to your business, but remember to look for that retraction and apology in tomorrow's issue of the *Times*."

The Colonel, his skin glowing pink with distress under his perfectly trimmed beard, gestured for Annie to sit down at the table with one of the detectives. He looked on the verge of a temper tantrum.

The young man, whose suit hung on him like a flour sack, stood up and greeted Annie, his bespectacled, intelligent eyes appraising her.

"Miss Oakley, I'm Detective Jonas. Please have a seat."

Annie sat, and Detective Jonas asked her a myriad of questions that she couldn't possibly answer about the deceased, Dick Carver. She explained that she and Bobby heard the woman scream, went up into the grandstand to see what had happened, and found Carver's body slumped next to the woman.

"That was the extent of it," Annie said.

"Do you know where we might find Bobby?" Detective Jonas asked.

Annie shook her head, still unable to comprehend why he would have fled.

"He must be around here somewhere. Perhaps the barn?"

"Thank you, Miss Oakley. That will be all for now." He jotted something down on his notepad.

Annie thought about getting up, but then thought again.

"Detective Jonas—" Annie debated whether or not to bring up something that could be disagreeable, but after her conversation with Emma she felt courageous and obligated to do right by her friend. "A few weeks ago, an Indian girl who worked for the show passed away, and I was wondering if you had heard about this, and if you had investigated her death?"

"No. Haven't heard anything about this." Detective Jonas furrowed his brows.

"So you haven't heard anything about a girl named Kimi?"

Before Detective Jonas could reply, LeFleur, who had been standing nearby, rushed over.

"I couldn't help overhearing, and I must reassure you that the coroner investigated and determined Kimi died from natural causes. Miss Oakley remains upset, as they were friends, but the matter has been put to rest, and there is nothing to be gained by bringing it up again."

"Well, if the matter was properly addressed, I see no reason to be concerned about it. But thank you for your time, Miss Oakley, and please be aware that we may want to ask you additional questions later."

Annie rose to leave, and LeFleur gripped her arm, escorting her quickly out of the tent.

Once they were alone, where no one could see them, he pulled her close.

"Don't ever bring up Kimi to the police again. Doing so risks everything the Colonel has worked to build. It can't get out that he fathered Winona."

"Let me go," Annie said, her teeth clenched.

LeFleur grabbed her other arm, shook her.

"And just what do you think you're doing with Frank Butler?"

Annie met his pointed gaze with equal intensity.

"That's none of your business, Mr. LeFleur. Now, let me go before I do something we both regret."

"I'm sorry, Annie." LeFleur released her. "I don't mean to be so brash, but you know very well that I have feelings for you."

"And I've made it clear that I do not return your feelings."

"I know you don't, but Frank Butler will bring you nothing but pain."

"Mr. LeFleur." Annie straightened her shoulders. "If you're trying to protect me, I appreciate your concern, but I'm in love with Frank Butler, and—"

"It's not good for your public image." LeFleur's face reddened. "You'll be the target of more bad press, Annie."

"The lies that were reported will be righted in tomorrow's newspapers, and I'm told that many women view my reputation in a positive manner."

LeFleur crossed his arms over his chest, and, to avoid looking into his eyes, Annie's eyes moved down to his hands, where she again noticed black stains on his right palm.

"Twila is furious that she discovered you in Frank's tent. You do know, I presume, that Twila and Frank were lovers."

Annie bristled. "I am aware, but I—*everyone*—is also aware that Twila is the Colonel's mistress, and has been for some time."

"This is not a woman you want to anger." LeFleur's eyes darkened to the shade of burnt coffee. He leaned in closer. "She is ruthless when it comes to getting her way. She uses whatever she can to make everyone—even the Colonel—do what she wants."

"Are you trying to tell me that Twila has something she can use against the Colonel?"

"I'm saying nothing of the sort, only that you don't want this woman as your enemy."

"I'm not afraid of Twila Midnight."

"Annie, I don't wish to create any animosity between us." LeFleur softened his approach. "But please believe me when I tell you that Frank is not the settling kind. He's only looking out for his own self-interest. He'll take advantage of you."

"And were you thinking about your poor, ailing wife when you kissed me?"

LeFleur's face blanched and his eyes darted behind Annie. She turned and saw Frank coming at them.

"You aren't giving Annie a bad time, are you, Derence?" Frank moved past Annie until he and LeFleur were face to face. "This is a woman who knows her own mind, and it'd be best for everyone if you—and Twila—keep your observations and opinions to yourself."

Annie watched the muscles below LeFleur's ears tense, his face turn redder. He butted his chest against Frank's.

"How dare you take advantage of this poor girl."

"Gentlemen, please." Annie grabbed LeFleur's arm and placed a firm hand on Frank's shoulder. "No one took advantage of me.

I'm not a 'poor girl,' and I am quite capable of making my own decisions."

"You see, that's just what I said, LeFleur. My intentions toward Annie are honorable, and this isn't anyone's business but hers and mine, so I need you to clam up, leave Annie alone, and don't rile Twila. She's got no claim on me, and never did. So I suggest you trot off now and leave us be."

LeFleur used both hands to jerk down the points of his vest, and stalked off.

Frank reached out and settled one of Annie's errant curls behind her ear. She leaned her face into his hand, then pulled away. They'd have to be more restrained in public, keep their relationship a secret, at least until things settled down.

"Is the Colonel in there?" Frank tilted his head toward the mess tent.

"He's hired a private detective team to help the sheriff. Do you think he's concerned that he'll be blamed for the murder?"

Frank sniffed. "Well, he certainly has a motive. When they split the business, Carver thought he got robbed, and he's come around every so often to look for something he could nail on the Colonel. He's tried to undermine the show many times. Don't guess anyone would be surprised if the Colonel finally had it—or that Carver finally had something that could ruin the show."

"You don't think the Colonel would stoop to murder, do you?"

"A man will do almost anything to protect his financial interests—or his reputation. The Colonel spent years building up the Wild West Show and now that it's been so successful, he sure wouldn't want Carver dipping into his pie."

Annie furrowed her brow. She could not envision it, even if he'd fought in wars—surely he wouldn't kill a man over a business deal, or a woman for bearing his child.

Frank winked and tipped his hat to her.

"Don't worry, Annie. They'll find the person who shot Carver, and it won't be the Colonel." He used a finger to lift her face and flashed one of his most charming smiles.

Frank could probably get away with anything, she thought—even murder.

CHAPTER 15

"Samson's Horse Traders in Need of New Horses.
Will Buy or Trade."

St. Louis Times, Evening Edition – April 18, 1885

Early that evening, with the afternoon performance cancelled, Annie retreated to her tent for a long overdue sleep. Still wound tight as a watchspring, Annie sought the soothing comfort of a warm cup of tea.

After she had the coals glowing in the little campfire outside her tent, Annie went back inside to find her tea tin and porcelain cup. Her eyes drifted to the corner above Kimi's bed, to the little pouch and porcelain cup she'd hung from the corner tent pole. Nakota told her that the pouch, filled with a lock of Kimi's hair and bits of food, must be hung where Kimi had lived, so that her spirit would be welcomed and nourished. She had added her own gift of some sweets, placed them in Kimi's teacup, and hung it next to the pouch.

Annie smiled at the notion of Kimi's spirit watching over her.

She went to her trunk and picked up the tea tin. She pried open the lid and was shocked to find the tin empty. It had been full only a few days ago, she could have sworn it. Did Lillie break into her and Kimi's stash? Didn't seem likely—Lillie didn't drink tea, only whiskey.

Annie put the lid back on the tin and set it on her trunk. She looked down at the rug where she had found the coin. The bits of tea leaves still remained. Annie reached into her pocket and pulled out the coin. She'd meant to ask Bobby about the gold flecks in the file, but the detective had been correct—Bobby couldn't be found. She put the coin back into her pocket.

Befuddled and too tired to stand any more, Annie went to her bed and crawled under the covers, fully dressed. She scanned the room, grateful for the silence. Her gaze fell onto the teacup and pouch in the corner, and she remembered the calico scarf she'd thrown in her wardrobe—Kimi's scarf. She had worn it every day. If Kimi had just dropped dead in her tracks, why had the scarf been so far away from her body? Did someone toss it away from her, or did it fall off Kimi in a struggle? There had been no ligature marks on her neck that might indicate it had been used to strangle her.

Annie closed her eyes, reasoning that she would think about it later, and when she awoke, she would wrap the scarf around the tent pole with the rest of Kimi's belongings.

Some time later, Annie woke to darkness when she heard what sounded like someone banging a pan near her tent. She sat up, rubbed her face, and ran her hands through her tangled hair. A glow from outside lanterns barely lit the room. Lillie's bed was empty. How long had she slept?

Annie got out of bed and lit the gas lantern, noticing an envelope with her name printed on the front lying on the desk. She picked it up and turned it over. It had been sealed with wax, but she couldn't make out the design embedded in the seal. She hastily opened it.

"When you get this, come to my tent. I need to speak with you. It's urgent. Frank."

Annie's heart leapt, and she quickly ran a brush through her hair, placed a bright blue ribbon at the nape of her neck, and tied it in a bow at the crown of her head. She then retrieved a rag from her toiletry bag and rubbed her teeth with it, then straightened her corset and pulled down her blouse. Her skirt, a wrinkled mess, hung limp. But did it really matter? His message said urgent.

She hoped that Chief Sitting Bull had spoken to the Colonel on Frank's behalf as he'd promised. Annie couldn't imagine the Wild West Show without the world famous Frank Butler, couldn't imagine herself without the man she had fallen in love with. She had enough burdens to bear. *Could she please just have this one piece of heaven to herself?*

After a brief, rushed moment at Lillie's mirror, Annie smoothed her hair and pinched her cheeks. She left the tent and ran through the night air, her path lit by lanterns and the stars twinkling in the midnight-blue sky. When she got closer to Frank's tent, she slowed, not wanting to arrive out of breath. Once there, however, she couldn't help rushing in.

Lit only by a dim light in one corner, Annie saw two naked bodies on the bed. The woman had long, black hair, but Annie's eyes were riveted on her lily-white hips, undulating above Frank, his hands gripping her, urging her on. When Annie gasped, Twila swung her head around and lifted her chin, grinning in such a malicious, hateful way that Annie fled, choking back sobs as she ran back to her tent. Once there, she flung herself onto her bed, buried her face in her pillow, and wept.

Frank had lied to her. Lied. He had told her that he loved her, that she'd stolen his heart, that Twila held no attraction for him—and now he was making love to her? What could have happened? Why would he do this? Why would he betray her? *Why?*

Annie felt like her heart had been wrenched from her body. She cried for what seemed hours. When the tears no longer came, her face ached, her throat burned, and her body felt as if it had been wrung out like a dishtowel.

She didn't know how much time had passed before she heard a rustling in the dark. Dim light beamed in as someone opened the tent flap.

"Annie, are you awake?" Lillie stumbled, knocking over something. "Ouch. Annie?"

Annie closed her eyes, holding her breath. She didn't want to talk to Lillie, especially a drunk Lillie. She listened as Lillie slumped down onto her bed and let out a rush of air so loud it sounded like a carnival balloon deflating. Annie lay quiet, not moving a muscle. Within minutes, Lillie's breathy snores filled the tent.

Annie curled onto her side, the pain in her chest so heavy she thought she'd suffocate from the weight of it. When she thought of Frank's face, his eyes, his smile, the strength of his arms around her, she could barely breathe. She thought of Frank's boyish charm, the tenderness in his embrace, his lips kissing hers . . . and now Twila's. Tears again streamed from Annie's eyes, seeping into the pillow, until eventually she fell into a fitful sleep.

"Miss Oakley, Miss Smith. Wake up." A male voice called from outside the tent. "The Colonel wants everyone at the mess tent in thirty minutes. Please hurry."

Annie heaved a sigh and blinked her eyes open. Her stuffy nose and swollen face reminded her of the nightmare of her heartbreak.

She pressed a hand to her pillow, hoping it wouldn't be wet with tears, hoping that what she'd seen between Frank with Twila had been a cruel dream. But the pillow remained wet, and she knew in her heart that she had been summoned to Frank's tent to witness his betrayal. She closed her eyes again. *Make it not be true*, she silently pleaded.

When the flap opened, sunlight pierced the tent's darkened interior.

"Miss Oakley, are you okay?"

"Bobby?" Annie leapt to her feet to hug him. "They said you disappeared. The sheriff and the detectives were looking everywhere for you."

"Yes, I know." Bobby lowered his head. "I spoke with them."

"But where did you—"

"I had something I had to do."

"Yeah, yeah, yeah," Lillie said, throwing off her blankets.

The light in the tent diminished as fast as it had come. Bobby vanished.

Not wanting to face Lillie, Annie went to her bed again, sat down and braced her elbows on her knees, placed her chin onto her forearms. Lillie rose from her bed, stumbling over clothing she'd abandoned on the floor.

"Damn it!" Lillie kicked at the mess. She then placed both hands against her temples. "Oh, my aching head." She made it as far as the vanity table and flopped into the chair. "Oh, dear. I look like hell. Too much hooch and too many cowboys. Hey, you're awfully quiet over there. Are you all right?"

Annie lifted her head and forced a smile, confident that Lillie was too self-absorbed to notice her swollen eyes.

"I wonder what the meeting is about." Lillie noisily moved items around on the vanity. "Maybe they found out who murdered poor ole Dick Carver."

"Maybe." Annie wished that Lillie would leave. She didn't want anyone to see her anguish. She didn't feel ready to face Lillie, let alone the entire show, including Frank . . . and Twila.

"Well, that's as good as the face is going to get this morning." Lillie stood up and groaned, as she wrestled herself into her corset. "Good God, I need some coffee." She glanced briefly in Annie's direction, waved her hands. "You better get going, Miss Annie Oakley. You know the Colonel doesn't like to be kept waiting."

After she left, Annie staggered to the vanity to view the state of her face. Her usually pale, freckled skin was stippled red and smeared with streaks of tears and dust. Her hair stuck out like porcupine quills.

She gathered water from the porcelain ewer, sank a cloth into the cold liquid until it was soaked, squeezed some of the liquid out, and pressed it against her sore and swollen eyes.

Next, she addressed her mass of wild curls, brushing them from the bottom up, fighting too many tangles. Braids would have to do today. She methodically plaited her hair, working slowly, trying to prolong the activity. Her heart felt so tender and bruised, she worried that she'd break down the minute she laid eyes on Frank, or she'd rip out Twila's hair in patches and poke out her cold, black eyes.

She changed her dress, not forgetting to take the gold coin from its pocket and placing it in the pocket of her clean dress. She might get a chance to ask Bobby about it, now that he'd returned, thank goodness.

Annie stood for a moment in the silence, smoothing the skirt, her composure feeling fragile in a way she'd never experienced before—not even when her father died.

She could hear someone ringing the cowbell outside the mess tent.

Showtime.

~

When Annie stepped outside, the sun's brightness striking the white canvas tents blinded her still-sensitive, irritated, tear-addled eyes. She wished the congestion high up in her nose would go away and relieve the persistent throbbing in her head.

Halfway to the mess tent, Frank came striding toward her.

"Morning, beautiful."

"How dare you speak to me, Frank Butler!"

"You're upset." He reached for her arm.

"Do not touch me!" Annie pushed his hand away.

Frank looked startled, but Annie didn't care. She kept walking, and he matched her pace.

"Annie. What is it? What's the matter?"

"How could you, Frank, after I—"

"What are you talking about?" Frank lifted his hands in question. His blue eyes implored hers, threatening to melt her resolve.

They reached the mess tent just as LeFleur flipped open the flap.

"You're late."

Annie lifted her skirts and ducked in under LeFleur's arm.

People gathered in small groups, holding hushed conversations. Annie's eyes immediately found Twila, talking to Lillie. Lillie blinked at her and sucked on a ridiculously long, mother-of-pearl cigarette holder. When Twila saw Annie, she narrowed her eyes and then laughed—the most evil laugh Annie had ever heard. Annie's stomach tightened. Apparently, Lillie, Twila, and Frank had all set out to make a fool of her—and they'd succeeded.

She felt Frank approaching behind her and quickly made her way through the groups of people to the other side of the tent. She glanced at him from across the room. His eyes had never left her. He looked genuinely baffled. *Did he think she would buy his innocent act?*

The Colonel stepped through the tent flap and everyone stopped talking.

"Attention, folks. As you all know by now, we had a situation yesterday. Someone shot my former business partner, Mr. Dick Carver, in the stands. The sheriff reckons the shooter fired the fatal shot during the performance when our people were firing their weapons. It seems no one near Carver heard anything and didn't realize he'd been shot until the end of the show.

"You may have already surmised that Mr. Carver and I did not get along. When we dissolved our partnership, he held a grudge against me and showed up from time to time to rustle up trouble. What I want you to know is that I had nothing to do with his death, and since we don't know who did shoot him, until we find out, you're just going to have to take my word on that."

A quiet murmur filled the room.

"I've gathered you here today because I want you to know that we are all going to speak to everyone in this room, and you may be pulled aside for questioning. If you saw or heard *anything* unusual yesterday—or if you saw someone acting suspiciously—I want you to let the investigators know immediately."

Annie's eyes fell on LeFleur, standing apart from the Colonel, arms crossed over his chest, stance wide, his feet planted. Bobby stood next to him, fidgeting. LeFleur uncrossed his arms to place a hand on Bobby's shoulder, but he shrugged it off.

"We've got some reporters nosing around," the Colonel continued. "As you also probably know, a week or so ago, a reporter wrote a story about Miss Oakley that did not paint a flattering picture."

Annie's stomach flipped, but when everyone turned to scrutinize her, she held her head high.

"That reporter had been misled by someone who wished to harm Annie's reputation. Even though the story was not true, it did not reflect well on the Wild West Show, and I can't have that. While we must give the investigators every consideration, when it comes to reporters, button up—do not tell them a thing. We can't control what they print in those damn rags, but we don't have to contribute." He paused to scan the room, looking into each person's eyes. "Do I make myself clear?"

Everyone murmured his or her assent. Rusty Post raised his hand.

"Pardon me, Colonel, for asking, but do they have any notion who shot Carver?"

The murmurings grew louder. The Colonel held his hand up to silence everyone.

"I don't rightly know. The detectives keep saying that they will inform me when they have a suspect, and since *I'm* likely a suspect, they aren't about to show their hand until they figure out that I had nothing to do with Mr. Carver's untimely death."

"What about that drunk old fool that's been following Miss Oakley around? Has anyone questioned him?" Mr. Post asked.

Annie again wanted to sink into the floor but lifted her gaze to meet the Colonel's eyes. He looked at her with such kindness she wanted to cry again, but instead gave him a reassuring smile. She knew that he didn't enjoy dragging her reputation further into this.

"I mentioned him to the sheriff, but they haven't been able to locate him." The Colonel's eyes swept the group.

"Well, he must be the shooter," someone shouted.

Annie's eyes shifted to Twila, who stared at the ceiling, as if bored with the conversation.

The Colonel held up his hand again.

"I know we'd all like to blame an outsider, but I don't want anyone making assumptions or wielding accusations. The Buffalo Bill Wild West Show is your family, and I expect you to treat your fellow performers and crew like they were blood relatives. Because of this calamity, and out of respect for the dead, we will continue our shutdown for two days, but I want everyone to continue practicing routines. When we open our doors again, I want us to give the people the best damn show they've ever seen. Are you with me on this?"

Everyone voiced their agreement.

Annie suddenly realized that in going to the far side of the tent to escape Frank, she'd hemmed herself in. She glanced around for a way out and spied LeFleur and Bobby engaged in another argument. Bobby's face bore a look of barbed defiance as LeFleur pointed a finger at him. Annie started to make her way over to them when Bobby yanked his hat off his head, slapped it against his thigh, and stalked past her in such a hurry that the wisps of hair on the side of her face moved from the breeze he'd created.

LeFleur glanced at Annie and he, too, strode past her, eyes focused straight ahead, as if on a mission.

What could they be fighting about? Where had Bobby disappeared to the day before, and why?

Annie's head pulsated with disappointment, hurt, and confusion, but she'd look into all this later, when her head stopped pounding. At least Frank had gone. She had no idea where, but felt relieved that she wouldn't have to face him . . . for a while longer.

CHAPTER 16

"Correction: It has come to the attention of the editors of the *St. Louis Times* that previous statements in a story about Wild West shooter Annie Oakley were untrue. Miss Oakley was dismissed of horse theft charges, and the injuries suffered by Vernon McCrimmon, at the hand of Miss Oakley, were deemed self-defense by Judge Brody of Darke County, Ohio.

It is with great respect that we, the editors of the *St. Louis Times*, apologize to Miss Oakley for the aforementioned mistakes regarding her good name."

St. Louis Times – April 19, 1885

Annie made a beeline for the stables. Once there she placed a halter around Buck's head and picked up the lead rope to take him out of the round corral. Listless, he followed behind her, his feet dragging, creating little clouds of dust as she led him through the gate.

She longed to ride him across the open fields, away from all her pain, but Buck still hadn't recovered from his illness. No matter, she just needed to see him—her only real comfort. A nice walk and some fresh grass might cheer both their spirits. A thicket of black gum trees in the distance beckoned. The two of them would keep walking, she reasoned, toward those trees, away from the show, away from Frank, away from her troubles.

As they strolled through the thick grass, Annie kept an eye on Buck, observing his behavior, trying to figure out what ailed him, what made him sick. He hadn't shown this sort of malaise since McCrimmon owned him, and then he suffered from malnourishment and abuse. Not the case now. His ailment didn't seem to be from anything on the outside of his body, so it must be something from the inside. She'd once heard Mr. Shaw from the North Star Mercantile say that his horse suffered from a poor liver. If that were true of Buck, wouldn't she have seen this behavior before? This illness hadn't appeared until they joined the show.

Annie remembered Twila asking if there had been a change in Buck's food, but there hadn't been since they'd come to St. Louis, and Mr. Post secured only the finest hay from the local farmers. Besides, all the other horses ate the same hay and drank the same water. Annie stopped in her tracks, letting Buck drift in front of her as he searched for the sweetest shoots of grass. The water. All the horses shared the same water—except Buck. Separated from the others because his fear of the barn, he drank from his own water trough.

"C'mon, Buck." Annie pulled on the rope, turned around, and headed back to Buck's corral. When they reached it, she led him inside, took off the halter, and walked to the wooden water trough. It was half empty. Light enough for her to tip over.

She ran back to the barn and grabbed one of the smallest glass bottles they used for shooting practice. She made sure it had a secure-fitting lid. Once back in the corral, she popped off the bottle's cork lid and dipped the small jar into the water, letting it suck the liquid in, filling it. She smashed the cork into the opening and pressed it down tight, then slipped the bottle into her dress pocket.

Grasping the side of the trough, she pushed, tipping out all the water onto the ground outside of the fence. When the water was gone, she let the trough fall back upright with a dull thud.

After several trips to the main water tank with a bucket, Annie filled Buck's trough half full, like before. Enough to keep him hydrated for the next several hours.

Sweating from the exertion, Annie brushed her hands together, satisfied at a job well done. Now she had to see Sitting Bull about getting the carriage to go into town.

Annie stood in the small reception area of the *St. Louis Times* offices, the crisp, punching sound of typewriters echoing throughout the large room as she waited for Emma Wilson. Reporters leaned intently over their typewriters, sitting in rows of desks neatly lined up like a farmer's neat row of produce. The smell of ink and paper wafted in the air, giving the atmosphere a heavy sense of importance. This was the epicenter of knowledge, the place where people spun the city's tales of politics, social doings, convenient lies, and the hard truth.

She spotted Emma Wilson heading toward her at a fast clip, today in a sage green dress with a white lace collar and cuffs and pearled buttons down the front of the bodice. The color of the dress made her eyes glow, more so now that she saw Annie there, waiting to speak with her.

"Annie!" Emma held out her arms and wrapped Annie in a tight embrace. "How odd that you've dropped by. I was just going to go see you. I have some news, but what brings you to see me? I'm honored." Emma's skin flushed pink, and her eyes danced with delight.

Annie, suddenly self-conscious at the attention Emma had inadvertently called toward the two of them, felt heat rush to her face and her palms grew clammy.

"Is there somewhere we can talk?"

"Of course, dear. Follow me."

Annie followed Emma down the aisleway between the rows of desks, trying to avoid the stares and whispers of the other reporters. When Emma reached her desk, she sat down and pointed to the chair positioned to the right of it.

"Here?" Annie looked around the room, her coat suddenly too warm with all the eyes staring at her.

"Appalling, isn't it?" Emma said. "This is the only space I'm allotted. I'm afraid it will have to do."

Annie took off her coat and sat in the chair. She folded her coat on top of her lap and placed her reticule on top of her coat.

A short, delicate-boned man appeared next to Annie's side. His triangular face, all angles and points, broke into a smile to greet her. He moved with a feminine air.

"Well, as I live and breathe—Annie Oakley! How do you do?" He bowed at the waist.

"Run along now, Harold," Emma waved her hand at him. "She's my exclusive. Go find someone else to pester."

The man sneered at Emma but moved on, much to Annie's relief.

"Now, what can I do for you, Annie?"

"First, I have to tell you, the Colonel doesn't want any of us to talk to reporters."

Emma, her face flushed pink, smiled warmly. Annie admired her creamy complexion, void of the unsightly freckles that covered her own nose. Miss Wilson cut a tall, lithe, willowy figure and—despite her avant-garde manner of dressing—she looked like she belonged in high society. Annie wondered what had drawn her to journalism. A lady like her usually married into another wealthy family and certainly did not stain her hands with work.

"I'm not going to ask you a single thing about the murder, promise. I was actually going to go see you because I have a surprise. I've arranged a shooting exposition downtown, an all-women's exhibition, Annie, in St. Louis. Won't that be spectacular?"

When Annie didn't reply, Emma reached out a hand to touch Annie's sleeve.

"My dear, what is it? You look positively wretched."

Annie forced a smile, surprised that her anxiety showed so transparently in her face. "Nothing. I'm fine."

"My dear girl. What is this all about? Why have you come to see me?" Emma leaned closer and the fragrance of lavender and vanilla filled the space between them. "Is it about the story printed about you? You did see the paper this morning, didn't you? The retraction and apology were there, front page center."

"I haven't. It was there?" Annie asked, glad to find some relief in her dim life.

"Of course it is. I gave you my word, and I am always true to my word."

"I am grateful, Miss Wilson."

"Emma, I insist you call me Emma. The story shouldn't have been printed in the first place. It's nobody's business who has, or has not, had an affair with whom."

"But that man was my enemy, not my lover." Annie tried to conceal her affronted astonishment at Emma's statement. "No tryst ever occurred. I despised him."

"I know there wasn't, Annie. I'm just pointing out that we're all human beings who occasionally have love affairs. You are almost a grown woman, so you don't have to concern yourself with what other people think."

Annie relaxed, somewhat appeased, and let her back rest against the rungs of the chair.

"Again, I thank you for the paper's retraction and apology—it means so much to me to have my reputation cleared." And that too would be gone, as soon as word spread about her intimacy with Frank.

"But that is not what you are upset about, is it? Please let me help if I can."

"It's Buck."

"Your horse."

"He's the most precious thing in my life. I'm afraid someone may be purposefully making him ill. Shortly after we arrived, his health changed. Some days he's better than others, but he's had a consistent malaise, and lately he doesn't have the energy to perform. Some days he barely eats."

"But who would want to harm your horse? What could anyone possibly gain from making Buck sick?"

"To get me out of the way or ruin me."

"Do you have someone in mind?"

"There is someone." Annie hesitated. Could she trust Emma with her suspicions? "But I have absolutely no evidence, just a hunch."

"Go on. It will be off the record, promise."

"Twila Midnight—or Vernon McCrimmon."

Emma's eyes lit with enthusiasm. Clearly she loved a mystery.

"How do you think he's being poisoned? His food?"

Annie shook her head. "Mr. Post keeps a good eye on the hay and grain, and I trust him completely. I couldn't imagine a single reason why he would want to harm Buck."

"McCrimmon I understand, but you think Twila would have reason?"

Annie nodded.

"Jealousy often leads to desperation," Emma said. "I would expect that more than one person in the show feels bested by the new—and extremely popular—Annie Oakley. So how do you think your jealous culprit is poisoning Buck?"

"Well, since we've ruled out food, I would guess someone is tampering with his water. He doesn't like the barn, so Mr. Post keeps him in a pen in the corral, which means his water is out in the open. Mr. Post and his crew are always busy in the barn mucking stalls or feeding the other animals, so it's possible that someone has been sneaking out there and slipping something in Buck's trough. I just need to figure out what's in that water, and then maybe we can find out who's making Buck sick."

"Oh, how intriguing." Emma tapped her lower lip with the end of a pencil. "I have a friend who's a scientist. Perhaps he could look into it?"

Annie's spirits lifted. She pulled the small glass bottle filled with water from her pocket.

"If we can get this sample of the water tested, could he determine if it's been tainted?"

"You clever, clever girl!" Emma's green eyes glowed. "Look, here's what we'll do. I'll figure out how to get it tested. If not the scientist, then maybe I can convince someone in the sheriff's office to help us. My ex-fiancé was a sheriff at one time, until he got into politics."

"Your ex-fiancé?" Annie asked, smiling for the first time that day.

"Oh yes, it's a long story. Mummy and Daddy wanted me to marry within my social class, so of course I chose someone they considered 'well beneath our station.' It was all quite scandalous."

"But you didn't marry him?"

"Heavens no. I didn't love him. I found my parent's stuffiness repressive and, as my father said, I 'felt compelled to rebel from the very things that had brought me the best that life can bring.' They disowned me, which is initially why I had to find work as a reporter, which, by the way, they also find 'unacceptable.'"

"I've never known a woman like you," Annie said, delighted by Emma's bravado. "You seem so confident, like you could take on the world."

"You seem the same." Emma grinned. "You just don't know it yet. Now, how about the shooting exhibition? Can we also make that happen?"

"I would have to discuss it with Mr. LeFleur, and possibly the Colonel. I'm not sure if my contract has specified limitations on what I can do outside the show, but I will look into it, I promise."

"Very well." Emma looked into Annie's eyes. "Are you quite restored, Annie? Have I helped you in any way with your current troubles?"

Annie smiled. "Yes, you have, Emma, and I thank you for it."

By the time Annie returned to her tent, she'd almost forgotten about Frank's betrayal—until she saw him, perched on her bed.

Of all the nerve.

"Well, there she is," Lillie said, sitting on her own bed, draining liquor from her flask, a cigarette bobbing in her ridiculously long cigarette holder. "Frankie here has been waiting for you."

"Mr. Butler, I would like you to leave." Annie clenched her fists at her sides, refusing to look at him.

"And I would like to speak with you."

"Well, I would like to rest before practice, so if you will excuse me."

"It's rather important."

Annie didn't want to argue in front of Lillie, who, sprawled across the bed, legs akimbo, stared at them through a cloud of cigarette smoke. Annie raised an eyebrow at her, in the hopes she would offer to leave, but Lillie ignored her—quite possibly on purpose.

"Well, if you won't leave, I will." She spun around and stomped out of the tent, Frank behind her. She walked until they were out of earshot of the rest of the camp, then turned to face him so abruptly he nearly walked right into her. She crossed her arms over her chest, breathing fire. Frank rested his hands on his hips.

"For the life of me, Annie, I don't understand why you're so mad at me. What in the world has gotten into you? One minute we were in love, and now you're walking around like I did something horrible. This is mighty confusing."

Annie sucked in a breath, every fiber of her being shaking with rage.

"I saw you with Twila," she said between clenched teeth.

"With Twila? When?"

"Hours after we—after I left."

His eyes shifted from side to side, as if trying to remember.

"I don't recall seeing Twila last evening. Around dusk, a bunch of the boys and I took a ride through the park, looking for clues to Carver's murder. We were out there for hours, and then I came by your tent, but you were fast asleep."

"I saw you, Frank. I saw you with her in your tent."

"Oh, come on, Annie. Why would I do such a thing? You must have been dreaming—"

"How can you stand there and lie to my face? I saw you." Annie could feel her heart pumping, her face flushing with anger, tears threatening to surface.

"Well, then you need to get your eyes checked, little darlin', 'cause it wasn't me you saw."

"I am not your *little* darlin'. You can't just show up at my tent. We were supposed to keep this quiet, but I find you sitting there with Lillie. Did you say anything to her about us?"

"Of course not. I don't go around talking to anyone about what you and I do together. I would never disrespect you, Annie."

Annie jammed her arms across her chest.

Frank shook his head, exasperation etched on his face.

"I came by to tell you that LeFleur wants to see you. Lillie had no idea where you were, and I started to worry about you and wanted to hang around until you showed up. We talked about the act, nothing else."

No matter what he said, Annie couldn't soften her feelings—his betrayal had been too deep, her anger too paralyzing.

"Annie, why are you so upset at me?"

"Because lying comes so easily to you, because you can't be trusted."

"I don't like being called a liar, Annie." Frank gave her a pointed look.

"And I don't like being lied to." Annie turned her head away, unable to look into those eyes she loved so well. "I don't think we should see each other any more. Outside of the show."

Frank took her arm and she shook it off. He took it again and gently turned her around to face him. She tried to ignore the pained look in his eyes.

"Is that really what you want?"

"It is."

Frank took his hat off and raked a hand through his hair.

"I didn't lie to you, Annie, and I don't know what this is about. All I know is that I love you, and I never loved Twila."

Annie drew in a breath and exhaled slowly, but did not respond. She had clamped her jaw so tightly her cheek muscles began to cramp. Frank settled his hat back on his head and stood silently, gazing at her, as if he wanted to say more, but instead, turned and walked away.

Anger and hurt pulsed through Annie's entire body. She sank to the ground, placed her hands around her knees, and rocked back and forth on her heels.

She'd been so foolish, so impetuous in climbing into Frank's bed. She'd sacrificed her good name and morality for what turned out to be a roll in the hay—and Frank could say he loved her all day long, but if he loved her, he would never have succumbed to Twila's seduction.

Annie thought about her father, who had always encouraged her to move forward despite life's impediments. She had to stop thinking about Frank and Twila and focus on more important matters, like the murder and her family. She vowed she would never let her passions rule her heart, ever again.

CHAPTER 17

"Spring Heat Wave over Last Two Years Responsible for 100
Years Drought. Farms in Ohio and Missouri in Trouble."

St. Louis Herald – April 20, 1885

The next morning, Annie found LeFleur emerging from the bath-
house. When he spotted her, he lifted his chin in greeting but
avoided meeting her eyes. He had a drying rag in one hand and his
shaving utensils in another.

"Mr. LeFleur, I need to speak with you urgently."

He nodded to her and kept walking. Annie winced at the uneasy
feeling in her stomach. She had to make him talk to her.

"You were right about Frank." She scurried to catch up with him.

He stopped, his back to her, and then slowly turned around.

"I made a mistake, and I know that now. I've behaved shamefully,
and I regret it. You were right about Frank being a scoundrel, that he
didn't care about me as much as I thought he did."

LeFleur moved the drying rag onto his other arm, squinted into her
eyes.

"You realize it's because of you that that rake still has a place in the show."

"Chief Sitting Bull must have spoken to the Colonel."

"He didn't speak to the Colonel, he raged at the Colonel. No one rages at the Colonel, so the Colonel raged at me."

"I am dreadfully sorry."

"So you two had a falling out? I must say that I am not surprised." He surveyed Annie with a cold eye. "Will this affect the act? Will you two be able to work together?"

Annie shrugged. She hadn't even thought about that yet.

"I'll do my best. I can't speak for him."

LeFleur grunted and headed toward his tent, obviously dismissing her. Annie trotted after him.

"Mr. LeFleur, I need to speak with you about my wages."

He stopped and looked over his shoulder.

"Your wages?"

"Yes, it's not related to anything that has happened. It's about my family, about my situation where they are concerned."

"Follow me." When they reached his tent, he abruptly turned and faced her. "Wait out here."

Annie waited for him and a few moments later, he reappeared, fully dressed.

"What's this about your wages? You don't really think this is the time to negotiate a raise, do you?"

"No, no, nothing like that. My family is doing poorly, and I'd like to get my wages early so I can send them to my mother. She really needs the money—to feed my brother and sister."

LeFleur held up his hand to silence her and then pulled a pencil and piece of paper out of his coat pocket.

"Write down where you'd like money sent, and I shall arrange to have it sent immediately."

Annie wrote down Mr. Shaw's address at the North Star Mercantile, in hopes he could give it directly to her mother, thereby denying Joshua the opportunity to drink it away.

"There is one more thing I'd like to ask." She handed him the paper and pencil.

"Really, Miss Oakley?" His stern face displayed his impatience, but she soldiered on.

"Miss Emma Wilson has arranged to host a shooting exhibition, strictly for women, at a venue downtown, and she has specifically invited me to participate. Would this be permissible under my contract? I don't want to do anything to betray your trust."

LeFleur's eyes fluttered in disbelief. Annie knew that at that moment, she had pushed his patience with her to the limit.

"I would like to help Miss Wilson, you know, give back to the community."

"Well, it could be beneficial for the show." He scowled at her—clearly, she'd have to work at restoring their friendship. "Spur some positive publicity—for a change. As long as it doesn't conflict with any of your performances with us, I see no reason to refrain."

"Wonderful, thank you." She turned to leave, but he grasped his hand firmly around her arm, making her flinch.

"You didn't speak with that reporter about Carver did you? The Colonel gave explicit instructions."

"No, of course not." Annie pulled her arm from his grasp. "I would not do so under any circumstances and explicitly told her so. Her interest in me is to pursue her women's causes."

LeFleur raised his hand in mock apology. "I see."

"Thank you, again, for wiring my wages to Mr. Shaw."

"Yes, of course." LeFleur's features softened. "Where were you all day?"

"I went to exercise and groom Buck."

"We have men to do that."

"Yes, but I love to be with Buck, and I thought maybe I could help him gain back his strength."

"And did that work?"

Annie shook her head, afraid to admit the truth.

"He's not quite strong enough to perform yet, but he will be."

"People love to see you shoot, but they really love to see you perform with Buck." LeFleur rubbed at his clean-shaven face. "It will be a shame if we have to find you another mount, but it's coming to that now, isn't it?"

"Please give us more time. I'm trying a new remedy."

"A few more days," he said, and turned his back on her.

Annie returned to her tent to freshen up and found Lillie passed out on her bed, drunk in the middle of the afternoon. Annie saw a pocket watch, probably left by one of Lillie's cowboys, on their vanity and checked the time. They had thirty minutes to get to practice.

"Lillie, it's time to get up. We have practice."

Lillie snorted then coughed. "I need breakfast." She rubbed a hand across her belly.

"It's 3:30 in the afternoon."

"Then I need a drink."

"What you need is a slap in the face, Lillie."

Lillie sat upright, her mouth gaping.

"Well, I declare, Annie Oakley, I don't think I've ever heard such harshness from you before! Why the change? Maybe you're just as bad as the rest of us."

Annie clenched her fists, amazed at Lillie's audacity. She would not let it affect her.

"I am nothing like you, Lillie. You need to be on your best behavior for practice today. There is a lot of pressure riding on this show right now."

Lillie stood up, then immediately grabbed the bedpost.

"Damn, the world's spinning."

"The world's not spinning, you are. Try washing your face. That'll wake you up."

"You are in a mood, Miss Oakley. Does it have anything to do with a handsome cowboy name of Frank Butler?" Lillie staggered over to the porcelain ewer.

"Mind your own business, Lillie."

"Tsk, tsk."

While Lillie splashed noisily at the ewer, Annie dressed in a simple deerskin leather skirt she'd made and a pristine, high-collared white blouse. She slipped on her boots and spats. When Lillie finally moved away from the mirror, Annie took her place on the vanity stool and glanced at her reflection. The swelling around her eyes had lessened, but her braids hung limp and disheveled, much in need of rebraiding. She pulled out the leather strings holding them together and ran her fingers through the plaits to loosen them. She didn't have the patience to braid it again, so brushed through her hair and plopped a brimmed hat, embellished with a silver star, onto her head.

"Well," Lillie said, running her hand down the length of her worn and wrinkled velvet riding coat, "this is as good as it's gettin' today."

"Yep. Here, too." Annie turned her face from side to side, glancing at her profile in the mirror. Since her time in the Wild West Show, the girlish fullness of her once innocent face had vanished, leaving her cheeks more hollowed and her chin more defined. Her freckles seemed less pronounced, and her eyes, staring back at her, shone with a new wisdom. Yes, she thought, this is as good as it's going to get.

Annie and Lillie walked to the arena together, toting their weapons. Annie balanced her rifle and shotgun on her arms, and her gun belt, with the beautiful pistols Frank had given her, rested comfortably around her tiny waist. Lillie carried only her rifle.

Several cowboys had set up their targets—an array of hat-shaped and cowboy-shaped metal props, colored glass bottles, a cage full of several dozen pigeons, and new clay pots.

The Colonel and Frank both rode into the arena, Frank on Fancy, and the Colonel on his beloved Isham. As soon as he saw Annie, Frank turned Fancy away from the Colonel and headed for the cowboys and targets. The Colonel urged Isham toward Annie and Lillie.

"Howdy, Colonel," Lillie said, her voice a little too enthusiastic.

"Lillie. Annie." The Colonel tipped his hat. He looked resplendent in a cream-colored deerskin duster, trimmed in ivory-colored conch shells. The front piece of his coat featured red-, blue-, and yellow-beaded birds circling bright orange corn stalks, and his thigh-high boots had strips of multi-colored beads and sprigs of eagle feathers on the outer sides.

Kimi's handiwork. Pure artistry. Annie again felt a pang of anguish at the loss of such a talented young girl.

"Annie, a word." The Colonel dismounted, and Isham, equally bedecked in silver and leather finery, stood still as a statue, waiting for his partner's feet to hit the ground. The Colonel pulled the reins over Isham's head, drawing Annie's attention to the horse's beautiful bridle, ornamented with the same lovely seashells that graced the Colonel's coat.

"Yes, sir."

"Please hand your rifle and shotgun to Miss Smith."

Annie handed Lillie her weapons. Feigning a smile, Lillie nodded to the Colonel and trudged off with her heavy load.

"This business with your horse—" the Colonel said.

"I'm trying a new remedy, sir. I'll get Buck back on his feet in no time."

"I'd like to see how you fare on Isham. He's well-known and loved by the audience, as are you, my dear. Our numbers have been low. If we were to advertise Miss Annie Oakley on Buffalo Bill's faithful steed, it might bring more crowds. I don't need to tell you what an expense it is to keep this show afloat."

Annie's stomach twisted into a knot. Riding Isham would feel like a betrayal to Buck, but if the show didn't do well financially, neither would she. Given the recent turn of events, everyone had to pull their weight, and more.

"I'll give it a try."

"He's quite sensitive to cues, will turn and stop on a dime." The Colonel gave her one of his rare smiles and handed her the reins.

Annie pressed her lips together in an attempted smile. She laid the reins against Isham's withers and set her right hand on the cantle of the saddle, raising her foot for a leg up. The Colonel's strong arms hoisted her into the saddle, as easily as if lifting a feather. While he adjusted the stirrups to fit her much-shorter legs, she organized her pistols in the gun belt.

"He's all yours," the Colonel said, with a slap on Annie's thigh.

Using her seat, Annie gently urged Isham into the arena at a steady walk, getting into the rhythm of his gait. She then raised her energy, encouraging a trot, posting with his movement, and took a couple of laps around the arena. From the corner of her eye, she could see Frank watching. She urged Isham on to a slow, rolling lope. When she shifted her seat and shoulders to the right, Isham turned right, and when she shifted her seat and shoulders to the left, Isham switched leads in mid-air and loped to the left. She sank her seat into the saddle and brought him to a quick stop.

LeFleur shouted for all to begin their target practice. With Frank and Fancy still on the far side of the arena, Annie decided to work the tripods for the mounted shooting stage. Isham did most of the work. After a few rounds, she brought the horse to a stop, relaxed in the saddle, and watched Lillie, Frank, and Bobby practice hitting their targets. She didn't want to be anywhere near Frank until they actually *had* to practice together.

Lillie ran towards the hedge for the pigeon stage but failed to clear it, falling flat on her face, her rifle firing off a shot mid-flight. Luckily, the bullet ricocheted off the ground and hit an old tree stump instead of one of the cowboys.

Lillie stood, dusted off her velvet riding coat, grabbed her rifle, and called for a pigeon to be released. The bird took air, flapping wildly to gain some altitude. Lillie shot and missed, and the bird flew out of range. One of the crew released another. Lillie shot again, and missed again. She finally hit the fourth bird.

Annie pulled in her lower lip with her teeth, thinking she'd have to watch Lillie during the hours before practice, make sure she didn't drink any more whiskey.

Bobby readied himself for his headstand routine and only hit two of the ten jars. She'd seen Lillie and Frank miss plenty, but never Bobby. Maybe the strain of Dick Carver's murder, coming on the heels of Kimi's death, caused everyone to feel off their game.

The cowboys righted Bobby, who angrily jerked his rifle out of the third cowboy's hand and fired at all the targets, hitting each and every one.

That's more like it, Annie thought, but Bobby's face looked like thunder. Annie knew he struggled with sadness over Kimi's death, but his actions spoke differently. His behavior did not reflect someone who suffered from a broken heart. It reflected someone in a rage. She'd have to find time to speak with him alone. Between her problems with Frank and Buck's lingering illness, she hadn't been able to think about anything else, but her pining for Frank would have to end. Annie had other more important things to tend to.

LeFleur whistled, motioning for her and Frank to come over to him. It was time for one of their card tricks, mirror tricks, or cigarette tricks. LeFleur gestured for crewmen to take the horses, then pointed at Annie and Frank.

They walked to the card table.

Lillie handed Annie a deck of cards, and Annie walked to the mark while Frank loaded his pistols. Annie turned to face him and waited patiently for him to be ready. After he'd holstered his pistols, he looked up at her. She tried to keep any emotion from her face and found it easiest to divert her gaze slightly over the top of his head.

Scowling, Frank pulled out his pistol, aimed, and shot. The bullet whizzed by, about a foot from the card. Annie held the card out in front of her to indicate that he'd missed. She held it out to the side again. Frank heaved a frustrated sigh, holstered his weapon, pulled it out, aimed for a split second, shot, and this time the bullet buzzed by Annie's ear. Adrenaline shot through her body. She probably should say something, but didn't want to humiliate him further. She just had to hope and pray his instincts would kick in.

She held the card out for him again. This time, he nicked the top corner of it. She raised the card for him to see. He shook his head in disappointment and walked away.

Annie glanced at LeFleur, who, with arms still crossed over his chest, now had a hand resting over his forehead and eyes, clearly disgusted with everyone's performance.

The Colonel spit chaw on the ground, turned his back to the group, and left, shaking his head. Annie fiddled with the deck of cards in her hands, wishing they could all start over.

"Well, that was a bust." Lillie brought Annie her shotgun and rifle. "How'd you do over there with the mounted shooting?"

Annie silently handed Lillie the deck of cards and took her weapons.

"Never mind," Lillie said. "Sometimes, Annie, I don't think this act would be worth a copper penny without you." Lillie looked down at the cards in her hand and shuffled them clumsily.

"Well, thank you, Lillie. That was kind of you to say."

"Aw, hell, it's the truth." She stuffed the deck of cards down her corset.

The sounds of gunfire made them both turn to see Frank and Fancy running the mounted course. His face, grim with determination, fell when he only hit a few of the targets.

"He's really losing his edge. I think he's got a broken heart." Lillie gave Annie a pretty pout and batted her eyelashes.

How could this girl be so kind one moment and so disrespectful the next?

"He'll be fine," Annie said, confident the great lothario Frank Butler would have plenty of pretty women and girls fawning all over him by the time they hit Kansas in two weeks.

Frank ran through the course again and missed every other target.

"That was a debacle!" LeFleur's voice bellowed throughout the arena. "Practice at oh-eight-hundred, sharp. Let's be a little more on our mark, shall we?" He turned on his heel and left the arena, his arms stiff at his sides.

Annie sighed. She couldn't disagree with Mr. LeFleur. Everyone, except her, missed their marks.

When she looked up a second later, Chief Sitting Bull was striding toward her, all of the paraphernalia hanging from his leather tunic swinging to and fro with each step. She hoped he wasn't coming over to talk about Frank.

He reached her, slightly out of breath.

"Watanya Cecilia, it's Nakota. He's fallen ill. He is asking for you."

CHAPTER 18

"Investigation into Murder of Dick Carver Continues,
No Conclusive Evidence Found."

St. Louis Times – April 20, 1885

Annie ducked inside the tipi to find Nakota wrapped in blankets, lying on a straw mat on the earthen floor. Michante, sitting on his heels next to him, rocked back and forth, singing a haunting tune.

Chief Sitting Bull came in behind Annie and gently pulled Michante to his feet.

"Come, Michante. We will go tell LeFleur and the Colonel about your brother, they will need to know." He took Michante by the arm and ushered him out of the tipi.

Beads of perspiration dotted Nakota's brow and the area above his chalky white lips. "Not the witch," he said, his voice cracking, but they had already gone.

"It's okay, Nakota, Twila's not here. It's me, Annie. The Chief said you asked for me."

Nakota nodded, shivering in his blanket. Annie looked around the tipi and saw a goatskin bag with a cork on it hanging from a pole. She uncorked it and sniffed.

"Water?" She held up the bag.

Nakota nodded and Annie held the bag to his lips. He drank greedily, and then coughed, almost choking on the liquid he couldn't get down his throat fast enough.

"I know—" Another fit of coughing took him.

"What? What do you know?"

"Kimi."

"What about her?"

"I know what happened. That's why I could not leave."

"You know how she died? Why she died?"

Nakota's teeth chattered and his eyes rolled back into his head. Annie worried that he might lose consciousness. She looked around for a cloth and poured water onto it.

"Nakota, stay with me." She swabbed his face with the dampened cloth.

"The trunk—" Nakota winced in pain and rolled to a sitting position as another coughing fit seized him. Annie pushed gently on his chest, trying to unfold him, make him lie down again, but his body remained locked. She rubbed his back while he coughed. Finally, he relaxed and slumped back against the floor mats.

"What trunk? What about the trunk?" Annie asked.

Just as Nakota tried to speak, Chief Sitting Bull entered the tipi, followed by LeFleur, Twila, and Michante. The Chief told Michante to lie down.

"He's burning with fever, too."

Annie risked a glance at Twila, who was either unaware of her presence or intentionally ignoring her. She kept her gaze focused on Nakota.

"How long has he been like this?" Twila asked Chief Sitting Bull.

"Michante came to me last night, when Nakota began shivering and mumbling in his sleep."

Twila ran her hand over Nakota's forehead.

"His fever is high. It may be a virus. Has he suffered from diarrhea or vomiting?"

Sitting Bull asked Michante the question in Sioux, and the younger brother shook his head.

"Do you have water?" Twila asked.

Annie held out the goatskin bag and Twila's eyes met hers, but she looked right through Annie and quickly refocused her attention on Nakota, urging him to drink more.

"What's *she* doing here?" Twila asked Sitting Bull.

"Nakota asked for her."

"Keep giving both of them plenty of water and keep them warm." Twila stood up, towering over the rest of them. "If you're up to it, when the fever breaks, you can sponge them down. It should pass in a few days."

"That's all you're going to do for him," Annie said, looking up at her.

Twila planted her hands on her hips, gave Annie a pointed look.

"I will assemble some herbs to bring down the fever, but there's not much more I can do. I cannot be expected to sit here and nurse them day and night. I have the baby who needs my attention."

"But we have practice in a few hours."

Twila shrugged.

"Witch," Nakota whispered.

Twila smirked at him and then turned to Chief Sitting Bull.

"Have one of your women stay with them and make sure the give them water, lots of water, even if they're vomiting. I'll come back with herbs, but you should also send for a doctor."

Chief Sitting Bull raised his eyes to her but said nothing.

With a flourish of her skirt, Twila left the tent, the tiny bells on her boots jingling.

"Nakota, what were you saying? About a trunk?" Annie leaned over Nakota, pressed her hand gently to his forehead.

Nakota looked over at the Chief, who was getting Michante settled with blankets, and shook his head, clearly relaying that he was unwilling to speak in front of the Chief, though Annie couldn't imagine why. Still, she'd have to come back later, find a way to speak with him alone.

They waited in silence for Twila to return with the herbs. Nakota fell into a fitful sleep and tossed and turned so much the blankets around him tightened around his neck. Annie tried to loosen them, but Nakota batted her hand away.

Chief Sitting Bull watched over Michante, who began speaking in Sioux.

"What is he saying?" Annie asked.

"Something about Bobby and LeFleur, but I cannot make sense of it."

Twila's jingling boots signaled her return. She entered holding a pouch and teacups in one hand, and a teapot in the other. The noise woke Nakota out of his fevered sleep.

"No, no! Get her away. She's . . . she's a witch," he murmured.

"It's all right Nakota." Annie gently shushed him. "She's here to help you. We all are."

Annie certainly understood Nakota's reluctance to trust Twila, but she couldn't imagine a reason for Twila to harm these boys, even if Nakota had information on Twila that pointed to Kimi's death—giving them poison would be too obvious.

"Look, he can take the herbs or not. He's already very ill and these herbs will help to break his fever." Twila handed the pouch and tea-cups to Chief Sitting Bull. "If you want to help, sprinkle a pinch of these herbs into some tea, and have them sip it slowly. It should reduce the fever in a few hours." Holding the handle, she thrust the scalding hot teapot at Annie, who reflexively reached for it, burned herself, and almost dropped it before she was able to set it on the ground. Twila gave Annie her usual close-lipped, feline grin as she left the tent.

Sitting Bull poured tea into a cup he placed at Michante's side.

"No." Nakota bolted upright. "Don't, Chief, don't . . ."

"Nakota, please lie back." Annie gently pressed her hand to his chest.

"Don't give him that witch's medicine." Nakota tried to rise when a fit of coughing again overtook him.

"Perhaps we should just give them tea for now, different tea," Annie said to the Chief.

"Yes. I also don't trust her medicine. I have tea and medicine I can give," he said.

Annie breathed a sigh of relief. She didn't want to give them Twila's herbs either, but she didn't want to explain why, not yet anyway. She needed proof that Twila had been poisoning Buck, and maybe Kimi—proof she could take to everyone, including the sheriff.

"Very well, then. Make sure the women who come to care for them understand. Nakota is upset about something, and I don't want him further disturbed."

"I will see to these boys, Watanya Cecilia. I will send for the doctor and make sure they are cared for while you are practicing for your show. In the meanwhile, I will give my medicine. You will return later to check on them?"

"Yes, I will, thank you."

She left with an unsettling feeling. The illness of the boys came on the heels of Kimi's and Carver's deaths. Was it coincidence, or something more sinister?

To Annie's amazement, practice began on time, with everyone present, clear-eyed, and ready to shoot. Frank tipped his hat to her, but she turned away, unwilling to give him any hope of friendship. She tried to ignore the tug at her heart when his face fell in disappointment, but involvement with Frank would lead to nothing but more heartbreak. She had to keep her heart closed and her mind focused on doing whatever she could to keep the show successful. Annie had to think of her mother, Hulda, and John Henry, and how much they needed her financial support.

After practice, Annie volunteered to ride Isham back to the stable. As they neared the barn, she glanced over at the outside pen and saw Buck kick up his hind end and then trot in circles, tossing his head. He stopped, snorted loudly, and then cantered a circle, snaking his neck. Her heart lightened—Buck was playing.

Overjoyed, Annie jogged with Isham trotting behind her, and they headed over to the round pen. When Buck saw them, he let out a long, loud whinny, and then continued to prance around the corral.

Annie brought Isham to a stop and unsaddled him, placing the saddle and blanket on the ground before leading Isham into Buck's corral. She slid the bridle off Isham's head, turning him loose. The two horses circled each other and then stopped to sniff at each other's noses.

Buck reared up and Isham followed suit. The two chased one another, nipped at one another, and stopped occasionally to nuzzle each other's withers.

Annie watched in rapt fascination. She'd often seen horses in the wild clustered together, playing together, and watching over each other. Her heart lifted to see Buck in such fine spirits, playing with a friend.

"Looks like your fella is feeling better." Mr. Post came up behind her.

"Yes, sure does. Do you think the Colonel will mind that I put Isham in with Buck? Just for a few minutes?"

"Nah. Isham goes out with the Indian ponies all the time. It won't hurt him."

Annie looked over to the camp, trying to spot Frank to see if he was lingering nearby, waiting to corner her again. Instead, she saw Emma talking to a group of people.

"Mr. Post, could I ask you to put Isham away for me? I need to take care of something at the camp."

"I'll let them play for a little while." Mr. Post winked at her. "You go on ahead."

Annie started to lift the saddle to put it away in the tack room, but stopped.

"Does Buck have fresh water?"

"Just filled it myself."

"Would you keep an eye on him, Mr. Post—I mean, more than normal? He's feeling so good today and I don't want anything to—"

"I'll keep an eye on him personally, Miss Oakley. You have my word."

"Thank you."

Mr. Post took the saddle from her arms and told her to go on, he'd take it from here.

"Ah! Annie," Emma said, departing from the group. "I was just asking where I might find you. I should have known you'd be in the stables."

"Buck is doing much better today. What did you find out about his water?"

Emma glanced over one shoulder and then the other, making sure they would not be overheard.

"We found traces of oleander. It stems from the dogbane family, and it can be highly toxic."

Annie's mouth dropped open, then she collected herself.

"Twila gave Buck a sedative when we first arrived, and I suspected that she might still be sedating him from time to time, trying to do it every few days so no one would suspect her of trying to harm him, but actual poison?" Annie blew out a breath of air. "I saw her in the barn the other day, and she never comes to the stables. I thought it strange at the time."

"Well, you will be fascinated to know that your snake charmer has had quite the past."

Annie felt a zing of excitement.

"I want to hear *everything* you have to say, but I don't want to discuss it here on the grounds. Could we go somewhere else?"

"We can use the carriage I arrived in to go into town, where I insist on buying you a very nice dinner at the Southern Hotel."

Annie rushed back to her tent and pulled a green velvet dress out of her trunk. Lovely white lace trimmed the square-necked collar, and the elegant, billowing sleeves reached to her fingertips. Not used to wearing a collar cut below her neck, when she slipped the dress over her corset and looked into the mirror she wrinkled her nose at seeing her upper chest so exposed. The longer she examined her reflection, the more the look grew on her. Her breasts appropriately covered with no cleavage showing, she saw no reason why she shouldn't wear the dress.

She pulled and twisted her hair into a tight bun and found a hat that suited the dress.

When she stepped outside, Emma waited nearby in conversation with Chief Sitting Bull. Emma sparkled when she spoke with the Chief, and Annie nearly laughed when she saw the Chief's silly grin. Emma had charmed him as she charmed everyone.

"Chief, how are our patients?" Annie asked. If Nakota could talk, she would slip in to see him before they left.

"Both Michante and Nakota are sleeping. Their fevers are improved. You go have dinner with your friend. I will be with Michante and Nakota while you are gone."

"They are in marvelous hands, then." Emma smiled at him, showcasing her enchanting dimples. She held out her arm for Annie to take. "Well, Annie, our carriage awaits."

Annie nearly gasped when she saw the gleaming black carriage pulled by two stunning chestnut horses, full white blazes down their faces, each with four white socks that gleamed in the sunshine.

They prepared to get into the cab when Frank appeared.

"Annie, please will you wait one moment? I must speak with you." His voice had an edge to it she'd not heard before.

"I'm sorry, Frank, but we are on our way to dinner, and it wouldn't be fair to keep Emma waiting."

"Just for a moment," he said, his eyes pleading.

"Don't be too long," Emma said batting her eyes at Frank. Annie wondered if she'd flirt with any man, given the opportunity.

Frank took Annie's hand and escorted her away from the horses.

"What do you want, Frank?" Annie didn't bother to hide her annoyance. What was there to say? He'd broken her heart and she had other concerns, more important concerns.

"I want to know why you are so angry with me. Why you broke things off with me."

"I think you know why."

"I swear to you, Annie, nothing happened with Twila—not yesterday, not a year ago. How many times, and in how many ways, can I reassure you that I hold no feelings for her?" He reached to take her hand again, but Annie pulled it away.

"I don't know what to believe, Frank."

"Believe me, Annie, believe in what we had together. I know you felt the same about us as I do. What I don't understand is what happened to change it. I did not have any relations with Twila. Hell, I can barely tolerate the woman. It's you I love, Annie, only you."

"I am so confused." Annie felt conflicting urges to run away from him and to fall into his arms. "I have so much on my mind—Kimi, Buck, my family, Mr. Carver's murder, the show, and . . . us." She straightened her shoulders and met his imploring gaze. "I can't think clearly at the moment, Frank, I just can't, so I am going to dinner with my friend Emma, and you need to let me be."

"That reporter?" Frank slapped his hat against his leg. "The Colonel made it very clear we are not to talk to the press."

"It has nothing to do with the murder. She's become my friend."

He gave her a dubious look.

"Well, goodnight then. I'll see you at the performance tomorrow," Annie said.

Frank pursed his lips, then tipped his hat to her. "Until tomorrow, then."

Yes, Annie thought . . . *until tomorrow.*

When they stepped out of the carriage at the Southern Hotel, people on the street noticed Annie and formed a circle around her, shouting, "It's Annie Oakley! May I have your autograph, please?"

After allowing about five minutes of Annie indulging her fans, Emma elbowed her way into the crowd.

"Sorry, folks, but Miss Oakley is late for a dinner appointment. She'll step out again later." Emma had to reach across people to grab Annie's hand and pull her towards the dining room.

"You want to be accessible, but only on your terms. Remember that," she said, once they were safely inside.

A maître d' escorted them to a small but lavish Victorian room, painted ice blue and accented with white wainscoting and molding. A miniature crystal candle chandelier hanging from the ceiling provided a glowing ambiance.

"Champagne? Tea?" The maître d' asked once they were seated on plush velvet wingback armchairs.

"Champagne." Emma dismissed him with a dainty wave of her hand.

"I'll have tea," Annie said.

"Finally," Emma said, after he left. "I was so busy prattling on about my family while we were in the carriage, I haven't had a chance to discuss my findings with you. I am sorry."

"I don't mind, I find your family fascinating. It's a pity they don't like the choices you have made in your life. I can't imagine my family disowning me."

Emma leaned in. "Well, she's the only one."

"Pardon?"

"As far as Mummy knows, I have been cut off from all finances, but Daddy can't bear to see his little girl suffer, so he provides a generous allowance. How else do you think I could afford these clothes, the carriage? The newspaper certainly can't afford my taste."

"And your father keeps this a secret, your mother doesn't know?"

"She has no idea." Emma winked at her.

Two waiters brought them champagne, tea, and a tiered platter of delectable baked goods.

As soon as they poured the refreshments and left them, Emma leaned in conspiratorially. "Now, about Miss Twila Midnight."

"Did you find something?" Annie scooted closer.

"First of all, did you know that Twila Midnight is thirty-seven years old?"

"Really? I had no idea."

"Yes, I thought she was much younger, as well. Her birth name is Rosalinda Verduci, and her family moved from Italy to America when she was a child. They lived in camps and traveled from city to city, often staying on the outskirts of town."

"Gypsies. Lillie Smith claims that Twila's family took her in, after the Shawnees killed her family."

"That much is true. I found a press report that validates that claim.

According to what I read, Twila's family found Lillie wandering in the forest and took her in. Not long after that, Twila joined Houston Tharpe's Wild West Review as a snake charmer, leaving her family and Lillie behind."

"And then what?" Annie sipped her tea.

"Twila traveled with that show for a couple of years, leaving a trail of broken hearts in her wake. During the time she traveled with Houston Tharpe's show, she met someone you'll find interesting."

Annie had taken a generous bite of a biscuit so flipped the fingers on her other hand to urge Emma to speak up.

"Dick Carver." Emma lifted her champagne glass. "And not only that, they became lovers, which infuriated Mr. Tharpe. He made it his mission to break them apart."

"And?" Annie could barely breathe.

"Houston Tharpe was found dead in a covered wagon, with severe bruising on his torso and neck, and broken ribs. His cause of death was ruled strangulation."

Annie drew a sharp breath. "Hank! Kimi had bruising on her body too, the kind of bruising that could have been caused by a snake wrapping around her torso—"

"—a snake that could break ribs and bruise a neck and torso," Emma said.

"A large enough snake could literally smother a grown man."

They sat in mutual stunned silence for a moment.

"So, did anyone suspect Twila for Tharpe's murder?" Annie asked.

"I found no evidence that they did, but Twila went on to have other lovers, and one of them also died."

"Of strangulation?"

Emma took a sip of champagne, shook her head no.

"Any bruising?" Annie asked.

"There's no record of it."

"Nothing about poison?"

"No. Nothing."

"So we still have no proof of anything." Annie slumped back into her chair.

"Well, we have confirmation that Twila's had a slew of lovers, and several turned up dead. That, my dear Annie, is a pattern."

"Do you think she killed Dick Carver?"

"Apparently, Twila and Carver reconnected when she joined up with Colonel Cody's and Dick Carver's Rocky Mountain and Prairie Exhibition. The Colonel quickly became Carver's rival—and she picked the Colonel. The rivalry became so heated that Colonel Cody forced Carver out."

Annie had been listening so intently she realized she'd been holding her breath. Thoughts spun around in her head, almost making her dizzy.

"The Colonel would have been a fool to shoot Carver." Annie put down her teacup. "Too many people knew about their rivalry. But it seems quite possible that someone wanted everyone to think he did shoot Carver. We just have to figure out who would benefit from implicating the Colonel."

"More digging to be done," said Emma.

"Did you find anything about what Twila might have on the Colonel?"

Emma shook her head and leaned back in her chair.

"So we need proof that Twila slipped oleander in Buck's water, and we need evidence that she may have killed Kimi, and maybe Carver, too."

"That sounds about right," said Emma.

CHAPTER 19

"Break-In at North Star Mercantile. Suspect at Large"

Greenville Gazette – April 20, 1885

Annie arrived back at the Wild West Camp long past dark, tiptoed into her tent so as not to wake Lillie, and discovered Lillie's bed empty.

Annie changed her clothes and set out for the barn to check on Buck. The full moon cast a beautiful glow on the long grasses undulating like waves on a silver ocean. In the distance, she could see Buck, standing quietly, probably dozing. Annie stopped for a moment and listened to the sounds of laughter from the tipis and music from the saloon drifting on the breeze. As she approached Buck, Annie's boot crunched on a twig, alerting her beloved horse. He answered with a soft nicker.

"Hey there, fella. All going well out here tonight?"

He placed his head over the fence and sought out her hand. She laid it on his forehead and stroked his white star.

The glow of a glass lamp lit up the barn.

"Hey! You get away from that horse!"

"It's me, Mr. Post, Annie. It's okay."

"Dang, girl. You gave me a fright." Mr. Post ambled over, light shining through his bow-legged walk. "I've been watching over Buck for you, just like I promised."

"I see that and thank you. I have recently found out that someone slipped oleander into Buck's water trough."

"Now who told you that?" He stood up taller, stuck his chest out.

"I don't blame you, Mr. Post, anyone could have come by and placed it in his water. We just have to prevent them from doing it again."

Post removed his hat and scratched at his sparsely haired head.

"I suppose I can bring him a bucket of water three times a day and stand by while he drinks it."

"That would be so helpful, Mr. Post. Just until I find out who it is—or can prove who it is."

"I ain't seen that McCrimmon fella for awhile." Post put his hat back on his head and hooked his thumbs in his belt.

Annie paused, trying to figure out if he would feel a sense of loyalty to Twila. She decided to broach the subject carefully.

"Mr. Post, I saw Twila in the barn the other day. Is that unusual, does she venture out here often?"

"I ain't never seen her out here. Do you think she's the one who gave Buck oleander?"

"I'm beginning to have my suspicions."

"But why would she do that?"

"I think she'd like to get rid of me, and she nearly has—if I weren't proving a draw for the crowds. The Colonel's already talking about finding me another horse."

"But what in tarnation could that woman have against you? You're plumb near the sweetest girl I ever met."

Annie shrugged her shoulders.

"Women." Mr. Post spat out a hunk of chaw. "Okay, then. I'll empty Buck's water right now and then give him a bucket in the morning. I'll stand right beside him until he's had his fill. Don't you worry, Miss Oakley."

"Thank you, Mr. Post. I appreciate your help. Say, have you heard anything about how Michante and Nakota are faring?"

"What's the matter with them?" His forehead creased downward.

"Oh, you haven't heard. They're ill. Some sort of fever, possibly a virus."

He let out a slow whistle.

"This place is going to hell in a handbasket."

"Never mind. You take care now, Mr. Post. I don't want you getting sick."

"Bah!" He swiped his hand in front of his face. "I ain't never been sick a day in my life, unless you count a night out with the jug. It can leave you feeling pretty poorly in the morning."

Annie chuckled. "Good night, Mr. Post."

"Night, Miss Oakley."

Annie watched as the old man walked over to Buck's water trough and emptied out all the water, then she headed for her tent, her mind humming with questions and information. She raised her head in time to notice Frank's tent brightly lit from within. He obviously hadn't gone to bed yet. Perhaps he had company. Pain stabbed at Annie's throat. No matter how he spent his nights, she was done with him. She picked up her pace, walking steadily toward her tent, determined not to think about Frank ever again.

~

The next morning presented the kind of day that made Annie want to lie in the grass, watching clouds float by in an azure sky. But she had neither the time nor the presence of mind to enjoy the beautiful, late spring weather that had finally cooled. She needed to speak with LeFleur as soon as possible about the oleander.

When he didn't answer, Annie slipped into his tent, resolved to write him a note, expressing the need to speak with him immediately. As she walked over to his paper-strewn desk, she noticed the large trunk she'd seen in there before, an odd, old trunk, with the forbidding lock. The top of the trunk hung open, the lock, open too, dangling from the clasp.

Annie scanned the desk for a blank piece of paper and a pen, but her eyes were naturally drawn to the trunk, sitting right in front her. *What could be in there that required such a lock?* She cautiously approached it and looked in to see several cantaloupe-sized burlap sacks, their necks tied with twine, a few books, a stack of dollar bills bound together, and guns—one, a unique revolver, a 9-shot cylinder with shotgun barrel attached below. She'd never seen anything like it before.

When she bent closer, trying to make out an inscription on the lower barrel, her eyes drifted to the burlap sacks. They looked just like the one's she'd seen in the paper, the story about the stolen Confederate gold. But what would LeFleur be doing with that? He had been a Union soldier in the Civil War, as had the Colonel.

Annie sighed, putting her hands on her hips. Burlap sacks were nothing rare and anything could be contained within them—likely money from the show's reserves. But she couldn't help wondering. Only LeFleur and the Colonel would have access to such riches. She leaned over the trunk to open one of the bags—

"Annie? What are you doing in here?"

Annie's heart nearly leapt through her chest. She spun around to see LeFleur, striding across the room, his face stiff and angry.

"I was trying to find some paper . . . and a pen, to leave you a note."

"In my trunk?" He stood towering over her. "How dare you pry through my personal belongings!"

"I wasn't prying, honest. I thought I saw a pen in the open trunk—"

"Well, I'm quite certain you would never find one in there." He snapped the trunk closed. "There's ticket-sale money in there, and if it came up stolen, I wouldn't want anyone to accuse our main draw."

"Oh, I would never—"

"Of course you wouldn't steal." He smiled, but Annie could see perspiration dotting his forehead. "Now, what was so urgent that you needed to leave a note?" He pointed to a chair, and Annie sat.

"I wanted to let you know that I obtained proof that someone tampered with Buck's water. Someone poisoned it with oleander. "

"Oleander? It sounds like a plant, not a poison."

"Lots of poisons are made from plants—mushrooms, for example, can be poisonous."

"And how did you get this proof?"

Annie bit her lower lip and then released it. "Miss Wilson, the reporter, offered to have a friend of hers—a scientist—test it for me, and he confirmed that the oleander in Buck's water was enough to make him ill, possibly kill him, if the amount increased."

"You got a notion in your head that someone poisoned your ailing horse's water—and you told a reporter?" LeFleur's eyebrows shot up. "What were you thinking?" The intensity in LeFleur's voice escalated. "The Colonel specifically told us not to discuss anything with the press, and I know you were there, that you heard him."

"Emma—Miss Wilson—and I have never discussed Mr. Carver's death, or Kimi's." Annie flicked her eyes up to see if he responded to her mention of Kimi, but he was so full of fury that she couldn't discern a spike. "Emma befriended me, because she wants me to participate in the shooting matches she's organizing for women, remember? I told you about them, and you said—"

"So you asked her to have Buck's water tested because you thought someone in the show was poisoning your horse, and it did not occur to you that she might find that provocative enough to print something in the newspaper about that?"

"Well, no sir, she promised me that she wouldn't—"

"And you trusted her because she's a nice person."

"Well, she's the one who printed the retraction about my humiliation, so, yes, I do trust her."

"Good Lord." LeFleur ran his palm over the side of his pomaded hair.

"I thought you would be pleased that I discovered what ailed Buck." Annie forced a smile. "Mr. Post agreed to make sure Buck only drinks the water he brings him, and he'll stick by his side until he drinks it. Don't you see, Mr. LeFleur? Buck will regain his strength and be able to perform again."

LeFleur's jaw flexed for a moment, then relaxed.

"Well, that is excellent news. Did you uncover any evidence about who might have given Buck the oleander?"

"No, that would be hard to prove, but I have something else to report."

"Pray tell."

"Miss Wilson knew quite a bit about Twila, and her past."

"Why in the world would you discuss Twila with Miss Wilson?"

"She brought it up, over dinner at the Southern Hotel. I took it as a woman gossiping, and I won't be revealing it to anyone but you, and only you, because I trust you to be discreet."

His eyes flickered and then steadied. He gave Annie a smile of encouragement.

"Twila has never been friendly to me, and I couldn't help but wonder if her past might reveal some reason for her to want me out of the show . . . why she *might* have slipped oleander into Buck's water to get rid of me."

LeFleur sighed. "And why would she want to be rid of you?"

"Because of Frank and me." Annie steeled herself for his reaction.

"But you told me you broke off relations with Frank, was that not true?"

"I told him we were through."

"Then we may safely assume Twila Midnight will have no reason to behave unkindly towards you or your horse."

"Perhaps. I'd love to think it's all behind us, but she does have quite the checkered past," Annie said, alluding to more information to see how he would respond. "I didn't say anything to Miss Wilson, of course, but I was surprised to learn that Mr. Carver was one of her former lovers." Annie could see the wheels turning behind LeFleur's dark eyes. "She said the newspaper had been digging to find out more about us all and discovered in old news reports that the Colonel bought out Carver's portion of the show when he fell in love with Twila and wanted Carver out of the picture."

"No, no, no, that's not right." LeFleur pointed a finger. "The reasons were solely financial in nature. Carver had gone broke before, and the Colonel didn't want his mismanagement to bankrupt their show." He trained his eyes so hard on Annie she could feel him thinking. "So does our Miss Wilson suggest that the Colonel may have shot Carver?"

"She leaned toward Twila, actually."

"What reason would she—"

"Perhaps Carver was blackmailing her." Annie cut in to keep him off balance. "Perhaps he knew things about her past that she didn't want anyone else to know?"

LeFleur leaned back in his chair, lowered his shoulders.

"My dear Annie, this all appears to be wildly speculative conjecture on Miss Wilson's part. She doesn't have any proof. She was likely trying to get you to tell her whatever you know."

"Well, I have the good sense to remain quiet. I wouldn't want her to accuse anyone unjustly. I was only interested in discovering what was wrong with Buck and to see if you might know who would want to harm him."

"Well, then. I thank you for this information."

"But what are you going to do with it?" Annie asked.

"I'm going to think about it," he said, gesturing for her to leave.

The next day, Annie returned to the stable to fetch Buck for a practice run. It had been a while since she'd worked him through the mounted course. When she spotted Buck in the distance kicking up his feet and playing in his pen, a thrill went through her. With each quick turn of his heels, Buck's long ebony mane whipped from one side of his neck to the other. He looked like an energetic colt.

After her time with Miss Wilson and her confrontation with Mr. LeFleur, Annie couldn't settle her mind. If someone could slip oleander into Buck's water, then what would prevent them from slipping it into someone's . . . tea? Annie's mind flashed back to Kimi's slightly over-turned, half-empty teacup at the campfire. Also, the empty tea tin that Annie could swear had been full. Her mind raced with the possibilities. If only she hadn't thrown the rest of Kimi's tea on the fire.

As she was about to open the gate to Buck's corral, Mr. Post emerged carrying Annie's saddle in his arms, and Buck's bridle draped over his shoulder. The skirt of her saddle had been embellished. Shiny silver Conchos, in varying geometric shapes and sizes, had been sewn on to create a beautiful pattern.

"Is that *my* saddle?"

"Sure is, kid. Put them on there myself. Don't it look beautiful?"

"Do I owe you for the silver?"

"Nope, it's a gift . . . and don't go bugging me about who because I had to promise I wouldn't tell. Just someone who wanted to add a little spice to your gear."

Annie's brow furrowed, but she knew Mr. Post was a man of his word—and wouldn't tell. She slipped Buck's bridle from his shoulder, noting that it, too, had been decorated with silver bars and conch sea-shells laid in floral patterns, just like Isham's bridle. It had to be the Colonel.

"Come on Mr. Post, tell me who did this?"

"Sworn to secrecy." He raised his chin and gave her a wink.

Annie ran her hands over the beautiful silver decorations on the saddle. It did enhance the beauty of the leather, and Mr. Post had worked hard to make it look just right.

Once he'd saddled Buck, Annie climbed on and headed into the practice arena, deciding to put her thoughts of murder on hold. She had some information to work with; she just needed to put the pieces together—but first things first. The show, lacking its usual luster, needed competent, focused shooters.

When she arrived at the arena, only a few of the cowboys were sitting around smoking and talking. No sign of Lillie, Frank, or Bobby—though this practice was optional. Not surprised at Lillie's absence or Frank's, she did find Bobby's nonattendance strange.

Annie tightened her gun belt around her waist and urged Buck to a trot. He moved steady and sure underneath her, his gait so full of impulsion she had to post to keep balanced, but she let him move out. With slight pressure from her left calf, Buck stepped into a right lead lope. When he stretched his neck down, she felt his back rise into her seat. The lope elongated into an easy canter. Annie steered him along the rail of the arena, delighted to experience the sense of freedom she had longed for in the last several days.

After a few easy laps, Annie decided to practice hitting the targets. She collected Buck into a more business-like lope and started through the course. They easily made the turns to hit the targets dead on, and then for the final line, she switched pistols and urged him forward to a full-on gallop.

Shooting on one side of Buck's head, and then the other, in perfect rhythm, Annie smashed all the glass balls into colorful shards. Once she holstered her pistol and brought Buck to a stop, she leaned down and wrapped her arms around his neck. Buck was himself again. Everything would be all right. She would get through this difficult time with the show, with Frank, and with her family. She suddenly felt an enormous sense of comfort. God had thrown Buck, the Wild West Show, and her together, and this is where she belonged.

CHAPTER 20

"Colonel Buffalo Bill Cody to Perform Today in Hopes That Dwindling Ticket Sales Will Return to Normal Numbers."

St. Louis Times – April 22, 1885

The Colonel told Annie there would only be one performance that afternoon. He and LeFleur wanted to make sure the stands would be filled to capacity for one performance, as opposed to having too many empty seats for both the morning and afternoon shows.

The Colonel opened the show "hunting down the buffalo." A dozen bison thundered into the arena to the whoops and hollers of the crowd. After a few minutes of watching the buffalo run around the arena in frantic circles, Buffalo Bill entered in all his famous splendor riding Isham, like a knight in beaded deerskin armor, firing his gun over his head.

Annie watched from the back gate, marveling that the man christened Buffalo Bill for his renowned feats of killing hundreds of the vanishing species now would only kill one or two of the herd to give the audience what they craved. He strove to preserve the proud beasts by starting his own breeding program.

Annie and Frank were up next for the mounted course. Annie

looked around for Frank and Fancy, but couldn't see them anywhere. In fact, she hadn't seen Frank for the last two days.

She turned around in her saddle and strained to see what was going on in the barn, and sighed in relief when she saw Rusty holding Fancy, helping Frank to mount. When she turned around again, she spotted Lillie and Bobby in conversation, comparing their weapons. At least everyone showed up. Annie hoped they would all give their best performances today. The show needed to be a success to keep the numbers coming in.

After the Colonel's act, as the buffalo and the Colonel exited the arena, several of the crew ran in with a flatbed cart to haul the two slain buffalo away. The announcer kept the audience entertained with tales of the famous Buffalo Bill and the time he scalped Yellow Hand in a major act of revenge for the murder of General George Armstrong Custer.

Finally, Annie and Frank took the arena. Frank hadn't even so much as looked at her while they waited for the gates to open. Annie tried not to let it get under her skin, but his indifference made her heart heavy, and she had to swallow down a lump forming in her throat.

The gates opened and Buck exploded beneath her as if he knew exactly what to do. Annie and Frank took turns running the course, both managing it with perfect marksmanship. The stands were completely full and the crowd roared their appreciation. When it was time for the horses to depart, Rusty Post and another cowboy came out to gather Buck and Fancy.

"I won't take my eyes off of him," Post said, as Annie handed him the reins. She smiled, secure in the knowledge that he would make sure no harm came to her horse.

The crowd cheered loudly as Lillie and Bobby came running into the arena, guns blazing, their show smiles plastered on their faces. They opened with Bobby shooting at targets while standing on his head, another crowd favorite. Then it was Lillie's turn to shoot a dozen pigeons with her stout rifle. Annie performed the mirror trick, and then Frank stood in as her target for the cigarette trick. The shooting exhibition ran much more smoothly than it had in some time, much to Annie's relief.

Annie handed Lillie a deck of cards, and Lillie held up the ace of diamonds. Taking quick aim, Frank shot the heart out of the middle of the card. Lillie held it up for all to see. Frank took his hat off and bowed with a great flourish. Lillie then handed Annie the deck of cards. Annie drew a card from the top of the deck and held it out to her left side, facedown. A hush fell over the crowd as they awaited the famous trick that had made Frank Butler the best sharpshooter in the world. Annie pinched the card tightly between her fingers.

Frank took aim and shot.

Everything went dark.

When Annie opened her eyes, her left arm lay stretched out to the side of her—covered in blood. An ice cold stabbing traveled from her fingers to her shoulder. Her body trembled and then convulsed, made worse by the sight of her crimson-soaked hand. The ace of spades lay next to her, perfectly intact.

Annie heard shouts and screams coming from the stands and the thunder of feet as the crew raced toward her, but she felt glued to the ground. All she could do was stare at her blood-soaked, maimed hand . . . as consciousness faded in and out. When she had the strength, she opened her eyes to see what appeared to be hundreds of faces staring down at her. She recognized Lillie and Bobby. Bobby had scooted his body under hers and held her shoulders and head in his lap. Lillie shouted at the crowd, "Step back, give her some air!"

Frank shouldered his way in through the crowd and knelt beside Annie, his face fraught with terror.

"I'm so sorry, Annie, I'm so sorry." He brushed his hand gently against her cheek. "I would never hurt you, ever."

"What the hell happened here?" The Colonel's voice boomed overhead.

At the sound of the Colonel's commanding voice, everyone except Lillie, Bobby, and Frank stepped back.

"Frank shot her in the hand," Lillie said.

"Get back, everyone!" The Colonel shooed onlookers and fellow performers away. "Someone go get the doctor. He's with Chief Sitting Bull, in Michante and Nakota's tent. Hurry." The Colonel pulled Frank away from Annie's side. "Annie, you hang in there, girl. You're going to be all right. We're going to take good care of you."

Annie tried to respond, but nothing came out. A damp coldness settled into her bones and her eyes rolled back in her head.

"Someone hand me a kerchief," the Colonel said.

"She's bleeding pretty bad," Bobby whispered.

Annie tried to lift her head, but everything spun. She could see familiar faces looking down at her, but they swirled in and out of focus. Her teeth began chattering and she had to fight to keep her eyes open. Where was Frank? She wanted only Frank.

As if he'd read her thoughts, Frank appeared next to her.

"You're going to be all right, Annie. I won't let you go. I promise."

Annie smiled at him, but when the Colonel lifted her hand to wrap it in a kerchief, pain shot through her hand and up her arm, and she let out a yowl like an injured animal.

"Hang on, girl. I know it hurts, but I've got to stop the bleeding." The Colonel's eyes implored hers.

The faces surrounding her faded out and coldness settled on her like a shroud. Annie could feel herself losing consciousness, her body floating toward the clouds. *Mama.* She wanted to apologize to her dear mother for having failed her. How would her family survive if she couldn't work, or worse, went off into the sky?

Acutely aware of her steady breathing, Annie tried to orient herself. Warmth and soft light surrounded her, and she felt as if she floated among the clouds in a perfectly cerulean sky. The fragrant aroma of roses washed over her. *Is this Heaven?*

Annie opened her eyes to discover that she lay in a stately, four-poster bed with luxurious bed linens soft as a kitten. She opened her eyes wider to see gold velvet wallpaper and furniture upholstered in burgundy satin. LeFleur sat in a formal wingback chair next to her bed, his eyes fully focused on her face.

"Annie?" He grabbed her uninjured hand.

"Where am I?"

"You are in a room at the Southern Hotel. The doctor has been to see you several times. You're going to be fine."

Annie wrinkled her brow. The room and LeFleur faded in and out of focus.

"The doctor has given you morphine, for the pain."

Annie looked down at the bandaged hand at her left side and tried to wiggle her fingers. A staggering pain shot up her arm. She held her fingers still and the pain slowly subsided, but its echo reverberated through her arm and into her shoulder.

"What happened?" she said, although she knew very well what happened. *Frank had shot her.* She blinked, letting the realization sink in.

"Frank missed the target and struck your hand," LeFleur said, his voice cool and measured. "He swears it was an accident, but—"

"But what?" Annie looked into LeFleur's eyes.

"People are of the belief that he did it on purpose."

"Why would you say such a thing?" Annie shook her head back and forth on the pillow. "Frank wouldn't shoot me on purpose, even if he was mad at me, he wouldn't hurt me." He'd held her in his arms and told her that he'd lost his heart to her.

"I just wanted you to know the truth."

"You mean the truth of what people are saying. Who are these people? Name them for me, because they are telling lies."

"I didn't mean to upset you." LeFleur leaned closer, ran a hand down her cheek.

When she flinched, he pulled back, clearly disappointed.

"It doesn't matter who thinks what," he said, straightening his shoulders. "The Colonel has decided that Frank can no longer shoot well enough to perform in the show. He's been given a few days to get his affairs in order. We brought you here to avoid publicity and to prevent Frank from knowing your whereabouts. He is forbidden to step one foot into this hotel. We'll make sure he won't be able to hurt you again, Annie, you have my word."

Annie's heart sank. Obviously, LeFleur had the upper hand in this situation and further protesting would serve no purpose. Still, she longed to see Frank, to at least let him know that she didn't believe he'd intentionally hurt her—he would never . . .

"Are you ready for a few visitors?"

Annie offered a slight nod.

Bobby came in first, a shy smile on his face.

"I'm so glad you came, Bobby. I've been meaning to talk with you." The words came out of her mouth, but at the moment she couldn't remember what she wanted to talk with him about. She blinked her eyes, trying to focus.

Bobby pulled his hat off his head and sat down. He folded his hands around the brim of his hat and placed it between his knees.

"I'm sure glad you're okay, Miss Oakley." His eyes briefly met hers, then flitted to the bedspread.

"Annie, Bobby. Please call me Annie."

A blush crept across his freckled cheeks. Annie smiled at his reaction.

"I remember you comforting me, Bobby. Thank you."

Bobby's eyes finally met hers. She thought she read confusion and a sort of desperation in them, but she couldn't be sure. His face moved in and out of focus.

"It all happened so fast. I couldn't believe it," Bobby said.

"Do *you* think Frank did it on purpose?"

"Mr. Butler? Shoot you on purpose? No, he wouldn't do that."

Annie drew in a deep breath and studied Bobby's hands as they twisted his hat between them. They reminded her of writhing snakes. Twila's snake. Bobby seemed terribly nervous about something. Suddenly, in a moment of clarity, it dawned on her what she wanted to say to him.

"Bobby, I've been meaning to ask you—" With her good hand, Annie reached into her dress pocket and pulled out the gold coin. She held it up to him. It shimmered and wavered before her eyes. "Does this mean anything to you?"

He stopped twisting the hat in his hand and stared at the coin, his mouth hanging open.

"N-no. I ain't never seen so much money." Bobby swallowed, his Adam's apple bobbing up and down in his throat.

"Are you sure?" Annie pressed, trying to gage his reaction, trying to see through the haze of her gauze-filled mind. "You see how the face of it, and the back, have been filed down? Don't you think that strange?"

"Yes. Very strange." Bobby let out a nervous laugh. In Annie's drugged state, his voice sounded heavy, slow.

Annie licked her lips, her mouth dry. She reached for the water glass next to her table and drank, stalling for time, trying to remember. Finally, it came to her.

"The other day, when you were filing Isham's hoof, you dropped the file. I picked it up and handed it back to you. Do you remember?"

"Yeah, I s'pose."

"There were gold flecks in that file."

The air hung pregnant with silence, but Annie could still hear her own words echoing in her ears. She shook her head, trying to clear it of the fuzziness.

"I don't see what you are getting at Miss—uh, Annie."

Annie laughed. "I'm not sure I do either. Um, had you used that file before?"

"Well, heck. I don't know. We use all kinds of files. I usually grab one from the barn. What does this have to do with me, Annie?" He seemed genuinely confused. "I really do need to get back to Forest Park. The Colonel is waiting on me."

"You seem upset."

He pressed his lips together, quickly stood up, snapped his hat back on his head, and thrust his hands into his pockets.

"I'm fine Miss . . . Annie. Truly." He flinched when the door opened.

"Okay, Bobby," LeFleur said, entering the room. "Miss Oakley needs her rest and the Chief wants to see her."

When Bobby drew his hands out of his pockets, Annie thought she saw something fall from one of them—but her head still felt so wobbly she couldn't be sure. Bobby tipped his hat to Annie and left the room.

Chief Sitting Bull entered and lowered himself onto one of the wing chairs, holding his spine perfectly straight, not touching the back of the chair, in the proud, regal manner he always displayed—even around a campfire.

"I am pleased that you were not more seriously injured, Watanya Cecilia, I could bear no more grieving today."

At the sorrowful expression on the chief's face, Annie snapped out of her daze.

"What's happened, Chief?"

"Nakota passed into the night sky."

Annie gasped and raised her good hand to her chest.

"I didn't want him to tell you," LeFleur said, stepping closer to Annie's bed. "I didn't want you further upset, but he insisted that you'd want to know, that you'd be strong enough to bear the news."

Annie looked briefly at LeFleur and then focused on the Chief.

"The Chief was right, I do want to know. I am so sorry, so very sorry. I thought the fever had broken."

"The doctor finally came and said Nakota had slipped into the dream world, that he would not return—and then Nakota stopped breathing."

Annie held her uninjured hand out to the proud Chief. Sitting Bull lay his warm, leathery hand on top of hers.

"You tried to save him. You did your best. And what of Winona? How is the baby?"

"I have heard nothing about the baby. I believe she is fine."

Good. She couldn't bear to have to worry about Winona on top of everything else. Her mind started to clear. Things came into sharper focus.

Emma and another man stepped into the room.

"What? How did you . . . what are you doing in here?" Mr. LeFleur's voice blustered, his face flushed with anger. "You do *not* have my permission to write a story about this incident, Miss Wilson. No reporters. No story. No press is permitted to speak with Miss Oakley."

Emma removed her gloves with a flourish and artfully draped them over her upturned palm.

"First of all, Mr. LeFleur, I don't need your permission. It's a free country. Secondly, I've only come to see my friend. The news has already spread about the . . . accident, and I've merely come to personally check in on Annie."

"But you brought the detective with you—this is an outrage."

Detective Jonas stood by the door. Emma gazed at Mr. LeFleur directly.

"People are claiming that Mr. Butler intentionally tried to wound Miss Oakley, so it's only logical that Detective Jonas should wish to speak with her. Don't you agree that it is in Miss Oakley's—and the show's—best interest to determine the facts regarding what happened? You've already had one person murdered on the grounds—and the Colonel himself hired the Theil Detective Agency to help sort out this mess, of which I fear Annie is but the next victim of foul play."

LeFleur's face clouded over with annoyance.

"Very well, but be quick about it."

Chief Sitting Bull stood up and leaned over Annie. He pressed his palm against her forehead.

"Rest well, daughter." He left the room, the small metal diamonds sewn into his buckskin coat tinkling like the sound of running water.

Detective Jonas and Emma trained their eyes on LeFleur, issuing a silent command that he leave the room. He focused his eyes on Annie.

"You don't have to say anything, Annie. We still don't know the particulars, and no one should expect you to remember the details when you suffered so much pain and obviously experienced a shock to your system."

Emma made a clucking noise, intended to dismiss his blathering.

"I'll be right outside the door," he said, before striding out of the room, glaring at the intruders as he passed.

"Annie, darling, how are you?" Emma perched on the bed, taking care not to jiggle Annie's wounded arm.

"Fine, for getting shot in the hand." She tried to lift her hand but winced in pain and lowered it again.

"Do you believe that Frank Butler had any desire to intentionally harm you?"

Annie shook her head, and then used her good hand to beckon Emma to draw closer, away from the detective's ears.

"I feel so confused. Frank had been having trouble with his aim, which began before I joined the show. The Colonel hoped I'd inspire him to improve his performance, and he did better, for a little while . . ." she stopped, glanced at Detective Jonas.

"I will be questioning Mr. Butler." The detective pulled on the brim of his hat. "But that doesn't mean we will automatically assume he wounded your hand on purpose."

"Annie, I brought Detective Jonas along because I wanted you to tell him about Buck."

"Oh, certainly. I've discovered, with Emma's help, that someone has been poisoning my horse's water."

"With what?" Detective Jonas got out his pad of paper.

"Oleander."

"Why do you think someone would do that?"

"To sabotage my act. To sabotage me."

"Is there anyone you know who would want to do what you've alleged?"

Annie told him about Vernon McCrimmon and about Twila. He busily jotted their names and their stories on his pad of paper.

"There's more," Annie said, and then waited for him to finish. He looked up from his pad of paper, his glasses halfway down his beak-like nose.

"I believe that the person who tainted Buck's water also meant to poison me."

Emma gasped. "Whatever do you mean, Annie?"

"Kimi and I shared a tea tin. I had just purchased some tea and filled the tin. We kept the tin in or on my trunk. When I came home from the saloon that night and found Kimi sprawled on the floor, I had seen a half-drunk cup of tea near the fire, partially tipped over. I think she drank poisoned tea. When I went to make myself a cup later, the tea tin was empty."

Emma and the detective shared a glance.

"This Kimi, is she the one you mentioned the other day when I was questioning you about Mr. Carver?" The detective licked the end of his pencil and scribbled something on his notepad.

"Yes."

When he was done writing, the detective folded his pad and placed it in his pocket.

"With this information, we may have reason to exhume the body of this young Indian woman. The coroner may be forced to conduct a new autopsy, as I am beginning to suspect, as you have, that she did not die of natural causes."

Emma grabbed Annie's good hand. Annie grinned at her and at the gawky detective. Finally, someone was taking Kimi's death seriously.

The throbbing in Annie's hand woke her. Glad to be rid of the hazy cloud of morphine that shrouded her thoughts, she sat up in bed and looked down at the nightgown someone had gotten her into. She didn't remember getting undressed.

Her memory of the visitors who came to her room the day before also remained fractured and unclear. She recalled Bobby and Chief Sitting Bull most vividly, and then Emma and Detective Jonas. She faintly remembered talking to Detective Jonas about her suspicions of Twila Midnight. She may even had told him that she thought Twila had poisoned Buck and possibly killed Kimi, and maybe Carver. Would he have taken her seriously about that, or assumed it was the morphine talking?

Someone tapped on the door and, seconds later, a young girl entered bearing a tray of food. The aroma of bacon and freshly baked bread made Annie's stomach growl with hunger. Given the uselessness of her left hand, it took Annie several minutes to push herself to a sitting position.

"Would ya like your breakfast in bed, miss?" The girl asked. She had red hair, freckles, and a thick Irish brogue.

"No. At the table, please."

The girl smiled sweetly and placed the wooden tray on the table.

"Would ya like a hand, miss?"

"No, thank you. I need to figure out how to get up and eat with one hand all by myself." Annie almost laughed at the irony of the maid's statement.

"Would ya like anythin' else, miss?"

Annie shook her head.

The girl backed out of the room, pausing at the threshold, offering Annie a slight bow before quietly closing the door.

Annie grasped the silk coverlet with her good hand and tossed it and the blankets to the side. She then slipped her legs off the bed and stepped onto the carpet, noticing an annoying prickle in the arch of her foot. She lifted it and discovered dried leaves and twigs of some kind. She vaguely remembered seeing something fall when Bobby pulled his hands from his pockets. She picked up the fragile fragments and laid them on the table, near her breakfast tray.

While she chewed the most delicious bacon she'd ever tasted, she stared at the leaves. They definitely weren't tea leaves. A number of people had visited the day before. The fragments could have traveled in on anyone shoes, or they could have been here before she was placed in this room. One sweep of the room with her eyes nixed that idea. The room was spotless, not even a speck of dust in the corners or coating the molding. No lint or stray fibers of any kind.

Her injured hand tingled as if a thousand nettles had worked their way inside the bandage. *Frank had shot her*. Fractured memories of his worried face above her swam in her head. She remembered the unbearably sad tone of his voice as he apologized, over and over.

After Annie had eaten every slice of bacon and every crumb of bread, she walked carefully to the small writing desk and retrieved a piece of the ivory stationary with the words "Southern Hotel" embossed on the top and returned to the table. She wanted to sweep the leaves onto the paper, but with only one good hand, that didn't work, so she set the paper down and very carefully set each fragile fragment of leaf and twig on top of it, wincing as they crumbled even more under her touch. After much effort with the dried plant, she folded the paper around the leaves, opened the wardrobe, and stashed the folded paper in her dress pocket.

With all the focused activity, Annie's hand ached and she suddenly felt very tired, so slipped back under the covers. She wanted to get back to camp to be close to Buck and rest in familiar surroundings. She missed the show, the camp, everything. Even Lillie. The thought caused her to snort in amusement. Clearly, the morphine *hadn't* worn off entirely.

When the maid returned for her breakfast tray, Annie noticed LeFleur standing in the hallway. He was clean-shaven and refreshed, and when he entered the room Annie noted genuine kindness in the way he looked at her. It seemed they'd been at odds for a while now, and she welcomed a truce.

"Good morning, Annie. How's the hand feeling?" He removed his beaverskin top hat.

"It hurts, but I feel much better. When can I go back to the show?" Annie pulled the bedcovers a little higher with her good hand.

"My dear, you won't be able to perform until your hand heals."

"But it's my left hand that's wounded. I can still ride and shoot a pistol with my right hand. The mounted course will be no problem. Buck is finally feeling himself again. I assure you I can do it." She offered her prettiest smile—though God knows what she looked like at the moment.

LeFleur pulled up a chair next to her bed.

"You are an amazing woman, Annie, and I—all of us really—so admire your spunk."

"When can I go back to the camp?"

"How about tomorrow?"

"Tomorrow," Annie said, groaning, "I can't sit in this bed all day. I feel fine, really. When is the next performance?"

"It won't be until Saturday, and it's only Tuesday."

"If you let me return to camp this afternoon, I promise I will rest in my tent until Saturday."

"No, Annie. You must stay here at least one more day. You need to be monitored by the doctor, and we need to get Frank safely on his way. No one wants the two of you to come within a mile of each other."

"Has he asked to see me?"

"Yes, of course, he asked multiple times, but I refused to tell him where you are. He'll not hurt you again, I promise."

Annie knew better than to push LeFleur on this topic. Perhaps it was best for she and Frank to go their separate ways. She didn't want him to feel guilty about wounding her, and she'd already decided not to continue their relationship. Still, she longed to see him one last time.

"Alright, Mr. LeFleur, I will agree to stay here one more night, but you must promise to move me back to camp tomorrow afternoon. I need to make sure Buck's still doing well, and I want to check in on the Chief. He's just lost another of his people, and I'll bring him comfort. Please." She reached over and grasped his hand.

"I can't find the strength to deny you. I still long to make you happy." LeFleur smiled, placing his hand over hers.

Annie released his hand and leaned back against the pillows. She felt faint, but didn't want him to know.

"Have your affections changed?"

Annie knew it would be prudent to be cautious with LeFleur—until she'd sorted out everything that had happened.

"Annie, you haven't answered my question. Do you have feelings for me?"

Annie thought it best not to reject him entirely.

"I am not in a position to love anyone. I've just ended things with Frank. It will take some time—"

"So, there *is* a chance?"

"You must permit me time to heal." Annie offered a shy smile.

"Well then, you must rest if you are to return to camp tomorrow." LeFleur snapped his hat on his head, ran his fingers along its brim, and prepared to leave, looking very much like a cat that had just captured a mouse.

Watching his hands run over the brim, Annie suddenly remembered seeing black stains on his hands the day of the shooting.

"Mr. LeFleur."

"Yes, my dear." He took off his hat, turning his attention back to her.

"I never properly apologized for looking into your trunk. I wasn't rummaging, I promise."

"Think nothing of it, Annie."

"I appreciate your gallantry. I keep thinking about a pistol I saw in your trunk."

"A pistol?"

"Yes, I remember it because it was so unusual, like nothing I'd ever seen before."

"What makes you mention it?"

Annie could hear skepticism in his tone.

"I'm not sure. I just keep seeing it in my mind. It reminded me of one of my father's pistols," she lied.

"Well, it is a very unusual weapon. It belonged to my father, who gave it to me when I was a lad. I haven't used it in years. It is a sentimental keepsake."

Annie smiled. "Of course, that makes complete sense."

"Is there anything else?" LeFleur's smile faded and coldness crept into his eyes.

"No, I was merely curious."

"I hope your curiosity is satisfied." He placed his hat back on his head.

"It is. Thank you."

LeFleur nodded and then silently left the room.

Annie tried to still the pounding in her chest. She'd touched a nerve.

CHAPTER 21

"Frank Butler Shoots Fellow Performer Annie Oakley.
Authorities Investigating Intent or Accident."

Missouri Chronicle – April 23, 1885

A nnie didn't see LeFleur for the rest of that day, which seemed to last forever. The doctor visited twice to check her hand for swelling or infection and to change the bandages. Luckily, the bullet had gone clean through her palm, between her thumb and forefinger.

"No broken bones." The doctor put his medical tools back in his bag. "I'm calling it a miracle. Might be some nerve damage though, should heal over time. You're lucky it wasn't your shooting hand."

That evening, when one of the hotel staff brought her supper, Annie insisted on eating at the table again. Her back and legs felt stiff from immobility, and, although her hand pained her, she could not stay in the bed one moment longer. The meal—a hearty steak, mashed potatoes, and sweet carrots, cooked to a delicate crunch—tasted delicious. Someone had carefully carved her meat into tiny, bite-sized pieces. A moist pound cake with raspberry sauce and a cup of tea for dessert delighted her taste buds.

Just as Annie stood up to ring the bell for someone to retrieve her tray, someone knocked at the door. She adjusted her dressing gown and ran a hand over her hair, which the maid had kindly brushed and pulled into a loose bun at the nape of her neck.

"Yes?" she called.

Bobby opened the door and stepped into the room.

"Bobby, so good to see you. Do come in and visit with me."

"I can't, Annie. Mr. LeFleur has forbidden anyone to bother you, but you received a letter today, and I thought you'd want it at once." He laid an envelope and a newspaper on the table. Annie noted that it was not the *St. Louis Times* but another paper, a much smaller one, one she hadn't heard of—the *Missouri Chronicle*.

"There's a story in there about your accident. I thought you'd want to see it."

"Thank you, Bobby. I am not surprised the press reported the story. The incident happened in front of a full house. There was bound to be talk."

"It didn't hit the *Times*," Bobby said, his voice hopeful.

Annie smiled. "My friend, Miss Wilson, most likely had something to do with that good fortune."

"We all miss you at camp." Bobby raised his eyes, full of admiration and sincerity, to meet hers.

She couldn't imagine this boy causing harm to anyone. But she'd also seen menace in that innocent face, knew he'd exchanged angry words with Kimi and LeFleur. Still, he'd been nothing but kind to her.

"I miss you, too. I'll be there tomorrow."

Bobby tipped his hat and turned to leave.

"Say Bobby, how is Michante?"

Bobby wagged his head from side to side.

"Aw, he's real broke up about Nakota. He lost his sister, and now his brother. I feel right sorry for him."

"Has he recovered from the illness?"

"Oh yes, he's doing much better in that way, he's just as sad as I've ever seen a man."

"I can imagine."

"Some of the other Indians came down sick, too, but doc says they'll all be okay in a week or two. The Colonel had the sick ones isolated from the rest, and Chief Sitting Bull is nursing them."

"Thank you for the news."

"Tomorrow then," Bobby said and rushed out the door.

Annie watched him hurry down the hall and then closed the door. Unable to handle the throb in her hand any longer, she poured some of the powder the doctor had given her into a glass of water and drank it down, grimacing at the bitter taste. She then climbed into bed and settled under the welcoming comforter. My, how far she had come from the two-room cabin and straw-tick mattresses she'd shared with her mother and siblings.

Annie quickly read the article in the paper. The story didn't cover much more than what Bobby had already told her, and it focused on Frank, dissecting his slow decline into mediocrity as a sharpshooter. The article confirmed that he had been forcefully dismissed from Buffalo Bill's Wild West Show.

She worried about Frank, who must be feeling so downhearted. Even if Mr. LeFleur and others were convinced that Frank had aimed for her hand and used that claim to dismiss him—and bar him from seeing her—Annie didn't believe it. Still, why hadn't he at least written her a note?

Her supper didn't settle well. She folded the paper, set it on her nightstand, and braced for the letter from home, fearful of what it might reveal.

Her fears not unfounded, the letter informed her that a riding accident had rendered Friend Mick Easton, her childhood sweetheart, unconscious for more than two weeks, his head wound so severe his doctors didn't know if he would ever wake. Plus, Joshua had broken in to Mr. Shaw's store to steal the money Annie had sent. This time, he'd used some of it to leave North Star. The bank had reclaimed the farm, and Mr. Shaw was allowing her family to stay in the back room of his store.

Annie leaned back against the headboard. Despite the pain-relief powder, her entire body ached, and she wanted more than ever to curl into a tight ball and sleep away her problems. In a few short weeks, she'd left her home, become a famous sharpshooter in Buffalo Bill's Wild West Show, fallen in love with a legend, witnessed two murders, been shot, and dealt with the possible loss of her beloved horse. Even worse, fate had now spoken.

Annie had no choice. She had to go home.

In the morning, the cheery Irish maid returned with a large box.

"What is this?" Annie got out of bed.

"A new dress. Your Mr. LeFleur had it sent to the hotel."

Panic seized Annie. Her old dress had the gold coin and dried twigs in the pocket. She ran to the wardrobe and opened the doors. Her dress hung neatly inside, untouched, still dirty and covered with blood.

"You want me to throw it away? You'll never get those blood stains out." The girl moved closer to the wardrobe.

Annie reached in the pocket and pulled out the folded paper and gold coin. She gripped them in her hand, hoping the girl wouldn't notice, and backed away from the wardrobe.

"Why, yes. I suppose it's ruined."

"I'll take it when I clean the room. Shall I open the box?"

"Please." Annie put her good hand, holding the coin and envelope behind her back.

The girl opened the box, revealing a deep burgundy satin dress with pink silk chevrons sewn at the cuffs and collar. Grasping the shoulders of the garment, the girl pulled the dress out of the box. A whoosh of the toile underskirts sliding across the comforter sent chills up Annie's spine.

"Oh, this is a fine dress." The girl held it up to the light, admiring the shimmering folds of fabric that would cover the bustle.

Annie noticed a matching reticule in the bottom of the box, and, grateful for Mr. LeFleur's attention to fashion detail, snatched the satchel out of the box and stuffed the envelope and coin inside it.

Annie let the girl help her dress, and together they gathered her belongings and checked her out of the Southern Hotel. The Colonel had paid the bill. Annie's hand still pained her, but, anxious to get back to the camp, she gritted her teeth against the discomfort.

The maid deposited Annie and her things in the lobby and then dismissed herself to continue with her work.

People milled about the lobby, some of them nodding their recognition. Annie smiled back, but tried to avoid their eyes in hopes of discouraging conversation.

"My dear, what a shock," a young woman said, approaching her. "How is your hand? Isn't it just like a man to be jealous of a woman's skill?" She tossed her tawny brown curls. "He deserves whatever he gets."

Luckily, a young boy came over and asked Annie for her autograph, pushing the rude woman out of the way. He had no pen and no paper, but gaped at her with such an innocent smile that Annie caught the attention of a bellhop, who scurried off to secure both. When he returned, Annie asked the boy to turn around so she could use his back as a solid surface upon which to sign her name on the paper. As she scrawled her signature, the boy looked over his shoulder.

"My ma says Frank Butler's going to hell for certain."

Annie turned him around to face her, bent down to his eye level, and handed him the slip of paper. "Mr. Butler did not hurt me on purpose. It was an accident. You tell your ma I said so."

A tall, well-postured doorman approached Annie.

"Mr. LeFleur sent the coach for you, ma'am." He gathered her small bag of belongings to take outside. "It will be brought around shortly."

Annie found it odd that Mr. LeFleur had not come in person to see her back to camp. Perhaps he had his hands full, trying to get the show back on track and dealing with Detective Jonas and his assistants amid the murder investigation. With the loss of Frank and Annie, he was likely scrambling to develop a new act. Just thinking of it made Annie feel guilty, particularly since she'd have to tell him that she was needed at home and would not be returning to the show. Regrettably, only she could help her family out of the mess Joshua had created—and it had to happen at home, hundreds of miles away.

The Wild West stagecoach arrived moments later. The driver

politely assisted her into the coach, then silently drove the horses back to camp.

When Annie alighted from the stagecoach, she was greeted by many of the cast and crew. Everyone wanted to know how she was feeling, did her hand hurt, how was she holding up? She noticed the Colonel, standing near his tent, smoking a cigar. He raised his hand in greeting. She didn't see LeFleur anywhere, which surprised her, given his devotion to her.

The crewmembers finally dispersed, allowing Annie to walk alone to her tent. She scanned the area for any sign of Frank but didn't see him. When she spotted Buck busily munching a pile of hay, her mood lightened—until she remembered that she had to return to Ohio, and she couldn't afford a train ticket for herself, let alone Buck. She ducked inside her tent to find Lillie sprawled on her bed, eating something.

"Look who's back?"

"Hello, Lillie."

Annie hoped her disappointment at seeing Lillie didn't show on her face. She'd wanted time to get settled in by herself, and Lillie tended to absorb all the energy in the room. As Annie set her reticule on her nightstand, she saw an envelope face down, discarded on the rug between her bed and Lillie's. She picked up the folded note lying next to the envelope and read it: "Candies for the Sweet, Sincerely, A Fan."

Annie glanced over at Lillie, who shoved another chocolate into her mouth.

"Did those chocolates come with this note?"

"Uh huh," Lillie said, mid-chew, "caramel inside. Simply *dee*-vine." She noisily licked her fingers, then probed the box for another morsel.

Lillie would *not* be someone Annie would miss.

"Want some?" Lillie held out the box.

Annie rolled her eyes and turned away.

"Ah now, sweetie, no one has ever sent me chocolates before, so I couldn't resist having a taste, but there's plenty. Have one." She stood to take the box over to Annie and staggered. "Oh, dear—"

Annie presumed she was drunk until she clutched her stomach and doubled over.

"Lillie? What is it?"

"My belly is cramping something awful. It hurts, Annie."

Annie rushed to her side and slid under her arm to lift Lillie and keep her from falling to the floor.

"Sit down, Lillie. Sit on the bed."

"I can't move," Lillie said, moaning. She tried to say more, but her body began to shake and convulse. They sank to the ground together, Lillie curling into a fierce ball.

"Help!" Annie shouted. "Somebody help!"

Lillie tried to speak but only succeeded in producing strained grunts and gasps.

Suddenly, Bobby was standing over them.

"Bobby, go get help. Lillie is terribly ill. Go quickly."

LeFleur and Twila came rushing in moments later, the Colonel two steps behind them. Twila immediately dropped to her knees next to Lillie, using a hand to shove Annie out of the way. Annie instinctively used her injured hand to rebalance herself and yelped in pain.

"What's wrong with Lillie? What have you done to her?" Twila glared at Annie.

Annie rose to her feet and stood clutching her injured hand.

"What do you mean? When I came in she was fine, then suddenly her stomach began cramping and she cried out in pain. I think it might have been the chocolates."

"Oh, dear God," LeFleur said, under his breath.

"She's convulsing and will slip into a coma." Twila craned her neck to speak to LeFleur. "We have to get her to the hospital right away!"

LeFleur seemed frozen in place, his face ashen.

"Derence, we need to move her, now!" Twila's voice rose in urgency.

"Yes, yes, of course. I'll get the stagecoach."

"Hurry!" Twila cradled Lillie in her arms. "Lillie, my sweet Lillie, it's going to be okay. I'm here. I will take care of you, darling girl—do not slip away, please, please."

Lillie's convulsions continued, rendering her speechless. Her eyes seemed to glaze over. The Colonel knelt down and placed a hand on Twila's back.

"Don't worry, my dear, we'll get her on her way quickly."

Twila shrugged off his hand, drew Lillie closer to her chest, and began to cry.

Bobby escorted Annie to her bed and sat down next to her, his face trained on hers.

"Are you all right, Annie? You look a little pale."

Annie nodded, biting her lip in an effort to reduce the throbbing in her hand.

"I'll be fine, Bobby. I'm just worried about Lillie."

Lillie let out a desperate groan and then went still.

"Lillie! Lillie!" Twila cried, stroking her face. "Wake up, Lillie, don't give up. Don't give up, don't give up . . ."

The Colonel placed two fingers on Lillie's neck.

"There's a pulse, but it's faint. Where is LeFleur with the damn coach?"

LeFleur burst into the tent.

"I've got it. It's right outside."

He and the Colonel lifted Lillie into the coach, Twila following in a labored rush.

"Wait," Annie said. "Bobby, take the chocolates. The doctor may need to test them, to save her. Take them, please."

Bobby sprang from the bed, gathered the box, and sprinted to the coach. Her suspicions rising, Annie walked to the discarded envelope, picked it up and turned it over, reading her own name scrawled across the front.

As she suspected, the chocolates had been meant for her.

CHAPTER 22

"Frank Butler Fired from Buffalo Bill's Wild West Show. Annie
Oakley Recovering Comfortably at Forest Park."

Missouri Chronicle – April 24, 1884

That evening, Annie, the Colonel, and LeFleur sat in the dim candlelight of the Colonel's tent in silence. Lillie remained unconscious, but they'd been told she was still alive. Twila had refused to leave Lillie's side. The remaining chocolates had been sent to the coroner for inspection, and Annie had just informed them that she had to return home to save her family.

"So, you see, I have to leave the show," she said.

LeFleur sat forward in his chair, his hazel eyes exhibiting an intensity she didn't wish to encourage.

"Isn't there something we can do? What if we gave you an advance on your salary? Would you be able to stay then?"

"I appreciate your generosity, Mr. LeFleur, but it's not just about my family anymore—those chocolates were meant for me."

"It hasn't been determined that those chocolates were poisoned." The Colonel raised his cigar to his lips and drew in smoke. "Hell, that girl's had a death wish since she got here. I haven't ever seen a woman, or a man, drink whiskey like she does. She could have rot gut."

"Lillie wasn't drunk." Annie shook her head. "I can always tell when she is, and I'm pretty sure the chocolates made her sick because someone also poisoned Buck. Someone has wanted to chase me away from the day I arrived, and this hatred nearly killed Lillie. Now Frank is leaving because of me. I've brought nothing but bad luck to the Wild West Show."

The Colonel puffed out a steady stream of cigar smoke and adjusted his weight in the chair.

"Miss Oakley, you have a public appeal the likes of which I have never seen before. The crowds love you—and that horse of yours. Frank's star, though it burned bright for a long time, has faded. I'd had it in my mind to release him earlier, but you appealed to Chief Sitting Bull on his behalf, and he wrangled me into giving Frank another chance. If I'd trusted my instincts and sent him packing, he wouldn't have been around to shoot you. Why, he could have killed you."

"But don't you see, Colonel? Someone *is* trying to kill me, which means that my mere presence is now endangering others. Lillie could die."

"I don't believe that, Annie." The Colonel shook his head. "Do you, LeFleur?"

LeFleur remained suspiciously quiet. When Annie finally looked at him, he'd set his mouth in a hard line, while his eyes flitted from her to the Colonel. He looked as if he were about to burst.

"You can't leave, Annie. The show needs you, especially now that we've lost Frank, and Lillie may not be fit to perform for a while. Other than Chief Sitting Bull, you are the best headliner we have. The Colonel is right, the public adores you—and we need you on the bill."

Annie sighed. "I have brought nothing but trouble and scandal to the show."

"What scandal?" the Colonel asked.

"That newspaper article? Old man McCrimmon prowling around, telling lies about me?"

"That was nothing to get all worked up about." The Colonel waved his cigar in the air. "It didn't change the public's—or my—opinion of you."

"What about Carver?" she asked.

"What *about* Carver?" LeFleur's eyes shot open. "You had nothing to do with that."

Annie shrugged her shoulders. "I still have a suspicion that he and McCrimmon may have formed some kind of alliance. He's just mean enough and crazy enough to do whatever he can to ruin the show, to get his revenge against me. It's not fair to have someone like him around, putting everyone in danger."

"Now wait a minute." The Colonel leaned forward. "Carver's death hasn't ruined anything. We don't know who killed him just yet, but the Thiel Agency will find the killer, and I'd be mighty surprised if this McCrimmon fellow was involved. No one has seen hide nor hair of him for days."

Annie sighed in relief, but knew in her heart that she had to go.

"All that may be true, Colonel, but my family needs me at home."

The two men studied her silently.

"May I remind you that you signed a contract," LeFleur said.

"I've not forgotten. It may take a while, but I will pay whatever penalty you feel is fair. Please, you can't ask me to stay when my family is in danger. I'm all they've got."

The Colonel stood up and walked over to a cabinet in the corner of the tent, rummaged around in a drawer for a few minutes, and then held up some papers.

"This was your contract," he said, ripping the sheets in half, letting the torn pieces fall to his desk.

LeFleur leapt to his feet, his fists clenched at his side.

"You can't do that. We can't afford to let her go. You have to make Annie stay."

"I don't have to do any damn thing I don't want to do." The Colonel clamped his teeth down on his cigar. "This is my show, LeFleur, which means I make the rules, which means I can break the rules. Now sit down before you pop your kettle."

LeFleur's jaw hung open and his face flushed beet red. He flopped onto his chair.

"I don't want you to leave because you think you are endangering anyone here at the show." The Colonel turned his attention to Annie. "That's nonsense. But I do respect your obligation to your family. It's my hope that if I let you go now, you'll get things right with your family and come back to us."

Aware that she'd never be free to return, Annie felt overwhelmed with gratitude, particularly after the Colonel had been so kind. She couldn't stop her lower lip from quivering.

"Now, now, my girl, don't you worry. We'll take care of your train ticket, and we'll see that Buck gets on that train, too." The Colonel squashed the butt of his cigar in a crystal ashtray. "Now you go on back to your tent and pack your things."

Annie wanted with all of her heart to thank him, but she couldn't form a single word. Instead, she offered the Colonel a tearful nod of acknowledgement and dashed out of his tent.

"Annie, you can't go." LeFleur ran after her. He grabbed her arm, wrapping his fingers tightly around it, so tightly she cried out with pain.

"Mr. LeFleur. Please let me go."

"I can't let you go, Annie. You have to stay."

"You're hurting me." She tried to pull away from his hand.

He loosened his grip, but still held on to her arm.

"I can take care of you . . . and I can take care of your family. We can send them money."

The look on his face made the hair on her arms and neck rise.

"*I* will take care of my family. Now please, let me go." She fixed her eyes on his with fury. "Let. Me. Go."

"You shouldn't do this, Annie. You'll regret it."

The next morning, the Colonel handed Annie a train ticket to Cincinnati, Ohio, scheduled to leave in two days time. He'd made the arrangements to transport Buck as well. Annie placed the ticket in her reticule and sat down to write a letter to Emma. She had to explain the situation of her circumstances and how she would not be able to fulfill her obligation at the Women's Shooting Exposition. She considered mentioning the twigs she'd found in her hotel room, but now the notion seemed silly. She did mention the teacup and tea tin, so Detective Jonas had all the information she could give him. She had to be content with the hope that he would find out who had killed Kimi and Mr. Carver.

When she finished writing the note, she folded the paper and placed it into an envelope, affixed a stamp, and slipped it into her reticule. She would be able to post it in town.

The stagecoach was waiting for her near the grandstand next to the arena. Annie wanted to visit Lillie in the hospital to say goodbye, and the Colonel insisted she use the show's stagecoach. She asked the driver to make a quick stop at the post office where she intended to deposit the letter, but on the way they passed an outdoor flower stand. She smiled when she spotted large white lilies.

"Stop the coach, please."

She would deposit the letter on her way back from the hospital.

The private hospital, once a spacious and lavish family estate, stood proud and beautiful on a large plot of thick, freshly mown grass. Annie marveled at the towering white columns and grand stairway leading up to the front doors.

A tiny, pixie-like nun, with sprigs of grey hair peeking out from her black veil, greeted Annie at the door.

"Welcome to St. Marks," she said, revealing remarkably white teeth for one so old. "How may I help you?"

"I am here to visit Miss Lillian Smith." Annie cradled the fragrant bundle in her arms.

"Yes. Right this way."

"How is Miss Smith doing?"

"She is resting. We had quite a scare. She almost didn't recover, but she's better now."

They climbed three flights of stairs, slowly, the nun stopping on every landing to catch her breath. When they reached the third floor, the nun led Annie down a long hallway. Thick molding framed the high ceilings, which were lit by dainty crystal chandeliers. Once a grand house indeed, Annie thought.

They found Lillie, reclining in a beautiful four-poster bed, and

Twila on a chair next to it, holding baby Winona. Annie steeled herself against what would surely become an unavoidable confrontation with the snake charmer. Twila fixed a cold stare at Annie as she approached.

"Well," Lillie said, her voice weak. "Is that the famous Miss Annie Oakley strolling through my door?"

Lillie, in a pristine white lace gown with long sleeves trimmed with pink ribbons, looked softer, more approachable, almost puritanical.

Twila, who wore her usual head-to-toe black, with a hint of white lace at her throat and sleeves, would never look approachable. Winona, wrapped in a light blue blanket, slept peacefully in Twila's arms.

"How are you feeling?" Annie tiptoed towards Lillie.

Lillie responded with a raspy cough. "Like I swallowed three hand-fuls of stickers."

Annie held out the flowers for her.

"Why, I do declare. Do you see, Twila? Miss Annie Oakley brought me flowers." She buried her nose in the fragrant blooms.

Twila raised an eyebrow but said nothing.

Annie pressed closer, smiled at Lillie.

"I know we haven't always gotten along, but I've grown fonder of you these last few weeks, and I wanted to see for myself that you're all right."

"That's kind of you." Lillie lifted her head from the bouquet. "The doctor says I should be fine."

"Do they know what caused your . . . ailment?"

"They aren't sure, but I had more than my fair share of lectures about firewater, which won't surprise you, I guess."

"It wouldn't hurt for you to let up every once in awhile. Not drink like the cowboys."

"Aw," Lillie waved her hand in the air. "Wouldn't hurt you to drink every now and then. Say, now that your hand's injured, Frank's out, and I'm here recuperating, what's the Colonel and LeFleur going to do about the show?"

"I'm not sure, but I've also come to say good-bye." Annie's eyes flitted to Twila, whose eyebrows arched. "I'm leaving the show."

"What? You're leaving? Why? Frank won't be around anymore," Lillie said, alarm in her voice.

"My family needs me, and I have to go as soon as possible."

"It won't be the same without you."

"I'm glad you're going to be all right, Lillie, and I want you to know that I wish you well," Annie said, touched by the sincerity in Lillie's voice.

"I think I'll miss you, too. Thanks for the flowers." She held them to her nose again.

Twila didn't say a word, but Annie caught a glimpse of that cat-like grin twitching at the corners of Twila's red painted lips.

When Annie arrived back at camp, Emma and Detective Jonas were waiting outside her tent, the expression on their faces grim.

"Darling Annie, I am so glad to see you looking so rosy and refreshed. How do you feel?"

"I'm fine, Emma, feeling much better today. I was about to post a letter to you, but I forgot." She looked at the detective. "Hello, Detective Jonas."

The stern, wire-bespectacled, impossibly thin man removed his Hamburg and nodded to her.

"Miss Oakley, may we step inside your tent? We have some information to impart to you."

Annie gestured for them to step inside.

"Sit down on your bed, dear," Emma said, "I will fetch chairs for Mr. Jonas and me."

Detective Jonas hitched up the legs of his too-roomy pants to sink into the chair, then leaned forward, his tie dangling mid-air between his crisp white shirt and his bony legs.

"We've had the body of Kimi exhumed," he said quietly. "She was indeed poisoned."

"Dear God." Annie let out a rush of air. She could feel her face blanch.

"You were absolutely right in your suspicions, Miss Oakley," Detective Jonas said.

Annie glanced over at Emma.

"So it wasn't the snake?"

"No, the traces of poison found in Kimi's body were the same poison that had been placed in your horse's water trough. The oleander didn't kill the horse, because he weighs over a thousand pounds. He would have needed a much bigger dose to kill him. Humans, on the other hand—"

Annie gasped. The thought that Buck could have been killed—that Kimi had been killed—overtook her.

"There's more, dear." Emma rested a reassuring hand on Annie's knee.

"We received word from the coroner's office." Detective Jonas cleared his throat, as if to impart more bad news. "The chocolates sent to your tent were laced with oleander."

"Well, I'm not surprised," Annie said. "But who? Who did this? It seems like it must be the same person."

"We followed up on your suggestions and looked further into Miss Midnight's life." Detective Jonas pushed his glasses up onto the bridge of his nose. "We even searched her and Colonel Cody's tent and found traces of dried oleander. We also found a gun among her belongings—a LeMat, a very rare Civil War pistol, primarily used by Confederate generals. The gun uses the same ammunition that was found in Carver's body."

Annie's body began to shake.

"We think she did it all." Emma leaned forward, pressing her hand more firmly on Annie's knee.

"So what happens now?" Annie asked.

"We have some deputies on the way to the hospital to apprehend Miss Midnight. They'll take her back to the sheriff's office for questioning. Now, please understand that we haven't proven anything yet, but I wanted to let you know that your instincts are impressive, and, if she's guilty, it will be thanks to you that this whole case came together. I could use you on all my cases." Detective Jonas smiled and promptly stood up. "Before I head back, I need to speak with Colonel Cody and Mr. LeFleur, so please accept my gratitude for your time and your assistance, Miss Oakley. I hope your hand recovers soon." Detective Jonas secured his Hamburg back on his head and turned to leave.

"Wait one moment, please," Annie said.

She went to her wardrobe, found the reticule LeFleur had given her with the dress, and retrieved the folded piece of paper and the gold coin.

"I want you to see something." She laid the paper down and carefully unfolded it. "I found this in my hotel room, after the shooting. It was on the floor, which means someone had it on them when they came to visit."

Detective Jonas peered down at the dried twigs and leaves. He gently lifted one of them and inspected it closely, held it to his nose. "I'm fairly certain this is oleander," he said.

"Why would it be on your hotel room floor?" Emma asked.

"I had a lot of visitors that day, you and Detective Jonas included. I thought perhaps someone had tracked it in on their boots or shoes unaware—or brought it in on purpose."

She mentally visualized Bobby pulling his hands out of his pockets, but couldn't bring herself to name him as a suspect. She had to speak with him first.

"More excellent investigating. I'll need to take this, as evidence."

"Yes, by all means." Annie sat back down on the bed. "And I have something else." She held up the gold coin.

Detective Jonas took it from her fingers.

"I found that on the floor below my trunk, where I keep my tea tin. I have no idea if it means anything, but I know it's not mine, nor was it Kimi's. I'm not sure how it got there."

"It's been marred by something." Detective Jonas looked up at her over his spectacles.

"I saw a file, with gold flakes in it. One of the cowboys was using it. It's kept in the barn."

Detective Jonas twisted his mouth. "I can't see how this has anything to do with the murders, but I'll hang onto it. Have you mentioned this to anyone?"

"No," Annie lied. She couldn't make Bobby's name come out of her mouth.

"Well, let's keep this under our hats. You see if you can get me that file."

"I will." Annie thought she could slip into the barn and find it before she had to leave the next day. "I'll leave it out by Buck's pen."

"Fine." Detective Jonas meticulously placed the twigs into the folded paper and placed it in his breast pocket. His brows knit in thought or concentration, he turned and left the tent, stealthy as a cat.

"Oh, my goodness," Annie said, looking at Emma.

"Quite a day, isn't it? You mentioned a letter?"

"Yes. I wrote to tell you I am leaving."

"No!" Emma's green eyes opened wide in alarm. "But why?"

"I have to. My mother is not well, and my brother and sister are too young to assume responsibility that is rightly mine. It's selfish of me to stay."

"Selfish? How?"

"My family needs me at home, but it would also be better if I weren't here."

Emma gave her a puzzled look.

"Someone found it necessary to poison Buck, Mr. Carver was murdered, and the chocolates Lillie ate were meant for me. I think the tea Kimi drank was also intended for me. It would be better for all if I left the show—the sooner the better."

Emma's brow crumpled with concern, her perfectly alabaster skin flushing pink.

"But we've identified the culprit. Twila Midnight is being apprehended. All the mayhem will vanish."

Annie shook her head. "I'm not positive Twila is behind everything."

"But why? She obviously despises you."

"Yes. But something just doesn't add up, like the oleander twigs being dropped onto the rug in my hotel room. Twila Midnight did not visit me while I was there, so she couldn't have dropped it."

"If you leave now, how will we ever find out the truth about all these happenings?"

"If I leave, everyone else will be safer." A wave of disappointment washed over Annie, causing her stomach to churn and her head to ache. "My family is homeless and penniless, Emma. That's not something I can take lightly. They depend on me, and they're in desperate need."

"Dear heart, you are such an inspiration, but promise me that you'll come back the minute things change." Emma reached out to touch Annie's arm.

Annie looked down at her hands in her lap. She didn't want to talk about home anymore. Doing so made her feel like the world was at its end. Emma must have picked up on her silent cue and changed the subject.

"Have you seen Frank Butler since you've been back? Is he still on the premises?"

Annie shook her head, pressed fingertips against her eyes to relieve the pressure behind them.

"No. I haven't seen, or heard from him since he shot my hand. I know he must feel bad about it. LeFleur wouldn't let him near me. Frank probably thinks I want nothing more to do with him and I . . . I don't." She looked into Emma's eyes and shrugged. "I feel so torn. I loved him, and I refuse to believe that he intentionally harmed me, but I'm not sure he's someone I can trust. It seems our romance is not meant to be."

"It's probably for the best, Annie. You deserve much better." Emma reached up to brush the back of her hand along Annie's cheek.

"Yes, I know." Annie reached up, took Emma's hand and and squeezed it.

"Well," Emma said, standing up, smoothing her skirts, "I will let you rest. When do you leave?"

"Day after tomorrow."

"I will be back before then, to say my farewells." Emma again brushed a hand across Annie's cheek, this time patting it. When she left the tent, the swishing of her taffeta skirts echoed long in Annie's ears.

Annie should have gone to the mess tent for supper, but only wanted to see Buck. On her way to his pen, she went into the barn, looking for the file. She entered into the dim coolness of the large wooden structure. Horses, their heads down munching on flakes of hay, popped their heads up as she passed. The smell of wood, oil, horse, hay, and manure mingled in the dusty air, and Annie breathed in, letting the scent infuse her body with its comforting earthiness. She would miss this place filled with hay dust, the sounds of horses moving about in their stalls, and Mr. Post, proud guardian of it all.

She stepped into the small room they used to keep tools and equipment, and Annie saw the pail with several metal files in it.

"Hey, Miss Oakley."

Annie nearly yelped as Mr. Post walked in behind her.

"Looking for something?" Mr. Post looked unusually tired, his hair and shirt mussed and his beard scraggly and uncharacteristically unkempt.

"Yes, actually. I am looking for a file. I wanted to clean up Buck's hooves before we leave tomorrow."

"I sure do hate to see you go." Mr. Post's watery eyes beseeched hers. "And I'm going to miss Buck."

"Yes, but I must leave. Thank you for all you have done. Now, about that file?"

"We can have one of the cowboys work on Buck's feet."

"I'd rather do it myself. You know—"

"I do. Right here," he said, pointing to the bucket. "Help yourself."

"Thank you, Mr. Post." Annie went over to him and embraced his skinny body, all bones and sinewy muscle. She felt his hand pat her gently on her back. Unwilling or unable to look her in the face, Mr. Post left the room.

Annie rummaged through the files, but couldn't find the one with the gold flecks. One of the cowboys must have it. She wished she hadn't promised to deliver it to Detective Jonas. It could be anywhere in the camp.

As she approached his pen, Buck came galloping to the fence. Annie patted his head, then reached into her pocket for the sugar cubes she'd taken from tea service earlier. Within seconds, Buck scraped the cubes from her hand and loudly crunched them.

The sound of someone clearing their throat startled Annie. She turned to see Frank, holding his hat in his hands, his fingers nervously smoothing the brim. Annie held her breath for a moment, not sure what to do or say.

"I hope you don't mind me coming here." He looked worn, like he hadn't slept in days, like a man who'd lost everything. "I just had to talk to you, Annie."

"I know." Annie steeled her resolve not to do something weak, like cry.

"How's the hand?"

"It's improving. No broken bones, so the doctor thinks it will heal fine."

"Annie, you have to know in your heart how sorry I am." His voice cracked. He cleared his throat again. "I wanted to come to you, but the Colonel and LeFleur absolutely forbade it. They put a guard outside your room."

Annie stood silent, focusing on her breath, breathing in, and breathing out. After all that had happened between them, the physical attraction remained strong. Part of her longed to throw herself into his arms . . . but she wouldn't. She hadn't known about the guard, but it didn't surprise her. LeFleur had staked his claim, empty as that claim was.

"You know I didn't mean to shoot you, Annie. I would never harm you."

To shield herself from the unbearable pain reflected in his eyes, Annie turned away. She couldn't bear to see those eyes shiny with tears. A man like Frank didn't cry, unless his heart and spirit were broken.

"I'm leaving the show." Annie modulated her voice to sound firm, resolved.

"No, Annie, don't leave because of me. I won't be here after tomorrow."

"It's not about you. My family is in dire straits. Joshua stole every penny I've sent, and the bank laid claim on the farm. They are destitute and living in the backroom of a store. I must try to rectify things."

"I'm so sorry. I guess we'll both be heading home. I have things to put right as well."

The finality of their words didn't sit well with her. He was so ready to leave her, escape *his* pain. But what about the pain he'd caused her—the emotional pain? A sudden surge of anger coursed through her. She turned to face him.

"Did you hear about Twila being called in for questioning?" Her tone carried a venom that surprised even her.

"Yeah, I heard."

"Well, are you going to tell me again that I have misjudged her?"

Frank's jaw flexed. "They haven't proven anything yet," he said, his voice deep.

"Just as I suspected—you're still defending the woman who caused me so much pain, who poisoned the horse I love. You've never stopped loving her."

"Annie, that's not true. I want them to find out who caused all this mayhem, but I don't think Twila's capable of killing someone. It's true that she can be a cruel woman, but it's also true that you set about building a case against her from the start of this mess. If you set your targets too soon—"

"You're a coward," Annie said, the depth of her rage bubbling out of her.

Frank turned away, looked somewhere in the distance, then slowly turned his head back around, drilled his eyes into hers. Clearly, she'd insulted him, but her words were unstoppable.

"You never wanted me to be in the show." Annie's voice lowered. "You resented my skill, my talent—a skinny little girl outshooting the great marksman Frank Butler was *unthinkable*. You couldn't keep them from hiring me, and you couldn't get your aim back, so you decided to make a fool of me. Well, you've won, Frank. In a day, I'll be gone, forgotten, back to Nowhere, Ohio, while you're off to live a rich life on your father's horse farm. You'll be able to start over. You'll never go hungry."

Annie closed in on him and drilled her eyes into his, demanding him to answer to her, to admit that he'd set out to make a fool of her. He lowered his eyes from her gaze.

"Look at me." Annie clenched her uninjured fist, rammed it into his chest. "I hate you, Frank Butler, I hate you, I hate you!" She pounded his chest in rhythm with her words, over and over.

He didn't move, didn't flinch, until at last he grabbed her wrist and held it firm, looked hard into her eyes.

"Let go of me." Annie tried, but couldn't look away from his gaze. Hard, steely, endlessly blue like the vast ocean.

Frank loosened but did not release his grip.

"You are going to believe whatever it is you have to believe, but know this, Annie Oakley, I love you. I loved you the minute you let me win that goddamned contest in Ohio, and I love you still, no matter what you say to me."

Annie jerked her wrist free, jammed her balled fist into his chest, and pushed him away.

Frank looked into her eyes one more time, then dusted off his hat and walked away without looking back.

"Good," Annie called after him. "That's good—you go ahead and walk out of my life—forever." She wanted to mean it, but could feel her heart folding in on itself. When Buck nuzzled her and lowered his chin onto her shoulder, she spun around and cradled his head. "You're the only one." she stroked Buck's neck. "You've always been the only one I could trust."

CHAPTER 23

"Private Funeral for Dick Carver Scheduled for Next Week.
Suspect Still At Large."

St. Louis Times – April 25, 1885

B y the time Annie crawled into bed that night, she had all of her belongings packed. She decided to take many of the dresses and accessories LeFleur had given her, as it would be a while before she could buy any new clothing. Some of the dresses could be altered to fit Mother and Hulda, so they would definitely be appreciated.

Once in her bed, Annie stared at the tent's canvas ceiling, hoping the murmuring voices and animal noises floating on the air would lull her into a sleepy trance. She would miss all her new friends, her fans, the excitement of performing, and most of all the enormous self-satisfaction that came with showing the world what a small girl from Darke County, Ohio, could do.

Back in North Star, she would be fighting every day just to put food on the table. She thought of Frank and regretted all the horrible things she'd said to him. But what did it matter now? Tomorrow she would leave, and she would never see him again.

Annie drew in a deep breath and slowly let it out, trying to focus on the murmuring voices and animal noises to force her muscles and her mind to relax. Try as she might, she couldn't stop thinking about the pain she'd seen on Frank's face—it had seared an image in her mind. Eventually, she fell into a fitful, restless sleep, only to be awakened by someone gently shaking her shoulder.

"Annie, Annie, wake up," Bobby whispered.

"What are you doing here? What time is it?" she asked, her voice thick, groggy.

"It's early morning. Sun's not up yet, but Buck's gone. He's not in his pen or the barn. Mr. Post had a bad night. I think he's got the virus. He heard something out in the corral, and when he finally got himself there, Buck was gone."

"Are you sure? You've looked everywhere?" Annie's heart drummed in her chest.

"Mr. Post came to the cowboy's tent, fever and all—guess it was closer than yours—and told me to rouse you. He's in a state, Annie. I have never seen the man so upset."

"Have you looked for Buck, Bobby?"

"I've looked all over the grounds. There's no sign of him."

Annie flung the covers off and pulled on a dressing gown she had thrown over the chair. She jammed her feet into her boots and fled from the tent. She could hear Bobby running behind her.

The breaking sun colored the sky pale peach, while stars above winked in the early morning light. Buck's corral was empty—the gate hung open. She ran into the barn to find Post sitting on one of the tack trunks, his head in his hands.

"Mr. Post, what happened? Where is Buck?" Annie knelt down in front of him.

The old man raised his head and looked up at her with weary, watery eyes. A sheen of sweat glistened on his face and his skin shone pallid.

"He's gone. Someone took him. I thought I heard something, but by the time I got up it was too late. I'm so sorry, Miss Oakley."

Annie squeezed her eyes shut, drew a deep breath, and bit her bottom lip to prevent crying or shouting at him.

"Let's get you back to bed, Mr. Post. You are in no state to be up."

"I have to find him," he said, his voice squeaking like a child's.

"I'll find him Mr. Post, you know I will. I'm not leaving until I find him. You need to rest or you will be no help to me at all. Do you understand?" Annie's words came out surprisingly firm and calm. Inside, she wanted to scream with panic. She had to go find her horse. She had to go now.

"Come on." She wrapped her good hand around Mr. Post's upper arm, gently urging him to get up. Bobby propped up Mr. Post's other side.

"I told the Colonel and Mr. LeFleur. They'll be along in a minute."

"Help me get him to bed, Bobby. We also need to wake Chief Sitting Bull. Mr. Post needs his medicine."

Together, Annie and Bobby helped Mr. Post limp to the tiny room he called home. The room, about ten feet by ten feet, housed a rickety cot, a small table, and hooks along the wall for Mr. Post to hang what little clothing he had. Annie's stomach churned at the filth in the room. The Colonel made lots of money from his show. She'd been shocked at the opulence and luxuriousness of her own quarters. How could the Colonel let Mr. Post live in this squalor?

They scooted their way through the small doorway and finally lowered the old man onto his cot. Annie picked up a tattered wool blanket and laid it over him, tucking it in around his body. Mr. Post let out a groan and shivered, his teeth chattering.

"I'll go get the Chief," Bobby said.

Annie nodded and knelt down on the floor next to Mr. Post. She hoped the Colonel and Mr. LeFleur would arrive soon. Every minute wasted, not looking for Buck, would mean he was getting farther and farther away. Annie held her breath, forcing down panic. Mr. Post laid his head back, his eyes closed and mouth open.

"What happened?" Annie heard the Colonel's voice in the doorway.

"Mr. Post is sick. He heard someone out in Buck's corral, but by the time he got there Buck was gone. He's gone, Colonel. Mr. Post thinks someone took him. I have to find him. I have to. I just have to—"

"Simmer down, girl. We'll send out a search party."

LeFleur arrived. "What's wrong with Post?"

"It appears he's caught the same virus Nakota and Michante had," Annie said.

Bobby and Chief Sitting Bull pushed their way into the small room. Now that the Chief had arrived, Annie rose and looked imploringly at the Colonel.

"Can we go now? Right away?"

"What's this about?" LeFleur asked.

The Colonel motioned for LeFleur, Annie, and Bobby to exit Post's room and gather in the barn's hallway.

"Buck's gone missing," the Colonel said. "I'll need you to get messages out to all the horse traders in this area, tell them to be on the lookout for Buck."

LeFleur nodded, but made no comment, his face void of any emotion.

"Colonel, I want to go with the search party," Annie said, her voice cracking.

"But Annie, your hand," LeFleur protested.

Annie ignored him, looking hard into the Colonel's eyes.

"Of course you want to go along. We'll find you a mount."

"Colonel, can we go now?" Annie's fear rose to a thunderous level.

"Bobby, get Isham saddled up and find a mount for Annie."

"She can ride Fancy," LeFleur said. Startled, Annie spun her head toward him. "Frank has gone." LeFleur stared at Annie with cold eyes, his expression flat. "His tent's been cleaned out, but Fancy's still in the stables."

Annie's mouth hung open. *Could Frank have been so angry at her that he would take Buck?*

"You don't think Frank took Buck?" Bobby asked LeFleur.

"Now, now." The Colonel looked into Annie's eyes. "Frank Butler may be a lot of things, but he isn't a horse thief. He'd never steal. He knows what *that horse* means to you. "

Annie felt her breath coming in short, shallow gasps.

"It could have been McCrimmon," LeFleur said.

Annie's chest tightened. *Yes, it could have been McCrimmon.*

"Can we go?" she pleaded.

"Bobby, tack Isham," the Colonel said, "and I'll help you with Fancy." The Colonel grabbed a halter and lead rope from the nearby hooks. After he retrieved Fancy and tied her to the hitching post, he followed Annie to the tack room to get her saddle and one of the Indian print blankets. Annie noticed Buck's bridle still hanging on a hook, but instead took the bridle she'd seen Fancy wear in the performances.

The Colonel placed the saddle blanket on Fancy's back and then swung the saddle on top of it in one fluid motion. They heard the clip-clop of Isham's hooves behind them as Bobby emerged, holding the saddled gray by the reins.

"Bobby, Annie and I will go on ahead in a few minutes. You rustle up anyone who might be interested in assisting, and you all follow behind. We're going to head north into the forest. Once everyone is there, we'll split up. Understand?"

Bobby nodded and handed the Colonel Isham's reins. They finished bridling Fancy and led the horses outside. Fancy was much taller than Buck, so the Colonel gave Annie a leg up before he mounted.

"We'll need to fetch our weapons—and you need to get dressed," the Colonel said, his voice somber.

Annie looked down at her dressing gown and night shift. She'd completely forgotten she hadn't dressed. They rode into the camp, stopping outside Annie's tent. The Colonel ground-tied Isham and ran to his tent.

Annie went inside hers, dressed, and grabbed the beautifully tooled gun belt and pearl-handled pistols Frank had given her.

Once the Colonel returned with his weapons, he helped Annie mount again, climbed aboard Isham, and they rode toward the forest at a brisk trot, moving into a rolling canter. Annie wanted to urge Fancy to an all-out run but realized it wouldn't do any good. She had to fight the frenzied panic rising in her chest, so she matched her breathing to Fancy's rhythm. The mare had a wonderfully smooth gait, and Annie forced herself to sink down into the saddle. Panic would serve no purpose here. She had to be sharp.

When they reached the tree line, they brought the horses down to a trot. They separated and began searching among the trees. Annie strained her eyes, searching for Buck's tawny golden hide among the thicket. Soon, they heard the thunder of hooves as riders charged toward the forest. Annie and the Colonel brought their horses to a halt to wait for the rest of the search party.

The Colonel removed his hat and placed it over the horn of his saddle. Without the hat, his thinning hair, which transitioned from soft brown to silver at his temples, betrayed his age. His eyes bore the weight of sadness, and Annie knew that sadness spread further than Buck gone missing.

"What's going to happen with Twila?" she asked.

"She was taken in for questioning."

"I didn't mean to cause you any trouble."

The Colonel sucked air through his teeth.

"That woman has a mean streak as long as the Mississippi. She's jealous as a she-wolf. Demanding. Doesn't understand the meaning of the word 'no.'" He paused, used his long fingers to brush dust off his hat's brim. "But she's not a murderer, Annie, simple as that."

Annie looked at the glowing horizon, searched for something to say.

"Who's taking care of the baby?"

"One of the Indian women." The sadness in his voice touched Annie. "It's probably for the best. She needs to be with her own kind."

Horsemen approached, halting their conversation. Bobby led the group.

"There are a dozen of us. What do you want us to do?" Bobby's face was flushed with excitement.

"You and Annie and someone else head that-a-way," the Colonel pointed east. "I'll take three and continue north. The rest split into two groups and head west and southwest."

Sensing the group's anticipation, the horses snorted and pranced.

Annie turned Fancy toward the east and took off at a brisk walk. Bobby and his mount came up beside her. The other cowboy stayed in the rear.

"We'll find him, Annie," Bobby said, hope in his voice.

Annie turned to him, swallowing down her fear.

"Yes, we will, Bobby. We have to."

CHAPTER 24

"Twila Midnight, Former Buffalo Bill Wild West Star, Taken in for Questioning in Dick Carver Murder Investigation."

St. Louis Times – April 26, 1885

Annie had lost track of the time, but her stomach told her it must be near noon. Not wanting to talk, she had ridden ahead. Bobby and the other cowboy followed behind her, talking in low tones. Although she felt heartsick over Buck's disappearance, the sunshine beating down on her, in tandem with Fancy's rhythmic cadence, calmed Annie. She had to believe they would find him, or she would go mad with terror.

"Annie, look," Bobby said.

She turned around in her saddle and followed the line of his finger. He pointed to a dilapidated old cabin with a sunken roof. Several logs had come loose from the frame and sprawled at awkward angles. Smoke poured from the chimney.

Bobby motioned for the other cowboy to catch up with him, and they maneuvered their horses in front of Annie, providing a protective wall of horseflesh. Annie rolled her eyes. She could outshoot both of these boys even on a bad day, but she appreciated their desire to be protective. Nevertheless, she laid her good hand on the butt of her pistol.

As they neared the cabin, they noticed a man sitting on the ground, his back slumped against a tree stump. Annie spotted the jug at his feet. When he saw them approach, he clumsily stood up.

"Who's there?" he asked, his speech slurred.

"We're looking for a missing buckskin horse," Bobby said.

"Ain't seen no horse." The man slowly rolled his head back and forth, his face slack with drunkenness.

Annie walked Fancy out in front of the boys and peered inside the cabin. Amid the logs and rubbish on the floor, she saw another man curled up on a pallet. Something looked vaguely familiar about him. Perhaps it was the sprigs of muddy gray hair that formed a messy halo about his head.

"Who's your friend?" she asked.

The man turned to look inside the cabin and then swatted his hand in the air.

"That's Vernon. He's been doing poorly for a couple weeks now. He's dying. Been like that for a couple of days."

Annie jumped off Fancy and pulled her pistol out of her holster.

"Annie, what are you doing?" Bobby asked, alarm in his voice.

The man at the stump stood up, a pistol held in his hand.

"Keep an eye on him, Bobby," Annie said.

Annie heard rustling, the man protesting as she rushed onto the battered porch, braced herself against the doorframe, and stepped over piles of rubbish to get inside. The stench made her want to vomit. She knelt down at the crumpled up body and confirmed that it was definitely Vernon McCrimmon, unconscious, a heavy rattle coming from his lungs.

A gunshot from outside startled her, but she ignored it.

"Vernon McCrimmon." She touched his filthy shirt at the shoulder and poked him. "McCrimmon, wake up."

The man's wrinkled eyelids flickered and then opened to narrow slits. He groaned. Annie covered her nose to block the vehement stench of stale moonshine.

Annie stood. If Vernon McCrimmon had been in this state for days, there was no way he could have taken Buck.

Just as Annie was about to leave, she felt something grab her ankle.

"You!" McCrimmon said, pulling hard, knocking Annie off her feet. Her elbow thudded against the floorboard and her gun flew out of her hand, skittering away from her.

McCrimmon flung himself on top of her, his breath hot and abhorrent in her face. She struggled against his weight to get her other gun, but Vernon shoved his pelvis over her hip. She couldn't get her good hand between him and the pistol. He clamped his hands around her neck and squeezed hard. Annie grabbed at her throat, desperate for air, but his hands kept closing in, tighter and tighter.

Annie thrust her arms outward and scraped them across the floor, searching for anything she could use to clock him. She kept rocking hard to throw him off balance and used those split seconds to scan the room. Her eyes lit on a knife at the end of McCrimmon's pallet. She thrust her knee into Vernon's groin to loosen his grip on her throat and gain leverage. As he struggled to wrap his hands around her neck again, Annie stretched her arm as far as it could reach and managed to wobble the knife into her grasp. McCrimmon pressed hard on her windpipe. Annie sank the knife deep into his back. His entire body tensed and then went slack. His weight rested on her like a stinking bag of potatoes.

"Annie!" Bobby rushed into the room.

"Get him off! Get him off!" She struggled under McCrimmon's lifeless body.

Bobby grabbed McCrimmon by the shoulders, lifted him, and Annie shimmied out from under him. She sat panting, ready to heave her last meal all over the floor.

"My God, what happened in here?" Bobby helped her to her feet.

"Where's the other man?" Annie bent over at the waist, rested her hand on her knee, and fought to steady her breathing.

"He shot at me but missed, and then the old sot was so drunk he fell over. Took us a while, but we were able to finally wrestle the gun out of his hand. He's passed out."

Bobby rested a hand on her back, but she shook him off and turned to see the man who had terrorized her for one long year, sprawled out on his back, a pool of blood soaking the floor beneath him.

When she stood up, Bobby held out her pistol. She took it, shoved passed him, and headed out of the cabin, straight for Fancy.

Annie led the mare over to a tree stump, which she used as a boost to hop onto the horse's back. Once in the saddle, she settled her gun belt securely about her waist. Bobby and the other cowboy, their faces pale with confusion and concern, got on their mounts, and looked to Annie for direction. She looked over at Vernon's friend, still unconscious on the ground.

"This lot will be of no help," she said. "Let's go."

Bobby and the other cowboy waited for her and Fancy to pass and then followed behind.

Annie clenched her jaw. She'd just killed a man. Again, she'd committed a grievous sin against her beliefs, her religion. But sometimes you had to take matters into your own hands. Finally that bastard McCrimmon got what was coming to him.

They returned to camp just before dark that evening. They'd stopped only once to eat the bread and jerky the other cowboy had brought along in his saddlebag. Annie's body ached with exhaustion and the weight of defeat. There had been no sign of Buck, and they had traveled at least ten square miles. She hoped the others had better luck.

As they rode up to the barn, the Colonel, on Isham, sidled up to Annie and Fancy.

"I'm sorry—we didn't find him, Annie."

Annie wanted to smile at him, but couldn't make her facial muscles cooperate.

"Thank you, sir. Perhaps tomorrow."

"I can't spare the men tomorrow, my dear. I am sorry."

"Oh, yes, of course." Annie blinked back her disappointment.

"Listen. I take it you're not going home till you find Buck."

Annie nodded. "I have to find him."

"Well, now, your family will still need money, so how about you stay on for a while, at least till we pack up for Kansas. I'll wire two months' worth of pay to wherever you want it wired."

"That's very kind of you. I won't leave without Buck." Annie swiped away the sweat and dust off her cheek.

"Of course not. When you and the boys aren't practicing or performing, we'll send them out in small search parties."

"Colonel, I can't tell you how much this means to me. That horse is—"

"I know, darlin'. I know." The Colonel leaned down to pat Isham on the neck.

"Have you seen Mr. LeFleur? Did he have any luck with the local horse traders?"

"No one's seen your horse. Maybe tomorrow."

By the time Annie ate dinner and made it back to her tent, she wanted nothing more than to crawl under her covers and get a few hours sleep. They had performances tomorrow midmorning and midafternoon, but she would take Fancy out in the early morning hours to search the forest again. Perhaps Buck would escape from his captor and head back. Annie vowed to use every spare minute to search for him.

Lillie stood by her bed, returned from the hospital, unpacking clothes. Annie noticed the white lilies she had purchased sitting in a silver pitcher on Lillie's nightstand.

"Well, there's the world famous Annie Oakley," Lillie said, with a throaty laugh.

"Hello, Lillie. I'm glad you're feeling better."

"Can't keep a good cowgirl down. Can't wait to celebrate. Want to come over to the saloon with me?"

Annie groaned. Almost poisoned to death a few days ago, and in her first few hours back, Lillie wanted to get drunk. Annie sank down on her bed.

"I don't feel much like celebrating."

"What gives, princess?"

"Buck has gone missing. We've been searching for him all day."

"What? He's gone? Just like that?"

"Mr. Post thinks someone stole him."

"Who would do that?" Lillie plopped down on her bed, still holding an article of clothing.

"Frank is gone, too."

Lillie's mouth fell open. "You don't think that he—?"

"Maybe." She didn't really believe it, but she felt so exhausted and frustrated, the words tumbled out. "I told him that I never wanted to see him again—ever."

"Are you saying that Frank may be seeking revenge? Even I find that difficult to believe."

"I don't know what I am saying." Annie sighed, lay back on the bed and placed the back of her hand over her eyes. "I am so tired and so worried about Buck I can't think straight."

"What about that McCrimmon fellow? He could have taken Buck."

Annie's stomach clenched. She shook her head.

"We found him in a cabin in the forest. The man was nearly dead with drink. There's no way he could have even walked this far to let Buck out. Anyway, he won't be bothering anyone anymore."

Lillie threw up her hands. "I never thought I'd say this to you, Annie, but I am truly sorry for your troubles."

"You may not feel so kindly toward me when I tell you something else." Annie steeled herself for what lay ahead. She sat up.

"Spill it," Lillie said, her eyes opening wide.

"The sheriff has apprehended Twila."

Lillie bolted to her feet. "What?"

"They haven't arrested her; they've taken her in for questioning."

"For Pete's sake, why?" Lillie positioned her hands on her stout hips.

"Remember when Buck was so ill? We couldn't figure out what it could be. On a hunch, I had a friend of mine take a sample of his water to have it tested. They found traces of poisonous oleander in it. The coroner exhumed Kimi's body at the request of Detective Jonas, and they found a lethal amount of the same plant in her system. It's also the same poison they found in the chocolates that almost killed you."

Lillie dropped the dress she held, her face in a grimace, and crossed her arms over her chest.

"And how does this involve Twila?"

"They discovered oleander plants in her possession, mixed among the other herbs. They also found a pistol in her trunk that uses the same ammunition used to kill Mr. Carver."

Lillie shook her head violently, shook a finger in the air.

"You're wrong, Annie, you're just wrong. Twila has a lot of unusual herbs in her possession, but she uses them for healing, not for killing."

"Things happened in her past, when she was with Buffalo Bill and Dick Carver's Rocky Mountain and Prairie Exhibition, that raised suspicion. Things that may have driven her to shoot Carver." Annie didn't want to reveal everything just yet, not until they were certain.

"This makes no sense at all." Lillie plopped down on the bed, struggling to process the information.

"The chocolates also had oleander in them, Lillie."

"If you're implying that Twila sent the poisoned chocolates, I don't believe it. She loves me like a sister—she'd never do anything to hurt me."

Annie looked down at her bandaged hand.

"Those chocolates were meant for me."

Lillie's mouth went from an opened gape to a soft *o* shape, but when the information finally registered, her expression reflected alarm.

"Twila is not the friendliest of women, Annie, but you cannot expect me," she pointed vehemently at her chest, "*me*, to believe she would try to kill someone. She just wouldn't."

"I'm not expecting you to believe anything, Lillie," Annie said, the weight of the world suddenly pressing down on her. "I'm just telling you what has occurred since you've been gone."

Lillie stood with her hands clasped together and her shoulders slumped forward, studying Annie. Annie flopped down onto her back and tugged the bedclothes over her body. She never even heard Lillie leave the tent.

Annie awoke to shrieking from somewhere outside. She sat up with the gnawing feeling that she'd slept longer than planned. Still in her clothes from the day before, she got out of bed and rearranged her skirts and corset. The skin on her torso had been rubbed raw next to the seams of the binding bodice. She never should have slept in her corset, she knew better, but she'd been so tired.

What *was* that horrible noise? She looked over at Lillie's bed . . . empty, and the bed covers typically scattered everywhere. So, she had spent the night there—and she hadn't murdered Annie in her sleep. Standing at the ewer, splashing cold water on her face, Annie caught sight of her image in the mirror. *Dear Lord, not a pretty sight.* She ran her fingers through her thick, knotted hair.

The shrieking continued.

Unable to ignore it any longer, Annie stepped outside. The yelling came from near the Colonel's tent. Annie strode briskly toward it and paused once she arrived, to inch around the corner. She saw

Twila, her finger held out in front of her face, screaming at the Colonel.

The Colonel stood with one hand on his gun belt. The other held a cigar, poised next to his cocked hip. He stood uncharacteristically still, enduring her tirade.

"I have given you the best of myself . . . for years," Twila moved closer to the Colonel, "and you can't give me this one thing—the one thing I've been denied over and over again. All those babies," she said, her voice raising an octave, "all those babies lost, but now you have one. One that is motherless. I can mother that child, Bill."

The Colonel raised his hand in the air.

"No!" Twila shouted. "You will not quiet me!"

"That child is where she needs to be, Twila, I won't discuss it further."

Annie watched the Colonel continue to calmly face the woman standing before him, her hair a disheveled mess, her face worn. Her torn and dirty clothes hung on her like rags. She looked like a wild Medusa.

The Colonel then turned and addressed the people gathering around to witness the commotion.

"We have a show in an hour and a half. What are y'all standing around gawking at? Get on with it." He jammed the cigar into his mouth and stalked off.

Twila stood her ground, her fists in tight balls at her sides. She turned and saw Annie staring at her.

"And you, are you happy now? I have nothing, *nothing*!"

As Twila moved toward her, Annie planted her feet and folded her hands neatly in front of her, placing her strong hand in front.

"Let me tell you something, *Miss Annie Oakley*," Twila spat in the dirt. "I admitted to the sheriff that I put that oleander into your horse's water. I figured you were only as good as that damn horse, and if he couldn't perform, then neither would you, and you'd be gone. And I wanted you gone. I make no bones about that, but that horse kept getting up and you wouldn't give up." Twila's face contorted into its familiar scowl. "All I hear is 'she's so charming, she's so talented, she's such a star.' Frank loves her, the Colonel loves her, and even LeFleur loves her." Twila put her hand to her temple as if her head pained her, squinted her eyes closed, popped them open, and trained them on Annie's face.

"And I may have lost my temper with that nit-witted Indian harlot, and I may have struck her when she kept simpering around the Colonel, pleading with him to love her. He was *my* man, and he was done with her. Done with her, so yes I got angry, but I did not give her poison, and I did not shoot Carver, and I did not poison those chocolates. So whatever you think you may have accomplished by talking to that damned detective came to nothing. *Nothing!*"

She fell to her knees. "I wanted that baby. I wanted to love that baby, and now he's taken her away—and it's your fault, Annie Oakley. It's your fault." She collapsed, and began sobbing and pounding the ground in front of her.

Annie remained rooted in her position, unsure what to say or do. Twila's confession had stunned her, and, as ugly as the tirade had been, Twila had bared her soul—and Annie believed her. The mask had finally been lifted, revealing a woman whose lover had betrayed her and denied her the respect she so craved, and the baby she so desired.

One of the Indian women knelt beside Twila and lifted her to her feet. Annie watched as they slipped into the Colonel's tent. As others began to move away, Annie followed suit.

The number of people in the stands surprised Annie. She had worried that the loss of Frank Butler would negatively impact the show's popularity, but the crowd swelled to full capacity and seemed more rambunctious and animated than ever.

After Buffalo Bill, his cowboys, and the Indian performers finished their enactment of "The Battle of Yellow Hand" with the Colonel holding his foot atop a fallen "heathen" and waving a black scalp in his hands, it was Annie's turn to shine. She leaned down and stroked Fancy's deep brown shoulder. The horse stood stock still, dozing, as she usually did before a performance.

While waiting for the masses of cowboys and Indians to exit the stadium, Annie noticed Bobby several yards away, under the stands, pacing back and forth, his hand to his chin. She'd never seen Bobby fret before an act. A natural performer, he'd never put much stock in rehearsals, although he'd never missed one.

The announcer delivered the Colonel's final send off, and the audience roared with appreciation. The Colonel sped Isham around the arena, a fake scalp still firmly grasped in his outstretched hand, before finally making his exit. He brought his horse to a sliding stop in front of Annie and Fancy, causing the mare to raise her head and widen her eyes. He stuffed the scalp into the pocket of his elaborately embroidered coat.

"Ready?" the Colonel asked her.

"Of course."

"They've been shouting your name in there. If I didn't know better,

I'd say your getting shot made them love you more than ever. You really are a heroine to them; they're waiting for your big entrance."

Annie tried her best to smile, but she wanted nothing more than to be sharing this moment with her trusted horse—and she couldn't help missing him, and Frank. The Colonel seemed to sense her unease.

"They know that you'll be riding Fancy rather than Buck, and they were disappointed, but if you ride her like a champ, all will be forgiven. It's you they really want to see."

Annie bit her lower lip.

"Annie, we'll send another team out to search for Buck. Some of Sitting Bull's people are trained trackers. If they have to stay out a couple of nights, we'll let them." The Colonel winked. "Don't worry, we'll get your horse back."

The announcer shouted Annie's name and the crowd came alive again, screaming louder than she'd ever heard them before.

Annie rode Fancy into the arena at a steady gallop, the reins poised tenderly in her injured hand, firing her pistol into the air with the other. She shelved her preoccupations and worries, flashed a pretty, girlish smile, and soared around the arena, making eye contact with her adoring fans.

After successfully completing the first course, while waiting for the crew to set up the next one, Annie walked Fancy along the railing, and began shaking hands with people jammed into the front rows of the ground boxes. Others clamored to get a glimpse of her, which made Annie's heart swell with pride. Perhaps, somehow, she *was* making a difference, if only by giving folks a diversion from their troubles for fifteen to twenty minutes at a time.

She and Fancy made their way down an entire length of the arena before the announcer called her back to perform her next course. Within minutes, she'd completed it perfectly.

The gates opened and Bobby and Lillie ran in, waving to the crowd. Behind them, one of Mr. Post's barn crew rushed over to collect Fancy. Annie dismounted with a lively bounce and joined Bobby and Lillie. When she grasped Bobby's hand, it felt wet with perspiration, and his face looked pale. Could he be coming down with the virus? She squeezed his hand to get his attention, gave him a questioning look that clearly conveyed that she wanted to know if he was okay. He shook his head.

The crew had erected the table with their weapons. Unable to use her rifle with her injured hand, Annie held the cards for Lillie. Soon Boomer the dog ran into the arena with his owner following behind, carrying a stool. Using her pistols, Annie managed to shoot a bottle, an apple, and a grapefruit off the canine's head. When she finished, the dog ran over to her, tongue wagging, and jumped up, placing his paws on her shoulders. Annie hugged him close with her good arm and reveled in the messy kisses he slobbered all over her face. Yells and laughter from the audience floated on the air, and, for a few seconds, Annie remembered what it felt like to be happy.

After a few more tricks from Bobby and Lillie, they gathered together, grasped hands, Bobby careful to hold her injured hand lightly, and raised them high in the air. Together they bowed low three times.

"Wow! That was a boon." Lillie said, breathless, as the gates closed once again. She leaned over to catch her breath. "Whoo! Those damn chocolates really took the spunk out of me. I'm one tired girl. Why don't we go get a drink, compadres?"

Annie shook her head. "I have to search for Buck."

"Oh, yeah. I suppose you do, huh?" Lillie's face crumpled. "You too, Bobby?"

"I'd like to help Annie."

"All right then." Lillie straightened her body. "I wish you two the best of luck. I'd offer to help, but me and the beasts just don't seem to get along."

Annie and Bobby exchanged a glance. No one had ever seen Lillie anywhere near a horse. They watched her amble toward the saloon. The stands creaked and thumped as people made their way out of the stadium.

"I appreciate you helping me look for Buck, Bobby."

"Aw, Annie, I'd do just about anything for you." Bobby looked away from her and pulled his hat off his head. His bottom lip quivered.

"What's wrong, Bobby?"

Bobby crushed his hat between his hands. His face contorted, as if struggling to contain an emotion that threatened to surface.

"I've got a secret that's killing me, Annie. I don't know if I can stand the strain anymore. My head feels like it's about to explode."

"What, Bobby? You can tell me." Annie pressed her uninjured hand to his shoulder.

Bobby twisted the hat mercilessly in his hands and shook his head.

"I can't. Truly. It'll just get you hurt. It *has* gotten people hurt. I just can't."

"I saw you and Mr. LeFleur arguing—several times. Does it have something to do with that? Why are you so angry with him?"

Bobby's face turned bright pink, darkening his freckles. His mouth turned down. He looked like he'd just seen something that filled him with disgust, and his breath came in long blasts out his nose.

"Yellow. Bellied. Traitor." Bobby's words came out behind his gritted teeth in a rasp. Annie gripped harder on his shoulder.

"Traitor? How do you mean? Did he betray you? The Colonel? Bobby, if you know anything about the murders, you have to tell me."

Bobby squeezed his eyes shut and pressed his thumb and forefinger to them, but tears seeped out anyway.

"No. I won't tell you."

"Bobby, when I was laid up at the hotel and you came to visit me, did you have oleander in your pockets?"

"How did you—?"

"I found it on the floor. What were you doing with it? I thought we were friends, Bobby."

The boy's eyes widened. "We are, Annie. It wasn't mine. I found it."

"Where?"

"Can't say."

"*Bobby*."

"I can't say. But I found it and I thought about giving it to that detective, but—"

"But what?"

"I can't, Annie, please, I can't explain. It will all come out, I reckon."

"Does Mr. LeFleur know about this? I saw you two arguing."

"I'm sorry, Annie." Bobby slammed his hat onto his head and sniffed. "I never should have mentioned it. Please don't say anything, to anyone. I beg you."

Annie watched Bobby compose himself. He wouldn't meet her eyes, but it was clear he was going to stand his ground.

"All right, Bobby."

As he left, Annie saw a group of cowboys mounting up for the search. Fancy awaited, all tacked up and ready to go.

CHAPTER 25

"More Bad Luck for Wild West Show—Buck the Wonder Horse,
Annie Oakley's Sidekick, Goes Missing."

St. Louis Times – April 27, 1885

They arrived back at the campgrounds well after dark, still no sign
of Buck. As he'd promised, the Colonel instructed the Indian
scouts to continue their search for the next couple of days. Annie grew
increasingly discouraged, dreading the day she'd have to accept that
Buck, like Frank, was never coming back—and she'd be headed back to
Ohio, whether she wanted to go or not.

Bobby hadn't ridden with her today in the search, which disappointed her. She wanted to know more about the secret that seemed
to be eating him alive. His admiration for Mr. LeFleur had sure taken
a fall—a bit surprising as both LeFleur and the Colonel treated him
like a son. But come to think of it, LeFleur's behavior had changed of
late. Once buoyant with enthusiasm, cheerful, and eager to share his
wisdom and knowledge, now he seemed moody, nervous, and agitated.
Perhaps that's just the way she saw him because she had rebuffed his
feelings for her.

In weary silence, the group of searchers removed the tack from their horses, brushed the horses down, and stabled them. Bobby finished first and quickly strode away toward the tents. Annie didn't know if he purposefully avoided her, but it made her determined to know what troubled him—particularly if it related to the murders.

Once she'd gotten Fancy rubbed down, Annie led Frank's horse into her stall where a fresh pile of hay and a bucket of oats awaited her. The mare gave a low nicker as Annie removed the bridle and, as soon as Annie removed the bit, plunged her nose into the bucket and munched noisily on molasses-soaked oats. Annie absently patted Fancy's neck.

On her way to the tack room, she decided to check on Mr. Post. She found him in his tiny abode, sitting on his soiled cot, sipping coffee from a tin cup.

"You're better!" she said, as she stepped into the room, careful not to tread on a pile of dirty clothing.

"Right as rain." Post raised his chin. The man still looked like a corpse, but his cheeks flushed pink and he'd lost the glassy-eyed look of the fevered. "Still no sign of your boy?"

Annie sighed. "Nothing. I fear he's gone, forever. The Colonel agreed to send trackers to search for the next couple of days, but I'm losing hope."

"I'm to blame, Miss Oakley, and I'm terribly sorry."

"Please don't say that, Mr. Post. Please don't feel that way. You were out of your head with fever. It's not your fault. It couldn't be helped." How she wished she'd bunked Buck outside her tent, like she'd seen the Colonel do with Isham from time to time. But there was no point in looking back.

They heard a clatter of boots outside the door, and one of the cowboys stuck his head in Post's room.

"There you are, Miss Oakley. You have to come quick. Something's happened. Lillie is out of her head, and she keeps asking for you."

Annie and Post stood up simultaneously, the wool blanket sliding off Post's shoulders and crumpling into a heap on the floor.

"Well, what is it that's got her going, son?" he asked.

"It's Miss Midnight. She was found dead in the kitchen. We can't be sure, but it looks like she was poisoned. She got awful sick before—"

"Oh, dear God," Annie hiked up her skirts and hauled her fatigued legs as fast as they could go toward the mess tent. She could hear the youthful steps of the cowboy and Mr. Post shuffling along behind her.

Annie reached the mess tent out of breath, sweat trickling down the sides of her face. She reached up to wipe away the moisture and felt the grit and grime of the day smear across her cheek. The Colonel, Bobby, Chief Sitting Bull, several of the cowboys, and a few of the Indians had gathered around a table. A couple of opened bottles of liquor and shot glasses littered the tabletop. The Colonel sat with his elbows on the table and his head in his hands. His hat slumped forward hiding his face. Annie heard soft sobbing.

The Chief met Annie's eyes and nodded his head to direct her behind the counter.

"She's been asking for you. Won't let us near the body, not even the Colonel. We are waiting for the detective."

The men remained silent as Annie hurried around the counter and found Lillie holding Twila's lifeless torso against hers, rocking back and forth, as if comforting a child.

"Oh, Lillie." Annie knelt down next to her.

"She's dead," Lillie whispered. Annie could smell liquor and vomit and nearly retched when she spotted the vomit next to Twila's body. Lillie's face burned bright red and her eyes looked wild with fury.

"I'm so sorry, Lillie."

"She's my only family . . . the only family I have left."

"I know, Lillie, but it's not good to stay here. Why don't you come with me?" Lillie drew Twila's body closer. "There's nothing you can do for her, Lillie, she's already gone."

"She's already cold, Annie, she's so cold." Lillie pressed her face against Twila's, and sobbed.

Several people rushed into the tent, Detective Jonas among them, his eyes searching the room and immediately alighting on Annie, who held up her hand to signal him to wait a moment.

"Lillie," she said softly, "the sheriff and Detective Jonas are here. They've come over now to find out what happened. Won't you come with me?"

Lillie violently shook her head. When she looked at Annie, her eyes had the haunted look of someone gone mad.

Annie reached out her hand. "Take my hand, Lillie, come with me . . . please. They have their jobs to do."

Lillie looked down into Twila's face, wiped a smear of vomit away.

Annie scooted closer, gently pried Lillie's hand from Twila's face and wrapped it in her own. "Look at me, Lillie. Come with me." Lillie began to wail again. "Let's go get that drink you wanted earlier, okay, just slowly release Twila and come with me."

Lillie locked eyes with Annie and began slowly releasing her grasp and lowering Twila's torso gently to the floor. Annie held tightly to Lillie's hand and drew them both to their feet. Detective Jonas stepped in to hold Lillie's other arm, and together they walked her out of the kitchen.

"I'm taking her to our tent," Annie said. "You can find us there if you need us."

Detective Jonas nodded his approval, and Chief Sitting Bull brought Annie a bottle of liquor. Annie nodded her thanks. As they passed into the cold night air, Annie noticed LeFleur speaking with a detective at the door, but she said nothing.

Once in their tent, Annie settled Lillie onto her bed, helped her change into a nightdress, and brought a wet cloth over for her to wipe her face. Lillie cried throughout and reached for the liquor bottle when she'd been tucked under the covers. She pushed her back against the pillows and swigged a long draw of whiskey, then held the bottle out for Annie.

Annie took in a long breath, staring at the bottle. What did that brown liquid contain that drew people in for comfort, but only ended up tormenting them? She thought of Joshua, McCrimmon, and Lillie. She wondered, what would it taste like? She raised the bottle to her lips and took a small sip. The liquid burned her mouth, and its bitter taste made her wince as she swallowed it down in one gulp. Normally, Lillie would have laughed at Annie's reaction to the liquor—but nothing was normal anymore. Still, Annie couldn't see the value in drinking oneself silly.

"I can't believe she is gone," Lillie said, staring straight ahead.

"I'm so sorry." Annie placed her hand over Lillie's. "I know you loved her . . . and she loved you." Annie had finally seen the goodness in Twila—she'd loved baby Winona with a mother's fierceness.

Lillie buried her face in her hands and shook her head back and forth. A few drinks later, she turned to Annie, a pained look on her face.

"I have something to tell you, Annie."

"What is it?" Annie braced.

"I don't know why you're nice to me. I haven't been nice to you. I gave you a hard time from the moment we first met, and you hadn't done anything to deserve it. Why do you do that, Annie, why are you always so nice to people?"

Annie shrugged. "I know you didn't mean half of it. You were siding with Twila from the start, so I didn't like you much in the beginning, but now I mostly worry about you."

"But I broke your heart." Lillie had downed another swig.

"I don't understand."

Lillie placed her hand on Annie's uninjured hand and squeezed it tightly.

"I helped Twila convince you that Frank wasn't being true to you. It wasn't my idea, but I helped her, Annie, I did you wrong."

Annie widened her eyes in disbelief, her heart thundering.

"Twila wrote the note, but I brought it to you, and I banged a pan outside the tent." Lillie's words came out in a rush. "I . . . I betrayed you, Annie. I did what I had to do so you'd rush over to Frank's tent, at just the right time, so Twila could put on a show, but it wasn't Frank—he didn't know anything about it. Twila made sure—"

"Wait, you and Twila—?"

"I am so ashamed," Lillie said, nodding, taking another swig of whiskey, "You've been nothing but good to me and I've . . ." she raised her head but glanced away. "I've been downright mean to you, Annie, and I am awful sorry about it now."

Annie's body began to tremble. She tried to stand, but her legs folded under her. She sank back onto the bed, fighting an urge to strike Lillie. They'd tricked her, made her believe that Frank succumbed to Twila's seductive powers—mere hours after she and Frank had first made love. And she'd judged Frank without clearly asking him if it were true. She'd thought the worst of him. She'd pushed the first man she ever loved away . . .

"If it wasn't Frank, who was it? I know I saw someone in bed with her."

Lillie raised her eyes to Annie's. "That man who's been following you, McCrimmon."

Annie's stomach lurched. She couldn't believe the depths that Twila would sink to in order to get back at her. So that's what Twila and McCrimmon had been scheming up together.

Lillie reached out her hand, but Annie turned away from her.

"Aw, damn it, Annie, say something. Call me a low down rat, a vile varmint—"

"Stop, Lillie, stop." Annie held her hands up to her ears. "I don't want to hear your ramblings."

Lillie whimpered like a wounded animal. Annie turned her back to her, fuming. Neither one spoke for a long while. Too mad to cry, Annie wanted answers, she wanted the truth.

"Look at me, Lillie," Annie said, and Lillie lifted her eyes. "I knew from the start that Twila was jealous and vengeful toward me, and I know you loved her, but what you two did to me . . . and Frank . . . was cruel."

Lillie nodded her head and closed her quivering lips to still them. Annie sighed, frustrated.

"I know Twila poisoned Buck," she said, clenching her fists. "She confessed to me and everyone who came out to see what all the yelling was about yesterday. So I want the truth, Lillie, I want you to tell me the truth, as you know it. Did Twila murder Kimi and Carver?"

"No, I swear no, Annie." Lillie shook her head. "She could be mean and vengeful, I know, but she could never kill someone. I don't think she had the guts. She couldn't stand watching you with Frank. She knew he'd fallen in love with you, and it just made her crazy with jealousy—but she didn't have it in her to murder someone."

"What about the pistol found in her belongings? Did she know how to fire it?"

"No, Twila didn't know how to shoot. I'd tried to teach her once, but she didn't cotton on to it. That's why I know she couldn't possibly have killed Carver. That shot took some aim, in between all those people. That was the work of a marksman."

Annie sighed, thinking back to that day. The day Frank missed all his targets, the day they made love, the day Lillie and Twila crushed her heart. She put away her anger for the moment. Lillie had a point. Shooting Carver in the head, during a performance, with all those people around, took some skill.

Since Frank, Lillie, and Bobby were performing at the time, the only sharpshooters left were the Colonel and LeFleur. She'd seen that fancy revolver in LeFleur's trunk. He said it was a rare, unusual keepsake, nothing more, but you could draw the same deductions about Twila's pistol. Annie regretted that she hadn't gotten a closer look at LeFleur's gun . . . it could have been the same weapon, but who used it to shoot Carver?

"I have to go back to the mess tent," Annie said, lying. She needed to slip into LeFleur's tent to get another look at that gun.

"Why?" Lillie sounded like a small, whining child.

"I just want to follow the trail."

"But, Annie—"

"Don't worry, Lillie." Annie placed her hand on Lillie's arm. "You just go to sleep and let me worry about this. I won't be long."

CHAPTER 26

"Miss Midnight Released on Her Own Recognizance.
Carver Murder Investigation Continues."

St. Louis Times – April 27, 1885

Annie urged Lillie go to sleep and tucked the blankets around her plump body. She didn't wait for Lillie's response. Lillie looked up at her, still sobbing, but didn't say a word and continued crying into a rag, wiping her nose and face repeatedly, like a cat cleaning itself.

About to step outside, Annie paused and saw her gun belt with the two pearl-handled pistols nestled inside. Listening to her instincts, she grabbed one of them.

The sky had grown dark, and the air crisp. Annie's legs felt like lead from the long day's ride searching for Buck, but she walked fast, her curiosity driving her forward. LeFleur would be with the detectives for a while longer. If what she suspected was true, LeFleur's gun would be gone.

When Annie reached LeFleur's tent, she stepped inside the darkness. She blinked her eyes, waiting for them to adjust.

On his desk, she spotted a half-burned candlestick in a silver-plated candleholder. She scanned the desk for some matches and found some in a metal box. She lit the wick and soon the tent glowed orange and yellow with the diffused candlelight.

Annie's eyes immediately went to the trunk, which was locked—of course. She perused the tent, looking for another way to break the lock—an ice pick, a file, a knife. Anything.

On a chair in the corner she saw a pair of pants flung over the back, and some boots below, on the floor. A boot wouldn't be strong enough to break that lock.

Annie walked over to the chair to look behind it, thinking maybe a tent stake had come loose and she could use that to force open the lock. She picked up the pants to toss them aside when she heard clinking come from them. Annie shoved her hand inside one of the pockets, and her fingers hit on something hard. She pulled out the object.

A gold coin.

She held it up in the dim light. The face and back of the coin had been etched clean of their markings. She dug her hand in the pocket again and pulled out another. She thrust her hand into the other pocket, which was empty, but her fingers fell through the loose seams. She turned the pocket inside out and stared at her two fingers, sticking out through a hole in the fabric.

Mr. LeFleur had lost the coin in her tent, next to her trunk where the tea tin resided.

Her heart hammering in her chest, Annie dropped the pants, gripping the coins in her hand so hard that her fingernails bit into her skin.

She had to get into LeFleur's trunk. She'd have to shoot the lock open. Far too late for target practice, a gunshot would definitely be heard and people would come running. Annie made her way to LeFleur's bed and grabbed the down pillow and one of the quilts. She wrapped the quilt around her pistol and held the pillow up to the lock. She knew the sound would be muffled, but not silent. She had to shoot the lock open on the first try.

Making sure everything lined up, Annie aimed and pulled the trigger. Downy feathers shot out of the pillow in a puff and wafted gently to the ground. She pulled the pillow away and grinned. She'd shot clean through the lock, and it hung open. Setting her gun on the ground next to her, Annie flung the pillow and blanket to the side and slipped the lock out of the hasp.

She opened the trunk.

As she suspected, no gun, but a farrier's file lay next to the burlap sacks. She picked it up. Glinting in the yellow light, Annie could see flecks of gold embedded in the threads of the metal.

Breathing hard, her hands shaking, she grabbed one of the burlap bags and pulled open the ties. Peering inside, she found gold coins. Hundreds of them. She pulled one out and inspected it. On the face, she read the letters *CSA 20 Dollars*. She blew her breath out in a whistle. There must be thousands of dollars worth of coins in the two burlap sacks.

"Confederate States of America," she whispered. But LeFleur and the Colonel were Union soldiers. She suddenly remembered Bobby and his words "yellow-bellied traitor." A traitor. Annie's father used to tell her stories of soldiers who would play both sides of the war, Confederate soldiers who would give information to the Union generals and vice versa. They were often paid, but would they have been paid this much?

It all started to come to her in a torrent of thoughts and images, crashing in her mind like tidal waves breaking over the rocky shore.

Annie looked up from the coin and saw LeFleur standing at the opening of the tent, staring at her. Annie's chest caved in, and she fought for air.

"What are you doing, Annie?"

Annie gulped, held out the coin.

"You're a traitor. That's the secret Bobby kept for you."

"Move away from the trunk, Annie."

"The oleander, in Bobby's pockets—he found it in your belongings. You must have stolen it from Twila. She admitted to tainting Buck's water, but the tea? She swore she didn't kill Kimi. You must have. You must have put the oleander in the tea. Then, after it took affect, you wiped the foam from her mouth with her scarf and threw it away from the body. She knew your secret—Kimi knew your secret."

LeFleur came toward Annie, holding up his hands.

"You've got it wrong, Annie. Step away from the trunk."

Annie bent down and picked her gun up off the floor. She aimed it at him. The tent flap opened.

"Mr. LeFleur, I—" Bobby froze when he saw Annie aiming the gun at LeFleur.

"Bobby, come over here." Annie's eyes darted from LeFleur to Bobby and back to LeFleur.

Bobby started to move, and LeFleur grabbed him and swung his other arm around Bobby's neck, choking him. Bobby's face turned pink and his mouth gapped open, searching for air.

Annie aimed her pistol to the ceiling and shot.

Surprised, LeFleur let his grasp slip from Bobby, let him go, then turned toward the tent flap to run. A loud click stopped him in his tracks. Bobby had pulled his gun and had it aimed at LeFleur's head.

"I wouldn't try that again, *Derence*." Annie said. "Bobby's a pretty good shot and all, but you know I won't miss. Back him up, Bobby. Clear the door—the others will be coming any minute."

As if on cue, the Colonel and Detective Jonas sprang through the tent flap. Immediately assessing the situation, Jonas pulled his gun and aimed it at LeFleur.

"What the Sam Hill—?" The Colonel's eyes grew wide. He raised an arm, the fringe on his coat swinging.

Annie turned her gun on the Colonel, dipped her hand into the gold coins and held them out to him.

"You know anything about these?"

The Colonel blinked. "Gold?"

"Confederate gold."

"Confederate—?" His eyes shifted over to LeFleur. "You son of a bitch. What are you doing with Confederate gold?"

"He was a spy," Bobby said, "a yellow-bellied, traitor spy."

LeFleur tilted his head back, biting his lips, probably trying to figure out a way to talk himself out of this mess, or run.

"That gold's been missing for years." The Colonel's shoulders slumped, his face crestfallen. "The government as good as gave up looking for it. And it was here, right under our noses." He looked up at LeFleur. "You bastard. You put all of it at risk, our partnership, our show, our people— our country."

"I was due, Colonel. I'd put so much of myself in the war. I was due." LeFleur said through clenched teeth.

"We *all* sacrificed in that war, Derence. You made an oath, a promise. And then you lied. You stole."

"I stole that money for the North, Colonel. I did, I swear. But then I realized it wouldn't solve anything. It couldn't fix the hate—but it could fix me."

Annie, adrenaline still racing through her body, lowered her pistol, now sure in the fact that the Colonel had nothing to do with LeFleur's gold. She saw a rifle leaning against the back corner of the tent, went to it, and tossed it to him. He gave her a nod and hefted it under his arm.

"I didn't put it together at the time," Annie took in a deep breath, "but when I came in here to look for the gun—"

"What gun?" The Colonel asked.

"The rare gun, owned by LeFleur, the one he used to shoot Carver. The same gun that was found in Twila's possession."

"A LeMat," Detective Jonas said. "A gun used exclusively by Confederate generals."

Annie walked around the side of the desk, her pistol at her side, and stopped, looking hard at LeFleur.

"You used my suspicions about Twila poisoning Buck's water to your own advantage, didn't you, *Derence?* After you shot Carver. You used the information I gave you, worried that I'd figure out that you'd poisoned Kimi, and planted the gun among Twila's things."

LeFleur turned to address Annie, and Bobby shoved the pistol up to LeFleur's head. "You can't prove I shot Carver," LeFleur said.

"We've already proven it was your gun," said Jonas.

"And I saw the gunpowder on your hands, before we discovered Carter's body," Annie said.

"That damn Carver wasn't looking to find dirt on me." The Colonel let out a bemused chuckle. "He must have had his suspicions about you. He'd been tracking you the whole time. He must have been getting close to finding out your secret."

"I found a gold coin in my tent." Annie leaned against the desk, trying to calm the shaking in her limbs. "On the floor next to my trunk. The image of the letters had been filed off. It was a strange place to find such a thing, and then I noticed the tea I had purchased was gone. You must have emptied the tin after you killed Kimi, so no one could trace the murder back to you."

"It's a lie, Detective. I had nothing to do with Kimi's death," LeFleur said.

"Bobby, tell the detective," Annie said.

"I saw the oleander on Mr. LeFleur's desk and snatched it before he could hurt any one else. She was gone. Kimi was gone, and I had to hide the poison so he couldn't—"

"So you put it in your pocket," Annie said.

Bobby let out a gasp and his shoulders shook. The pistol slipped from the side of LeFleur's head. In a split second, LeFleur turned, grabbed Bobby's gun, shot Detective Jonas, and put Bobby in a head-lock with the gun next to his temple.

"Detective Jonas!" Annie started to run toward him as he sank to the ground, but LeFleur lifted the gun from Bobby's temple and trained it on Annie.

"Don't do it," the Colonel said.

Annie looked over and saw the Colonel aiming his rifle at LeFleur. She raised her gun again, and also pointed it at LeFleur.

"You are outnumbered, Derence. Put the gun down," the Colonel said.

Annie stole a quick glance at the detective, who was sprawled on the floor next to the tent flap, unconscious, blood pooling beneath his body.

"I tried to tell you, Annie," Bobby croaked.

"Shut up, boy!" LeFleur jerked Bobby's head back further, tightening his grip on his throat. Bobby gasped.

"Let up, Derence," Annie said. "He's just a boy. Let him go."

"Yes." LeFleur's face took on a sneer. He must have loosened his grip slightly, as Bobby was no longer gasping, but his face stayed rigid with fear. "A boy. A boy I treated as my own son, just like you did, Colonel. We're his only parents, for godsakes. Can you imagine what I felt, just now, when he pointed that gun at my head—my own boy."

"You killed Kimi! I'll never forgive you." Bobby started gasping again.

"Let the boy go, Derence," the Colonel said. "I won't feel sorry about shooting a goddamn traitor."

LeFleur laughed, his voice like the hiss from a snake.

"You'd never risk shooting this boy. Now, if you'll excuse us, we're going to leave, and you won't make a move because you might hit your only living son, right, Colonel? You have a blood daughter now, but she's a half-breed squaw. Nothing like this precious boy to carry out your legacy and run this damn circus when you're gone, if he behaves and I don't kill him first."

LeFleur started to drag Bobby out of the tent, and Annie raised her pistol. She squinted her left eye shut, aimed, and shot LeFleur right above his ear. His head jerked forward, his arms released, and Bobby fell to the floor, gasping.

"Bobby, are you alright?" Annie ran to him.

"I was going to tell about the gold, Annie. I swear I was. I wanted to tell the Colonel. I just couldn't find the right time or enough courage. Mr. LeFleur was like family to me, and I didn't want you to turn him in. He would have hanged. Hanged for sure. But I didn't know he'd actually kill someone, and once it started, he threatened to kill me." Bobby's words came out in a rush. His body shook, his limbs nearly flopping. His face had gone white and his lips blue.

The Colonel came over, his face clouded in anger.

"Why didn't you say something, Bobby? LeFleur was a traitor, a Confederate traitor. He killed my . . . Kimi, my daughter, my—and you didn't come to me?"

Annie held up a hand. "Colonel, not now. He's in a state of shock. Get a blanket and check Detective Jonas."

The Colonel went to LeFleur's bed, dragged the other quilt off it, and brought it to Annie. She bundled Bobby in it the best she could as he slumped against her.

"Still alive," the Colonel said, leaning over Detective Jonas. "Shot in the arm. I suspect he's unconscious from hitting his head. He'll come to in a bit."

"I kn-kn-know where Buck is," Bobby said through chattering teeth. "Mr. LeFleur took him over to Samson's, a horse trader on the other side of town. I t-t-told him not to do it, I begged him. I know what that horse m-m-means to you. But he was angry with you, awful angry, and he said he'd kill me—and you—if I opened my mouth. He'd already killed Kimi and Carver, made Lillie sick—"

"And also killed Twila?" Annie asked, looking at the Colonel, who lowered his head and held a hand over his eyes.

"I believed we were next, if I said a word."

"Yes. He tried to kill me with the chocolates, but Lillie had opened the box and began eating them before I got back to my tent."

Bobby wiped his nose. "He was half out of his mind that night. He'd almost k-k-killed Lillie, but couldn't forgive himself for almost killing you. He was in l-l-love with you, Annie. And as soon as Frank left, he f-f-felt you two had a chance. After that, he felt safer having you here, under his nose. He thought he could control you, so he took Buck."

Annie pulled Bobby closer to her, trying to steady his shaking body. Everything made sense now. A sense of relief washed over Annie, but something else tainted it. She could taste it in her mouth—the tangy, metallic taste of evil. She shook her head. All this death and mayhem— over a little gold.

CHAPTER 27

"Stash of Confederate Gold Found Thanks to Anonymous Tip.
Stash Awaiting Transport by Federal Marshals to
Louisiana Mint."

St. Louis Times – April 28, 1885

O n the way back from Samson's, the stagecoach rocked back and
forth on the gutted dirt road. Annie swayed with the motion,
her heart broken and her soul dampened, the life squeezed from it
like water from a soiled rag. Buck had been sold the day he'd arrived,
and the horse trader refused to tell who'd bought him. She'd lost
everything.

As the stage passed through the gates of Forest Park Camp, Annie
steeled herself. She'd already packed her bags, but now she'd leave without Buck and face an uncertain future back in Ohio. At least no one
had been charged in LeFleur's devilry—or his death. Bobby had been
cleared of any involvement, and the sheriff didn't press any charges
against Annie, as she had stabbed McCrimmon and shot LeFleur in
self-defense. A betrayed and despondent Twila, they concluded, had
actually committed suicide. Emma had written a long story about the
murders that newspapers across the country and in Europe picked up.

Luckily, she toned down the drumbeat that would have kept Annie's name in the spotlight, for which Annie felt grateful.

The coachman stopped in front of the Colonel's tent, and Annie entered to find the Colonel and Bobby. Both of them stood up upon seeing her.

"No, please sit down," Annie said. They'd been treating her like some kind of hero—both swore she'd saved their lives, and in a way she had, but she still didn't like being treated like a saint.

She told them she hadn't been able to retrieve Buck.

"Look here," said the Colonel, "I know you're sad about losing that horse—you loved that horse like your own family—we often do—but one of these days, you'll find another one that suits you. You can trust me on this, Annie."

"Thank you, Colonel, but that doesn't seem possible—"

The Colonel's face brightened, his blue eyes renewed with life.

"We'll all get a fresh start in Kansas City. What do you say?"

Annie drew in her top lip, hating to speak, hating to squash his new chance at hope.

"I'm not going, sir. I must go home."

"I was afraid you might say that." The Colonel took off his hat and held it in his hands, studying the crown. "We could sure use you right now, Annie. Bobby and Lillie are fine entertainers, but the people are hankering to see Annie Oakley. We've taken a hard hit at the show, and I swear you are the only one who could sure make our audiences forget we ever had spies and murderers among us."

His words tugged at her heart.

"I just can't, sir. Please understand."

The Colonel put his hat back on his head, opened a desk drawer, and pulled out a wooden box. After setting it on the table, he opened it and reached inside, retrieved some paper bills and handed them to Annie.

"That's two hundred dollars, your monthly salary and a bit more for good measure. You have your train ticket, and this should be of some help to your family when you get home."

Annie took the money and folded the bills in her hands.

"Thank you so much, sir. It will be a good start. I appreciate it."

The Colonel smiled with his lips closed.

"Would you ever consider coming back to us?" Bobby asked.

Annie turned to him. "Perhaps, someday."

"It's been a pleasure working for you, sir—even for a brief time." Not one to belabor sad moments, Annie stood up and held her hand out to the Colonel. "You changed my life, and I'm ever so grateful."

The Colonel raised himself from the chair, swept his hat off his head, and placed it over his heart. He then took Annie's hand in his.

"The pleasure has been all ours, Annie Oakley, best little sharp-shooter in the entire United States, and a hell of a cowgirl, too. I'm sorry to lose you, and you write to me when things improve."

Annie's breath caught in her throat as she shook the Colonel's hand. She then turned to Bobby, offered him a trembling smile, and tousled his hair, much like she would John Henry's. Without waiting for another word, she turned on her heel and quickly left the tent, afraid she would crumple up like a rag doll.

She fought off tears as she slipped into her tent for the last time. Lillie sat at the vanity, her head bent over pen and paper.

When she heard Annie enter, she rose and faced her.

"You're back. Did you find your horse?" Lillie seemed more animated.

Her bright and rosy skin glowed. She wore a finer gown than Annie had ever seen her wear, and her eyes were no longer red and droopy. Lillie appeared to be sober. Annie smiled inside, but then told Lillie about Buck.

"What are you going to do, Annie?"

"I'm going home."

"I suppose you would, especially if you couldn't find Buck. I'm sorry to lose you, Annie." She paused to smile, dimples creasing her plump cheeks. "I can't believe I'm saying this, but I'm going to miss you."

Annie smiled in return. "And I, you, Lillie. You're all right."

"I'm mending my ways, Annie. You've inspired me. I and about a thousand girls want to be just like you."

Afraid she would burst out in ridiculous sobs, Annie planted a hand over her mouth and drew in a deep breath.

Lillie seemed to be fighting back tears too, but her face took on a different demeanor—like she was about to deliver important news.

"Now, I know it's none of my business and that I shouldn't pry, but I have something to give you." She held out a small piece of paper.

Annie took it, read what she'd written on it, then looked up at Lillie, waiting for an explanation.

"That's Frank's family's address in Lexington. Before he left he made me promise to give this to you. He said he'd welcome a letter, if you felt inclined, once you finished being angry with him."

"I don't think so, Lillie, but thank you." She handed the paper back to Lillie.

Lillie frowned, but didn't pressure her further.

"I think I'd like to go to bed," Annie said. "I would like to get to the train station some time tomorrow, so I'll have to get up early to pack."

"I should probably get some shut-eye, too." Lillie ran her hand along her bed, made for once. "I hear we'll be packing up and getting things ready to go ourselves. Kansas City, here we come."

Annie walked over to her wardrobe and slowly undressed. She drew her night shift over her head and crawled into her comfortable little bed in her rustic little tent for the last time.

Snuggled into the covers, her eyes scanned the sanctuary she had called home for the past few weeks. She remembered how the opulence of this abode overwhelmed her when she first arrived. Never had she slept in a bed so comfortable and never had she had such fine clothing. It would all change in North Star, Ohio. There's she'd be focused on getting food into everyone's mouths and providing shelter. A bath in the creek would be a luxury. Her stomach churned at the thought of what lay ahead.

Suddenly very sleepy, she closed her eyes and drowsily listened to mumbling voices floating on the wind, lulling her into the twilight of dreamland. She relished how warm and secure she felt in her bed, falling asleep to Lillie softly snoring.

They all waited for her at the stagecoach—the Colonel, Rusty Post, Bobby, Lillie, Michante, Emma, and Chief Sitting Bull. Annie swallowed hard, afraid she would cry like a little girl. If only she could have stolen off into the night.

They each took turns saying goodbye. Bobby couldn't look her in the eye, and Lillie had nearly soaked a hanky clean through by the time they hugged. The Colonel and Rusty Post were sweet and kind, but as dignified as ever. Emma chucked Annie under the chin, said she'd be in touch, and Chief Sitting Bull stood some feet away from the rest, his dancing eyes dulled with sadness. Annie approached him.

"Will you stay with the show?"

"Only in the hope that you will return, Watanya Cecilia."

"I'm going to miss you, Chief," Annie leaned closer to him, whispering, "more than I'll miss anyone. You believed in me."

"I still do."

When his stoic face softened, Annie dropped her bag and flung her arms around the proud Chief's torso. He wrapped his arms around her and patted her back three times. Those pats were loaded with the Chief's sort of praise—at least to Annie.

"You must forgive Frank Butler." The chief stood back and held Annie by the arms. "Even my medicine couldn't fix his failing eyes."

"Yes. I suspected it was poor eyesight. But Frank is gone. It's too late for us."

Once seated in the stagecoach, Annie looked out the window at the buffalo fighter, Indian chief, cowboy shooter, suffragette, and the wildest woman she'd ever known. They had become her family, and she would miss them terribly. When the stage jerked forward, Annie pressed her hand to the window and kept it there long after they were no longer in sight.

CHAPTER 28

"Sale—Cut Rate Prices: North Star Mercantile—
Large Selection of Fowl and Game."

Greenville Gazette – May 30, 1885

Six Weeks Later

The bells on the door of the Mercantile jingled as John Henry burst through, his face red with exertion and his hair matted to his forehead.

"Annie, I finished stacking the wood for Mr. Shaw. He said I could have a lollipop."

Annie put down the broom and wiped her hands on her apron. She went behind the counter and reached into the jar of sweets.

"Where is Mr. Shaw?" She handed John Henry a red lollipop.

"Dunno. Can I go to the creek and fish for a little while? Maybe I'll catch something for our dinner!"

Annie tousled his sweaty hair and smiled.

"Yes. Be careful. Mind the slippery rocks."

John Henry turned and raced out the door, causing a melodious cacophony of bell ringing.

Annie resumed sweeping the floor, enjoying the whoosh-whoosh of the brush against the wooden planks, grateful that few people had visited the store that day. She didn't want her quiet melancholy disturbed. She just wanted to tend to the mindless business of sweeping.

She and her family still lived in cramped quarters at the back of the store. Annie had given Mr. Shaw all the money she had left over from the show and resumed her task of hunting birds and game for the mercantile. He said they could stay as long as they needed, but Annie felt the call to move on to their own place. She just didn't know yet how they would manage.

She stopped sweeping and lifted her nose into the air to enjoy a wonderful aroma wafting out of the store's small kitchen. Annie looked up and saw her mother waving a towel in the air, shooing away smoke. Her face looked so offended by the smoke that Annie laughed.

Her mother turned. "Oh, Annie! I'm glad you're here. I think I used some wet wood. See if you can find some drier logs, would you?"

"What are you doing, Mother?"

"Why, I'm making dinner, sugar." Susan stopped her fanning and placed her hands on her hips.

"But—"

"Oh, stop gaping and get me that wood."

Annie welcomed the bossiness in her mother's voice. She hadn't been up and around that long.

"But how are you feeling, Mother? Are you all right?"

"I'm fine, lovey, just fine." Susan's face softened and her eyes drifted over to a tin vase filled with wildflowers. Annie stared at the flowers, then turned back to her mother.

"I have an admirer," Susan said.

"What?" Annie hoped to God it wasn't Joshua.

"Oh, don't look so shocked, Annie. It's Mr. Shaw. He brought me those flowers earlier and told me it was a glory that a fine woman like me was feeling so renewed."

Annie blinked, not quite sure she could believe what she heard.

"Well, I, um, he's right. So you're—"

"Yes, my dear, I am restored, and I am thanking Mr. Shaw by making us all a hot meal. Do you think he'll be pleased?"

Annie dropped the broom, rushed to her mother, and drew her into her arms.

"Yes, Mother, I think he'll be very pleased, we'll all be very pleased."

The bells on the door sounded again and Mr. Shaw entered, his blue eyes dancing under thick brows, and a smile creasing his heavy cheeks. He wore a fine wool suit.

"Well, don't you look dapper," Annie said, smiling.

"It's a special day, Annie. I have a surprise for you."

Annie cocked her head. "What? What do you mean, Mr. Shaw? It's enough that my mother is feeling restored, don't you go teasing me."

"I am not teasing you, young lady. Now, go get your finest dress and put it on."

Annie knit her brows. She'd been hunting, fishing, cleaning, and cooking since she got back. Her old sackcloth dress had been more suitable than those fancy clothes. She hadn't even opened the trunk full of dresses she'd brought back from St. Louis.

"Go, go, and hurry up about it."

Annie quickly washed her face, changed her clothes, and brushed her hair. She'd even pinched the apples of her cheeks. When she returned, clothed in the green velvet dress, Mr. Shaw had just finished securing the "closed" sign on the door.

"There we go," he said, shrugging, "we can close for a couple of hours."

Susan came up behind them. "I can mind the store, if you like."

"I wouldn't want you to take time away from that wonderful cooking of yours." Mr. Shaw removed his hat and smiled at Susan.

"Oh, Mr. Shaw." Susan's face turned an appealing shade of pink.

"What's this surprise all about, Mr. Shaw?" Annie asked.

"Well, if I told you, it wouldn't be a surprise, now would it? You look real pretty in that dress, Annie, so let's head on out."

They climbed into his wagon and headed toward his farm.

"Where are we going with me in this fancy dress?" Despite her protest, Annie's mood felt lighter than it had in a long time.

Mr. Shaw laughed and clucked to the horses.

"You'll see, my dear. You'll see."

Another mile later, he drew the horses to a halt and turned to face Annie.

"You know Annie, your mother is doing well, and I see a future here for us together, her and John Henry and Hulda, but I can't say the same for you."

Annie sighed. "I don't know where I belong anymore."

"I do." A note of mischievousness tinged his voice. "You belong in the Wild West Show, where you shined like a star."

Annie noticed a man working on a fence in the distance.

"Who's that?"

"A cowboy I hired to mend fences. I've been so busy at the store, I haven't had time to repair them."

Annie pulled at the lace at her neck. The sun beat down on the fabric of her dress, burning her skin, and she again wondered why Mr. Shaw felt she needed to be dressed up.

"We've all been busy, and I don't understand why I had to put on a fancy dress to ride into the fields."

Mr. Shaw chuckled. "Just take a look over there." He pointed to a field on their right.

Annie saw horses, one a deep chestnut color and the other—a buckskin with four white socks. Annie peered harder.

"Buck," she whispered, as she leapt off the wagon.

"Buck!" She shouted out to him, and the horse raised his head, whinnied loudly, and galloped towards them. They met within seconds at the fence. He nuzzled her as Annie ran her hands through his mane. "Buck, Buck, it's you!" she exclaimed, bursting with happiness.

Annie lifted her gaze and saw the man who had been repairing the fence walking towards them. When he took off his hat and ran a hand through his thick blond hair, Annie gasped.

"Frank!"

He broke into a run and rushed to her, his hands stretched out and grabbing hers the instant he reached her.

"Hello, Annie, don't you look beautiful, as always!" His startling blue eyes looked deep into hers.

"Frank Butler, what are you doing here?"

Frank flashed that gorgeous smile she loved so well.

"I had to bring a girl her horse. And, I have a question for you."

"Yes?"

"Will you marry me, Annie Mosey?"

EPILOGUE

Annie ran out to the field behind the Mercantile where Frank worked at building the frame of their new house. They'd married two weeks ago during the Friends Monthly Meeting. It had been a simple ceremony, each reciting their vow to take each other as life partners with friends and family looking on.

She reached him out of breath, excited.

"A letter from the Colonel." She thrust the letter at him.

Frank raised a hand to push his spectacles further up his nose.

"You read it, you've got better eyesight." He winked at her.

Annie ripped it open, scanned it fast, and then, with her heart racing, looked up again at Frank.

"So, what's the old codger got to say?" he asked, grinning.

"The Wild West show has been invited to London—to perform for the Queen! Queen Victoria herself asked about me, said she'd like *me* to stay in her palace, as her personal guest. And the Colonel wants us *both* to come back, you as my manager and me as the headlining sharpshooter."

Frank studied her face, and she his.

"What do you think?" she asked.

"Manager of the famous Annie Oakley. London." Frank shook his head, a look of awe in his eyes.

"Personal guest of the Queen," Annie said with a laugh.

"Sounds like we have no choice." Frank pulled Annie into his arms and swung her in a circle, their laughter echoing across the golden fields of North Star.

Acknowledgments

There are so many people who were instrumental in helping me to create this book centered on a plucky young girl from Ohio who became one of the most famous American women of all time.

First, I would like to thank Annie Oakley herself, for proving to the world that a woman can shine on her own in a career and vocation dominated by men. She was a maverick of her time, and a woman who persevered regardless of the challenges life presented to her. She was and continues to be an inspiration to me.

Next, I would like to thank my dear friend Becky Hopper, her husband, Don Hopper, and Jake Kettenacker of the Rio Grande Renegades chapter of the Single Action Shooting Society (SASS) for teaching me to shoot period weapons that Annie herself used. They also helped me with some of the research for other rifles and pistols that might have been used by Annie's contemporaries and fellow showmen. I would also like to thank my equine veterinarian, Dr. Matt Paxton, and his wife, Laurie, for assisting me with my own horses and some of the research on equine health and hazards. They helped me put poor Buck through his paces, but the Wonder Horse lives on!

I would also like to thank my friends Debra Speck and Linda Cecil, who have been my some of my biggest cheerleaders and allies. Thank you for your belief in me and in my work. It is so appreciated. And thank you to Jon and Julia Patten, who always asked me to tell them what was happening in my writing life. Your interest and support has been wonderful.

Also, my undying gratitude goes to my two amazing critique partners, Dana Killion and Shelley-Blanton Stroud, who are incredible authors in their own right. You have been through it all with me—the ups, the downs, the tears, the frustrations, and the joy in this passion that we share! You are the best, and I hope we can continue to support each other throughout our careers. Write on, my friends—your talent needs to be shared with the world.

Most of all, I would like to thank my husband, Kevin, and my children, Jessica and Michael, for their continued belief in me, and for the times I was unavailable or inconsolable as I pursued my passion. You are my rock, my joy, my life. I love you. And thank you to my parents, Jim and Geri Cramer, who bestowed upon me a creative mind, a diligent work ethic, and a belief in myself that has made my dream of becoming an author possible. I hope I've made you proud.

And last, thank you to Brooke Warner, Lauren Wise, Crystal Patriarch, Tabitha Bailey, and the wonder team at Spark Press and Book Sparks. You have been amazing to work with.

About the Author

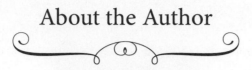

E mpowered women in history, horses, unconventional characters, and real-life historical events fill the pages of Kari Bovée's articles and historical mystery musings and manuscripts. Bovée is an award-winning writer: She was a finalist in the Romantic Suspense category of the 2012 LERA Rebecca contest, the 2014 NTRWA Great Expectations contest, and the RWA 2016 Daphne du Maurier contest for her unpublished manuscript *Grace in the Wings*. She was also honored as a finalist in the NHRWA Lone Star Writer's contest in 2012 with the unpublished manuscript of *Girl with a Gun*. Bovée and her husband, Kevin, live in New Mexico with their cat, four dogs, and four horses. Their children, who live happy lives as productive entrepreneurs and professionals, are their greatest achievements.

SELECTED TITLES FROM SPARKPRESS

SparkPress is an independent boutique publisher delivering high-quality, entertaining, and engaging content that enhances readers' lives, with a special focus on female-driven work.
Visit us at www.gosparkpress.com

A Dangerous Woman from Nowhere, Kris Radish, $16.95, 978-1-943006-26-7
When her husband is kidnapped by ruthless gold miners, frontier woman Briar Logan is forced to accept the help of an emotionally damaged young man and a famous female horse trainer. On her quest to save her husband, she discovers that adventures of the heart are almost as dangerous as tracking down lawless killers.

Hidden, Kelli Clare, $16.95, 978-1-943006-52-6
Desperate after discovering her family murdered, a small-town art teacher runs to England with a handsome stranger in search of safety and answers in this suspenseful, sexy tale of treachery and obsession—perfect for fans of Sandra Brown and Ruth Ware.

Learning to Fall, Anne Clermont. $16.95, 978-1940716787
A behind-the-curtains peek into the glamorous but often heartbreaking world of competitive show jumping, *Learning to Fall* is a universal story of healing, hope, and what it means to love.

Found, Emily Brett, $16.95, 978-1940716800
Immerse yourself in life-changing adventures from a nurse's perspective while experiencing the local color of countries around the world. *Found* will appear to not only medical professionals but those who are drawn to suspense, romance, adventure, and self-discovery.

The Year of Necessary Lies, Kris Radish. $17, 978-1-94071-651-0
A great-granddaughter discovers her ancestor's secrets—inspirational forays into forbidden love and the Florida Everglades at the turn of the last century.

ABOUT SPARKPRESS

SparkPress is an independent, hybrid imprint focused on merging the best of the traditional publishing model with new and innovative strategies. We deliver high-quality, entertaining, and engaging content that enhances readers' lives. We are proud to bring to market a list of *New York Times* best-selling, award-winning, and debut authors who represent a wide array of genres, as well as our established, industry-wide reputation for creative, results-driven success in working with authors. SparkPress, a BookSparks imprint, is a division of SparkPoint Studio LLC.

Learn more at GoSparkPress.com